+Horror Library+
Volume 1

D1225957

+Horror Library, Volume 1+

First Edition Trade Paperback, May, 2006

All rights reserved

Cutting Block Press, LLC.

1408 E. Del Mar Blvd.

Laredo, Texas 78045

cuttingblock.net

Editor in Chief:	R.J. Cavender
Assistant Editors:	Dawna Bailey
	Vincent VanAllen
Editing Team	Ginger Hamilton Caudill
	Jeff Cercone
	Mark Edward Deloy
	Michelle Garren Flye
	Theresa Cecilia Garcia
	Chris Mahn
	Alex Spires
Cover Art and Design:	Groundfrost Illustration and Design
	www.groundfrost.com

This book is dedicated to the authors whom I've included in this collection. Without you, I'd have nothing at all to publish. You are the best, and I wish to present nothing but the very best. I'd like to take this opportunity to thank Ruth and Josh Heinz for letting me take over their living room and personal computer in my own insidious bid at world dominance. And, a special thanks to -[angel] and Rebma, my online muses, for inspiring me to persevere, even when I felt things were at their very worst. And, lastly, thanks to all those who have doubted me along the way. Your skepticism and pessimism has fueled a world of creativity within myself. Without your doubt I would have ended my quest long ago.

R.J. Cavender
Founder of the Terrible Twelve Authors
Owner of +The Horror Library+
www.horrorlibrary.net
www.myspace.com/horror_library_net

+ TABLE OF CONTENTS +

FOREWARD and ONWARD

Maybe it's a testament to 'modern times' or maybe just a commentary on how reliant I personally am on today's technology, but this story starts and ends with a website.

It was early May, 2002 when I first came across Zoetrope.com. I'd read about it in *Zoetrope All-Story* Magazine, a publication owned and maintained by Francis Ford Coppola. Here was this website that was designed for artists to workshop, network, and collaborate. It was like nothing I'd seen before. I was hooked immediately.

As I developed a portfolio of fiction and formed relationships in the process, one thing became clear; horror writers like myself, were drowned out in a sea of other genres. It became evident that it was time to seek out the 'darker' writers from the bunch and start up my own group.

On June 6th, sharply at 6pm (only a horror fan would recognize the significance of the date) I opened my own 'office' on Zoetrope, where we met to discuss topics, projects and agendas. I named it +The Horror Library+.

Exactly one year later to the day, I created a cyber-showcase, a place for members of my office to display their work; +The Horror Library+ web site, located at www.horrorlibrary.net and thus the +Terrible Twelve+ authors group was born. With our first foray into cyberspace we unleashed thirteen blood-curdling, exquisitely horrific stories. The idea for an anthology was already brewing then. But, first, we had to figure out a way to put our 'zine out monthly. That was a chore in and of itself. It seemed just as we'd finished workshopping our stories for one month, it'd be time to start workshopping for the next.

Well, shortly after this book hits the market, my website will be celebrating its third anniversary, and we'll be bigger and more popular than ever. We've gained and lost a few contributors along the way, as any community will, but, we thrive upon the talent and energy of each other to remain strong and grow.

It's been a battle for sure, but as our popularity online rises, so does our productivity.

I subscribe to the philosophy that if you have ambition and drive, and you surround yourself with like-minded individuals, you can accomplish anything. This book is that case-in-point. It is a collection of thirty stories, the very best creations of each of the writers who have helped me along the way. I'm proud to know people like this.

Their work speaks for itself.

And the best thing about doing what I do is that +The Horror Library+ website is always open to new writers, and bringing them to a reading market is what we do.

This collection is what I consider to be the best of the best. Prepare to be horrified. And remember, at +The Horror Library+ there's always room for more...bodies.

R.J. Cavender
www.horrorlibrary.net
www.myspace.com/horror_library_net

Palo Mayombe in Matamoros

by Boyd E. Harris

This is your night, David Yates. You are on your game, and tonight you'll be the one to score. You're determined to make spring break history, and fate agrees -- you will.

Mike approaches and reminds you that it's really getting late and the others are probably waiting at the car by now.

One by one, spring breakers bump you as they stumble in procession toward the international bridge, your portal back to the United States. You try to hold your wristwatch steady.

It is late.

You nod and insist on making your final move on the blonde in the bar across the street.

She steps out of the Tequila Frog Cantina, sees you and smiles. The klutz who's been a nuisance much of the night follows her out, says something to her, and walks away in defeat. You see your window of opportunity and you work your way across the moving crowd of intoxicated students, who are on their way back to South Padre Island.

Bearing your naturally boyish charm, you grin on approach, and she says, "Hello, David Yates, pre-med student at Baylor University".

You laugh, but since you are under the heavy influence of cerveza and tequila, you can't remember her name, school or major. You only remember that she's from somewhere in the Midwest, and earlier today she almost won the Meridian Hotel tan-line contest. But you are a smooth drinker, and you work your way into a flirtatious conversation.

She leans forward and your heart races. Her golden skin, covered by very little in the warm, humid night, moves close to yours. She gives you her hotel room number. Your bodies finally touch, as the two of you pull together for a rousing kiss.

Fully expecting to close the deal, you wink and promise you'll see her later. You head toward the bridge, looking for Mike, wondering why he left you behind.

You find yourself staring glassy-eyed at several Latin men, who observe you from the cab and bed of a late model pick-up, as the vehicle moves along your side. These men are about your age, and their communal stares make you nervous.

The driver asks if you want a ride to the bridge, which is only a block and a half down the crowded street. Concerned with the motivation behind the offer, you refuse and walk on.

The truck eases along at your walking pace, and the men insist on you coming with them. Something's wrong. Just as you decide to run, the three in the bed leap over, and the one in the passenger side lunges out. They tackle you and pull you to the ground. Two grab your feet and two more grab your arms. Dirt-caked, greasy hands cover your mouth. They drag you, kicking and squirming, into the dark side alley. The pick-up stops halfway down, and they lift you feet first into the back. The truck speeds off, the engine revving and gravel grinding under the tires. As they hold your face against the black plastic bed liner, you feel the first true waves of panic from the claustrophobic early moments of this hostile abduction. The terror of the unknown paralyzes.

Though you pick out some Spanish words and some pieces of the conversations during this bumpy ride, you haven't the frame of mind to understand any of what's going on or the plans they discuss. They seem hyper, angry at something. They speak too fast and yell at each other. They argue, disagree.

The truck stops briefly. Several of the men stand up and begin arguing with others outside the truck. Only one remains to hold you down.

Is this is your big chance?

You bite the kidnapper's hand, break free and climb over the truck bed. You sprint away from the truck, down the dirt road toward the orange dawn. They fall farther and farther behind and your adrenalin pumps hope.

You approach the main road and spot a vehicle on the horizon heading toward Matamoros, but it passes the intersection before you get there. The driver continues by, oblivious to your screams and flailing arms.

The passing sounds of the vehicle are drowned out by your pursuer's truck, which rambles up from behind. The angry men jump out. They curse you in Spanish and chase you on foot.

You alter your course; take to the bull grass and cactus of a dark field, stumbling over mounds of soft dirt and scratching your bare legs and sandaled feet in the thickets of brush and mesquite thorns.

They tackle you into a patch of prickly pear cactus and beat you from all sides. They pound and kick, screaming words that you don't recognize.

##

It's a wooden shed. The room is dark, devoid of windows. The only light comes from various cracks in the walls, where slivery beams of sun break through onto a dilapidated floor.

Sitting up is out of the question. Your throat is tightly roped to the very bottom of a beam on a back wall, your head forced perpendicular to its body. It throbs from the battering in the cactus field.

But your swollen face doesn't alter your sense of smell. You've smelled rotting flesh before. You recall the rodent that died and decomposed behind the side wall in your dorm room, but you've never before been forced to take lungful upon lungful of fumes like the ones oozing from the metal cauldron eight feet way. A small beam of sunlight illuminates the brim, which crawls with a variety of insects.

Hours pass. Well after the light fades from the cracks, voices rise and fall outside, all in Spanish.

Without an inkling for their plans, you know one thing for certain. These are dire straights. You need to put your thoughts together. You must keep thinking. You need to stay sharp, because at any moment, one of these men could come in. You need to prepare for the worst. You need your faith.

You pray for strength to face what may come. You offer consent to His will, but remind Him of your dreams of medical school and becoming a surgeon. You remind Him of how good you will be at healing people and bringing your faith into your practice.

You pray for the sake of your family; Mom, Dad and Sheila. You remind Him how tough it will be on young Sheila in this world without you.

You ignore that He is all knowing and His plan is set.

Over the last dozen hours or so, completed thoughts have become impossible and your desperate prayers come in bits and pieces. You wonder about your future in school, your plans to become an MD and your dream of that nice suburban home with a beautiful wife and two kids. Two or three, and at least one of them a boy. Are these the things you really want? Or are they just dreams you've been raised to believe are right for you? You know you want to live to see tomorrow. To have this destiny to explore.

What do these men have in store for you? Could this be about ransom? Why were you not warned about this type of thing? Why has this happened to you?

The voices begin to rise outside, and a newer, flickering light breaches the shed's cracks. Your pulse quickens and your heart races. Blood throbs against your skull.

It's been the better part of a day, and by now your friends have notified the police in the U.S. and Mexico. They should be sending search parties out to find you. Your family has connections in customs. Your uncle is in immigration. They are contacting every agency and office in Mexico that could possibly help. You wonder if your disappearance is important enough for the Mexican *Federales* to step in and do sweep searches.

Could they be negotiating price with a reasonable figurehead of this group of *desperados*, who might want nothing more than to see a nice bundle of cash in payment for your safe return home?

You try to convince yourself that friendly forces are making progress. You just need to ignore the putrid fumes in this hot shed and hang on for a while longer.

The voices outside gain rhythm, chants form in an unknown tongue. The door bursts open, and four silhouettes appear in front of a raging bonfire. The figures encircle, pick up the cauldron by its rim handles and carry it outside.

Then they return and approach you. Breathing heavy, but immobilized from being tightly bound to the post, you are at their mercy. They detach the collar and drag you outside to a thick wooden table. As they hoist you up, you notice the scuffed surface darkened by blotchy stains. They set you down and hold each limb to a corner, pulling your wrists far above your head.

A fearsome man appears, his eyes swelling at the sight of you, his legs quaking in rhythm to the chants. He is Latin like the others, Mexican, you assume, and the top of his jeans are dark with sweat. His bare chest glistens in the light of the fire. His neck tendons show through, and the veins in his temples bulge. His grin widens, jaws trembling to the deafening sounds his mouth produces; rhythmic grunts followed by bongo drums pounded by people you cannot see. He raises his hands high, punching his fists at the sky. Across his breast is a large necklace with rough, pointed edges, whitish gray in the firelight, the texture and color of bone. The beads appear to be made from some animal's vertebrae, possibly human. He is unquestionably the psychotic leader of this group, and you are most certainly more frightened than you were a moment ago.

But it is what you see next that brings sheer terror to this night. A rack of various dangling knives and scissors is positioned close by, as a tray of instruments might be placed for you in an operating room someday, if you live through this to become a surgeon. Knives of varying shapes, grades and edges are dwarfed by a thick, steely cleaver with a gleaming edge that twinkles in the firelight.

You plead with him, beg for mercy; whimpering in a way you never thought you'd been capable of as a child, much less now. Your trembling voice becomes prepubescent. You are a sniveling wimp, begging as though he was your mommy.

Your whining only increases the excitement of the men around you. Their chants rise and their eyes enlarge.

He chooses a small knife and leans over the top of the table with it, his sweaty chest pressed against the side of your face. You cannot see what he's doing, but you feel sharp pain in your left hand, in your fingers, and you scream to the night. The pain moves to your thumb. You continue to plead with him, but you no longer even recognize your own quavering voice.

He howls. Leaning back into view, he spreads four fingers and a thumb on your chest, and grins into your eyes with his face close up, searching deep for your terror. Then he circles the table to the right and the same pain seizes your other hand.

You've shrieked incoherently for the entire moment. *God* and *Mommy* are the only two words that make sense. With ten digits lying on your chest, erratic breathing chokes out your screams, which in turn fade into dull moans.

The men holding your limbs roll you over to your belly. You feel your shorts being pulled and then pain in your waist as they cut the clothes free and tear them away.

A rough hand clenches your scrotum. Pain surges as the testicles are pulled tight, and the agony is multiplied, even cubed as the sack is sawed with what feels like a jagged blade. You scream again, this time louder than you thought humanly possible. You squirm and fight with every bit you have left. Next to your face, a fleshy, bloody mass of skin and meat is set down. Within the mush, you recognize your penis.

You are not sure, because due to the pain in your hands and groin, other sensations have become clouded, but for in the next moment, you think you are sodomized. The man lies on your back and breathes across your neck. Your body moves forward to his humping motion, but you could be in shock; you're not quite sure. You struggle for air, but you groan with his movement.

They roll you over, this time so you can see the cleaver in the psycho's hands.

While the four continue to hold you down, two others slip ropes onto each of your legs, sliding them up to your thighs. There is a knot in each rope, with an iron pipe running through it. They twist the ropes into tourniquets, choking off the blood flow to your lower legs. They tighten them until the pain seems to equal what you feel in your hands and crotch, and then beyond.

He raises the giant knife. With a forceful grunt and one clean chop, your left leg rolls off the table. He circles and removes your other leg with the same ease.

Much closer you realize someone else is cutting your abdomen open with a pair of shears. Two men pierce their hands into your belly and dig around. One bundles your small intestine, heaving it up to clear the way for the other's digging, who holds your spine and cuts the meat around it. You now realize pain comes in increments. The agony in your lower torso far surpasses any of the other things you've yet experienced.

Your weak head falls to the side. There is no strength left to hold it up. You stare at the cauldron. Three men stir it with long sticks, and they grin at you.

The dumbest question runs through your mind. "Am I going to die?" You've been thinking it all night, but now it's merely a waste of precious brain waves.

Someone turns your listless head up and you see him again, standing behind you, still quaking. From over the top of the table, he stares down, holding the cleaver high. His eyes widen again, seeing you have no more terror for him to consume. You follow the shiny, glistening blade as it bears down on your forehead.

But you are not twenty-two-year-old David Yates and this is not March 12th, 1990 on the small Santa Cruz ranch outside of Matamoros, Mexico. You probably never have even been concurrently in the same town as Fernando Alderate, the Cuban-American, bisexual, drug-smuggling cult leader who has crafted this heinous torture so he could summon *Palo Mayombe* black magic to ensure safe transportation of his drugs into the United States.

Four weeks later the authorities do not dig your body out from a shallow grave. They do not find your spinal column separated from your torso in the sandy loam above it, placed there by the sect to be cleaned by nature's elements for later use in a ritualistic necklace. They do not find your eyes, genitals and brain in a *Gnanga* cauldron --a potion of blood and human body parts mixed with poisonous insects and reptiles used to ward off threats from enemies by this twisted religion.

Of the countless acts of random violence around the world that occur daily, many of them too close to home for comfort, this is what happens to the other guy, someone else.

You are not twenty-eight-year-old Colleen Reed, washing your car in broad daylight in an affluent area of Austin, Texas on December 29th, 1991, when Kenneth Allen McDuff abruptly seizes and shoves you into his late-model Ford Thunderbird, speeding off in a cloud of exhaust, to later kill and dismember you in a neighboring town.

You are not twenty-three-year-old Kelly Smith or seventeen-year-old Amber Michaels serving coffee at a espresso shop in Marietta Georgia, on February 7, 1995, when you are abducted and stuffed into the small trunk of a vehicle before having your throat slashed through the bone to the point where your head hangs from your shoulders by tendons and skin by binge-slaughtering Stuart Edward Briggs, whose restaurant worker slaying rampage across several states has gone on for two months since being fired at Basil's Cafe in St. Louis for throwing a temper tantrum.

You are not forty-three-year-old Mark Lansing on a weekend fishing outing with your ten-year-old son in DeSoto County, Mississippi on September 12, 1998, when you are gagged, stabbed and shot to death in your boat by Franklin Thomas Pearson, a man who feels that just stealing your truck doesn't stir enough adrenaline for his taste.

You are not fifty-two-year-old Gregory Biggs, legally crossing an intersection on October 26, 2001, in Dallas, Texas, when twenty-seven-year-old booze, pot and ecstasy-induced Chante Mallard runs you down and drives home with your mangled body lodged in her windshield, before leaving you in her garage to die for two slow, agonizing days.

You are not fifty-three-year-old Dean Harold Meyers stepping out of your car to pump gas at a D.C. area gas station on October 9, 2002, when you are shot in the head by snipers John Allen Muhammad and John Lee Malvo from a distance of over 100 yards.

You are not one of the 1,100 taxi drivers throughout the world who have been randomly slain since 1997 for various minute reasons, including being the first person the perpetrator comes in contact with after having a heated altercation with someone else.

Yes, bad things do happen. David Yates is just one of millions whose fate serves to remind you of your paper-thin right to be. To this, you wonder about David's brief time here, and how often he told himself, *that's what happens to the other guy.*

Note: "Palo Mayombe in Matamoros" is a creative non-fiction story. Some details of occurrences and some names have been changed. The author only speculates on any behavior or suffering of the character, David Yates, and makes no claim to its accuracy.

Oren's Axe

by Jed Verity

There was a knock on the front door. A single knock. It was neither insistent nor timid, nor did it appear to wish to summon someone. It sounded more like a thrown plum. Oren, dozing in his rocking chair a few yards down the hall in the den, kicked a foot in the air and fumbled the book off his chest, at once wider awake than he ever could have been in the absence of such a midnight disturbance. He blinked the sand away from his eyes and leaned back to glimpse the great oak door cast in darkness at the end of the hall.

What was that? he wondered. A faint ring, the whirr of his organs filled his ears.

Oren's house was situated on the fringe of a deciduous forest, at the foot of a moraine. During an inclement three months many summers ago, Oren constructed the cottage from a pile of local oak timber and a chunk of limestone. Though the resulting structure had looked weathered and trodden from the first moment of its completion, it suited Oren's needs perfectly. There was more than enough room for one person, and it couldn't have been further from the suffocating clusters of human habitation. He could let his beard grow out, sleep all day if he wanted to, masturbate in the living room or while breathing the clean air out on the deck. After thirty-six years in the company of family and friends and enemies and strangers, skin and eyes and teeth everywhere he looked, Oren had stepped off of the stoop of his old home, turned the corner, and walked until his feet were black. He hadn't said more than a few words to another person in the years since, and even after all that time, he embraced whole-heartedly the opportunity to indulge in such indifferent solitude.

His ex-wife was the only human being he ever admitted missing. And that was only when the temperature was just right and the breezes smelled of coming snow. On such intoxicating mornings, he wanted to tell her that he had been an ass. That his leaving didn't have as much to do with her as she probably thought it did. They had had their problems -- she thought social work made a difference, he thought wars made a difference -- but if his things-are-just-as-they-are attitude hadn't made it so easy for him to leave, they might have been okay. It wasn't about her. It was about them. The frowning, needy faces, helpless to be helped. The blood-suckers and life-zappers, buying and drinking and eating and smoking everything in sight, spreading blah. He'd tell her all of this if he could. If she hadn't died years ago, he would've invited her over right then. They could fold into each other under a heavy blanket, like they did when they were kids, crying and apologizing, leaving the midnight disturbance on the stoop, safely forgotten.

Silence.

I'm not expecting anyone, am I? It was a ridiculous question, but Oren's memory wasn't what it used to be. He had long since forgotten the names of his old friends. He could still see the vague shape of some of their faces, but the names were gone or buried under humongous blankets of time.

The darkness was overwhelming. Oren leaned instinctively towards the lamp and strained to hear further noises on the other side of the door, now deciding not to move a muscle for fear of drowning out critical auditory clues.

Just as he was relaxing, sure that it had been nothing more than his mischievous subconscious, the sound came again. A dull but unmistakable thud. Oren, nearly as shocked as he'd been after the first knock, clutched the arms of his chair and inhaled.

Who could it possibly be? He wondered. *And why aren't they using the knocker?*

The shadows at the end of the hall were dramatic, affording only a rough sketch of the door with its single, face-sized window. Oren leaned back in his chair once again, as if the view of the door itself or of the darkness that flowed through its window would reveal the origin of the noise. But then paranoia set in, and Oren imagined that whoever this intruder was, he or she would surely be peeking through the window, watching his every move.

He climbed out of his chair and moved further into the den, steadying himself by grabbing the edge of a bookshelf. He listened. He wondered why the noise, if intended to be solicitous, wasn't more representative of a conventional knock. Who would ever attempt to receive attention at someone's door, especially in the middle of the night, by rapping once, a single knock, every twenty seconds? It was absurd.

He walked to the edge of the hallway and peeked his head around the corner. The bulb that normally would have shed light on the stoop and its temporary tenants had burned out just three nights ago, popping as soon as Oren had flipped the switch. Now, needing that light for the first time in months, Oren cursed his indolence.

Nearly three minutes passed in silence.

What do I do? Oren asked himself. *Do I just open the door and peer out into the darkness? Do I turn off the light inside and try to look out the window to see who it is? Do I call out, asking the knocker to identify himself?*

He looked around the room, at the thousands of dusty books that populated the shelves, at the Sioux relics that adorned the walls, at the lamps carved from rosewood that glowed golden through their shades, at the foot table fashioned from a tree trunk. He glanced over all of the objects in the den, hoping that one of them would speak to the proper course of action. They were all just as suffocated by the silence as he, however, and helpless to offer the consultation he sought.

"Who is it?" he yelled from the corner of the den and hallway. The quantity of wood and textiles in the house prevented his voice from reverberating, wrapping it in an eerily present, nightmarish, blanket.

There was no response from the other side of the door.

Oren laughed silently as he thought, *It's probably a bat who's had his antennae clipped. Or a bird who's gone blind.*

These thoughts provided some comfort. Given the odd singularity of the knocks, the animal collision theory made sense. But he was still incapable of shrugging off his paranoia. A bat or bird would have to be fairly strong to survive, with flight mechanisms intact, what sounded like a high-speed impact with the solid oak door; and it would have to be maniacally stupid to back up and do it again.

Oren looked with renewed interest at the wall that displayed the relics. He decided he would take the tomahawk, walk to the door, and ask again if anyone was there. He peered at the three inches of wood that separated indoors from out, sanity from madness, order from chaos.

Taking the first step around the corner was more difficult than he had expected. After thirty seconds of failed attempts -- *is that the gray semblance of a face that I see pressed against the window?* -- he gripped the axe with a thousand pounds of pressure and shuffled slowly towards the door.

The hall was at once longer and shorter than usual. Oren made slow progress at first, but decided that he didn't want to appear timid if someone was indeed spying at him through the window. He wanted to be intimidating. After all, no one would be able to break down such a thick door that was locked redundantly, three times over, with iron bolts the size of baseball bats. He picked up speed and arrived at the door within moments, eyes ablaze and fixed on the window.

"Who is it?" he yelled in his deepest voice, still holding the window relentlessly in his vision. He put his ear to the door.

A series of faint, muffled moans answered. They were formless, labored, exhausted, frightened. Then the knock came again, slightly louder this time, not just from Oren's proximity to the door, but wielded with greater force and urgency.

Oren stared at the window with unblinking intensity. He could see nothing through it, but held it in his gaze nevertheless, prepared to react appropriately if the knocker should reveal his intentions.

"Who's there?" he asked again. "Please announce yourself."

Two knocks sounded off immediately. A series of louder, more intense, drawn-out moans followed closely behind.

Oren shuddered and felt his skin tighten around his flesh. He grabbed the bolts and let go. Grabbed them again and let go. After pacing in front of the door, he said, "Please. I'm asking you to identify yourself."

Another moan, more broken this time, and a soft knock.

Oren grabbed his chin and looked at the window. Then he got on his knees and tried to look underneath the door. After a second's thought, he put his hand on the bolts and kept them there for ten seconds. Then he dropped his hand to his side. Then he lifted the tomahawk in the air and started unbolting the door, his fingers fumbling with the rim locks. After all bolts had been pulled, he grabbed the knob, tightened his grip on the axe, and opened the door.

Fighting midnight's darkness as it poured into the opened doorway, light from the den traveled down the hall and illuminated the threshold and stoop.

There, barely visible amidst the profundity of shadow, was a man, or a woman, or a being that might once have been a man or a woman, lying on the ground, propped up against the stone wall to the right of the door. Its mouth was sewn shut with thick black cord, muffling the screams that fell from its nose. Suddenly aware that the tomahawk was scaring the creature, Oren dropped the axe to his side, overwhelmed by the pitiful sight of the thing on his doorstep. In addition to the threaded lips, the recumbent abomination had no legs of any kind, the flaps of skin in their stead stitched together with the same black cord. The being's groin region and both arms were bandaged with gray, bloodied, earthy cloth, reminiscent of those that could be seen wrapped around the skeletons of exhumed mummies. Underneath the bandages, the creature's arms were inhumanly small and knobby. They appeared to have a breadth no greater than that of naked bones, ending in hands that were caked with mud but otherwise intact. Its torso was bruised and chewed up and stitched, missing chunks of flesh in the pectoral region and gut. Its neck was also too skinny, with more black thread running up either side, stopping right below the jaw. The emaciated face and head were as gray-white and ashen as a tombstone, sharp, and devoid of hair except for a couple of yellow-grey tufts on the scalp.

Oren raised a hand to his mouth and coughed, looked at the being and then away, holding his neck, his arms, dropping the tomahawk and leaning on the frame of the door. The thing watched his every move with wide, wet eyes, exhaling and moaning through its nose.

"Good God," Oren exclaimed at last, not capable of containing himself.

The thing moaned in response, wincing. All of a sudden, it rolled over and landed with its belly on the threshold. From this position it let loose a flurry of muffled guttural exclamations and started to crawl through the door. The process was nauseating to behold. The thing threw its skeletal elbows out in front and lifted itself up, dragging the rest of the body one or two centimeters before dropping down in exhaustion, its skull thudding on the wood, its hands plopping lifelessly on the floor. After a second's rest, it would shimmy up and repeat the whole process.

Oren instinctively stepped aside, avoiding all parts of the thing's body as if their condition were contagious. He considered shutting the door before the being had a chance to weasel its way any further into the house, *but how can I do that?* he thought. *I can't slam my door in the face of such a suffering creature, can I?*

As the thing made its way three centimeters more through the doorway, Oren noticed, for the first time, the staples on the back of it's skull, the stitches at its temple, and the pungent, sour, rotting odor that rose from its physical exertion in a putrid cloud. Vomit stung the back of Oren's throat and would have continued upwards had a breeze not suddenly taken flight to carry the odor away from him, replacing it with the clean smell of a humid evening meadow. He inhaled deeply and found himself scratching his own scars and hairline.

Oren didn't have a telephone. He had never bothered to figure that one out. A part of him had known that he'd pay a price for not spending the time to bring modern convenience to his cottage, but this wasn't exactly what he'd had in mind.

"What do you want me to do?" he found himself saying to the thing. "Should I go get--"

The creature moaned and turned on its side, staring at Oren through the constant tears that rolled down its cheeks. With monumental effort, swinging its head and shoulders from side to side, it brought a hand to its mouth. Over its threaded lips, it made a V with its index and middle fingers. Three times in rapid succession, until its arm could no longer support it, it pinched its fingers together and returned them to the V-shape once again.

Oren, perplexed, watched it do this. After it fell over, he reached for his keys, thinking of nothing other than getting somebody out here to help this thing as soon as humanly possible. As he made for the door, however, the creature's pantomime flickered again across his eyes and the revelation froze him in his shoes. After another second had passed, he rushed to the den, returning at once with a pair of scissors.

He looked upon his visitor with refreshed eyes. The trip to the den, the removal of this dismembered thing from his vision and preoccupation, even for a mere second or two, instilled within Oren renewed horror and sympathy. What in the world was this thing doing in his hallway, and how could he have just stepped aside and let it in? What tremendous torture had befallen this poor man or woman, and why? And who were the tormentors? While Oren raced through his own mind, his body continued unabated in its practical tasks.

He bent over the thing and asked if it wanted to hold and use the scissors itself, or if it wanted him to do it. Propping itself on an elbow with tremendous effort, the creature made a feeble "give it to me" gesture with its free hand, moaning and gurgling, its head bobbing from side to side. Oren handed over the scissors and took a step towards the wall.

Lying on its back, the creature clutched the scissors with all ten fingers and slowly snipped the threads that incarcerated its mouth. Oren watched, eyes wide, succumbing to the mental and physical numbness that had forced itself on him since the moment he had first viewed the monstrosity on his doorstep. After ten seconds, all threads had been cut and the creature opened its mouth nearly to the point of unhinging, panting and coughing and spitting and gurgling and moaning ecstatically. Oren felt a sudden explosion of pride in his stomach, realizing that he was probably rescuing this dolorous and wronged being from a recent past that was probably more hideous than anything he or the majority of the world had ever contemplated.

The pride intoxicated and emboldened him. At long last, it seemed, there was a sense of balance in the heavens and earth. A chance to atone for any wrongdoings in his life.

"What else do you need?" Oren said, urgency shortening the words. "Water? Are you thirsty?"

The thing coughed and nodded, managing to whisper a ghost of a "Yes," the stitches' remnants jutting from above and below its lips like barbs or antennae or whiskers.

Oren ran to the kitchen, grabbed the chipped blue mug from beside the sink, filled it with water from the faucet, ran back to the hall, and kneeled by the creature. "Here you go," he said. "Drink it slowly, or it might not stay down."

The thing lifted itself onto its bandaged elbow joint. Oren cradled an arm around the healthiest-looking part of its back, attempting to support it. It looked up at Oren with its haunted eyes and, for a moment, looked as grateful as any being could ever appear.

But the look in its eyes started to change. A subtle glimmer of uncertainty flashed behind the wet gel of its eyeballs, and it began to observe Oren with a menacing vigilance, as if it were a vicious beast whose young had been threatened. Oren's arm hair prickled and he felt an army of icy ants crawl quickly over his body. In the same moment that he was thinking *why is it looking at me like that?* the thing spun with surprising strength and agility out from Oren's supporting arm.

"Shh, it's okay," is what Oren had just begun to say when the creature wheeled its arm around and sank the scissors, up to the screw, into Oren's temple.

Oren's eyes searched from left to right and top to bottom, rolling around in their sockets as hot crimson streams flowed down his cheek. His gaze finally came to rest on the creature. In that moment, he noticed the effortless way it supported itself with both arms, leaning back slightly, watching Oren with those wide, cold, curious, somehow familiar eyes.

Ten seconds passed, during which Oren wondered absurdly whether he had scared the creature into defending itself, tried to imagine whence the thing came before knocking on his door, considered that there was no possible way he would live through the night with a pair of scissors stuck in his skull, death was probably a mere moment away, how ridiculous to have three bolts on a door only to release them for an ominous moan, ha ha, good God, this, this, this was a... And then he passed out. In a kneeling slump, his shoulders hunched over, his head down.

He awoke an indefinite amount of time later and casually observed in the two remaining seconds of his life, as if he were only having a nightmare, that portions of the flesh on his torso and arms had been carved away. The stitches all over the creature's body had been partially unlaced, without bleeding; and the creature itself was, with a sparkling eagerness in its haunted, sad eyes, diligently hacking Oren's legs off with the tomahawk.

Flamenco Amputee

by Paul J. Gitschner

The judges sat in a semi-circle around the performance area. A small piece of masking tape marked the center. Beside them sat those who had come to play in today's contest. The contestants squirmed and held their instruments, waiting nervously. Cellos, oboes and violins would compete with bongo drum, banjo and even a simple acoustic guitar. All were welcome to show their talent and commitment today. At the center of the group of five judges sat the senior judge. His wooden chair was more ornate with a taller back than the others.

The senior judge appeared to be a kind man. With a sympathetic smile and a soothing voice, he welcomed them all to the annual event and requested that the first candidate step forward. Prior to the event, a drawing of lots determined the order in which they would perform.

A shaking, middle-aged man in a drab gray shirt and matching pants rose and limped to the front of the group. He stationed himself exactly on the mark. The senior judge squinted at his registration number and noted it on the clipboard awkwardly held on his lap. His eyebrows arched as he added the word "guitar."

"Please begin when you're ready," he said, pressing the start button of a stopwatch with his thumb. The other judges nodded and prepared to grade the performance according to the rules. Presentation and originality, as well as execution, would all be major factors. This man had already lost points on his choice of dress.

The player addressed his audience.

"Today, I'd like to play a Spanish piece on my guitar. I'll just need a moment to prepare."

He took a deep bow and set the instrument on the ground. The house lights reflected off the lacquered wood of the guitar like the flash of a knife blade. Standing straight, he clapped his hands three times rapidly to set the mood of a flamenco dance and stamped his feet twice in staccato on the hardwood stage. He dropped down, and his hands moved in a blur that obstructed his next action. A metallic thud was heard as he stooped over the guitar. He gingerly picked it up. Calmly, he stood with the instrument and began to play the chosen piece.

Unique sounds of flamenco guitar filled the chamber. Arpeggios, scales, and individual notes flowed forth, and it sounded as if the man had thirty fingers, each working individually and in coordination. A blood drop landed on his face and began to run down his cheek.

The other contestants sat quietly. They're faces showed concern as they made mental notes on how their own performances could be improved to win today's prize. The banjo player gripped the neck of his instrument with white knuckles and knew there was no way he could muster that level of dexterity, speed or commitment. The fat man with the oboe searched the judges' faces for clues. The bongo player knew he too was a dead man.

They all stared in awe at the feet of the playing man and the four small objects lying there in the blood. Sweat poured from the guitar player's forehead as he focused his fingers on the guitar's six strings to produce notes that ran like scales. The riffs were interrupted by spasms of hard strums that accented the intensity as he changed tempo. He occasionally stamped his boot heels on the hardwood surface as a form of percussive accompaniment.

The concrete walls of the hall echoed the sounds, heightening the effect. Blood dripped from his flying fingers to prove his commitment to winning today. The junior judges seemed impressed, but the senior judge remained stone-faced.

Blood pooled on the floor by the player's feet, spattering his boots as he released another salvo. The piece of tape could no longer be seen. His exhaustion started to show. He'd been playing for eight minutes and had begun to repeat himself. The originality factor was being lost. Sweat stained his prison-issued shirt and darkened it to the color of his registration number.

The senior judge looked down at his clipboard, and the player's eyes widened in terror. He wasn't going to win today, despite his efforts and sacrifices. He kept pounding the strings in desperation. The blood continued to pour, spurting from his index finger in rhythm with the pounding of his heart. It would have been hard enough on his fingertips if he hadn't severed them prior to starting. The four, half-inch long pieces of flesh lay at his feet. Plucking the strings brought excruciating pain to the fresh stumps that had been left. Tears streamed from the corners of his eyes. The four pink fingertips lay on the floor with the machete. A deep scratch marred the hardwood where the blade had impacted only seconds before he began to play. How he had gotten the knife would remain a mystery to them. He'd thought his extreme act would show them how much he wanted and deserved to win today.

Sure, it was drastic. But the parole board only met once a year and only released one inmate. He was sentenced to life with no hope of parole, and if he didn't get out this year, he was sure he'd go crazy. He'd had to try something desperate. By entering today's contest, he'd been given a single chance to win his freedom at the risk of joining all the losers in a mass execution. One man went free, the others died. That was how it worked. It was how they freed up cell space in this overcrowded prison system.

The contest had started a few years ago based on true musical talent, but soon the gimmicks had taken over. Contestants would now try anything to get the judge's attention. The beauty of the contest was that it was all volunteer. There was never a shortage of willing artists. Since the winner ran as far away as possible and the losers never talked, no one had the valuable knowledge of what had been the clincher in previous years. Sure, there were rumors, but they were heeded at the candidate's peril. He'd thought he had something today that would so impress the judges that he would be the one set free. He'd thought wrong.

The player stopped, knowing it was over. He knew he'd been cheated when he paid for the information. He thought he'd paid to find out how others had won. There was a moment of quiet. The senior judge spoke up. "Thank you very much, who's going next?"

The player gathered his guitar and machete. Fumbling, he picked up his finger tips. He walked away from the bloody mess on the floor with his head hung low. An inmate with nails driven into his arms and face timidly raised his flute into the air. Again, no costume had been allowed other than the standard prison uniform with a registration number on the chest.

The senior judge pressed the stop and reset buttons of his stopwatch and held back an urge to laugh as he raised his other arm and used his thumb to direct the second contestant to the performance area. It was the only digit remaining on the judge's right hand, and although it had won him his freedom many years ago, there were days when he wished he'd had his fingers back.

"Start when you're ready," he said.

Little Black Box

by Eric Stark

1

Harold stepped out, as he did every morning, for the paper. Only the most stubborn stars remained in the sky, and they but briefly, as the coming sun burnt away the blackness. He sucked in the chill remnants of last night's air and stretched his arms out, groaning as his joints popped softly, and then blew out between pursed lips. He coughed. The air seemed stale. Rarified.

He usually enjoyed the fresh taste of daybreak, before the flatulent neighborhood automobiles were led out of their stables, and the near quiet just after the nightshift cricket-lust and just before the dayshift bird-gossip.

Harold frowned at the still-curtained eyes of the nearby houses and, as he did every morning, took pleasure from being up before his younger, but lazier fellows, up even before the sun. He lived by his father's adage: the earlier worm avoids the bird. Even after he had begrudgingly accepted retirement, he couldn't avoid the determination that work was something to be greeted as a challenge, that the day was to be battled and won rather than simply accepted and appeased.

He had come out for the paper though, and it was in none of its usual locations: on the step, or somewhere along the stone steps that arced around the arbor vitae towards the driveway, or anywhere on the well-groomed lawn; it was not in Lenora's flowerbed or under the hag-haired tendrils of the willow; it had not been tossed irresponsibly onto the neighbor's less-well-groomed lawn. It had not arrived at all.

Late. Again. He did not tolerate tardiness; it implied disrespect for one's valuable time, disrespect for structure, for foundation, for walls and borders and properties. There was a reason Time had been divided into such infinitesimal units. In a world of nanoseconds and Cesium clocks, there was no excuse for tardiness. He glanced at his wrist, but his watch lay on the kitchen table waiting for its daily winding. Certainly it was after six.

And it was Sunday, his least favorite day of the week. Some folks would be lounging in bed, getting up only for a heavy breakfast or professional sports. Others would be dressing for church, buttoning up their once-a-week collared shirts and spirituality. Harold had always believed, like his father, that the good Lord would rather have seven days worth of steady, quiet faith than one of boisterous repentance. Harold huffed and slipped back inside.

The coffee maker burbled and caffeinated the lamp-oranged air. Harold heard the bathroom faucet hissing as his wife began her morning ritual. Soon she would join him in the kitchen and prepare his breakfast: two slices of wheat toast sparsely decorated with margarine, low fat of course. Then he would half-jokingly order eggs and bacon, and she would remind him that such things were strictly forbidden -- doctor's orders -- but he might enjoy the other half of her grapefruit, which he would politely refuse.

Harold sat at the kitchen table and wound his watch before latching it around his wrist. Yes, it was after six—fourteen minutes after, in fact. He waited and listened for the familiar thwump of the paper hitting the step so he could catch the paperboy and have another discussion regarding the importance of punctuality and the resulting effect upon salary arrangements. He wondered by what factor he would threaten to decrease it this time, and whether it would make any difference. Children were so abysmal at math these days.

Lenora joined him in the kitchen, tugging her robe snug. She put her hands on his shoulders and leaned and kissed him on the cheek. "Good morning, dear. You need a shave." Indeed, it was time for his week-beginning shave, which he performed every Sunday after finishing the paper and leaving it folded over the back of the kitchen table so Lenora knew it was ready to be put in the recycling bin, so they might do their own small part to save the earth. Not today, of course, and Lenora noticed the scowl on her husband's face and said, "Why the sour puss? Where's your paper?" and then she zipped open the shades. The gathering light fell to the floor.

"Hasn't come this morning. I swear that boy has it in for me."

"Oh, Harold. You know I'm the only one who has it in for you."

"I'm serious. How many times have I warned him? Does he want to be paid or not?"

"Just a few times, dear. Honestly, it will still be news by the time it gets here."

"A few? You let them get away with it once, twice, four times..."

"Yes, I know," she cut him off, "and four becomes sixteen and sixteen becomes two hundred and so on. Arithmetic progression."

"Two-fifty-six, dear," he corrected. "And it's called geometric progression. You multiply each number by the preceding one, and very quickly you reach an exceedingly high number."

"You and your numbers. You'd keep them as pets if you could."

Harold ignored the jab. "You know, I used to deliver papers when I was a boy. And our parents weren't around to drive us all over town. We pedaled our butts from one end of our route to the other. And if we were late we weren't paid."

Lenora rolled her eyes. "Yes, dear. Even in the sleet and snow. Uphill both ways, to boot."

She poured two cups of coffee and offered one to her husband, who always took his with neither cream nor sugar, not sweetened and diluted, "Just like a woman," he said and grinned.

She swatted him playfully on the arm and said, "I don't know why you bother to read that thing every morning. So full of murder and war and sensationalism. Too depressing for me."

Harold sipped his coffee, licked his lips, and said, "It's not sensationalism. Murder and war is the natural state of mankind. Always has been. Besides, there has to be some way to curb our population."

"If so, then it's hardly news, right?" Lenora wet a rag and wiped down the coffee maker.

He knew she hated when he said things like that. He tried to offer a smile, but she ignored him. "Besides, how else is one to know what's going on in the world?"

Lenora twisted the rag empty and rinsed it. She looked thoughtfully out the open window and said, "I can see what's going on in the world just fine by looking outside. I see the lawn needs mowing, for one thing." The smile she had prepared collapsed as she pondered the motionless trees in the back yard. Everything seemed clear-coated in the shadowless light. She shivered. "Today is certainly going to be gray."

Harold finished his coffee and set the empty mug in the sink and then coiled his arm around his wife's waist, pulling her close despite her feeble resistance. He followed her gaze out the window to her garden in the back corner of the yard. It was just a few carrots, radishes, green onions, and tomatoes, but she tended it with care and patience he couldn't fathom.

Since he retired, the garden had also served as her sanctuary. They both had their places away from one another. He had his workshop in the garage; she had her garden. Like most unspoken agreements in a marriage, it had evolved from necessity rather than conscious effort. "No sun for my babies today," she said and slid the window closed. Harold knew she liked listening to the morning birds as she did whatever women did in the early mornings before the day of men buttoned up its shirt and got on with business. That there had been no singing that morning, he hardly noticed. But the closing of the window bothered him. It was not how things were usually done.

Harold shrugged and let his gaze wander to the cedar jungle gym that he had assembled, a grandchild-safe distance from the garden. It stood lonely -- its chained swings still -- and the nearby stone birdbath, usually occupied by the singing bathers of dawn, stood empty. Indeed, the sky had gone a monolithic gray that sucked the color from everything. Then Harold glanced at his watch. The sun seemed to be taking its sweet time this morning. Of course, that was an absurd thought.

Lenora's head cocked suddenly to one side. "Did you hear that?"

"What?" Harold held his breath and listened.

"Just now. That sound. Like a pop."

Harold pecked his wife's cheek -- it twitched -- and said, "Must be the paper. About time."

Harold did not find the newspaper. He found a little black box. The contrast, a focal point on the concrete slab, demanded his eyes. He stood over it and stared. The thing had been mathematically placed at the median, its sides parallel to the descending steps. Harold crouched for a closer look and groped for his glasses, which he perched upon his nose. Gifts, packages, and deliveries were sometimes placed with near-equal care, but this was too small, too insignificant, and too precise.

He plucked it between index finger and thumb, rotated it on its axis, and frowned at each of its six, uniform sides. Two by two by two inches. Light and solid like wood, but smooth and cool like metal. Its edges were sharp, without visible seams or welds. He let it lay in his palm. Matte black. He shook it near his ear and then tapped it with a fingernail. Then he stood, his knees popped, and he grimaced, sure he had never received anything so ordinary.

Or so out of place.

He jammed it in his robe pocket. He plodded down the steps and surveyed his neighbors' porches. So it wasn't just him; no one would be informed today. He looked down the street. No cars. None like himself gone out to check for their papers. No one yawning and stretching while the dog did its business. The houses were still, eyes and mouths closed. The morning stood so silent, so calm. As if pausing to listen with him. No birds, no breeze.

Harold glanced at his watch. Six-thirty? Couldn't be. No, the second hand was motionless. He held the watch to his ear; it had stopped. Why not? Nothing else was going right today. But hadn't he just wound it? Harold shook his head and plodded back up the steps.

2

Inside, the back door was sliding shut. At least the cat was on schedule for her morning prowl. Nora stood with furrowed brow, one hand holding the door closed.

"What's the matter?" Harold fingered the box through his robe.

"There's something on the back porch." She shook her head and brushed past him.

"What kind of thing?" But before she could answer, he was at the glass door. "Goddamnit." He jerked the door open, kneeled down, and nabbed the second box.

"Harold!"

He closed the door, turned, and revealed his own box, identical to the other, and held it up for her. "Front porch."

"Two? Is it some kind of prank?"

"Prank?" He set the two boxes on the kitchen table and plopped into a chair. "Burning bag of dogshit -- that's a prank."

"Stop being vulgar, Harold. But what are they?"

"Two little black boxes. What else?"

"Sheesh, Harold, I could've told you that."

"I'll bet the paperboy did it. To get back at me for not tipping him."

Lenora squinted at the twin objects. "I don't like this." She wiped her fingers on her robe. "When I touched it, it felt cold and tacky. Like drying paint. You should have left it outside."

"Don't be silly, Nora." Harold stroked one of the boxes with a finger. "Feels smooth and polished to me. Besides, it's a harmless prank, but I've half a mind to call that boy's father right now and cancel my subscription."

"Leave the poor boy alone. And I'm not being silly. They give me the creeps. Toss them out." She gave the boxes a sideways glance. "I'm going to take my shower." She scurried down the hallway.

Harold got up, poured himself another cup of coffee, stretched, and glared down at the boxes. Nothing creepy about them.

Normally he would sip his bitter coffee and scan the bitter headlines. The world never changed. Different names and faces, but always the same issues; the ridiculous constancy of the inane. But he couldn't recall any stories about little black boxes that arrived unannounced on people's front steps. Unless, of course, it was all over today's front page.

Time to do some investigative reporting of his own. He palmed the cubes and walked to the attached garage. The garage smelled of sawed wood and turpentine, gasoline and greasy rags, furniture polish and paint. The smell reminded him that here he had everything he needed to make sense of things, to fix what was broken, to put his hands to good use.

Retirement could be unkind: all that time and nothing productive to do with it. But he knew the key was to prioritize, to schedule, and then see it through, though today's schedule seemed doomed. Once he had thought only in terms of syllabi and theorems and angles, both acute and obtuse, or integrals; where others had seen only jumbles of seemingly random numbers, he saw beauty and logic, a cold elegance that could explain everything. Almost everything. Of course it had never explained to him the workings of his wife's mind, had never quantified her joy at the birth of their son, William, or her sorrow when he had, so many years ago it seemed, refused to have another child. He had tried to explain it to her. There was only one species that reproduced at a rate approaching geometric progression. It had been a different time, a more idealistic time, and he had considered it his small duty, with his knowledge of population curves and logarithms, to prevent such an outcome. In retrospect...but there was no time for that.

He clamped one of the boxes into a vice. He examined the wall of hooked tools and pulled down what he needed: a rubber mallet, a chisel, and a handsaw. It would ease his mind to saw the goddamn thing open and see what it was made of.

4

From inside the house, his wife shrieked a high, sharp sound of surprise. He abandoned his project and fled up the stairs into the house. "Nora?"

Probably just a cockroach. Filthy things, but only when combined with the natural filth that humans seemed to acquire. Like most insects, and like all paragons of survival, there was something beautiful about them. He had read they could survive even nuclear fallout. But no matter how many times she made that awful noise, it always alarmed him. It wasn't something one got used to -- even after thirty-five years. Usually she would be treed in the kitchen, balanced on a chair and jabbing hysterically at a creature far more afraid than she. He would scold her afterwards and say, "How do I know whether to come running with the gun or a can of Raid?"

When he met her in the hallway outside the bathroom, a half-grin on his face, he expected what he found: her hands over her mouth, trembling, her skin gone pale. When she stammered, "Bathtub," his grin widened. When he went into the bathroom and drew back the shower curtain, he expected nothing less than a roach the size of a field mouse. But what he found, sitting harmlessly on the white porcelain, was a little black box.

Then Lenora was at his side and she whispered, "Harold, something's in the house."

"Someone," he corrected. "No. I don't think so. Must be William. He has a key to the house." She looked at him suspiciously, and he turned away and reached into the tub for the box. It was cool and smooth in his hand. He tossed it and caught it and then smiled. "Who's afraid of a little black box?"

But she wasn't looking at his smile. She was scowling at the thing in his hand. He folded his fingers over it and dropped his hand to his side. "Throw that thing away," she said. "No! Not there. Outside." Then she marched out of the room.

Why should she be upset by something so harmless? And William enjoyed practical jokes from time to time. Nothing like this though. Just the same, he would give his son a call. "And now to get rid of. . ." The sentence evaporated. There was another one. In the middle of the sink. Had it been there when he'd come in? Lenora hadn't mentioned it.

"Harold," Lenora called.

He snatched the box out of the sink and stuffed them both in his pocket. "Coming."

Lenora paced in the bedroom, the phone to her ear. She gnawed at a fingernail, something she hadn't done in years. "Harold? Harold, the phone is dead!"

"Here." He took the phone from her trembling hands and put it to his ear. Silence. He banged it against his palm, and the numbers flashed to life then went dead. "It's just this darn phone. Nora, do calm down. We'll use the cordless in the kitchen."

"Should we call the police?"

"The police? Nonsense. What would we tell them?"

"That something is in our house." She set her jaw and glared at him.

"No one is in the house, Nora. No one. How long have we lived in this neighborhood? Nothing ever happens here."

"Okay," she whispered.

He rubbed her shoulders and smiled. "Besides, what kind of criminal runs around planting little black boxes all over someone's house? It's really the most asinine thing." Or the most psychotic, he didn't say.

She forced a smile. "No, you're right. I'm sorry. Just a little frazzled is all." Her finger went to her mouth and she chewed an already-ragged nail.

"That's my girl. We'll call William and straighten this thing out." He took her hand away from her mouth and squeezed. Then he half-tugged her out of the room and into the hallway.

16

Harold pulled the cordless from its base and pressed speed-dial for his son. Lenora sat in the living room, on the edge of the couch, her hands folded stiffly in her lap. Busy signal. But he hardly noticed. He was sure he had taken those two little black boxes into the garage, but there they were on the kitchen table. And when he turned to hang up the phone, black shapes flashed in the corners of his eyes.

One in each basin of the sink. Two more on the linoleum floor. One in the windowsill, partially hiding behind a small, green fern. Two perched upon the refrigerator as if eyes looking at him. And four placed equidistant from one another along the kitchen counter below the wood cabinets. He summed them immediately. Ten. Plus two in his pocket, plus two on the kitchen table, plus the two he was sure sat in the garage.

Sixteen.

"Harold?" Lenora called from the living room. "Is he not home?"

He heard but could not reply. He stared at the boxes, his forehead creasing almost painfully. They had only been out of the room for a few minutes and had heard nothing. It was a small house. There were few places to hide. The floors creaked, the doors sometimes growled on their hinges. Keyed up as she was, Lenora would not have missed the slightest or strangest of noises. But there they were, scientifically aligned, obsessively precise in the way that only a psychotic would find meaningful. Not a prank, then.

Something pinched his right arm and he started. Lenora had come into the kitchen. She let out a high-pitched moan. "Harold!"

"I know."

"There's something in the house."

"I know." She was right. There was someone in the house. Harold's head darted from side to side as if trying to catch up with some peripheral movement.

Lenora dug her fingers into his arm. Her gaze followed after his. "Call the police, Harold." She whispered near his ear. "This is no prank."

No time. The gun. "What about the phone? The phone," Harold's wife protested as he pulled her back down the hallway to the bedroom and slammed the door shut. He flung open the closet and reached up.

"What are you doing?"

"Getting the gun. Just in case. And then I'm going to check the house." He pulled out the black .22 pistol. It wasn't going to stop an army, but a gun's a gun. He flipped out the cylinder and loaded the gun, one shaking bullet at a time. Then he handed her the gun.

"Oh! Oh, no. I can't."

"Nora, please. I can handle myself but I want this with you for your own peace of mind."

"Look. I'll take this putter with me." He pulled a putter from a bag of clubs that sat dusty in the back of the closet. "It's good enough for the behinds of neighborhood punks." He tried to smile. "I'm just going to check the house."

"Harold. Don't be brave. Please, don't be brave right now." Her eyes blossomed, round and white. The gun wilted in her hand.

He touched her arm. "You remember how to use this, right? Single-action. You have to cock the hammer before you shoot. Don't jerk the trigger. Squeeze."

"I remember."

"I'll be right back with the cordless. Then we can call the police. Ain't nobody gonna come through the door with this pistol-packin' momma in the room. Right?"

She grimaced. "Right."

"That's my girl." She flumped onto the bed. Harold hefted the putter and opened the door.

"See, I told you those clubs would come in handy when you retired," she called after him.

He turned and winked at her. "Be right back."

"I love you, Harold."

"I love you too, Lenora."

He stepped outside the room and closed the door. She was so much stronger than she seemed. Maybe all women were. They squirmed and shrieked at the smallest bug or beast, but any man who tried to break through that bedroom door would get a six-pack of lead for breakfast.

256

Harold crept low against the hallway wall. There was someone in the house. In his house. This house in which they had lived so many years now felt tainted, unsecured, and he, the protector of the house, was reduced to slinking through his own hallway, locking his own doors behind him, jumping at the groaning of his own floor.

The familiar calm of the house was suddenly restive. Gray light sneaked through the living room curtains, and dull, limp shadows huddled into corners. Each piece of furniture threatened to hide something. And he couldn't shake the sense of eyes, of being watched, that at any moment he would feel a rough hand on his shoulder, or that someone would pounce from a corner, arms perhaps loaded with little black boxes. Harold shook his head. Nonsense. Probably they had already fled the house, laughing and slapping one another on the back.

The living room appeared empty. Harold dashed across the room and locked the front door, then spun to spy into the kitchen. Nothing. No movement. Nothing coiled to strike. He could even see outside to the indifferent, motionless trees in the backyard. He chastised his hammering heart for being so foolish. Still, as he crept toward the kitchen, he wagged the golf club like a batter waiting for a pitch.

As he passed into the kitchen, he cast a glance down the hallway from where he had come. Empty. The kitchen, too, was empty. Well, not exactly. All along the countertops, across the table, even on the seats of the chairs, sat little black boxes. Scores of them. Too many to count. All lined up so carefully -- some solitary, some in single file one after the other, perfectly spaced. How could anyone have done such a meticulous job in so little time and make so little noise? Surely he had only been gone a few minutes, and the boxes were not casually tossed about but preordered in a grid as if according to some unknown formula. Dolloped as if by invisible machines.

No, William had not done this. Nor the paperboy, and yet it seemed like such adolescent foolishness. Was it though? Weren't they both terrified? By little black boxes. Like a child's alphabet blocks, almost. Though placed by someone who had invaded their space with such ease and right under their noses? He needed an invader, someone to confront, to attack, to punish. Someone who needed a lesson beaten into him.

Only the basement, garage, and back doors were left to check. In passing, he locked the sliding glass door, then eased open the basement door. It creaked maliciously. Harold froze, peered through the scant opening and down the dark stairs. Perfect hiding place. Windows large enough for teenaged boys to squeeze through. Harold shut it and locked it. If they were down there, they would stay there. For now.

Finally, he locked the nearby door to the garage. He put his ear to the wood. Nothing. He tried to smile. Master once again. Then he turned, let out a breath, and returned to the kitchen. Jesus. Were there more of them?

He groped for the phone, tore it off the receiver, and speed-dialed William. This time it rang.

"Hello?"

"William." He tried not to shout.

"Dad?"

"Will. Yes, it's me."

"You sound strange. Something wrong?"

"No. Course not." He swallowed hard. "I, uh, was just calling to see how you were this fine Sunday." It sounded hollow in his ear and he felt childish embarrassment.

"Funny you should ask. It's the damnedest thing. Trudy went out this morning to walk the dog and she found this little black box on the step." Harold stopped breathing. The phone crackled with static. "Dad? You still there?"

Standing there, putter in one hand, the phone in the other -- squawking and crackling at his ear -- Harold realized two things. First, there was no one in the house. No one locked in the basement or in the garage or skulking from shadow to shadow. The golf club slipped from his hand and clattered to the floor. Second, he understood why some men snapped, lost it, locked themselves in a room and blew their brains out or hanged themselves from a rafter with no explanation, why they brought guns to work and started shooting. The same reason young children huddled in their beds at night, sure that something lay hidden beneath the bed or in the closet, lay waiting until the loneliest part of night to ooze forth. And parental assurance meant nothing. Scientific fact meant nothing in a world that allowed for such things.

It didn't happen to all men or even many men. But some. Women and children had a method for dealing with such things. With things that defied explanation. With visions transmitted from eye to brain that could not be explained. With things that made no sense, that dashed reason to dust. They could scream and empty whatever toxic gas infused the blood. But men couldn't scream. Not most men. No, a scream would mean acknowledgement or worse -- acceptance.

Harold stood with whitened fingers clawed around the phone even when the line went dead, stood trapped between fight and flight, between anger and apathy. He could not engage what did not exist nor flee from what did not give chase. His mind, a mess of miscalculations, could not rally to this gathering army of innocent black boxes.

There were too many to count by eye, but he thought he knew exactly how many he would find if there were time to count by hand. One, two, four, sixteen, two-fifty-six. And then?

A scream. Lenora.

65,536

Harold dropped the dead phone and leapt into a hallway now paved baseboard to baseboard with little black boxes. He plowed through them, sending them flying down the hallway and clicking off the walls, though the contact sent phantom slivers through his slippers and into each toe. At the bedroom door, he twisted the knob and pushed. It opened a few inches and then stopped as if braced from inside. Through the crack, he saw the boxes stacked nearly thigh high. The door was barricaded. He threw his weight against the door, but it did not give. "Nora, I can't get the door open."

"Harold," she moaned from within. "They're everywhere."

"Nora, come to me. The door won't budge."

"No. I won't touch them. I can't."

"Nora!" He strained against the door, but it only creaked and bent, and his feet slipped on the smooth surface of the boxes. We have to get out of the house. Please."

"Why did you bring them in, Harold? Why?"

"The window. Go to the window. I'll pull you through from outside." He yelled into the crack.

"Hurry. God. Please, hurry."

4,294,967,296

Defeated by the door, Harold turned to find himself nearly walled in. The boxes had piled up to his waist. Silently. Impossibly. Mercilessly. He struggled to the top of the pile, his hands and feet slipping as if across an icy surface. As he scuttled across the pile, he heard a clattering sound. It grew louder towards the kitchen and living room. Little black boxes were tumbling from the kitchen table, which was almost buried. They tumbled from the countertops, from the refrigerator. The living room furniture was drowning in them. A black flood in his house, every crevice filling with black cubes. A slow, solid entombment with the inevitable force of water.

He scrambled for the door. The boxes were stacked to the doorknob of the front door. How would he get out? Dig, he told himself, dig. He pawed through them. His hands sliced open on their sharp corners even as they flew and clattered behind him. Tick, tack, clackitat -- all around him -- a scuttling of unseen appendages. He dug furiously with both hands, pausing to wipe the blood from his hands. If he could only get outside. Lenora. He dug. Darkness loomed around him. But there would be light outside.

Harold's hands, slick with blood, slipped on the doorknob. He wiped his hands on his robe and felt hard masses against his waist. Looking down, he saw his robe pockets bulged with black boxes; they spilled out.

He clawed himself out of the robe and used it to grip the knob, and then he heaved, nearly falling back with the sudden opening of the door -- just enough for him to squeeze from the jagged pile of boxes and out into the flat, gray light.

Outside.

Harold's triumphant yell was murdered in his throat. The well-groomed lawns, the street, the sidewalk, the roofs of the neighborhood houses were covered with little black boxes. All so perfectly square, one after the other like the shiny carapaces of a shiny insect swarm. And he was alone. None had escaped. Perhaps they had lain in bed as the boxes had gathered, secretly silent around them, and when they awoke it was too late. Buried alive.

But how could there be so many with no one to put them there? That there could be so many, and placed with such precision, indicated some sort of intelligence, some sort of logic. Where there was logic, there was reason, purpose. Perhaps it was some kind of cosmic joke: one little black box for every single man, woman, and child on the planet, as a kind of wake-up call. See what it's like to be overrun by a force that cannot be controlled? Sure, Harold thought, there was some kind of perverse logic to that. Sure. It was almost funny. Almost. And once we get it, once we get the joke, well it would simply be a matter of division, or of subtraction.

Then the living room and bedroom windows shattered outward and spilled great masses of boxes that clattered almost musically against themselves. Harold jumped off the step and waded to the bedroom window, kicking the boxes away. "Lenora!" Only her white hand, cut with thin red lines, was visible in the flow of cubes. And her ring. Her muffled cries. He reached for her hand, grasped it and pulled. From the rooftop, the boxes tumbled down around him like hard rain. He tugged. More boxes spilled around him as she was pulled forward. He braced one foot against the side of the house and strained, groaning and clenching his teeth. Please, God. Please.

Their blood-slicked hands slipped apart. Harold flailed. For a moment he thought he might regain his balance, but then fell backwards, his feet slipping and rolling on the boxes. He fell among them. They cut into his flesh. He thrashed, arms and legs twisting for purchase. The boxes gathered, spilled over him. He screamed. For Lenora. For God. But only the boxes heard his cries and they flowed over him, cool and smooth against his skin. They poured from nowhere, from everywhere, a sharp, solid deluge. He fought frantically to keep them away from his face, but still they piled, spilled, and clattered about until they were all he saw and all he heard.

They were tasteless on his lips. Pinpoints and slivers of light between them grew fainter and fainter as every fissure was fused. And the imperceptible gathering weight pressed against him. The gathering silence. Gathering darkness.

18,446,744,073,709,551,616

The gray above eventually lifted, and light reigned with the silence and weight of air. And from the darkness below, something stirred, its carapace shiny against the darkness. It groomed itself and was warmed by the morning light, so late in coming.

LEMONHEAD

by Vincent VanAllen

On the drive back from Mexico, the engine surged for a few seconds then choked, then surged and choked again, repeating the cycle over and over. The accelerator felt like a dead chicken under Keith's foot, and the air conditioner had expired hours ago. He turned off the radio and listened to the motor. Dragging a sweaty forearm across his brow, he prayed the Pontiac LeMans would limp the remaining two hundred miles to Texas.

Pontiac Lemon! The whole damned car had gradually fallen apart once the odometer snuck past 22,000 miles. First, the computer chip burned out and the vehicle wouldn't start. Then, there were electrical problems with the thermostat and ignition. Days after, the oil gaskets had to be replaced. Followed by broken transmission fluid lines, a faulty alternator, cracked CVC boots, brake repairs, fouled battery cables, on and on and on.

The engine surged one last time and died. Keith pulled onto the highway shoulder, exited the car, and yanked tumbleweeds from the grill. When he raised the hood, heat erupted from the exposed engine, blasting his face. He dropped to his knees, wheezing. The tumor in his skull throbbed, stretching black fingers across his brain. Over the past four months it had doubled in size, pulsating with anti-life and poking him like a voodoo doll to provoke blurred vision, new headaches, and violent seizures.

The desert sun smacked him on the back, and Keith spat at the front bumper. He crawled into the slice of shadow on the driver's side of the LeMans. Spying his molecular biology textbook under the front seat, he tore out the chapter on cell division and used the pages to wipe new sweat from his face before tossing the rest on the highway.

Six months to go: that's all he had until graduation and a now meaningless bachelor's degree in biology. So many tedious assignments, late nights of study, hours of lab work--all for nothing. The tumor made him unemployable; worthless.

Ear infections, appendicitis, brittle bones, tonsillitis, migraines, asthma, and scoliosis: God had dealt him a lemon for a body. He had struggled through childhood, adolescence, and somehow survived to adulthood--so many pills, doctors, needles, x-rays, scalpels, and stitches. Why had he fought? Cancer had certainly been inevitable, given his fragile existence. The malignant mass migrating though his skull was a slap in the face to Keith's years of fortitude. He was tired of patching up a broken-down body.

Chemotherapy had kicked his ass and bankrupted him, but he had stashed just enough money for a self-indulgent trip to Mexico involving two weeks of unabashed but unfulfilling revelry, seasoned with cocaine, tequila, and Mexican prostitutes. All his life he had been as sickly as this contemptible car. For Keith, it was a faulty set of genes. For the LeMans, it was a disgusting set of blueprints.

Keith intended to complain.

He took a swig of water from a plastic milk jug then went to work on the engine. Five minutes into the project, he determined the battery posts were corroded. Again. A few good whacks with a hammer, and the LeMans started as though it hadn't missed a beat.

It knew that the time had come to roll back into Texas and take a stand.

#

Keith crossed the border into his tiny hometown of Edinburg, Texas, and drove up to a DX gas station. He slammed the gearshift into park and stepped out of the LeMans' dim interior, grazing his head against the automatic seat-belt clip that hadn't moved forward along the window track. The tumor rattled, and pain shot down his neck. Damn the local Pontiac dealership for selling him this piece of shit!

The diamond-shaped DX gas station logo was clean and new. The scent of freshly laid asphalt rose up from the parking lot, and the station's galvanized pump nozzles glistened in the autumn sun. Not so the Pontiac LeMans: coffee stained seats, cigarette-burned upholstery, crinkled beer cans, crumpled pornography in the back seat. Was there a home for battered cars, a salvage yard where they all met and bitched about their abusive owners? Keith chuckled as his cousin Mike strolled up to greet him.

"Hey Bro, you're looking kinda pale." Mike offered his hand. "You all right?"

Standing a foot shorter than Keith, Mike had tousled blond hair that matched the sulfur of his teeth. Grease-soiled, denim coveralls clung loosely to his thin frame, and he stunk of petroleum and soot. A squished pack of Marlboros protruded from his breast pocket. Though he smelled like an ashtray dipped in motor oil, Mike was one of the best mechanics in town.

"Where's the hit?" Keith asked.

"Luke's got it." Mike craned his neck toward the attendant sitting behind the pay window. Luke flipped on the switch to pump number three for a lady driving a blue Camaro, then gave Keith a thumbs up.

"Great," Keith said, rolling his eyes. "So you told him?"

"Yeah, well. Kinda had to. Said he wouldn't sell unless he knew who it was for. Said he'd go half-price if he could watch when you take it, but I figured you wouldn't be interested."

"Good figuring." Taking his first, probably last, hit of Front Page wasn't something Keith wanted to do in front of an audience.

Besides, Luke wasn't exactly a cherished pal. Oh, he could fix a guy up all right. Whether it be a high-tech hit of Front Page or a homegrown ounce of pot, Luke was the go-to man. But he was still a dope-slinging fiend, and Keith didn't like him.

Mike's forehead creased with concern. "Hey Bro, can't you do this thing sober, I mean, without the bells and whistles? That shit is like smoking jet fuel, buddy."

"Hell no. I told you before--this fantasy's way out there, man. Couldn't get up the nerve."

But Front Page delivered nerve and more. Fascinated with the drug while enrolled at Texas A&M, Keith had signed a waiver allowing him to participate as a test subject in a controlled study, but by the time the grant money rolled around, the Feds had put a lid on any further human experimentation. Though most of the research had been performed legitimately, a few rogue scientists coupled the drug's instinct-inhibiting enzymes with a powerful derivative of morphine. The public result: pain-free maniacs who held no fear of death.

"This isn't gonna be like firing up a joint," Mike said.

"I know, I know," Keith pulled a Marlboro from the pack in his cousin's breast pocket.

"I just don't see why you have to---"

"You were there! You're the one who took me to the doctor in the first place." Keith hunched over, stretching his bony arms out. "Do the words 'malignant' and 'terminal' ring a bell?"

Mike looked away.

Keith flicked open his Zippo and took a long drag from the cigarette. At the pay window, the lady in the blue Camaro handed Luke a wad of cash, then he gave her a rolled-up cellophane baggie filled with something dark.

"Yeah, I know," Mike said, kicking a bottle cap across the asphalt. "You know, if it were me---"

"It's not you. It'll never be you. It doesn't matter anyway. I've had my vacation and party time--Mexico kicked ass--and now all the money's gone, and this is all that's left. I'm not gonna rot in a hospital bed, sucking food through a tube in my face while some nurse wipes my ass every time I crap myself."

"All right, all right, you got it, Bro." Mike hurried over to Luke with a crumpled fifty-dollar bill.

This was going to be a cheap ride. Keith hot-boxed the cigarette and flicked the smoldering butt at the LeMans, where it glanced off the front tire in a shower of sparks. When Mike returned empty handed, Keith crossed his arms and scowled.

Mike appeared grave. "Okay, it's in my pocket. But first you have to tell me you're not gonna kill yourself."

"Stop playing games, man."

"Just tell me, Bro."

"Maybe, maybe not." Keith ground the heel of his boot into the asphalt. "I don't wanna die, but if I go, I'm going out big."

Mike arched an eyebrow.

"Just give me the hit, dammit."

Mike dug into his pocket and handed Keith the fat, yellow pill. Keith marched to the pay phone on the side of the station and made a call. "Tell Channel Eight News about the bomb that's in your showroom; they won't wanna miss this."

"Oh shit!" Mike threw his hands up. "You didn't tell me anybody was gonna get killed."

"Relax," Keith said, hanging up the phone. "That's why I made the call." Smiling, he bit down on the rubbery yellow pill, allowing its oily contents to spill into his mouth. He swallowed hard and grimaced at the citrus flavoring. So this was it--the tangy taste of Front Page. Lemon-lime loathsomeness. Why did medications always have to be artificially flavored like some nasty, fruit wannabe? Nevertheless, numbness coated his mouth and crept down his throat. It wouldn't be long before the pain-killing properties of the pseudo-morphine in the drug swept throughout his body. He leapt into the LeMans and kicked an empty beer can away from the brake pedal.

"What in the hell are you gonna do?" Mike asked, frowning.

Keithed grinned and winked. "Grab a newspaper tomorrow morning. You just gave me Front Page." He cranked the LeMans ignition half a dozen times before it caught, then pulled out into the lunch hour traffic. "Adios!"

The fulgent Texas sun wrapped Keith's face in white light as he turned on the radio and brought the LeMans up to forty miles per hour. A death shroud? Transfiguration? He contemplated the Shroud of Turin, wrappings of a risen Christ. Would Keith rise from the dead in three days? Visions of Moses and Elijah, the Garden of Gethsemane, divine revelation—he grinned so hard that his cheeks hurt. So this was Front Page: profound, dreamy thoughts overflowing with a genuine sense of well-being. No wonder so many people got off on it.

His fingers tingled with the shimmy that reverberated throughout the steering wheel. The LeMans always shimmied at forty miles per hour, a nuisance that lingered until it smoothed out at sixty. Damn this piece of shit car. And damn Sean Murphy for selling it to him. Oh, what a silver-tongued devil in a three-piece suit. Damn him, damn him, damn him! Keith stomped the gas pedal. The car coughed and sputtered, wearily speeding up. It peaked at sixty-five miles per hour just before starting its descent of 21st Street, the steepest hill in town.

A police officer parked at a Mocha Mama espresso-stand roared out into traffic behind him. Halfway down the grade, Keith had just run a red light at seventy-five miles per hour when the police car zoomed up behind him. He spied the cop's determined face in the rearview mirror.

That's when the Front Page really kicked in.

He gritted his teeth and fought the urge to slam the brakes. Just to see the shock plastered across the cop's face as he tried to dodge the trunk of the LeMans--oh, so beautiful! Keith's foot hovered over the brake pedal, shaking uncontrollably. The desire to cause such a wreck was almost overwhelming, but he had other plans today. Plans he'd been dreaming about for years. He stomped his foot back down on the accelerator and let out a defiant scream that flowed into a delirium of laughter.

Sirens blared from behind, accompanied by the squealing tires of another police car joining the chase. Keith's head hummed with the noise. He turned the radio volume up. Ozzy Osbourne screamed out the lyrics to *Crazy Train*. Keith grinned and bobbed his head in time with the music.

Suddenly everything seemed to decelerate. Dashed white lines on the road launched themselves at the LeMans like lethargic torpedoes: one shot past starboard, another narrowly missed port. The music began to drawl as well. Ozzy sounded as though he desperately needed a fix; his words drooled out of the speakers. Heavy-metal molasses.

Then came the blackness. Keith's eyes inverted within their sockets, looking inward through the orbital fissure, peeking through a bone keyhole into a sacred place marred by unholy intimacies--an altar, a priest, a prophetess. And there, on the altar, sat a grapefruit-sized tumor, pulsating with anti-life. The priest raised the tumor overhead, slamming it onto the naked bosom of the prophetess. Spittle fell from Keith's lips and spotted his shirt. An orgasmic wave swept over him. He cried out in a garbled mess, like he'd just had a stroke. Delighting in this new language, his voice grew louder in a series of tongue-twisting grunts and moans. He imagined himself speaking in tongues, preaching to the masses of his Front Page disciples.

Keith bit his lower lip to quiet himself. Taking a deep breath, he forced himself to concentrate on the road. He changed the radio station. And now he remembered the episode of Cops he'd seen where a speeding motorist had T-boned a tractor-trailer rig at eighty miles per hour. What a beautiful way to die. No open casket funeral for that guy. Slide his pancake ass into an empty Beatles album jacket and send him to *Strawberry Fields Forever*. Keith mouthed the words as the song played on the radio. The taste of strawberries filled his mouth, washing away the horrible lemon flavor.

The LeMans shuddered and clanked, threatening to fly apart when it reached the bottom of the hill. Traveling at a hell-bent one-oh-five miles per hour, the engine sputtered one last time and died. Screw it. Keith dropped the gearshift into neutral. There was no way he would stop now. His pale fingers clenched the steering wheel, nails biting into the vinyl-coated rubber. The smell of burning oil filled his nostrils. Godlike intuition allowed him to diagnose the problem as yet another cam-cover gasket leak. "Front Page kicks ass," he mumbled. Maybe if he survived this, he would become a mechanic like his cousin.

And then it appeared--the showroom window of the Sean Murphy Pontiac Automotive Dealership.

With a quick jerk of the wheel, the LeMans broke free from the road. Three of its four tires ruptured on impact with the curb. Keith's skull hit the headrest at the moment the trunk clipped a telephone pole in two. The collision ricocheted the vehicle into a single roll immediately before sending it airborne. "Mayday...Mayday..." he calmly said with a chuckle as the LeMans launched itself at the showroom window. A new tranquility washed over him. He could see himself at home as a child, standing beside his mother, her soft hands peeling potatoes. Or were they lemons?

Instinct urged him to close his eyes and protect his face, but the Front Page held him in thrall, eyes wide open, hands locked onto the wildly gyrating steering wheel. It was going to happen. He was going to watch it happen, every bit of it. It was going to be beautiful.

Keith's eardrums burst when the LeMans plowed through the showroom window of the Pontiac dealership. A chandelier of tinkling glass spread over the hood. Smells of fresh paint, new leather interiors, squeaky-clean engines: the disintegrating LeMans snuffed them out, desecrating the showroom air with the stench of spewing gasoline, anti-freeze, and motor oil. Metal grinding against metal; the hissing of broken hoses; a chorus of car alarms and air bags deploying in unison—they became the sickening clamor of a junkyard orchestra.

By the time the car slammed to a halt at the far end of the showroom, the overhead sprinkler system had begun to shower the destruction. The LeMans engine let out a few, feeble, spastic coughs; then fell silent. With the taste of dusty dashboard in his mouth, Keith spat a pair of bloody incisors into the now open glove compartment. Won't be needing those anymore. Ashes to ashes, teeth to dust. Baby food--that's what they feed the patients in a mental institution, right? Bananas and strained carrots, peas and processed turkey, lots of flavors to choose from. But most of all lemons--lots of lemons--he hated lemons.

With the hot rush of Front Page coursing through his veins, Keith struggled to extricate himself from the engine that now sat upon his lap. He imagined his internal organs to be a tomato goulash sloshing inside his chest. Laughing, he released the safety belt and crawled through the broken windshield. Drenched in his own blood, he snaked his way out of the wreckage, as if born of it. He took on the persona of Jonah, and the LeMans became the Great Whale. And now he was to be belched out...out of the bowels of the big, yellow, lemon whale. Soon he would preach to the ungodly at Nineveh.

As he looked around the showroom, the smoldering carnage of new automobiles sanctified him as a self-appointed, Holy-rolling prophet. Transfiguration, yes!

Deuteronomy--vengeance. And there before him stood a wide-eyed Sean Murphy, mouth agape, exposing the gold crowns of so many rotten, neglected teeth. A man with bad teeth wearing a fine suit should never be trusted.

Sean Murphy wasn't God, but he would do just fine.

Keith puffed up his chest and slogged over to him, pressing the bloody keys of the

LeMans into the auto dealer's hand.

"Trade in!"

GARCES CIRCLE

by CJ Hurtt

There was a surprising amount of traffic on the road for it being eleven thirty at night. Not really the kind of thing Claire and Paul were expecting. They were hoping that by the time they got to Bakersfield the roads would be clear, the night would be quiet, and they could just get some rest after a long day of driving.

"Like a sandwich?"

"No thanks."

Claire looked at Paul. She knew he was tired and hungry. She also knew he wouldn't eat. He didn't want to be on this trip, in this situation, and he was just going to pretend that he wasn't. As if eating would have made it more or less real.

"I'm glad you came."

Nothing.

Claire's mother, Denise, had never liked Paul. He hated Denise right back. And here he was, going to the funeral.

Up ahead, Claire saw the statue that stood in the middle of Garces Circle. Its stone arms reached heavenward.

"Do you know the legend about that statue?" she asked.

"Hmm. No."

"There are a lot of accidents here. A lot. The lanes are pretty fucked up. The circle is poorly designed. Anyway, they say right before an accident, you can see that statue move."

"Weird. Say, who was this Garces person anyway?"

"I don't know."

Claire looked again at the statue. Hundred of cars circled around its feet. The expression on its face was one of tried patience. Its outstretched arms looked not like it was delivering benediction as the sign said, but like it was asking God "Why?"

What a weird thing to put in the middle of traffic, thought Claire.

"Damn radio. All they have here is country," said Paul.

He shouldn't have come, thought Claire. He was trying to be nice, but he really should have stayed home.

As they went around the circle, Claire could have sworn she saw the statue move.

THE GROVE

by Michelle Garren Flye

Manuel Gutierrez turned his eyes out the window of his corporate jet. Though nearly lost in the folds of age, those eyes still surprised new acquaintances with their sparkle. *We're getting close*, he thought, picturing the cacao groves beneath the cloud layer. Those trees had belonged to his family for generations, and would for generations to come.

He straightened. "Lisa," he called, not too loud, because she was always attentive to his slightest whisper.

"Yes, Grandfather?" Lisa turned from her seat across the aisle where she tapped away at a laptop computer.

"Put that thing away and come sit with me," Manuel said. His gruffness hid some of his pride. Her long black hair was much like her grandmother's, though her bone structure resembled her Caucasian mother's. But her shrewd intelligence came straight from Manuel, a fact that gave him much satisfaction. *Thank heaven there's nothing about her father in her*, he thought.

They spent the remainder of the plane ride discussing the cocoa bean harvest, the rainfall over Central America, and the upcoming purchase of more cacao groves. Lisa knew as much about the industry as her grandfather, which made up for her late father's ineptness. This satisfied Manuel. The death of Lisa's father a decade before had been inconvenient, as Manuel had planned his own retirement much earlier than this. His heart had not been in his work since his wife had passed away, but he'd been unable to let go of the business without a proper replacement. Lisa was that replacement.

Manuel squirmed a little as he thought of telling Lisa what she didn't know about her father's death. He still had nightmares at times, horrible memories of Carlos' screams echoing back from the shielding branches of the cacaos. Carlos had been worse than useless – he'd been lazy and extravagant. But he had been Manuel's only son. Manuel always woke from the dreams certain the dampness of his sweat was his son's black blood.

"Grandfather, why did you want me to come with you this time?" Lisa asked, breaking into his thoughts. "I could have stayed to supervise the shipments – you know you don't like to leave that to George." Lisa's cousin George was a pale shadow in the corporate world when compared to Lisa. He seldom did anything the way his grandfather wished.

Manuel tented his fingers and looked over them at Lisa. She was a strong woman, but would she be strong enough? "I have something special to show you this time, Lisa. Something you will need to know when it is your turn to run this company, and that time is fast approaching."

Lisa covered her grandfather's hand, grown silky with age, with her own smooth one. She didn't deny death, as many would have. She accepted it, just as he did. It was a fact of nature, a turning of the wheel, just another part of life. But with the simple touch, she let him know his life was valued and he would be missed.

Manuel sat back in his chair and reflected on how far he had come in his seventy-five years. From a simple laborer swinging a scythe in his family's grove of cacao trees to a part of the corporate world of America, supplying many of America's chocolate manufacturers with cocoa beans unrivaled in flavor and richness.

The plane circled to land, and Manuel looked out the window just as they broke through the fluffy layer of clouds to reveal the city below. "Jorge says the jeep is ready for us, Grandfather," Lisa said. "He offered again to have someone accompany us. Are you sure you would not prefer that?"

Manuel sat up straighter with an effort. Lisa was worried about him because he hadn't been able to maintain his concentration in the board meeting in the city. But now that he was here among his cacao trees with their foot-long tan cocoa pods hanging like bizarre Christmas ornaments from the branches, he should regain some of his strength. "I'm certain," he said. "It is important that we do this on our own."

Lisa helped him into the jeep, then climbed into the driver's seat. Following Manuel's directions, she steered eastward, the sun warm on their shoulders as it dropped toward the horizon. Manuel knew Lisa wouldn't be afraid of the dark out here, and it would surely be dark before the jeep could make it back. She knew the groves nearly as well as he did.

Deeper into the groves they went, the road fading to a grassy path and then to nothing. Finally, Lisa had to stop, unable to find a way through the undergrowth. "What now, Grandfather?"

"Now we walk," Manuel said, stepping out. The moment his foot touched the earth, he felt a surge of energy. His shadow stretched long and black ahead of him, covering the grass and weeds. Yes, they were very close now.

Lisa went ahead of him, pushing aside the undergrowth, and their shadows mixed into the growing twilight around them and became one with it. Manuel followed, perhaps a little faster than he'd walked in the city, perhaps a little more eagerly than at home. So close now.

And then the undergrowth ended and Lisa stumbled out into the middle of a clearing. Manuel caught her elbow and steadied her. Lisa took a deep, awed breath, looking all around her at the cacao grove they'd entered. "Grandfather?" she whispered. The cacao trees here were old, their trunks more gnarled, and the pods hanging from the twisted branches looked more like sleeping vampire bats than Christmas ornaments. The branches formed a kind of cavern over them, blocking out whatever sunlight was left of the day.

Manuel walked from one tree to the next, touching their trunks, caressing the enormous pods and whispering as if to old friends. He reached the largest of the monstrous trees and knelt among its roots, taking some of the rich black soil in his hand and letting it run through his fingers. Then he stood and went back to Lisa.

"This is where I will stay, Granddaughter," he said. "My death awaits me here, as yours will someday."

"I don't understand, Grandfather," Lisa said. "You seem so much stronger than you did just an hour ago."

"Only because I am here," Manuel said. "You see, this is where it began, Lisa. I worked these trees when I was a boy, and my father before me and his father before him. It is my turn – these trees and the love of them have claimed so many lives – my father, my father's father, and – and your father, Lisa."

Lisa shook her head. "No, Father died of a heart attack. You buried him here because they wouldn't let you take him back across the border. I've-I've visited his grave."

"You've never visited your father's grave before today, Lisa," Manuel said. "You see, I had to give your father to them – they were ready for me, but I couldn't go. Your father was a fool when it came to business. None of my children ever knew enough. But you, you were different. I knew if I could wait until you were ready... And so I gave your father to them instead of myself."

"Them?" Lisa whispered. Her eyes flickered around the cavern of cacaos.

"The trees," Manuel said. "They need our family to survive, to continue to produce. They need our blood, our sweat and our tears, but mostly our blood."

Lisa made a horrified sound and took a step back, stumbling a little on a protruding root. Manuel caught her elbow. "You must stay, you must watch and understand," he said. "It is not horrible, it is not evil. It is the way of things, just as life and death are the way of things."

He kissed her tenderly on the forehead and turned, ready for it to be over. He walked to the central cacao tree and lay down among its roots, waiting.

It didn't take long. The cacaos were hungry. Lisa's father had been nothing more than a stopgap. His blood had not the ripeness of age that Manuel's did. As Lisa watched, one root after another ripped from the earth, rearing over Manuel's supine form, then stabbing through him and back into the earth below. Lisa's screams were lost in the sucking, squelching sounds of the cacao's feeding.

Though Manuel felt his energy seeping away as his life became nourishment for the cacao grove, he also felt himself growing stronger, stronger than he'd ever been, even as a young man working in the grove. Just before his consciousness left him, he was the grove, along with the many generations who had gone before him.

One Small Bite

by John Rowlands

I spent most of June, 1918, in Brazil doing field research on the exotic plants of the Amazon River Basin. It seemed hotter there than on any of my previous visits. The humidity was oppressive. Was it the progressive result of global warming, a new theory being discussed in scientific circles in England, or was it an anomaly? I made a note to research this once I finished my current project. My impatient editor rushed me to complete the first draft of my latest botany book describing the fascinating flora of the Basin.

One afternoon while sitting outside my lean-to editing my field notes, a large mosquito bit me. Needing blood to boost her egg output, she neatly punctured the skin of my arm and pierced a capillary. With two powerful pumps from her head, she drew blood while simultaneously discharging hundreds of parasites into my bloodstream. Within half an hour, the parasites were safely established in my liver where they multiplied asexually for six days. On the morning of the seventh day, they burst free to attack my red blood cells, and I exhibited all of the classic symptoms of malaria - delirium, chills, vomiting, diarrhea with a 108 degree fever in the shade. I gathered bark from a Simarouba tree, boiled it to make a tea, and drank it. The Papallata Indians had told me about its curative powers for ague and tropical fevers.

I was alone and isolated in the depths of the jungle. Inside the shelter on a narrow camp bed, I lay for five days shivering and feverish in turns -- my spleen dangerously enlarged. During the day, as fast as the sun dried my clothes, sweat from within me rewet them. Early on the afternoon of the sixth day, the fever and chills left me. The tea worked; however, I was still extremely dehydrated and weak.

Only one thought befuddled me – how would I return to civilization? Summoning what little strength remained, I gathered a meager pack and staggered, full of misgivings, into the dense jungle. Time was the most precious thing in the world to me, and I moved as quickly as I was able, trying in vain to avoid the razor-sharp ground foliage. The jungle was unspeakably dismal, as it never ceased raining. The soggy swamp and escalating heat posed a daunting trek for even the healthiest man.

Yet when night fell, I huddled under my heavy, rain-soaked blanket in a relatively clear spot, trying to generate enough body heat to ease me into sleep. Delirious, I saw green and blue flashes in the night sky, then fell into an uncomfortable restless sleep.

I awakened with a severe itching all over my body, generated partly from the multitude of foliage scratches I had received and partly from the jungle insects. Weak and hungry, I stumbled to my feet. I rolled my blanket into a sodden log and pushed myself further into the jungle.

Over the next few days, I barely survived by eating grubs, cola nuts, and turning my mouth up to the ever present rain for water. I couldn't believe my good fortune when on the third day I came across a deep stream. I cupped my hands and drank my fill, then slumped into the cool, comforting water.

Floating in bliss, I felt a small amount of energy return to my ravaged body. I allowed myself to drift, then eventually took up my trek from the opposite shore. After what seemed like hours, I encountered a similar branch of the creek. I traversed it a second time, but midway lost my blanket, which had nearly pulled me under in the unexpected swift current. Once again I dragged myself onward, my feet nearly numb, my clothes badly torn, my body covered in festering bug bites. At times, I encountered a strange plant I had never seen before in that jungle. Parts of it looked edible, but hungry as I was, I was not about to add poisoning to my list of recent maladies. What was this plant? How did it get here? Was it a new species? Questions for the researcher in me, I could not answer.

Later that same day, I came upon the meandering stream for the third time. Crossing it again was more a chore than refreshment. On the further bank I turned upstream and found fresh footprints -- my own. I stood on the same spot where I had taken to the water before I had spent an entire day wandering in a complete circle!

Dispirited and disoriented, I turned my back on the stream and staggered off in a new direction. It was nearly dark when I crumpled to the ground to rest. I fell asleep almost immediately, shivering despite the heat, and nearly delirious with hunger and exposure.

When I awoke, the pangs of hunger had left, but I knew debilitating weakness would soon overcome me if I didn't eat. In desperation, I managed to uproot a tiny palm, and with my pocketknife, cut out the crisp, tender, celery-like heart. My stomach was in no condition to keep it down, however, and the vomiting left me weaker than before. The scratches on my arms and legs had turned septic, infected by a microbe that caused a maddening irritation. The skin on my legs, irritated by the constant moisture, had broken out in ringworm-like sores, and my feet were a mass of festering wounds. The heat was unbearable.

Stepping gingerly on benumbed feet, I continued my trek. I must have paused to rest every half-hour. By nightfall I was thoroughly exhausted, and it was with great difficulty I managed to lay a bed of leaves before I collapsed. That night, the rain fell more heavily than ever.

I awoke the next morning in a puddle of rainwater. The jungle sauna steamed everywhere. With my last vestige of strength, I managed to stand and totter weakly off. About midday I came up against a dense wall of bamboo, and with no energy left to stand, my knees gave way and I sank to the ground defeated. As weak and disoriented as I was, however, I clearly noticed the same odd plant I'd seen days before. My last thought before I passed into oblivion was that the plant seemed to sway with me, mirroring my movements. Was it tracking me?

Illness, according to the Indians, passed through distinct stages: first one feels hot, then feverish, then ill, then dead, then absolutely dead, and finally dead forever. When the Papallata Indians found me, they took me for dead. I was not, however dead forever, not even absolutely dead, and they set about nursing me back to life with medicines derived from wild native plants, including the one that I thought was tracking me.

Utterly at peace with the jungle that sustained and sheltered them, the Papallata lived with no belief in evil other than that of their enemies. Not surprisingly, they sang songs of praise to the jungle that provided them with sustenance. They were singing just such songs when, having seen me through my crisis, they carried me on a litter to the nearest settlement. They handed my care over to Don Juan Ramerez, a wealthy dealer in rubber and slaves, who fortified me with quinine, then put me on one of his steamers to Belem. With my delirium gone, I laid recuperating on deck traveling down the Amazon, my strength and eyesight slowly returning.

I arrived at a hospital in Belem, and a doctor explained to me that, while malaria was rarely fatal, its nickname, "benign tertian fever," was really a misnomer. A malaria victim suffered eight to ten relapses, each with a long series of chills and fever, followed by profound prostration and debility. Terrific -- I could look forward to a life as a semi-invalid, never to set foot again in the Amazon jungle to continue my life's work. My editor would be so pleased to hear that. It was ironic; the jungle in which I had known my deepest tranquility was the same jungle in which I had contracted the disease that drove me out forever.

My roommate in the rustic medical facility was a skin and bones monkey who became so attached to me he never left my side. When some three weeks later I boarded a liner home to England, he remained with me. The ocean voyage was long, and while I seemed to draw some strength from our companionship, the creature seemed to draw only weakness from me. When at last we arrived at our destination, I wobbled slowly down the gangway, one steward at my elbow, another close behind carrying a large bamboo cage with my monkey huddled shivering in a corner.

A three-day overland trip took the last energy from the poor little fellow, and by the time my brother Robert met me at the station in Newcastle, the monkey was dead. Robert, a warmhearted bear of a man, reached into the cage and stroked the matted fur as I told him of our companionship. In thanks, a nasty flea, having taken all it could from the monkey, hopped onto Robert's wrist and bit him before I was able to reach out, smack it dead, and flick it off my brother.

When we walked to his well-tended garden to bury the monkey, I noticed Robert absently scratching his wrist where the flea had bitten him, removing the small crusty scab that had formed there.

We spent the rest of the week lingering over far too many glasses of scotch, talking about old times and past adventures, visiting with Robert's friends and a few of mine who came over to welcome me back. It was obvious Robert was well liked in the community. From his devoted friends, I learned of the many local charitable societies he supported. My brother lived a happy, enviable life.

One Small Bite

On Monday, I sat in the kitchen huddled over a cup of tea when Robert stumbled in coughing up blood and what looked like lung tissue. Against my wishes, he took a crowded one-hour train ride to London to visit his doctor, spraying sputum all the way, unknowingly infecting hundreds of passengers with whatever he had contracted. By the time he arrived at Paddington Station, he could barely stagger to a taxi. Upon examining him, his doctor immediately put him in one of the six beds in a hospital ward. My brother died by nightfall. I was devastated. We were just getting to really know each other again. Robert had been a vibrant man, living a grand life when I arrived on my recovery from death's doorstep, and now he was gone.

Several days after Robert's death, I read in the *London Times* that ten unrelated people in the same hospital had come down with similar symptoms. When two of the five patients who had shared the ward with Robert also died, and the other three became violently ill, the doctors belatedly called for a quarantine. So quickly the virus overwhelmed the body's natural defenses. Unknown to the completely baffled doctors, an epidemic was spreading and would soon be out of control.

Profoundly saddened, I remained in our family home in Newcastle in complete seclusion. Contemplating once again putting pen to paper, I mused on what in the world was happening.

Perhaps now was the time to start my new research before it was too late, and switching my focus from botany to ecology would not please my editor. But then, maybe he was no longer alive.

Momma's Shadow

by Mark E. Deloy

Maitland, TN 1966

Eldred Gamtree sat next to his wife's bed holding her frail hand. Bobby, their eight-year-old son, stood on the other side of her, watching her eyelids flutter and her sore-ridden mouth twitch.

Rita's breathing was shallow, interrupted occasionally by a harsh, raspy cough that made her sit straight up in the bed and curse her illness, her bed, and sometimes God himself.

Bobby watched his father's brow furrow with worry and his face twist in the agony of grief. His parents had had their problems, but they loved each other. The boy got up and looked out the window in an attempt to hold off his own tears. The farm looked overgrown and unkempt. It had been raining for the better part of a week, and puddles pooled in the yard. The world seemed fully saturated and much too green.

"Bobby. C'mere for a minute son," his mother said, and then erupted into another fit of terrible hacking coughs.

Bobby went to his mother's side, but she kept on coughing. She doubled over and gripped the bedcovers with her claw-like hands. Bobby watched as his father put his hand on his wife's back, trying to do something, anything. Doc Windsor said that her emphysema had reached a critical stage, and it was only a matter of time before she succumbed to her illness. Bobby rubbed his mother's thin arm through her sweat-soaked nightshirt. He suddenly realized that he was going to lose his mother. She would never go to his high school graduation, never go to another of his baseball games or school plays. She was leaving him here with his alcoholic father in this drafty, lonely house to live the rest of his life out without her. There would be no warmer, soft hand on his shoulder or encouraging voice in his ear.

Rita gasped, tried to catch her breath but failed; instead, she wheezed and pulled at her neckline attempting to get some air. Spit flew out of her mouth, and Bobby watched a drip of saliva settle onto the bedspread. It seemed to take forever to seep into the brown material. He thought to himself, *this is what shock feels like. I'll stay like this forever, with my eyes stuck on the last drop of my dying mother's spittle.*

She lay back onto her pillow and struggled again to breathe. Her eyes bulged in her head, and the tendons in her neck stood out like steel cables. Her face turned ashy, then pale and then blue. Finally, she gripped Bobby's hand and died with her eyes wide open and his name on her lips.

Eldred dropped his head to Rita's limp hand, his tears tracing tracks on her thin, wrinkled skin. Bobby had finally shaken himself out of his stupor. He reached up and shut his mother's eyes as he'd seen people do on TV, and then he kissed her goodbye.

##

Bobby watched his father wrap his mother in a clean white sheet, tucking in the corners, completing her shroud. Eldred then called both her parents and his father. They all lived nearby and arrived in the yard an hour later. Bobby wondered if his mother would want anyone else there, but he couldn't think of a single person whom she had called "friend".

The boy sat with his grandparents, listening to their stories about Rita, her childhood, and how sad it was that she had only had one child. They gripped Bobby's hands, kissed his cheek and wiped the tears from his eyes, telling him that he favored his mother with his dark hair and light skin. He smiled and tried not to lose her face in his mind, but it faded slowly like a perfumed smell or a sweet taste. He cut his eyes over to his mother's covered body every few minutes expecting her to twitch or struggle against her cotton confines, but she never did.

Outside Bobby's father dug her grave in the family plot. The small graveyard bordered a short cedar fence. In the center a large magnolia tree shaded the departed family. Under the tree rested Uncle Greg and Aunt Florence. They had died in a car wreck five years ago. Also included were Bobby's great grandparents who had been dead his whole life. Some of Bobby's earliest memories were of playing happily around their rough granite headstones in the early summer sunshine.

The sounds of the steel shovel impaling the earth coughed in through the open windows. More than anything, Bobby wanted that sound to stop.

After about an hour, the chuff-chuff sounds ceased, and his father came back into the house sweating and covered in dirt. His arms hung at his sides, and his face looked flushed and haggard. Bobby knew that face, his father had been taking pulls from his flask, and now he was drunk. But he couldn't blame him. Bobby would have escaped himself if he only knew how.

"I'll go change my clothes, and then we'll lay her to rest." His voice was very weak, and for the first time in Bobby's life, he looked not just drunk, but old.

##

Ropes were placed under Rita's body and she was lowered into the hole. Eldred said a few slurred words about what a good wife and mother she had been. Her parents wept openly as they held Bobby close. He could smell their starched clothes tainted with mothballs and breath mints. Gordon Gamtree, Eldred's father, went on about Rita's place in heaven and God's will. To Bobby, all of his words sounded like excuses, raw and unfair ways of explaining something that really he knew nothing about.

The wind picked up as Bobby's grandfather shoveled dirt onto his daughter. The trees over the family plot swayed back and forth. Eldred said he couldn't watch her be covered up and went in the house to lie down. Bobby stayed with his grandparents and prayed to God that his mother would be happy in heaven.

Bobby took one last look at the bottom of the grave. The last patch of white sheet was being covered by loose black soil when he thought he saw the sheet, and more importantly his mother's body, move. He stared hard until she was completely covered, then convinced himself that his eyes had been playing tricks on him and followed the adults inside.

The next day, Bobby woke up with his mother's name on his lips.

"Mommy, mommy, mommy." It was the sacred mantra used by all children to summon goddesses and chase away demons even in the darkest night. But this time the spell had failed.

He sat up in bed, and his heart shattered all over again as he realized that his mother was no more. He wanted to slide back down in his bed, cover his head and never face the world again. He wanted to yell to God and tell him that he'd made a mistake. He wanted to tell him that his mother didn't deserve to die.

After lying in his bed crying for twenty minutes, Bobby finally dragged himself out from under the covers and set to find his father. It was nearly nine o'clock.

He found the old man huddled under the covers apparently sleeping off a hangover and talking in his sleep. Muffled mumbles came from the bed. Bobby could make out a few words including his mother's name. He left his father to his troubled dreams and went to make breakfast.

The sun cut through the kitchen windows, filling the room with glowing amber light. Today was a day that his mother would have loved. She would have been singing as she went about her daily chores. He could almost hear her soft, melodic voice floating in on a summer breeze.

Bobby got a cereal bowl out of the cabinet and started reaching for the box of corn flakes atop the refrigerator when he saw the worms on the kitchen floor.

Three thick, bulging earthworms coated with dark soil writhed on the faded linoleum. They wriggled like mad to get back to where they came from. Bobby bent down to pick them up. He started to bring them back outside when he heard a shuffling sound coming from the porch. He looked up and saw a flash of white move past the old, rusty screen door. Standing up slowly, he pushed the creaking door open. More dirt clotted worms squirmed on the front porch. They worked their plump brown bodies across the dry peeling paint, struggling to escape the sunlight as it invaded the shadowy sanctuary.

Looking to his left, Bobby spied his mother, swaying like a drunkard and covered in black earth. Her eyes were wide open, and her once beautiful black hair hung in a matted filthy mess. She had been buried only in a cotton shroud, and now it lay draped over one shoulder, torn, covering almost. The milky white skin which had been the envy of every woman in town was now scratched and streaked with mud. Her full breasts sagged against her swollen stomach, and her legs were bruised and bloody.

Bobby ran to her and wrapped his arms around her waist, his fingers sliding through the mud and the muck to find her soft skin. That sweet heavenly mother smell was still there even under the thick, cloying earthy smell of death. But she wasn't dead. She was alive.

"DAD! DAD! Get down here! Momma's alive! She's alive!" Bobby called back into the house over his shoulder.

"Uh...Bob. Bobby," she said weakly and tried to return his hug.

"Momma. How Momma? How?"

"I wasn't dead. I...I woke up. Something told me to dig. I..." She collapsed onto the porch. Bobby tried to hold her up, but she had passed out.

"DAD!" he called again.

There was a thump from upstairs as a bottle tipped over, and Bobby heard the clumping of heavy feet coming down the stairs. His father burst through the screen door and just stood there with his mouth open.

"How...did..you..."

Bobby knew what his father had almost asked. He thought Bobby had dug his mother up.

"Dad! She dug her way out. She wasn't dead yet. She came back."

"But I checked. I..I.."

"Dad! Help me!"

That seemed to snap him out of his stupor. He rushed to his wife and picked her up in his arms. Bobby noticed that his father did not hold her closely, but almost at arms length as if he still didn't believe in her resurrection and believed that the earth would rise again to reclaim her. As they brought her inside, Bobby thought that he saw something out of the corner of his eye, a black shadowy shape that slid along the wall, but it was gone when he looked in that direction again.

Eldred set her down on the sofa, then bent down and put his ear to her mouth.

"She's alright. Still breathing. Bobby, go and run your mother a bath."

"Yessir," Bobby said with a smile. He ran upstairs and turned on both faucets, spilling mostly hot water into the claw-footed tub. He dumped in some Calgon bath crystals for good measure. Then he ran back downstairs. He was afraid that when he went back that she would be gone again. He was terrified that his father would say that it was all just a dream.

When Bobby went back down the stairs, he realized he hadn't been dreaming. His mother was sitting up now, sipping water. Bobby and his father helped her up the stairs and into the bath. Bobby was embarrassed by his mother's nakedness, but she didn't seem to mind. He didn't want to, but he left her in the bathroom and sat outside the door in the hallway, his knees pulled up to his chest. He giggled and cried, thanking God.

After her bath, Rita looked a little more like herself. She had combed her hair and wrapped herself in a thick, white, terrycloth robe. She pulled Bobby to her and hugged him for what seemed like an hour.

"I love you momma."

"I love you too, honey."

Eldred wrapped his arms around them both, and they stayed like that for some time.

"I'm so glad you came back to us," Eldred said. "We'll need to call your parents and my father. God, we were sick with grief. You don't even seem sick anymore. How do you feel?"

"Like a new woman. Why did you bury me?" she said. Her face looked as if it was set in stone.

"Honey, you were dead," Eldred said, his face worried now.

"No. I don't think that I was. I was someplace. I had gone someplace, but I wasn't dead. You shouldn't have buried me."

Bobby saw a shadow like the one that he'd seen out on the porch slide into the corner by the table. It bobbed up and down as if getting excited. He wanted to say something to his parents, but he was afraid his mother already knew that it was there.

"Honey. I...I'm sorry. If I had known, I never would have...done...that." Eldred looked as if he was about to cry. His eyes were bloodshot, and Bobby smelled the whiskey on his breath.

Her face broke into a slight smile. "I know you tried."

"Well, I'll call your parents. Are you up to seeing them?"

"Sure dear. I just feel so tired."

"You sit down and rest. They will be happy to know you're alive. They'll think I went crazy, but they'll be crying with joy."

Phone calls were made, and Rita's parents did cry with joy. They hugged her and then hugged Bobby. After dozens of questions and another round of weeping, they left with a promise to return soon to help out until Rita got back to one hundred percent. Shortly thereafter, Bobby's paternal grandfather arrived. He clutched a crucifix to his chest. His long grey hair fluttered in the breeze, and his eyes were wild and electric.

"Pawpaw, what's the matter?"

"'Tis the work of the devil Bobby. No one comes back, no one."

"But Pawpaw, she wasn't dead. She dug her way out. Look!"

Inside the family plot was a mound of loose, black earth where Rita Gamtree had lain for seven hours before clawing back up to the surface through three feet of rocky soil.

"She's got to go back son. It's for the best. You'll see that in time."

The elder Gamtree gently pushed Bobby aside and mounted the porch steps in his lopsided, limping gait.

Rita sat in the kitchen smoking a cigarette and drinking coffee. Eldred stood near the kitchen counter, reading the paper, wondering if any newspaper would pay for his wife's story. Paw Paw Gordon opened the screen door and let out a savage howl as he ran at his daughter-in-law. Bobby was right behind him, but he was too small to stop the big man.

Rita jumped up and covered her face. Something black and spider-like leapt out of the corner near Rita's leg and landed on Gordon's face. He screamed and clawed at the black creature, but it held on. Its huge fangs sink into his grandfather's neck.

"What's wrong Dad? What are you doing?" Eldred said.

Bobby saw the creature as clearly as if it really was a giant black spider instead of a wisp of shadow as dark as night and as mean as old scratch himself.

"Ahhh, ahhh, get it off! It burns!" he said waving his arms around his head, trying to brush the creature off, then he gave up being gentle and bashed himself in the face with the crucifix.

Rita sat calmly, saying nothing.

Finally Gordon ran back outside, knocking the porch door half way off its hinges. He ran across the yard as if on fire. Eldred rushed out after him.

Bobby looked at his mother. She puffed on her cigarette and watched through the front door as Eldred finally got his father to calm down. The creature had detached itself from the old man's face and was crawling back towards the house.

"Momma. What is that thing?"

"I'm not sure, Bobby, but it came back with me."

"Back from where, Momma?"

"From wherever I was when I died. It was the one that told me to dig," she said guiltily. "It whispers to me when no one else is around and tells me that no one will hurt me again. It tells me that it will protect me and you too, if you want it to."

Bobby dropped the conversation and changed the subject.

"Will Pawpaw be alright?" he said, as he watched the old man collapse against his car.

"Ya' know Bobby, if your father wasn't such a miserable drunk, he might have been able to afford to call the doctor when I died instead of just burying me."

"Momma, there was nothing that anyone could do. You were dead."

"Apparently not, Bobby."

The next day was Sunday, and Bobby and his parents got dressed in their usual Sunday clothes and headed to town. The shadow-spider sat on the back seat next to Bobby. It seemed to enjoy riding in the car and even scrambled up the door at one point to look out the window. A strange dark smell came from it, barely perceptible, but very distinctive. It smelled like burnt toast. Bobby considered getting his father alone and telling him about the creature, but he wasn't sure if he would believe him, so Bobby kept quiet and waited. Maybe if the shadow knew Momma wasn't going back where he had come from, it would go away.

They arrived at church and were greeted warmly by everyone outside. When they started up the church steps, the creature scrambled back and forth. It looked as if it was afraid to follow them into the church. The thing lifted one foot and mounted the steps. Its long, slithery leg sparked at the moment that it touched the stairs. It fled to the car where it hid near the front tire. Rita didn't even seem to notice the creature was gone as she entered the church with the rest of her family.

Their pastor apparently didn't have the same opinion of Momma as Gordon Gamtree because he declared her return a miracle, right up there with Lazarus. He said people would come from miles around to talk to her when word got out. Rita's face went from polite amusement to embarrassment, to anger. Bobby had always known her to be a very private person.

They left church. The shadow-spider jumped up excitedly like a dog as they came outside. Bobby's mother acted as if she didn't even notice the creature.

On the drive home, Bobby pondered just what was sharing the Ford's backseat with him was. He reached out and tried to touch it. He expected there to be some form, some shape to the shadow that he could put his hand on, but there was nothing. The black air that made up the creature was slightly cooler than the outside air, but was the only indication it was even there at all. The shadow-spider crept across the seat and seemed to snuggle against Bobby's leg. A cold shiver went up his spine, but he didn't try to move away.

They arrived home, and Bobby changed out of his church clothes. He heard the phone ringing downstairs and crept around the corner to eavesdrop. His father's voice grew grave and shaky.

"Yes, of course. I'll be right there. Thank you. Goodbye."

"What's wrong, dear?" Rita asked.

"It's my dad. That was his neighbor, Mrs. Jefferies. She said that Da' was raving about last night with all of the lights on, yelling about the end of the world. She said she finally had to call the law to get him to quiet down. She went over this morning to check on him, and he was dead."

"Oh my. We should go over there right away."

##

When they returned that night, Eldred had already been drinking for three hours. They had found his father face down in the kitchen. His skin was a bluish-black color and had started peeling away from his bones. The coroner at the scene told Eldred that he had never seen anything like it. It was as if the corpse had been injected with battery acid. His body would have to stay at the morgue overnight until they discovered what had killed him.

Rita retreated to the kitchen where she chain-smoked as the spider-shadow wound around her legs like a black cat. Eldred wandered around the yard, talking to himself. Bobby wanted to go to him, but he'd earned more than a few bruises by bothering his father when he was drunk. Finally Eldred burst into the kitchen and looked at his wife through blood-shot eyes.

"You killed him. Somehow you killed him, you bitch."

"You don't know what you're talking about. Go lie down," she said, not even looking at him.

"You can't talk to me like that. You shouldn't even be here. Daddy was right; you ain't supposed to come back."

Eldred grabbed a knife from the drawer and started towards his wife. The shadow reared back on its hind legs and boxed the air, ready to strike.

"Daddy, no!" Bobby grabbed his father's arm and pulled him towards the door.

Eldred swatted at him, and Bobby fell to the floor, crying. Rita went to him and covered him with her own body. The shadow moved in front of them and hissed.

Eldred stopped, threw the knife down, and stomped back outside. It had started to storm. Bobby watched his father fetch a bottle from where he had it hidden under the porch and wander out into the high stalks of corn.

"Did he hurt you Bobby?" Rita said, checking him over. "Are you alright?"

"I'm fine. Where did the shadow go?"

A slither of blackness slid through the screen door and moved out into the night.

Rita held Bobby close, sitting on the dirty linoleum as the storm roared outside.

##

The sun crept through the cracked windows as it began its relentless path. Bobby leapt up, remembering what happened last night. He and his mother had slept on the couch.

"What's wrong, Bobby?"

"Dad never came in. I'm going to look for him."

"He probably fell asleep on the hay in the barn. You know he hates being woken up with a hangover even more than he hates being bothered when he's drunk. Leave him be."

"I'm going to find him," Bobby repeated and ran outside barefooted.

Bobby checked the barn, but his father wasn't there. He checked the yard and even inside the car, thinking he might have crawled inside when the storm started, but it was empty, too. Finally, he headed out into the wet corn plants. His feet slid in the mud, and the cuffs of his pants were immediately soaked. He searched up and down the aisles for an hour. He saw a leg poking out into a row. He ran to his father's ruined body.

The corpse looked as if it had been turned inside out. It wasn't much more than a blackish-red blob. Bones stuck out in some places, and his body had swelled to twice its size. Bobby vomited into the black soil and then collapsed, crying next to his father. His mother found him twenty minutes later and carried him into the house. She ran a bath and placed him in it. The shadow spider clung on the back of the toilet, watching him. Bobby had never felt more naked.

"Bobby," Rita said. "My friend has been whispering to me again. He says it's time to go. She sat on the floor and cupped his head in her hands. The creature jumped up and down and then hopped down from the toilet and crept into Rita's lap.

Rita took a straight razor from off the sink and opened the vein on her left arm from her wrist to the bend in her elbow. Blood dripped onto the tile floor, pooling in the grout canals.

"We are going together this time." She slid the bloody blade across her other wrist opening a flap of skin. Then she grabbed Bobby's shoulders and forced him under the water. He fought desperately, flailing his arms and kicking his legs. He opened his eyes under water and saw his mother's blood mixing with the warm water. Above that he saw her face shimmering with madness.

Bobby sucked in a lungful of water and coughed. He tried to get his head above the water, but his mother had him pinned to the bottom of the tub. He grabbed his mother's wounded wrists and tore at them, opening the slits even more. She didn't seem to feel it. She kept pushing him down with all of her weight. The water was now dark with blood, and he couldn't see his mother's face. Then, all at once, her strength waned and her arms went limp. Bobby used all of the strength to push her off from him. He sputtered to the surface, and spewed bloody water onto the floor.

He crawled past her and fell onto the floor, trying to make his lungs work again. His mother remained slumped over the tub with her head floating in the gore-saturated water.

Bobby saw movement out of the corner of his eye. He had forgotten about the shadow. It nudged Rita's leg as if to say *wake up*. *This wasn't how it was supposed to go*. Then it gripped her ankle and pulled. Rita slid out of the tub and her head hit the tiles with a dull, soggy thump. Red water leaked from her mouth. The creature dragged her slowly out of the bathroom and into the hallway. Bobby breathed heavily and pulled his knees to his chest. He sat on the cold floor shivering as he watched his mother die for the second time in a week.

Suddenly her eyes sprang open, and she grabbed a handful of Bobby's hair in a clenching grip.

"Come with us son. Come with us. It's so beautiful down there, down where the dark things are. They roam free and always end the day with a full belly." She cackled madly, looking him right in the eye.

"Momma, noooo."

He backed away, struggling to be out of her death-grip. Her hand finally pulled free, taking a clump of his hair with it. She slid away, leaving a trail of blood and water behind her.

Bobby heard the front door slam and he crawled to the window. The shadow dragged his mother's body across the lawn, she was still laughing hysterically. Her arms spurted more blood onto the grass and the driveway. Bobby had never seen so much blood, and he couldn't believe that a body could hold so much.

The creature pulled her all the way to her overturned grave. She had finally gone limp as her body slid into the hole, disappearing into the earth once more.

A Hell of a Deal

by Marcus Grimm

"Listen," Roger's father said, "whatever you do, don't sign a goddamn thing."

"I'm not going to sign anything, Dad," Roger said from behind the sports page. "I'm just going to look." If this appeased the elder Monroe, he didn't show it.

"God only knows what the hell's wrong with it," he continued. "The basement could be full of mold..."

"Radon," Roger's Mom sing-songed from the kitchen sink where she was washing the dishes from their Sunday dinner, the only meal of the week when supper food was substituted for lunch food, and had been for as long as Roger could remember, which, incidentally, was too long.

"Right!" Roger's father agreed. "Radon." When this failed to get a response from the boy, he continued.

"Termites," he said. "Check for termites." Despite Roger's sincere attempts at avoidance, he surrendered, dropping the newspaper like a foolish village lowering the drawbridge for an invading army of worry.

"It's just an Open House, Dad," he said. "You come, you look, you leave."

"To you!" his father agreed, enthusiastically, obviously thrilled to be able to finally talk some sense into the boy. "To that realtor, you're a lunch ticket, a paycheck, a commission, a..." In the living room, the old cuckoo-clock started whirring like a wind-up toy, finally culminating in a single declaration of insanity. One o'clock. At last. Roger stood.

"Time to go," he said. His father rose, too.

"Don't," Roger said. "Please." The old man opened his hands to the world. These kids!

Sensing his father's understanding of how very much he was wanted on this trip, Roger felt the closest thing to love he could muster.

"Dad," he said gently. "I won't sign anything. I promise. Really." His father looked at him, wondering when this boy went from being his pal to being so goddamned independent. Like most of the answers anymore, this one was lost on him as well.

"Ballgame's on in half an hour," he said finally. Roger walked past him, kissed his mother on the cheek.

"I'll be back by the third inning," he said over his shoulder.

"Radon!" his Mom called out the window, and Roger waved back, as if that were how she always said goodbye. And once he'd left the scene, his parents were quiet, like two lost souls, unsure of how to move or speak without him around.

##

In his car Roger felt immense relief, as he always did when he left the house. This relief carried with it a fair amount of guilt - *it can't be good to hate your parents this much* - but the relief was more than worth it.

Roger felt his nagging independence was natural for a man his age. He was twenty-five after all, more than a year or two beyond the point when most young adults move out. But without a steady girlfriend in his life and a graduate degree that rendered him practically unemployable, he hadn't honestly noticed how much his parents had been wearing him down until the money came, and he realized his life now could be different.

When Roger's grandfather died six months ago, he'd left the boy eighty thousand dollars. Not ten million dollars. Not one million. Not enough to retire on, either. But enough, Roger quickly realized, for a sizeable down payment on a house. Enough of a down payment that the resulting mortgage could be paid for by his woeful job at the paper factory. Roger couldn't say for sure, but it'd only taken him about five minutes after he'd done the math before he'd officially gotten sick of living with his parents.

They hadn't taken it well, of course. In their world, their sick twisted world, Roger would grow old with them, possibly before them, without ever moving out. He gave them entertainment and purpose and lawn care. Without him, how would they get along?

These were the things they felt. They voiced these feelings in different ways, though.

"The closing costs will eat you alive."

"Mortgage rates are bound to rise."

"You have no idea what the upkeep on a house can do to a man."

But in the end, Roger had ignored it all. Not that he expected **this** house to be **the** house. From the curb outside, he already saw half a dozen things he didn't like about the small rancher. But he was fine with that. It was the first house of many, he felt, on the road to independence. A road he couldn't wait to hit.

##

The sign outside the small rancher read, "FOR SALE – IMMEDIATE OCCUPANCY – TRIDENT REALTY." A smaller sign on top of the first sign said, "Open House, 1-4." Roger tapped on the sign for good luck as he made his way up the sidewalk.

The rancher was located in a development, but not a newer one. He guessed it had been built in the 70's. The architecture was of the time period – kind of that retro-modern look, when houses (and people) were trying to look techie about fifteen years before they would have the cell phones and laptops to warrant such George Jetson appearances.

The siding was sort of a mustard color and the shutters were brown. The sidewalk was made of slate stepping stones and had settled into an uneven wobbly pathway. Roger felt slightly off-center as he followed it to the front door. The interior door was ajar, and Roger opened the screen door and stepped inside.

The first thing Roger noticed was the carpet, which absolutely positively, no two ways about it, would have to go. It was middle brown, not the worst color, but worn beyond belief. In some places, the fibers were practically gone. It didn't smell so hot, either.

"Welcome," a voice said, and Roger turned to the hallway where a slightly overweight man in a wrinkly button-down shirt was walking towards him. "Franklin Hindsight." He put out his hand, which Roger accepted. It was cold and clammy. Not, Roger thought, an ideal realtor handshake.

"I saw the sign," Roger said, trying instinctively to sound as uninterested as possible. "It's on my way home from work, so I thought I'd drop in." The realtor nodded.

"Good," he said. "Glad to hear it. Very glad in fact. You're new to the housing market?"

Roger considered this. Except for the arguments with his parents, he didn't know if he'd actually voiced his intentions to anyone else. But, he admitted, the idea sure *sounded* good.

"Yes," he said. "I am."

"Excellent," Hindsight said. Roger noticed the realtor's forehead was wet with perspiration and his shirt was soaked through. The combination of sweat and polyester sent a scent off him that was artificially sweet and sick, like perfumed, wet cat hair.

"Can, I, uh, look around?"

"Please, do." The realtor made a grandiose gesture, as if showing Roger this could all be his. "And let me know how you feel about the house, too."

Roger had started walking across the living room floor, but stopped.

"Come again?"

"How you feel," the realtor said. "Finding a house is like finding yourself. Honesty is always the best policy."

"Huh," thought Roger, who had increasingly been lying to his parents more and more just to get by. The idea of honesty, frank truthfulness, tickled him. "I'll keep that in mind." He made his way across the threadbare carpet, and then, prior to walking into the kitchen, stopped and turned.

"That carpet," he said, slowing with clear enunciation, "sucks." The realtor, for maybe a half a second, registered something that looked like the pain Roger had seen in his own mother's face many times. But in an instant it was gone, replaced by an understanding smile.

"Sucks?" Well, Roger figured, in for a penny...

"Awful," he said, "barely anything left to it." The realtor looked down, turned his head as if to see the wear of the fabric in a different light.

"You're right," he said, looking up. "What color would you have it?"

"Color?"

"Yes, what color would you have it?"

"I don't know, I haven't thought about it 'til now."

The realtor flashed a wide grin.

"Well now that you're thinking about it, what do you think?"

Roger, realizing it was pointless to argue with a trained salesman, sighed.

"Tan," he said.

The realtor removed a little spiral notebook from his breast pocket and licked the tip of a pencil he'd pulled from behind his ear.

"T-A-N," he spelled out. "Got it."

The kitchen cabinets were a basic medium oak finish, not awful per se, and at some point they may have been nice, but time had caused the veneer to warp in some places and peel in others. Roger ran his finger along one of the edges and grimaced at the roughness.

"No sweat," the realtor said. "We'll take care of that." Roger turned and watched him writing in the book.

"You seem awful confident that I'm interested in this house. I haven't even seen half of it."

"You'll love it," he said. "When we're done here, you'll love it."

"Look," said Roger. "I don't want you to get the wrong impression. I've just started looking."

"Huh?" The realtor put his hand to his ear.

"I've, uh, I've just started looking."

"Trust me, Roger, you've also found the house of your dreams." The realtor winked and Roger felt himself go cold, though he couldn't figure out if the reason for his sudden chill was the surety of Hindsight or the knowledge that he had never given the realtor his name.

"Let's show you the rest of the house," Hindsight said.

As they toured the rest of the home, Roger surrendered to the process. There were better than twenty things Roger found to hate about the house, and Hindsight seemed to notice every time Roger winced, scowled or even paused. The wallpaper was torn in some places, and god-awful ugly in others. Sometimes Roger said things, but more often than not, he'd just think it and the realtor would be scribbling in his pad.

"You're quite..." Roger paused here, "perceptive. You know your clients well." This seemed to please Hindsight, who smiled hugely.

"Yes, well, all part of the process, you know."

"The process?"

"This," the realtor gestured at the surrounding room, "the process. It's all about finding you the perfect home. Come, let's go out to the back porch for a moment."

The porch was screened in, with two beaten but functional chairs sitting empty. They each sat in one, and Hindsight gestured toward the back yard.

"Nice property," he said. Roger looked out. Where he assumed the property ended was a dark line of fir trees that all but obscured the midday sun. It wouldn't have been a stretch to call it pleasantly shady, nor would it have been one to call it completely overgrown. The grass itself was a good eight inches long and reminded Roger to ask one of the questions on his mind.

"Where are the people who moved out?"

"The Simpsons?" Hindsight said, as if Roger would recognize their name. "They decided it was time to sell." He shrugged. "Good people, though. I sold them this house."

"Huh," Roger said because he didn't know what else to say. Hindsight, as he seemed to take everything, took this slight action as a sign to react.

"That's the way it works," Hindsight said. "Customers like you, and they stick with you. You'll see."

"I'll see?"

"You're going to love working with me, Roger."

Roger sat up, feeling a bit uncomfortable.

"How do you know my name?"

"You signed the book when you came in." The realtor motioned over his shoulder into the house.

"The book?"

"The open house registry."

Roger thought long and hard. He knew that signing in for an open house was a common procedure, yet had no recollection of doing it at all. Had he? He was still thinking this through as the realtor pulled out the notepad.

"Here's what I got, Roger," he said. "I've got one threadbare carpet. The wrong color." He made a little check mark beside it in his notebook. "Kitchen cabinets..."

"What are you doing?" Roger asked.

"Going over the things you don't like about the house, of course."

"Why?"

"Because Roger, they're going to need to be fixed if you're expecting to live here."

Roger stood and Hindsight did too, blocking his entrance.

"I can't live here!"

"Of course not," Hindsight tapped the notebook, "not with these problems."

"Listen..."

"No, you listen!" The realtor suddenly grew serious. "This list is everything that sucks about the house, right?"

"Right."

"These things make the home unbearable, right?"

"Right."

"You signed the paper when you came in here, right?"

"Right?"

"Right!"

"Okay, right." Roger felt himself growing uneasy. *Don't sign a goddamn thing* his father had hissed.

"If these things were fixed, say beyond your wildest dreams, would you have cause to complain?"

"Well..." Roger didn't know what to think.

"Well what? If this house had carpeting you loved, and cabinets you loved, and air conditioning you loved, and, and..." he slapped the notebook, "all of these things! What would you do then?"

"It's an absurd question."

"Roger," Hindsight's eyes bored into him. "If all of these things were taken care of, and you never had to deal with your parents again, what would you do?"

Roger paused. "What do you know about my parents?"

"Roger." Hindsight's voice was barely a whisper now. "What would you do?" Roger considered the absurdity of everything the realtor was asking. What the hell, he decided.

"Mister," Roger smiled. "If you could do all that, I'd never leave this goddamn house."

The realtor regarded Roger, and the smile that blossomed on his face seemed to come from his entire self, his entire soul.

"Roger," Hindsight winked. "You just gave the perfect answer." The realtor stepped aside. "Why don't you go on in and have one more look around."

Roger walked past Hindsight, wondering what the grin was about, and into the house. The first thing he noticed was the smell. Previously the house had smelled musty, lived in. Now, it smelled like paint and plastic. Like...

Like new shit.

Roger couldn't believe it. The carpet was exquisite. The cabinets pristine. A soft hum from a new central air conditioning unit pumped cool air throughout. The house was immaculate. Roger felt the realtor beside him.

"How did you do this?" Roger asked.

"You like it?" The realtor moved in front of him.

"How did you do this?"

"Contractors," Hindsight shrugged. "Economy sucks. Put a little pressure on them. Works every time."

Roger walked along the wall, knelt down and felt the edge of the carpets. They were nailed down perfectly.

"This is unbelievable," he said finally. "Definitely, something to consider."

"What did you say?"

Roger motioned at the house all around him.

"This is awesome. I'm seriously going to consider this house."

The realtor shook his head slowly. "Roger. Roger. Roger. We have a deal."

"What deal?"

The realtor snapped his fingers, and a voice echoed from all around.

"If you could do all that, I'd never leave this goddamn house."

"Wait a second!" said Roger. "This is all fine and good, but this is a big decision. There's things wrong with this house. I want to talk to my parents."

"Your parents," the realtor bellowed, "are gone, per your request!" Voices from minutes ago echoed throughout the house.

"If all of these things were taken care of, and you never had to deal with your parents again, what would you do?"

"I'd never leave this goddamn house."

"I'd never leave this goddamn house."

"I'd never leave this goddamn house."

Roger moved to the door and found it without a doorknob. He turned and found the realtor grinning at him, fangs showing now. He ran to the window, saw someone walking a dog and banged upon the glass, but the person just kept going, oblivious to his fists, which bounced off the pane without a sound.

"What have you done to my parents?" Roger cried. "What have you done to me?"

The realtor regarded him, shaking his head. "Roger, my boy, I'm just closing a deal." He walked close to Roger while the young man drew back, shrinking into the corner. Roger, shaking and horrified, watched as small horns grew from the realtor's head and his salesman's beer belly rose up and swelled into a massive muscular chest. Roger tried to scream, but nothing would come out. Nothing at all. The realtor beast paused a few feet from him.

"One clarification, though," he snarled. "This house is damned, all right. But trust me: God had nothing to do with it." The beast moved forward, formally welcoming Roger into the neighborhood forever.

THE MATTRESS

by John Peters

This is insane.

The thought flashed while she pulled his left arm straight out from his side. With practiced quickness she tied the rope to his wrist, looped it around the bedpost and pulled, stretching his arm as far as she could before tying off the rope. His right arm was already pulled straight out, that wrist firmly tied to the opposite bedpost.

Can this be real?

The night had started innocently enough for Jack Kellum. With his wife and kids visiting relatives for the week, he had decided to spend the evening at O'Shanty's, an Irish-wanna be bar on the riverfront. The Irish motif was a bit ridiculous in the deep south of Savannah, but the food was good, the air conditioning worked, and there were a dozen televisions around the bar all tuned to the Braves game or some other sports channel.

Jack had been there an hour, sitting alone at a tiny table in the back corner when she walked in.

Stunning.

Jack could only think that simple word when she slipped through the door. She was not movie star beautiful. Fact was, Jack really couldn't tell much about her figure - she wore a long-sleeved, loose-fitting, dark blue dress that nearly reached the floor. A white crocheted shawl draped over her shoulders. It seemed too much clothing for a late spring Savannah evening.

He was enthralled with her appearance - wild, shoulder-length black hair, pale skin, and full red lips. She climbed onto a stool at the bar facing Jack, ordered a drink, took a few sips, then stood. She talked to no one, acknowledged none of the other patrons. She simply disappeared into the crowd.

Jack stood, craning his neck to catch another glimpse of her.

Nothing.

He sipped his drink for another half hour. He asked for the check, left a twenty on a ten dollar tab, then stepped away from the table.

"Where ya going?"

Jack whirled around. There she sat. Silently, Jack sat down, staring into her brilliant blue eyes.

She leaned over, her fingers brushing his hand. Jack flinched.

"You don't like?"

"No, that's not it," Jack stammered. "I...it's just..." His voice failed. He wanted to say her touch was electric, that he felt a jolt shoot up his arm. "Nothing, nothing at all," he stammered.

She grabbed his hand, stood and pulled. He followed. Jack didn't notice that no one else in the bar gave the woman even a second glance. He couldn't look away from her, couldn't resist as she guided him from the bar.

Outside, she gracefully raised a slender arm, the sleeve falling away to reveal milky white skin. Seconds later a horse-drawn taxi pulled to the curb, the kind tourists and newlyweds ride through the city's historic district. Jack couldn't remember if he'd ever seen one out at night. He helped her up, then, with a bit of effort, pulled himself into the carriage. She leaned forward, whispered something in the driver's ear and settled back against Jack, wrapping her arms around him, laying her head on his shoulder.

Jack lost track of time, the clop-clop-clop of horses' hooves the only sound. The carriage traveled through the central business district, then through a neighborhood of huge, immaculately renovated homes, some more than two centuries old. Next was a more run down neighborhood, with boarded-up businesses and metal bars protecting windows of claptrap houses that lined the road.

The cab stopped in an ancient neighborhood on the outskirts of town. Jack hadn't noticed any of the places they passed, but the realization that it was completely dark in this neighborhood caught his attention. No, not completely dark - a feeble light flickered at the end of a long brick walkway where an old-style gas lantern stood.

The woman deftly stepped over Jack, then leapt to the ground. Instinctively, he reached for his wallet, but the woman grabbed his hands and guided him from the carriage. Jack was a big man - a bit overweight, but even with a belly the two-hundred-and-seventy-five pounds on his six-foot-three-inch frame was impressive, and he intimidated most people. He towered over his diminutive escort, yet he felt weak, almost helpless. When she touched him, without saying a word, without exerting any real pressure, she led him as if he were a child.

She took the lead down the brick walk, and Jack followed to an enormous, dark Victorian home. The two climbed the porch stairs, slipped in, then walked another long flight of stairs to the second floor. Jack panted, struggling to catch his breath and to see in the dark. She held his hand and his body understood where to step, how to go as long as she led.

At the top they continued deeper into the house, down a long hallway. Without realizing he had stepped into a room, Jack felt her step behind him. A door shut, a key turned.

"Wh--"

"Shhhh," she whispered, placing her finger against his lips, gently kissing his neck.

Jack wanted to protest, to say he couldn't stay, that he had never been with another woman since marrying his wife two decades ago. Instead, he caressed her shoulders, leaned down and kissed her lips. She returned the kiss, her hands on his chest. Then she pulled away.

Her movement was so sudden Jack stumbled forward. She laughed softly, her form silhouetted against a window, the faint light of the rising moon creeping in. She pulled the shawl from her shoulders and flung it across the room. Jack watched her reach behind her neck. With a simple flick of her fingers the dress fell to the floor.

Now, your turn.

The words startled Jack. Not because she said them, but because she had not said them. They were her words, he was sure, but they seemed to come from his own head. He hadn't so much heard them as understood her thoughts. He pulled his shirt up. As it covered his face, he felt her next to him, loosening his belt, unzipping his pants. His trousers fell to the floor. Despite the sticky spring humidity, Jack felt a chill crawl across his skin. She kissed him, her lips pressing hard against his. Her hands played, touching his hips, one slipping briefly against his penis. Again she stepped back, grabbed his hands and led him to the bed.

Jack kicked off his shoes, struggled to get his pants off his feet as he sat. She pushed him down, straddling him. He felt an uneven lump in the mattress, started to sit up, but she held him down, kissing him, and the lump faded. Jack began to caress her breasts. She laughed, then grabbed his right hand, slid off his stomach, and stretched his arm toward the bedpost.

"Hey, wha-" he protested when he felt rope loop once around his wrist.

"Shhhh," she whispered, cutting off any more protest with a deep, passionate kiss.

She sat up and began tying again, wrapping the rope around his wrist until he lost count of the loops, then pulling the arm tight while she fastened it to the bedpost.

The woman - Jack realized he didn't know her name - climbed over him, pausing as her breasts brushed lightly over Jack's chest. She pulled his left arm as far and tight as it would go and began tying his wrist to the bedpost.

No, I can't do this.

"I have to go," Jack said.

"No, you don't," she said, her voice a deep whisper. She leaned back, pulling the rope tight.

"No!" Jack shouted, the rope biting into his skin, nearly cutting the circulation to his hands. He pulled with both arms, tried to sit up, but he could barely lift his head.

"You can't do this," he said.

She straddled him again, placing a finger against his lips. She slid down his stomach, and Jack felt himself slipping inside her. She began moving up and down slowly at first, gradually picking up intensity. Jack's breathing quickened. He pushed his hips upward in rhythm with her movements. With each thrust, her breasts touched him. The moonlight bathed the room and lent her skin an even paler complexion.

"Oh god," Jack whispered, arching his hips, his body shuddering. "Oh god!"

"No," she said. The woman slipped off Jack, her hands grabbing his balls, squeezing hard.

Jack screamed in pain, trying to roll away from her grip. She squeezed harder, then let go.

"You don't climax until I say you do," she whispered, a hard edge to her voice.

Jack lay there, sharp pain crawling up inside his stomach.

She stood, grabbed his ankle and pulled until his leg stretched as far as it would go. Again Jack felt rope, this time binding his leg to the lower bedpost. She repeated the process with his other leg, then she climbed on him, massaging where she had earlier inflicted pain.

The next three hours were like that. She touched, kissed, caressed, brought Jack to the edge of losing control, only to bring a quick and dreadfully painful end to his pleasure.

Finally, shortly after midnight, she took him in, began moving, thrusting, moaning. Jack tried to hold back, afraid of what she would do, but eventually his body took over. Tied so tightly he could scarcely move, he still thrust his hips upward, over and over.

He called out, she screamed, her hands on his chest. Sweat covered their bodies. Jack could barely catch his breath, she couldn't stop gasping. They shuddered against one another, reaching release together.

Jack's breathing slowed. She sat atop him, her face hidden behind her hair. She slipped off, lying beside him, her head resting on his arm. They lay silent for several minutes.

"I can't feel my hands," Jack said.

"Shhh."

"No, I can't feel. You have to-"

She straddled him again, her lips pressed against his.

"No talk," she whispered. "No talk."

"But, I have..."

She pushed something rubber and hard into Jack's mouth. He jerked his head back and forth violently as she pulled what felt like leather straps around his head, snapping them in back.

"I said no talk," she whispered.

Jack protested, his words nothing more than garbled noises.

She laid back down, her head on his shoulder, arm across his chest. Jack struggled, jerked, tried to talk. He felt her hand slowly move down from his chest, over his belly, then close around his balls, just tight enough for a hint of pain.

"Be still," she commanded.

Jack obeyed. His feet tingled, his hands were beyond all feeling, but he was afraid to do anything other than lie silently.

Gradually her grip loosened, then relaxed altogether. After several minutes, her breathing grew quiet and deep. She slept.

Eventually Jack nodded off as well. Three times during the night he was awakened as she mounted him, her hands pressing on his chest, her body white in the moonlight. Each time, he began thrusting his hips in rhythm with her movements, muffled screams of ecstasy escaping his mouth. Each time, she remained silent, her rapid breathing the only sound. The first two times they'd moved in perfect harmony, climaxing together as sweat rolled off their bodies. She'd fall back onto the bed, her head on his shoulder, and drifted back to sleep.

The third time, as he began to lose control, he felt others. Who, he wasn't sure, and how, he wasn't sure, but Jack could feel other people, men and women, moaning, screaming, thrashing. He opened his eyes. She was there, on top of him, her face hidden by her long, wild hair. Jack closed his eyes again and felt pain, felt burning, but not his pain -- the pain of others. He felt darkness around him, holding him.

He opened his eyes again, watched while she threw her head back and screamed as she reached orgasm. He did not climax. He lay there, his hands and feet dead, the back of his legs and arms burning. He tried to scream, the pain more than he could bear. A muffled, saliva-filled gurgle was the only sound he made. He slammed his head back against the mattress.

She climbed off and disappeared into the darkness. Jack tried to lift his hips, tried to sit up, but he couldn't move. He tried lifting his head, but it felt glued to the mattress, a burning sensation running the length of his body, from head to feet.

Jack's world began to turn gray, then blackness darker than the dead of night enveloped him.

Sunlight streamed through the sheer tattered curtains hanging over the floor-length window. Before Jack was aware of the light, he felt pain.

Intense, deep, burning pain. Fire.

He opened his eyes. It was late in the day, perhaps even afternoon, but Jack barely noticed the light. He felt as if his skin was in flames, as if he burned deep inside, as if his very soul was alight.

Jack tried to move but could not budge, though the effort sent waves of intense, bone searing agony throbbing through his body. He tried to scream, but couldn't.

He noticed a mirror in the ceiling, and a chill ran the length of Jack's body. Despite the burning pain, his body turned icy cold. He saw his reflection, or at least the reflection of what remained. The mattress was absorbing his body. Most of his belly still protruded above the fabric, but his legs, his arms, his hips were more than half gone. Even his head was nearly halfway into the mattress.

Despite the gag Jack screamed so hard he tasted blood in his throat. He tried to thrash about, to break free, but pain exploded in his head. Then he heard the voices again. Felt, more than heard, men, women, screaming, burning, lost in dark torment. Jack's mind faded to gray, then his world went dark again.

##

The rusty hinges squealed as the door swung open. Jack opened his eyes.

Darkness.

He tried to turn to the side, pain the only reward for his effort. He tried to scream, but not even a muffled, gurgled cry came forward. His body burned, the agony intense. He heard the others, could feel their presence, their pain.

Out of the corner of his eye, he saw them. He heard the door shut, lock.

"Wh--" a man's voice came.

"Shhhh," she whispered. He recognized her voice.

He could barely see them, off in the corner, near the door, their bodies pressed against one another as they kissed. She stepped back, leading the man toward the bed. Jack tried to scream, to move, to warn the man. He watched while she pulled the shawl over her head, reached behind herself and, with a quick movement of her fingers, the dress fell to the floor.

Now, your turn she whispered without uttering a word.

Jack watched, tears of pain and frustration spilling from his eyes while the man pulled his shirt over his head. When he did, she stepped forward, unbuttoned his pants. Jack could hear the voices of the others, all screaming in agony, calling out to the man, pleading for him to run. Jack watched her kiss him. Her hands played, touching his hips, her hand slipping between the man's legs, out of Jack's view. She stepped back, grabbed his wrists and led him to the bed.

Jack's body convulsed with pain when the man sat on the edge of the bed. She pushed the man down. Jack's world turned black as the man fell on the mattress.

Jack felt the man shift his weight. "What's tha..." the man said, trying to sit up.

"Shhhh." she said.

Jack felt them brush against him, bump him, grab him. The others, the men, women here before. They moaned, cried out, screamed, and Jack joined them. Screaming, weeping, enveloped in darkness.

Under the Floorboards

by Cordelia Snow

When Agatha first heard scratching in the walls, she thought the rats had come back. Last summer they'd invaded after the Health Department cleaned up all the garbage piled up in the parking lot next door. They'd tunneled through the walls and chewed holes in the kitchen pantry. Every morning her mother put poisoned cakes out for them in aluminum trays. Every night the trays were chewed through. Agatha could hear them screaming and thrashing inside the walls. The smart ones didn't stick around. For weeks after, the stench seeped through the cracks in the floorboards.

So when she first heard the scratching, she'd thought the rats were back.

"Don't worry lambkin," her mother told her, "they won't come back. That dump is gone and Daddy took care of them."

Agatha knew it was something alive. In a way, she was glad. She was lonely that summer, especially at night. Sometimes when she heard the scratching, she imagined a rat boy in there. Nazrat was his name. He was like Tarzan, but he was a rat boy, not an ape man. He tunneled through pipes and walls, compressing his bones just like a rat could, and he lived off of dead snakes and bread crumbs under the house. Sometimes Nazrat was her friend, sometimes he was her enemy. She couldn't decide.

Before the scratchings, the summer nights had all bled into one long, hot night. The air conditioner was almost busted, so Agatha's mother said they had to turn it off at night. She poured baby powder on the sheets so Agatha's legs wouldn't stick and told her to leave the windows opened. One Saturday, she took Agatha to Service Merchandise and allowed her to spend fifteen dollars on whatever she wanted. Agatha picked a plastic horse and named him Flicker. She also picked out a fan that was just high enough to blow over her bed.

But it was still too hot for sleeping. Agatha put Flicker at the foot of her bed and called him her little doggie. She wanted a puppy, but her Dad said a puppy would crap all over the place. So Flicker was all she had until Nazrat came.

Aggie counted the nights. On the third night, she pressed her hand against the wall. It was almost like touching Nazrat, because all that was between them was a thin sheet of wall. The next night, she scratched back.

The scratching stopped. A shock jolted right through her body. It was real, it knew she was there. Agatha scratched again.

It didn't scratch the way the rats had. These scratches were light, like footsteps or raindrops pattering. Agatha tapped her fingernails against the wall. She tapped for hours, and Nazrat tapped back. She fell asleep with her body pressed against the wall to the sound of his tap-tap-tapping.

The next day she looked for the duct-taped rat hole in the back of her closet. She found it behind the clothes. It was just big enough for her to slip her hand through. She pulled a half-empty jar of maraschino cherries from the back of the pantry and placed it in the back of her closet for him.

She thought about Nazrat all day. He only came out at night, so she stayed out of her room because otherwise she would have just stayed waiting by the hole. Until Nazrat, she'd spent most of her time trying to get out of the house. Her Mom was home, and now that she wasn't working, the house was dirtier. Sometimes her mother just sat in the kitchen sipping scotch from a jelly jar, looking out the window where the dump used to be.

Agatha's father was a painter. During the day, he painted houses. At night, he painted in the garage. He painted murals on the walls of the tumbling down house. "It's a disgrace," her mother had told him once, pointing to the overgrown Augustine in the front lawn, to the tumbling columns, to the peeling paint. "Why don't you paint the goddamn outside of the house instead of the inside?" The house, once eggshell white, now looked like dirty fingernails. But the walls were brilliant, Agatha thought. When her mother was feeling good about things that was the word she used for Dad. Brilliant. He painted a roiling ocean in the living room and a big red desert in the kitchen. Agatha's walls climbed with sunflowers and a big red monster flower her father told her was called Loveliesbleeding. Sometimes the flowers gave her a headache and it felt as if they were crawling around inside her brain, but other times they looked as if they leaned over her, ready to pop out of the wall and into her hands.

Everything besides those paintings seemed fuzzy and gray, safer than outside, but dimmer. That summer nothing was right. Agatha had fallen into the habit of looking too closely at things, even at the embedded dirt in the grout between tiles and the dead bugs in the light fixtures. She yearned for cactus yellow siding, curtains like butterfly wings, for an orange so bright it hurt her eyes to look at it, for a blue she could fly into.

The day that her jar was waiting, she just had to get out. "Who knows where your Daddy is," her mother said, "you should ask him to take us out when he gets back." Her mother was happier when Dad was home, even if it meant more fighting. Agatha wasn't sure anymore. It was quiet now with him gone. One night before school was out, he'd caught Agatha crossing the street without looking both ways. It felt good to have him catch her, at first. His eyes were on her, and it felt like what she did mattered. But then he'd looked into her, hard, and punched. Afterwards, she sucked the blood in through her gums and sipped Coke through a straw. Her mother stroked her hair and spoke softly. "That wasn't your father," she said. "You know it wasn't him. He loves us. How could he be so angry, if it isn't love?"

Agatha stopped listening. The Coke mingled with the blood, making it taste sweet and achy.

When he came back the next night, he spun Agatha in circles. He'd brought a bag of rice candies from downtown and he talked into the night about a mural he was going to paint on the east side of town. Then he talked about the house he was working on. Bougsie colors, he said, piss yellow they call Yellow Cake, for a gingerbread house. The woman he was working for was a lush. She wanted to paint the trim blue, and when he'd asked her what shade, she'd told him a "blue blue." He'd spent an hour and a half trying to find the elusive blue blue for her. Yuppy bitch, he'd called her, and Mom had laughed. Mother's eyes were small and mean when he said that. "What's her name?" her mother had asked him, "And how old is she?"

Now he had gone to entertain the rich lush, mother said. Mother had seen her, once, at one of those posh groceries downtown buying sea bass. "Sea bass is a trash fish," her mother said. "She's not that pretty, just skinny. And she goes to spas, you can tell. You know what those women do there, Agatha? They get poop shot out of their bottoms."

Agatha went outside to play in the side yard. It was hot, so she squeezed inside the crawlspace under the house. There were things down there from people who'd lived in the house before. Once, she'd found a glass disc full of colored blue water and pale sand. There were old shoes, baby bottles, rat skeletons, garter snakes. She wasn't supposed to go down there. Her father had seen a coral snake in the yard once. But it felt better down there. It was cool and dark, her own cave. When she closed her eyes, she could feel Nazrat with her. His eyes were the deepest black. She felt his breath on her neck, but when she opened her eyes, he was gone.

When she went to bed, Agatha checked the rat hole. The jar of cherries was empty. "Are you there, Nazrat?" she whispered. She listened for scurrying. After awhile, she heard breathing. "I won't tell," she whispered. She hunkered down and pushed her hand through the hole. She waited. She heard her mother in the kitchen putting away the dishes. "I won't tell," she said again.

It made her flinch, at first, when she felt Nazrat's hand placed in her palm. It was a small hand. She felt its cool fingers and smooth nails. She stayed perfectly still until her hand fell asleep. "I'm going to bed," she said then. She squeezed the hand and let go.

She wondered the next morning if it had been real. How could he survive in there? And had he always been there, or had he only just arrived? And what did he eat? Apple cores? Did he lick the chocolate bar wrappers she brought home and threw under her bed after her Mom took her grocery shopping at the Lewis and Coker? When she thought of him, her heart beat wildly and she felt a taste in her mouth. It was like blood and Coca-Cola and cold metal. Maybe she was in love. But she was too young to be in love. She wanted to bring him things, to pull him out of the hole. She didn't go outside.

"No reason to molder in here just because I am," her mother told her at lunch. Her Mom had made cream cheese and honey sandwiches on special bread from the bakery. She cut the crusts off the sandwiches and served them on the special green glass plates. She even poured a capful of vanilla into Agatha's Coke.

"I think we should go to the library and get you some books to read. Doesn't that sound nice? I think they have story hour. Don't they always have story hour in the summertime?"

"I don't know," Agatha said.

"Well, I need to get some things at the store. Do you want to help me shop? You can read the list to me."

"I have a project," Agatha told her.

"What project?"

"I'm building a fort," Agatha lied.

"Well, okay. I'll go then and you build your fort. I'll be back in a jiffy."

But she wouldn't; Agatha knew that.

As soon as her mother was gone, Agatha got the hammer from her Dad's toolbox. She found the duct tape and brought it too. Knocking down the closet wall was easier than she thought it would be.

How could it be? There she was, a small girl. She sat hugging her knees and staring at Agatha from out of water-blue eyes. Her skin was as white as paper, and her long hair was so blonde it would have seemed white, but for the pale skin it fell against. She wore dirty pink corduroys and a tee shirt with yellow daisies on it.

Agatha put the hammer down. "Don't be scared," she said.

The little girl said nothing, just stared at Agatha with those big, creepy eyes.

"Why are you here?" Agatha asked her.

Once when they'd gone camping, her father had taken her flashlight hunting. That meant looking for animals in the dark with your flashlights. When something scuttled or scurried, you tried to catch the wild animal's eyes in your flashlight beam. She'd seen lots of armadillos and possums that way. That was what this girl's eyes were like.

"Don't be scared," Agatha whispered. She held her hand out flat for the girl, just the way she would have if she were meeting a strange dog. The little girl dropped her arms from her knees, but she still said nothing.

"What's your name?" Agatha said. After awhile, she said, "My name's Aggie." As soon as she said it, she felt it was her true name. It was the name of a girl who had friends, who knew how to blow bubbles, who could throw a ball and flip-flop backwards.

Aggie tried to coax the girl out with toast and honey, but she wouldn't come through the hole. "Aren't you hungry?" she asked her, and finally she just handed her the toast. The girl ate it in such a pretty way, Aggie thought she looked daintier than a kitten lapping up a bowl of milk.

Where were her parents? Did she live in the walls and under the floorboards? Aggie asked her every question she could think of, but the little girl wouldn't speak.

"When my Mom comes home, you can come out of there," Aggie said. But as soon as she said this the girl crawled away. Aggie went to follow, but then she got scared. What if there were still rats in there? What if she fell through the walls and died under the house, like a poisoned animal?

When her mother came home, the sun was almost down. She had bags and bags of groceries. There were bags of fruit that Aggie didn't even know the names of, although some she recognized. Kiwis, star fruit, mangoes and cherry plums. There was also a bag of liquor.

"I'm going to take a shower, Sweetness," her mother told her, "and then I'm going to make you a lemon chess pie. And we'll read from your Little Golden Book. Won't that be fun? Pour me a little Kahlua and milk, will you honey?"

Her mother had been drinking, but she wasn't drunk. The house smelled of peppermint as she showered because she'd bought a bottle of Dr. Bonner's Peppermint Soap. Agatha put the fruit away.

That night her mother lit candles and cooked mushroom stroganoff. She looked beautiful in the candlelight. Her hair was copper, like Aggie's, and fell down to a smooth point in the small of her back. It was clean and damp from her shower. She wore a dusty rose slip and a coral necklace. Her freckled skin seemed to glow from inside like the candles. "Isn't this fun," she said, "just us two?"

"Yeah," Aggie said. How could her father stay away when her mother looked like that?

Afterwards, they had milk and lemon chess pie.

"Mom," Aggie said, "I have to tell you something."

Her mother tapped her fork against the china, then leaned back and waited.

"There's a little girl in this house."

Her mother swallowed. "No there isn't," she said.

"There is Mom. She's lost, I think. She has long yellow hair. She's littler than me."

Her mother stood to clear the table, took Aggie's plate of half-eaten pie.

"Don't make up stories, Agatha. It's nasty."

"I'm not. Let me show you. She's scared, but she might come out if we're quiet."

Her mother turned on the lights and started stacking the dishes in the sink.

"We have to help her, Mom," Aggie said. When her mother turned around from the sink, her eyes narrowed.

"Alright, Agatha."

Aggie took her mother's hand and led her into the bedroom. She opened the closet door as softly as she could. Then she turned on the light bulb, fast.

The girl sat there on her knees in the big hole. She was frozen.

"There she is," Aggie said.

"What are you talking about?" her mother said. "There is no one there, Agatha."

"Yes there is," Aggie said. "She's right there, staring at us. Don't you see? She's right there."

Her mother folded her arms across her chest and walked away.

After that, Aggie wondered. She knew the girl was real in a way that Nazrat wasn't. But maybe she wasn't as real as Aggie was.

Nothing had ever been so exciting before. The little girl only came out at night now, but during the day, Aggie collected things for her. A bird's feather that, when you held it up to the light, looked like a prism. A tiger's eye marble. Flicker. A bag of Pop Rocks from Lewis and Coker. A plastic necklace that, in the right light, looked like pink pearls. She found most of these treasures under the house; they weren't anything the littler girl couldn't find, but when the girl took them from her, her eyes were grateful. It didn't bother Aggie anymore that she didn't speak. Aggie thought that nobody, not even a dog, could speak so well with eyes.

"Your name is Daisy," Aggie told her. She told Daisy stories about Nazrat. He could crawl through the city's pipelines and he knew how to rescue dying animals. He could cause some serious damage to the bad guys if he wanted to - he could start fires by gnawing on wiring, he could enter buildings by enlarging gaps in the walls and foundation, around plumbing pipes or through other holes in the structure. He had been raised by rats, and he had rat superpowers. If he wanted to, he could come up from the sewer through the toilet and bite bad guys' butts.

Daisy just blinked and listened. After awhile, she came out of the hole, but she wouldn't go very far. Aggie brushed her long hair and wiped her face with a washcloth. Daisy smelled sour, like spoiled milk, and there was a lot of dirt under her fingernails. But even so, she was prettier than any girl Aggie had seen in real life.

When Aggie's mother left during the day, Daisy came out from her hiding place and into Aggie's room. Aggie had never liked dolls, but Daisy did, so they pulled Aggie's old Barbie Dream House out of the closet and dressed Barbie in all of her outfits. Once, Aggie raided her Mom's closet, and they tried on her old prom dresses, Chinese slippers, and Chanel No. 5. They ate peanut butter and chocolate frosting sandwiches and drank some of the stuff in the liquor cabinet. They also ate all the fruit. Aggie knew they had to eat it quickly or it would rot. Daisy wouldn't leave the bedroom. Aggie wasn't sure where she went to the bathroom. Probably under the house.

It started to feel normal, having a little girl inside the walls. Even nice. Daisy was all Aggie's and nobody else's. She was better than a dog, better than a friend. She was better than a sister, too, because nobody else knew about her.

When Aggie's Mom was home it was hard, because Daisy wouldn't come out or even tap on the walls. And Aggie's mother was depressed. Sometimes she spent the day in her ratty bathrobe, sitting at the table, sipping scotch.

Sometimes she called Aggie to the table and made her sit in her lap. She ran her fingers through Aggie's hair and talked about life.

Time for me to be maudlin, Agatha, she'd say. She talked about love, said it tasted like blood. That's the good thing about scotch, she said, it makes you poetic. She talked about how, when she was a student, she'd felt sharp and quick. Why, she asked, was she so good at being a student, but so bad at keeping a job? Don't follow in your mother's footsteps, she said. Don't be a lover.

Once, she opened the robe and told Aggie to touch her breasts. Aggie cupped one of them in her hands. It was heavy, like a melon. The nipple was almost as dark as lips, and little blue veins ran through the pale skin. It was like seeing blue through a hard-boiled egg.

When your father met me, she said, they were small and perky and stood up. More than a mouthful is too much, he said. Can you believe that, Agatha? More than a mouthful.

That night, Agatha felt sick. Even in the dark, the flowers on her walls were scary. They looked as if they might grow right into the room and strangle the dolls, the furniture, and her.

She pressed her hand against the wall. "Daisy?" she said "Daisy? I'm scared."

When she went to the closet, Daisy was out of her hole. She came out into the bedroom and crawled into bed with Aggie. Aggie held onto her the way she used to hang on to Flicker. Daisy was stinky, but it was a good stink. She loved the way Daisy smelled, the way a cowboy probably loved the way cow paddies smelled. Aggie breathed deep, and fell asleep fast. When she woke up, Daisy was gone.

Her mother was up and dressed already, brewing coffee. "Your father called," she told Aggie. "He's coming home tonight with a big fat check. Did you hear me? He's coming home, and we're going to go to Astroworld this weekend. Then we'll have a picnic with strawberries and champagne."

But when he didn't come by nightfall, her mother changed into her nightshirt and told Aggie to go to sleep. Aggie ate some old fruit and went to her closet. But Daisy wasn't there. She knew because the room was dead quiet. She waited for a long time and then went to bed.

Agatha woke with a thick taste in her mouth. Her sheets were wet with sweat. She heard her father's voice. She couldn't hear what he was saying, but it was rich and low. There was the sound of ice clinking and a chair pulling back.

Aggie tiptoed into the hallway. Candles flickered. The light was warm and bright and unlike any light she had seen before. The table was set with the green glass plates. Everything seemed softer, burnished, as if someone had polished the air. Even the rickety old table looked varnished. Her father was there, leaning back in his chair, white shirt sleeves rolled up to his elbows. And across from him was Daisy. Her hair was brushed clean and pulled back off her neck with a black velvet ribbon. She wore a red dress, white lace tights, and patent leather Mary Janes. She nibbled a big slice of white cake and swung her stockinged legs under the table.

They were more beautiful than any two people Aggie had ever seen. She rubbed the crust from her eyes and watched. Her father laughed, and he looked at Daisy as if she were his girl. Daisy kicked the table leg and looked right back at him.

Watching them together was almost like looking into one of those little plastic snow globes her mother put out at Christmas time. Another world, lovelier and smaller than this one. If it could come outside and into this world, it wouldn't be so magical. But Agatha wanted to get inside it just the same.

She'd seen her parents like this when she was a little kid. They would dance together even though there was no music playing. Her mother would rest her head against her father's shoulder and they'd waltz through the rooms. Sometimes her father would sing. "Loving her was easier than anything I'll ever do again," he'd sing, or, "Love is like a dying ember, and only memories remain..."

She shivered a little. Her throat was scratchy, she had the chills. It felt like strep throat was getting inside her again. She didn't want them to see her, so she went back to bed.

When she woke up, her mother was sitting beside her.

"He was here," Aggie said. It felt as if little shards of glass were stuck in her throat.

"Shh," her mother said. "You have to get better soon, or else I'll have to take you to the pediatrician."

"He was here last night, with Daisy," Aggie said.

"I know," her mother said. She laughed. It was a hard, brittle laughter. Aggie didn't want to hear anymore.

"My head hurts," she said. "Can I please go back to sleep?"

The sickness stayed with her for a few days. If she'd been well, she would have thought it was worth it because her mother wasn't drunk. She brought Aggie medicine and checked on her every few hours. When she did, she felt her head and kissed her hairline. She made sure Aggie drank even when it hurt her throat, and she pressed cold washcloths against Aggie's forehead.

When her fever was gone and she felt like eating more than Popsicles, Aggie noticed that the sounds inside the walls were gone. She went into the closet. The hole was still there, but Daisy wasn't inside.

The house was clean. The kitchen looked different. There was a microwave on top of the refrigerator. Plastic drop sheets covered the floors, and buckets and brushes blocked the doorway to the living room. Half the foamy sea was painted over in a glossy bright white.

"Look who's come out of her lair," her mother said. There was juice and toast on the table. Her mother's eyes were hard bits of glitter.

"I've started on the inside, and when I'm done, the outside will be painted too. What do you think of Cake Yellow, huh? Or maybe Arctic Blue?"

Aggie didn't answer. The toast was almost burned, and ice was already melting in the glass.

"Can I go outside?" she asked.

Her mother shrugged her shoulders.

"Oh, go on," she said.

Aggie had to find Daisy. Could she have left? Had she left with her father? Or was she all alone, hurt somewhere? If she had to, Aggie would climb through the hole and search inside the walls. She could go up into the attic, even though there were mummified rats up there. But first she would check the crawlspace under the house.

Her arms and legs tingled. It was not the excitement she'd felt down here in the beginning of the summer, when she'd closed her eyes and felt Nazrat behind her. She knew she had to find Daisy, but she was also afraid. She was beginning to think maybe Daisy had never been there.

She'd crawled farther than she ever had before when she saw the lump. Something bigger than a cat or a dog was wrapped inside an old flowered sheet, which was wrapped inside of one of the plastic floor drops. It was difficult to unravel. But the hard work was good; it meant she could concentrate on the unwrapping and not what was inside.

Daisy's yellow hair was matted. There were little hatch marks up and down her arms. She was whiter than paper, heavier than she'd ever felt in life. Aggie brushed the hair from her blue blue eyes. She was naked.

Aggie wanted to stay inside that moment under the crawlspace forever. She lifted Daisy's broken body up as much as she could manage and held her tight. It wasn't Daisy though. It was hollow, just a body, just a skeleton with flesh on it.

Aggie closed the eyes and tucked the dirty sheet around it.

She went into the house. Her mother was there at the table with an empty jelly jar in front of her.

"She's dead," Aggie said flatly.

Her mother just sat there.

"Daisy is dead. Under the house." Aggie's voice rose from her throat. She started to cry. "She's scratched up and her hair is dirty."

Her mother came to her and pulled her close. Aggie felt the floppy breasts against her face.

"She got killed," Aggie cried.

"Hush now," her mother said. "It's all right now."

"She's naked!" Aggie's body was stiff, but her mother held on anyway. She ran her fingers through Aggie's hair. Her voice was close, but seemed to come from a long way away.

"Shhh, Agatha. I know, I know. It had to happen. She couldn't stay." Her voice was sweet and low, not a real voice, but the voice she used when she was singing. She tried to pull Aggie down into the chair, but Aggie stood straight. She rocked back and forth, and as she rocked she pressed Aggie's face against her breastbone.

Aggie made her body go stiff, just like the body down there. Her mother smelled right, like soap and perfume and make up. It didn't seem right that her mother smelled normal and Daisy was dead.

##

In the months that followed, Aggie didn't want to leave the house. Her mother found a job as a library assistant, and her father stopped calling. When school started, she sat next to a girl who painted her fingernails with liquid paper and wore a monogrammed anklet. She said she had a boyfriend named Charlie at her old school. Her name was Trina, and she lived in an apartment that smelled of new carpet and pine air freshener. Aggie spent weekends with her sometimes, and they rented scary movies.

Her Mom painted over the flowers, and now Aggie's bedroom was purple and yellow. She also fixed the wall in the closet. Aggie told Trina Nazrat stories. But they were just stories now. She couldn't make it feel as if Nazrat was there with her when she closed her eyes.

She cried at night when she thought of Daisy. But she did it quietly, and she never said anything about Daisy aloud. She knew she was down there, wrapped in the soiled sheet. She wanted to cover her with velvet, to write her name in letters across her notebooks. But she was beginning to believe a person could think different thoughts about a thing at the same time, and they might be all true. But the truest was the secret, the thing that went unspoken. A little girl lived under the floorboards. Her eyes were jewels, her skin was like milk, her hair was long and bright. She wore pink corduroys and a flowered tee shirt. Her name was Daisy.

A Sunny Day Turns Dark

by Chris Perridas

It started as a scratch.

It was a sunny Gulf Coast day. I looked down as I crunched across the gritty sand in search of pink-tinted seashells. I warily scanned for stinging, stinking jellyfish ambushes across the bright bleached sand, my skin slathered with sun block. Who cared if passersby cackled at my zinc-white nose and droopy hat? This was one pale, plump old son-of-the-south determined to go home melanoma-free.

I'd just reached up to keep the brisk breeze from tugging off my hat, when my flip-flop flapped and a small seashell slit my great toe under the joint. I wobbled on one leg examining my foot scaring off a flock of Ibis. The slice appeared no worse than a paper cut, though the salt water burned.

What could come of such a small cut?

Back at the hotel, I reexamined the wound. The toe now throbbed, oozing pus. I rubbed on some antibiotic salve, put on a Band-Aid, and lay on the couch for a nap.

No! That damnable dream came again!

It started as always, with me hiking through the woods back home in Kentucky. Outside of that nightmare, I was the great armchair explorer who loved to watch National Geographic specials, but hated getting bit by bugs.

In the distance, a woodpecker rapped. I was alone and my bladder was full, so I unzipped to relieve myself. Halfway through, I glanced down. A mosquito was poised in the most inconvenient place, its long black thread legs straddling my member, the long proboscis slurping my blood. My pee-valve tensed, a pain cascaded to my prostate, which caused me to do a woodland dance. I ended upended in a creek.

I removed my wet, soiled clothes and sat on a soft mat of green moss with my back propped against a tree. Just when I thought I might rest, I felt the pinch of an ant picking at my toe. My cut dripped green goop onto the velvet moss. The faster it spread, the more ants came to feast at the banquet. A long, black line wound through the woods, reminding me of the crowd at last month's Baptist potluck picnic.

Sweat beaded on my brow, which attracted a cloud of gnats. The fuzzy dots flew straight up my nostrils. I coughed when they crawled past my tonsils. A large butterfly lighted on my eye and sucked juice from my tear duct. A fat black beetle waddled its way down the curve of my buttocks.

I tried to brush the bugs away, but my useless arms were numb. On the ground lay my hands, covered in fuzzy fungus like that on week-old bread. A mouthful of moths smothered my scream. Just as a praying mantis crawled over my brow and started to nibble at my ear, I awoke.

"Ah, finally awake? Good. That last procedure wasn't so bad, was it?"

I lay in a hospital bed. A perky, buxom nurse peered down at me.

"I have more forms for you to sign," the nurse said. "Naturally, with the amputations, you will have to make an 'X'. Here, honey, let me put the pen in your mouth. I checked with administration, it's perfectly legal."

"My God, woman! What have you people done to me?"

"Oh, I see", she replied with a knowing smile. "The anesthesia sometimes makes the memory come and go, but you'll be to yourself in a few minutes. I'm your nurse, Ashley, remember?"

Tubes hung all around me; wires were glued onto my body. Tangled in the medical spaghetti was the string of a Budweiser-shaped balloon that stated, "Get Well Soon." It was from the boys at the bowling alley back home.

"Your infected toe has made you something of a celebrity here," Nurse Ashley said. "All the doctors are baffled. You've been the talk of the break room. Doctor Alvarez and Doctor Guillermo have a wager on what the infection might be; the loser has to caddy for a month!

"You really made the doctors work, honey." She leaned and pinched my cheek—the one that remained. "Why, every time we thought we'd snipped enough of you away, well, that pesky fungus just climbed a little higher up your leg. Then there was that small mix up where we amputated the wrong leg. That's never happened before at Clearwater Memorial. You broke our perfect record.

"The doctors did save about half of you. We think this will stop the infection for a while. Of course, as we discussed yesterday—you do remember, don't you?—it seems to be mutating. That forced us to switch to that other treatment we discussed. I'm so excited. I haven't seen maggots used to clean wounds since the nurses' seminar in Orlando. The doctors got the big, genetically-enhanced maggots to treat you. You're just the luckiest patient! They're so much better at eating decayed tissue."

I wanted to retch, but my stomach was gone—replaced by more tubes. Then a thought struck — did I still have my frank and beans?

My memory ebbed back. I remembered being embarrassed as a candy striper daubed the open cavity between my legs. So, yes, they were gone. Damn, they were my best features.

With no hands or legs, suicide seemed impossible. Or was it? I twisted my head to the left, took an IV tube into my toothless mouth, and gummed it in hopes of cutting off my life.

"Honey, what do you think you're doing?" Nurse Ashley asked. She put one competent hand on her curvaceous hip. "I'm going to have to keep my eye on you, aren't I?" she said, moving the tubes out of reach.

My momma raised me to be polite, so I knew I shouldn't kick up a fuss with Nurse Ashley. I'd be a good son of the south and accept the parade of greenhorn interns who would learn surgical technique by whittling away at me.

Just then, a prim man with a white jacket and stethoscope came in with a group of medical students, all of them twenty-something women.

"Now, this is an interesting case," the doctor said. "You don't mind if we take a peek under your sheet?" Without waiting for an answer, he pulled it back to reveal the remains of my pubic area. The blonde in the front put her hand to her mouth as she ran out of the room. The doctor chuckled, "I remember that happening to me back in '71."

It was time for my next treatment. Nurse Ashley, came in with a covered stainless steel tray. She leaned over to set the tray down, accidentally showing three inches of cleavage. Her thin white blouse left little to the imagination in the heavily air conditioned room. Somewhere, down the hall in a large vat of formaldehyde, I had an erection.

"Oh, honey, I've always wanted to be an M.A.S," she said, removing the lid from the tray.

"What's that stand for?" I asked.

"Your poor memory just comes and goes. It means 'maggot application specialist'."

She used long forceps to pick up a squirming, cream-colored bug from the tray, carefully positioning it on a gooey portion of my gray flesh. I watched, but there was no pain as the white worm gobbled what was left of me. She continued to move the wrigglers, one by one, to other places I couldn't see.

I groaned. I squirmed.

"None of that from you," she said sternly. "The ingestion organisms have a lot to eat...I mean neutralize...today. Our team will be working around the clock, so you just get used to it.

"Are you looking down my blouse? Shame, what would your mother think? I thought you were a nice patient. Well, there's not much left of that eye anyway, so let me just fix it so you can't ogle me anymore."

The angry shadow that passed over Nurse Ashley's face was the last thing I saw before her long nail moved to my one good eye. As my vision went dark I felt only the whisper-breeze of Nurse Ashley's warm breath; and the wet feel of my eyeball leaking down what remained of my face.

THE REMEMBERING COUNTRY

by Kevin Filan

Two weeks after Jennifer Peterson died, Doug McKenna sat on his front porch and stared out at his father's land. Behind the storage shed the black gum thicket sparkled burgundy in the sunset. The door banged against the lintel in the autumn breeze. The torn screen scratched a backbeat on the cracked storm window.

I'm home, Doug thought as he sent a cigarette butt between the porch boards. The end glowed ember-orange for a brief second, then faded to Georgia-dirt red and was swallowed by blackness.

You're home, the crumbling marble angel in the front yard agreed.

Shut up Doug said as a fat crow landed on the wrought iron gate.

Are you finally going to go back in the basement?

Overhead the moon brightened as afternoon became dusk. Lengthening shadows turned the angel's eyes to black pits. The crow rose from the gate and flew three lazy wing-beats to her shoulder.

Shut up Doug told it again.

The crow nuzzled the crack in the marble angel's cheek. Doug smelled the roadkill stench of carrion and tar on its feathers.

What's wrong? the angel smiled at the stinking crow, or maybe it was smiling at Doug. *Don't want to follow in your father's footsteps?*

"There's a sledgehammer in the basement," Doug said aloud. "If I go down there I'm coming back and smashing you."

The shadows covered the angel's mouth and she was silent. The crow puffed out its chest and raised his wings, then flew away with an indignant *CAW!!!!*

"I guess you told him."

Doug started in the direction of the voice outside his head. A slender girl watched from the road. Her hair was the color of the moon above the kudzu-choked slave quarters. Doug wondered why she held antlers in her hands, then realized she stood astride a bicycle. She waved to him, then set off down the road. Doug waved back, but quickly put his arm down when he realized he was showing his scars.

##

"So tell me about your mother."

Jancowski wiped his glasses and leaned back in his chair. Outside it still rained.

Doug smelled the dampness soaking through everything and thought the staples in his forearms might rust.

"What do you want to know?"

Jancowski shrugged, his smile exposing small, unevenly spaced teeth. He picked up his pen from the crack between the half-finished Princess Sardines tin and the grimy water jug. "I'm a psychiatrist. We're supposed to ask that question."

"Fine." Doug lit a cigarette. "She died right after I was born. That's what dad told me, anyway."

Jancowski placed his glasses back on his flat, broad nose. "And you think perhaps your father was lying?"

"I don't know."

Dr. Jancowski leaned back a little further. The buttons on his shirt moved one step closer to popping. Lightning struck not too far away. The sky brightened to the color of Jancowski's pale, hairless belly, then darkened again.

"You don't know?"

"Dad always told me my mother died right after I was born. When I was thirteen I found out she died giving birth. To me." Doug took a long drag from the cigarette. "It was my birthday. I really wanted a 12-speed, just like Jimmy Phillips down the street had. The whole day goes by, and there's no card, no cake, nothing. By sunset I'm trying to figure out what's going on. So I figure there's going to be a surprise party. And I go all over the house looking for him, and finally I see him in the library."

Doug blew out smoke. Thunder rumbled in the distance.

"And he's sitting in his big leather chair. He's got a photo in one hand, a glass of Scotch in the other. The bottle is sitting next to him. Or what's left of the bottle anyway."

Jancowski frowned. "Your father wasn't a drinking man when I knew him."

"He wasn't. That's the only time I ever saw him drunk."

Jancowski leaned back still further. His chair creaked in protest as he put his wide stubby feet up on the black leather ottoman. "I see. I'm sorry, I shouldn't have interrupted you. This is your story, not mine."

"And he sees me coming in, and before I can even say, 'Dad, it's my birthday,' he says, 'it's because of you she's gone. Why should I get you a goddamned thing?' And right after he says it he realizes what he's done and he gets up and he comes after me crying, 'Doug, Doug, I'm sorry.' But I'm running down the stairs."

A long fierce drag.

"The next morning neither of us say anything to each other at breakfast. And when I go out to the garage there's a brand new 12-speed sitting there."

Lightning struck, closer this time: for a second the sky was as white as the radiator beneath the window. The glass shuddered as if the rumbling might crack it, but held steady. Doug chuckled and shuddered with the glass.

"It's funny. I remember how I felt when I didn't get a card. I remember how I felt when I was going up the stairs. I remember how I felt when I saw the bike. But I can't remember how I felt when I found out I had killed my mother."

"Your father loved your mother very much," Jancowski said, his basso profundo voice rumbling soft as the last of the thunder's echoes. "But they..." He paused; lightning struck close again. "It wasn't your fault. And your father knew that."

"I can't remember how I felt," Doug said again. "I can remember a lot of other things."

Don't say a word a voice hissed through the radiator's steam. *You know we can make it hell for you.*

I'll cut myself again, Doug warned, feeling the hair bristle on the back of his neck. *Maybe this time I'll do it all the way. Then you won't have anyone to talk to. You'll be all alone in the dark again.*

Maybe that's what we want, the steam hissed back spitefully. *Did you ever think of that?*

Dr. Jancowski peered intently with his bulbous Marty Feldman eyes. "Other things?"

Maybe that's what we want.

Doug put out his cigarette. "I don't remember."

Jancowski chuckled. "You will."

Over the waitress's head, Elvis leaned against a microphone stand. A man with a scraggly goatee laid out Tarot cards on the corner table. Doug smelled civet amidst the baked goods and clove cigarettes. He tried to tune out the lunch-rush chatter and peered into the corner shadows. The moonlight-haired girl looked up at him and smiled, then turned back to the Celtic Cross.

"You have a lot of secrets," said the man with the scraggly goatee as he pointed to The Moon. He looked up at the girl as his finger moved past the Nine of Swords to the Eight of Wands. "And a lot of suffering. It's in the past now, but you're still running from it."

Doug stared at her for a second then turned back to the menu, trying to decide between Almost Wintertime Hot Fudge Pie and Thanksgiving Leftover Pumpkin Cheesecake. In the next room the band continued their sound check.

"But there are a lot of changes coming soon," the Tarot reader added as the sound guy adjusted the treble.

The slender girl smiled but didn't reply. Doug looked away from the menu to see the Two of Pentacles coming down beside the Eight of Wands.

"One-two-three..." the vocalist shouted from the other room. The guitarist played an ice pick staccato pattern; the drummer filled in the empty spaces. Doug winced at the feedback: the tiny waitress beneath the Daily Specials board winced with him. The vocalist gestured angrily. Doug could see his hand through the archway, his polished fingernails black as Elvis' background.

"We're getting distortion."

"No shit," the vocalist said. "These ceilings are too low."

"Dude, what do you want?" the sound man asked. "It's a basement."

"Can I help y'all with something?" the waitress asked as she peeked into the performance area.

"I think we're good, Christine," the vocalist replied.

"Okay." Christine passed the Tarot reader and returned to the front stand. "Let me know if you need anything."

"Let's see what's coming next," said the man with the goatee. The moonlight-haired girl laid her hand on his. Her onyx ring glistened in the incandescent light.

"Don't tell me. I like surprises."

"Again! One-two-three..." Doug winced at the noise. The bass joined the guitar and drums: Doug waited for it to start mocking him with each thudding downbeat, but it remained meaningless noise. He closed his eyes and tried to lose himself in the empty rhythm as he lit a cigarette. For a second he thought he might dissolve into a 3/4 puddle, then somebody touched his arm.

"Hello again."

The slender girl leaned forward. Doug smelled patchouli and civet and something else, something sharp as the feedback from the next room as she drew closer.

"They're not very good, are they?"

"No," Doug said, trying to look away from her aqua-green eyes. "No, they're not."

"Noisy as marble angels," she said, or maybe she didn't say that at all, Doug thought, maybe it was the guitar trying to fool him. As she waited for his reply, she smiled: Doug couldn't tell if she was being friendly, pitying or mocking. Finally she turned to the waitress.

"Get Don whatever he wants."

"You want the Captain Bligh Tuna Platter, right?" the waitress asked as Black Velvet Elvis panted benevolently at them.

"Can I get extra fries with that?" Don packed up his cards and put them in the stained front pocket of his bowling shirt. "And a chocolate milkshake?"

"Two scoops with whipped cream, right?"

The vocalist began a long droning howl, weaving around the music like kudzu growing up a wall. The drummer hit a rim shot, then accented it with a cymbal as if he could chop away the vines as they grew higher. Doug winced as the noise scraped against the inside of his skull. The slender girl leaned forward again.

"Noisy as marble angels," she said aloud, and this time there was no mistaking it, it was clear even through the tangled noise. She leaned closer again: Doug thought she might kiss him, but she just pressed her face against his, then turned and left a ten-dollar bill at the waitress's table. As she reached the doorway she stopped, waiting for Doug to say something. When he didn't, she turned and went up the stairs, and then there was only the afterglow of civet and the scars on his forearms and the vocalist in the next room waving his arm again and yelling cut, cut, cut.

"Can I get you something, sir?"

Doug jumped: his cigarette dropped to the table and made a new burn beside the old one. The tiny waitress hesitated, her South Georgia accent even heavier than before.

"Ah'm sorry. Ah didn't mean to startle you." Her lip quivered. "Ah can come back if you want."

Doug smiled. "It's okay."

She giggled. "You sure?"

"Positive." He handed her the menu. "I think I'd like the raspberry tart. And you don't know if the owner would be interested in selling this place, do you?"

"Would you like to talk to me about the voices?" Jancowski asked, then, when he saw Doug stiffen, "I'm sorry. I didn't mean to make you uncomfortable."

"It's all right. You didn't make me uncomfortable." Doug lit another cigarette and tapped his fingers against the arm of the chair. "It's just that I'm not supposed to tell you."

Jancowski stared silently ahead. The fluorescent lights above buzzed faintly, like mosquitoes. Doug smelled the rain outside, then turned back to his cigarette and tried to shut every smell out with a long drag.

"The last time they got mad at me they screamed for three days. They wouldn't let me eat or sleep or anything. Night and day they screamed."

Another drag, inhaling deep, trying to bury the cold red mud outside, not the warm catfish and cottonmouth North Georgia swamp dirt smell, but close enough.

"I don't want them to start screaming again."

The rain picked up, blowing against the windows. Doug thought they might give, but the walls held steady and the radiator kept the muddy air warm despite the wind, adding a metal steam tang to the wet dirt and plaster dust clumping on the moisture beads around the window.

"So do all the voices scream?" Jancowski asked, still staring with those unblinking eyes.

Doug tried to concentrate on the taste of his Marlboro Light, tried to ignore the mosquitoes buzzing like fluorescent lights around him, drawn in by the blood on the briar-wounds.

"Sometimes..."

Jancowski waited. Doug felt the staples in his arm prickling, prickling like the briar scratches on his chest and legs, prickling like the fangs in his mouth. Another short drag, the tobacco bitterness brought him out of the swamp and back to Jancowski's office.

"Some of them are helpful. Most of them just leave you alone."

Jancowski leaned back toward the shadows around his bookcase.

"You tried to tell your father that, didn't you?" Another pause, Jancowski almost hidden in the darkness, only his bulbous eyes and full half-smiling lips visible above his belly. Doug ground out his cigarette. Jancowski drew in breath. Doug thought he would wait him out this time, but he spoke before Doug expected it.

"I'm sorry. This is your story. You tell it as you see fit."

"It's okay." Doug waited for the lights to begin buzzing a warning, but they remained silent. "When I was a kid, dad always asked me about the voices. Every night after he told me a story. But then, when I was seven, he stopped telling stories. And he told me I shouldn't talk about the voices anymore."

The scent of the mud faded as the ice crystals covered the mud. Doug crumpled the empty pack in his hand and talked toward Jancowski's faintly widening smile.

"'Those voices are not real,' he'd say. 'They have nothing to offer you.'" Doug mimicked his father's ringing baritone. "'You're much too old to be talking about nonsense like voices.'"

Jancowski chuckled. "That certainly sounds like Sebastian McKenna."

"They were real to me, you know. But he made me think they weren't."

"So you stopped hearing them?"

"I stopped paying attention to them." He threw the empty pack into the wastebasket. "After dad killed himself, I stopped hearing them altogether. For a while. Most of the time. Then it started again. They told me to go home. When I wouldn't go, the screaming started."

"And that was when you cut yourself?"

"And that was when I cut myself."

The sun disappeared into the clouds before going down altogether. Brown magnolia leaves fell heavy on the McKenna land. Doug read while he sat between the old oak's roots. Atop this week's *Halfmast* the headline read DOWNBELOW STATION CHANGES HANDS. SEE SONDERBERG ON PAGE 3. Doug tried to read the story, but the print was too small in the dimness. He leaned back against the bark and lit a cigarette and waited for the new sodium yard lights to come on.

"You're in the news."

He started as the slender moonlight-haired girl sat down beside him.

"You should be more careful." She smirked. "Didn't your father tell you there were only three times one should have his name in the paper?"

Doug tried to place her accent but couldn't. Not southern – maybe Russian or Scandinavian. But maybe he was just guessing that from her high cheekbones and higher forehead and impossibly aqua eyes.

"Actually, he did." Doug smiled. "But he was always getting mentioned in the business section anyway. So I'm doing what he did, not what he said."

"You should be careful," she said again, not smirking this time. A bat fluttered overhead. "You weren't here when Jennifer Peterson got killed, were you?"

"No. I was still back home. Back where I grew up, I mean. Well, where I grew up from when I was twelve. It's a long story. Anyway, I didn't get here until two weeks ago."

"Good." Her smirk returned. "Then they can't blame you for that one." Doug chuckled. "Should I be worried about the villagers?"

Again the smirk vanished. "Yes. People are scared. And nobody remembers the McKenna family. Not even the professors' kids who grew up here."

"I'll watch out for pitchforks. And torches."

The stone angel chuckled in response. Doug tried to ignore its malevolent cackling. Finally the slender girl smiled, a real smile, not a smirk. Doug noticed the faint scars on her reconstructed upper lip. She jerked away when she saw him looking.

"I'm sorry."

She looked down at the ground, her lower face almost hidden by her long hair.

"I don't remember the surgery," she said finally. Doug noticed the faint sibilance over her still-untraceable accent. "I was very young."

"They did a very good job. The doctors, I mean."

"Thanks." She touched the scars on his forearm. "They did a good job with you too."

"I did it so I wouldn't come back here. I guess it didn't work."

She smiled. "So how do you like Athens now that you're here?"

"It's fine." He smiled again. "You don't need to trade behaviour points for smoking privileges."

She wrinkled her nose. "I don't smoke."

"I'm sorry." He put out his cigarette two drags early. "So you've read about me in the papers. But I don't even know your name."

She leaned closer. The smell of civet overpowered the springtime humus. "I'm Miranda. And you're Doug McKenna. Is that the McKenna/Clarke County Preserve McKennas or the McKenna Road McKennas?"

"They're the same McKennas."

She shook her head. "McKenna/Clarke County is named for Edmund McKenna; McKenna Road is after his brother George."

"Edmund was my grandfather." The sodium light clicked on. Miranda's eyes shone amber in the glow. Doug looked past the chuckling angel toward the moon hanging above the yew hedge. "So when did you graduate from Journ school?"

"Very good!" She grinned. The caps on her front teeth glistened plasticine orange in the yard light. She looked down. When she looked up she refused to meet Doug's eye. "Three years ago. I was a Sebastian McKenna Memorial Scholar."

"Sebastian was my father, you know?"

Miranda finally met his eye again. "Yes."

She touched his shoulder, then stroked upward. Her hand was warm on his neck, the skin glossy like hot wax paper. He closed his eyes, trying to concentrate on the civet and the hot moist warmth of her breath on his face. She leaned toward him. He kissed her once, then opened his eyes as he nuzzled her ear. As she stroked toward his chin he noticed the thick scar tissue on her fingers. He stiffened. She pulled away.

"I wasn't so young when they operated on my hands."

She stood, her head hanging low and her hair completely covering her face now.

"I'm sorry. I need to go."

"Miranda!"

She took two more steps, then turned at the gate.

"I'll talk to you soon?"

Still staring at the ground. "I'm sure you're very busy with the new restaurant. Maybe I'll see you around?"

"Yeah. I'd like that, I mean."

"I think I'd like that too." She smiled. "Goodbye, Doug."

"See you, Miranda."

"They're much smarter than people think," Doug explained to Jancowski as he pointed to a bedraggled squirrel seeking shelter from the rain.

"You mean squirrels," Jancowski asked as he scratched notes on his pad.

"I mean animals in general."

The squirrel climbed an ash tree, trying to hide beneath the few remaining leaves.

"Why do you say that?"

Doug used the butt of his cigarette to light another cigarette. The squirrel curled against the tree, a drizzle-trickle of water soaking his left shoulder as he turned balefully toward Doug. *Don't tell him anything*, the squirrel whispered in his head. Doug put the butt in the overflowing ashtray and took a drag from the fresh cigarette. The MARLBORO on the paper disappeared to embers before Jancowski finally broke the silence.

"Are you afraid they'll punish you?"

Doug looked out the window. "He's watching me."

Jancowski snorted, then turned his head and stared with Doug out the window. The squirrel stood transfixed as Jancowski stared, water pouring down both its shoulders now, matching Jancowski's silence with its own as it fell into the mud below.

"The bad ones make noise. But they can't hurt you." Jancowski was smiling with the lower half of his face as he turned back to Doug, but his eyes were still dark and quiet. "They retreat from us if we confront them. They can be ignored. The other voices, the ones that want to teach us, those are the important ones."

"No. No, you can't trust them either." Doug felt something sting his hand, then realized his cigarette was burning his knuckles. He dropped it into the ashtray. "You can't trust the other voices."

"Why do you say that?"

"'When the men came, the lords of the animals hid,'" Doug leaned forward. "That's what it told me. They hide in the places between places. And sometimes they put on skin."

"Put on skin?"

"That's what they call it," Doug leaned forward, his voice soft. "Coming back to this world."

Jancowski nibbled on his pen. "And when did you hear this?"

"Right before my father died. It took me to a place in the woods. We ran together. Everything was shining. I heard my father calling for me. I could hear him even though I was miles away. So I ran back toward him. On the way, I passed through some swampy land and got caught in briars."

He tensed his hand on the chair's arm, using the pain from his newly unstitched wounds to keep back the memories. Jancowski wrote a quick note, then returned to nibbling.

"Dad asked me what had happened, and I told him." Doug paused, gripping harder till his scars stood out bright red on his skin. "He wouldn't let me finish. He told me to forget everything." A harder grip, as if he might split the cuts open again. "Three days later he shot himself."

Doug felt the tears rolling down his face before he realized he was crying. Jancowski pushed a box of tissues in his direction.

"Something about that voice scared dad so much I killed him. Like I killed my mother."

"Your mother and father knew childbearing was unwise for them," Jancowski went on, ignoring Doug's sobbing. "They made their own choice, Doug."

"But..."

Jancowski reached for the half-full glass and swallowed the slimy water in one loud gulp. "They. Made. Their. Own. Choice." His voice was harsher now, his second and third chins quivering with each sharply enunciated syllable, as close to angry as Doug had ever heard him, then sad and hurt as he repeated. "They. Made. Their. Own. Choice."

"Fine. Fine," Doug said as the pain began to slip away. "It was their fucking choice, all right?"

"That's right," softer and darker. Doug's tears melted away in the rumbling bass voice and the *dark brown eyes, the eyes that left you sitting there like a squirrel waiting to drop...*

"Your father refused to listen to that voice, Doug. I want you to tell me that voice's story." Talking dark and cold now, *cold like a puddle.*

"That voice gave you a story."

Like a puddle coming up to meet you, not even able to flinch as your head hits the ground and your brainstem whacks your spinal cord like a hangman's knot.

"Repeat that story for me."

"They hide when they come," Doug said as he tried to pull himself from the mud. "They can look like anything they like. Sometimes they put on animal-skin. Sometimes they put on tree-skin or mountain-skin. And sometimes they put on man-skin. Some of them are friendly. Some are hostile. Most don't care one way or the other." He inhaled stale tobacco, trying to forget wet mud and paralysis. Jancowski sat silent, his hands crossed over his belly. "They're the ones talking in my head."

Jancowski looked out the window at the squirrel lying ear-deep in muddy water. He put his pen down beside the stained pitcher then turned with a thick-lipped grin.

"I told you that you'd come to the memories."

"So I'm the first one in the new Downbelow Station?" Miranda said as Doug unwrapped an after-dinner brie-and-fruit platter. "I'm flattered."

"I didn't have to change anything but the plumbing. And I brought the electrical system up to code. And put in an automatic dishwasher. But other than that, I didn't do a thing."

"Not a thing." She laughed. "So where did you learn about restaurants?"

"I worked at the Blackwater Diner for eight years. That's in Pennsylvania where I'm from originally. Well, where I was from after my dad died." He shook his head. "I'm sorry. I'm sure I'm not making much sense."

"Who said you have to make sense?" She leaned forward. "Go on. Tell me more."

"Is this for publication, Miss Sonderberg?"

She rolled her eyes. "While Downbelow Station buys half a page weekly, nobody at *Halfmast* is going to say anything bad about you. Besides, I thought my article was very flattering."

"I always wanted to be a 'mysterious stranger with hometown roots,' I guess." He put some smoked salmon around a celery stick. "So if I buy a page a week, am I guaranteed a good review from your food critic?"

Miranda snorted. "Don gives a glowing review to anyone who gives him a free meal."

"Don who reads Tarot cards?"

"He has a few jobs. You should get to know him. He's very entertaining. And sincere."

"Then he eats free forever." Doug handed her the salmon. "Maybe Downbelow Station can be a salon for sincere people."

"But who would come?" Miranda winked as she bit down. "You said you worked at the Blackwater Diner for eleven years. And you started in ninth grade?"

"Yeah, washing dishes. I was making food orders by the time I was a junior."

"And then you went to Penn. Where your father went?"

"Is this for publication?" he asked again, not smiling this time.

"Not unless you want it to be, no," she said.

"I went to Penn for two years. That's where my father went to law school: he got his degree from UGA, but I didn't want to be anywhere near Georgia."

"I see. So you only went for two years?"

"When I was twenty I had a breakdown. Well, when I was nineteen I had a breakdown. I was twenty when they put me in the hospital."

"And that's when you cut yourself?"

"No, that was a different time. Then I came back to Blackwater and worked at the Diner for a while." He looked away. "I'm sorry, can we talk about something else?"

"That's fine." Her smile grew bitter. "Do you think I really want to hear about hospitals?"

"Oh, shit, I'm sorry..."

"Please." She put her hand on his. He felt the warmth and tried to ignore the missing nails, the glossy pink nubs at the end of each fingertip. She gripped harder as if she might poke through him with her mutilated claws. Doug smelled civet and leaned toward her. She smiled shyly, then pulled away.

"Go on. I want to hear more of your story."

"I worked at the Diner for four years. By the end I was doing their books. I was always able to work at the restaurant. Even when I was sick. Well, most of the time anyway. So

I thought I should get a restaurant here. Then I could always come to work and pretend I was better until I was."

He looked down at his slashed arms. "That's the short version, anyway. And then Dr. Jancowski said I should come back here."

"Dr. Emil Jancowski."

He tilted his head. "You know Dr. Jancowski?"

She smiled and reached for more salmon. "Know him? He sent me to school. He's the chairman of the Sebastian McKenna Memorial Trust."

"Yep, that's him." He smiled. "I didn't meet him until I went to the hospital. The fourth time I went to the hospital, I mean. I'm sorry, I only told you about two."

"That's fine." She stared intently at him now, the faint thin lines around her mouth baby-pink against her baby-white skin. "You don't have to tell me anything if you don't want to."

"No, that's fine. I think I only met him in the hospital. Sometimes I think I remember him. When I was small. Dad was standing behind him and he was telling me a story."

"'And the Priest of Frogs stayed in the swamp,'" Miranda said. "'and he remembered where we were, and where we are, and how we got there.'"

The hackles rose on Doug's neck as he spoke the story's next line. "'And most of all, he knew the way back to the Remembering Country.'"

Miranda smiled. "And most of all he knew the way back to the Remembering Country."

##

"I don't know what's wrong with the yard light," Doug said as they walked up the trail to his house. "It should have been on hours ago."

"Don't worry about it," she said, looking up at the full moon. "We can see just fine."

Miranda ran suddenly, then ascended the McKenna porch steps in one floating stride, her legs stretched in a quick *pas de deux* as she hit the landing. Her smile gleamed in the full-moon light.

"How long were you a dancer?"

"Please don't ask me about that." She hesitated, then stretched out her hand toward Doug. "Come on. You do it."

Doug reached toward her fingers then leapt. The porch boards creaked as he landed beside her, touched her shoulder to get his balance. Doug put his hands in her hair, natural platinum to his Scottish red and longer, past her shoulders and almost to her waist. She reached up and kissed him on the ear, her lips hesitant against his skin.

So are you ready to go back in the basement? the marble angel asked. Doug couldn't tell if it was being malevolent or encouraging or just curious. *Do you want her to see what's there?*

"Those damned marble angels are making noise again." She nuzzled her face against his, drenching him in the sweet musky scent of civet. "Don't you have a hammer in the basement?"

Doug froze, his heart racing like he had just jumped a skyscraper, not a porch. Everything shone in the moonlight. The cool rot of the leaves and the faint scrape of newly bare branches mingled with Miranda's rumbling, hesitant breathing. He waited for her next words as she moved backward slowly, opening the new front door even though he knew it had been locked, *it should have been locked but it was open...*

"Come on!"

Into the shadows in two steps now, he wanted to stop but instead found himself following behind her, everything bright even though the lights were out. He moved past the old dresser, past the china cabinet, past the pile of bills and receipts on the kitchen table to the place where she stood opening the deadbolt.

"Let's go get it."

Dad never left the cellar open. I called for him but he didn't answer.

His mouth felt strange, like someone else's mouth he had borrowed and never returned. He tried to scream at Miranda, tried to tell her to come back, to stop, but his mouth wasn't taking orders, nothing was taking orders. He stumbled toward her, down the narrow stairs and once green-and-white Sears ivy-vine-patterned wallpaper, past the stain...

He was sitting by the water heater on a stack of milk cartons, the shirt he wore to the office, tie in his front pocket and unbuttoned to his chest...

Doug walked onto the concrete, toward the faint dark stain by the water heater. The blood sang in his ears. He reached out for a 2x4 to catch his balance as black flowers bloomed at the edges of his vision.

And I tried to catch my balance but I fell. The floor was slippery and I couldn't concentrate on anything but his shirt unbuttoned halfway down his chest, the head mostly gone, the shotgun still held in what was left of the jaws, the suit soaked like the floor around him...

He tried to ignore the vertigo, tried to ignore the scent of civet, tried to ignore everything but the stairs leading out, the stairs with the faded wallpaper and the stain, the handprint where he had caught his balance when he saw.

"When you saw that his neck was still there. And his chest. And they were covered with striped fur."

##

Doug tried to leap up the stairs but slipped on the fifth step. He hit his side hard as he fell, whimpering with the sharp blow of the handrail against his ribs. Jancowski stepped toward him from the shadows, not wearing his usual suit but something else now, a warty olive one-piece outfit with a white throat that swelled every time he spoke.

"And the animals hid in the places between places. But the dreams stayed behind. And so the animals came back to dream."

He ran into the yard, then leapt over the stone wall separating McKenna property from the wetlands. Everything was hot and heavy and smelled of swamp water. *I'm dreaming*, Doug thought, then backed into briars and realized he wasn't. The stinging on his arm joined the dull bruise ache on his side. He lurched forward; something snarled in the distance. *It's not an outfit*, Doug realized as Jancoski shuffled closer. *That's his body.*

"Do you remember that part of the story now, Doug?" Miranda asked as she jumped from a tree and landed beside him. He saw the faint pale hairs which covered her body and realized she was as naked as Jancowski.

"I remember," Doug said, his tongue thick and his teeth impossibly sharp. He tore off what was left of his tattered pullover with one slash of his claws, claws?, and stood shirtless in the swamp. The scars on his arms looked like stripes.

"But the dreams were different now," Miranda said as she moved pale and downy toward him. "Men had learned to dream. And the animals learned to dream like men."

Doug began moving backward, back toward the house, back toward the stone wall. Jancowski moved toward him, clearing what had to be thirty feet with one bound and making a four-point landing in a puddle.

"And some of the animals got lost in the dreams and believed they were men," Miranda said as she walked past the rotting willow tree toward the path. Her eyes shone aqua-green, vertical-slit pupils wide open to catch the moonlight. Doug looked away, then flinched as he saw Jancowski beside him.

"And they stayed in the man's world and learned to love its noise."

Jancowski thrust a hand mirror in Doug's face. The eyes which looked back at Doug were amber and cat-slit too, the mouth too large, the teeth...

"The King of Tigers made a woman his Queen. And when he lost her he went mad and decided he was a man," Jancowski continued. Miranda moved closer to Doug. Her scars were barely visible beneath her fur as she touched his chest.

"But the animal dreams wouldn't leave him," she said, a new element to her accent, something throaty and rough. "He tried to run from them. And finally he ran to the place where there are no dreams."

Doug looked down at his claws and the stripes on his arms.

"And so we lost the King of Tigers," Jancowski said, "But we watched over his son. We waited for the time when the noises hurt his ears."

Miranda removed Doug's jeans, *mrrwling* fiercely as she ran her scarred fingertips over his orange fur. He barely noticed her body against his as Jancowski continued speaking.

"And the Priest of Frogs brought the Prince to the Remembering Country."

Miranda breathed in his ear; Doug smelled coppery blood-salt and the faint sweet hint of decay over the moist warmth of her lips. "And the Lady of the Cats brought him to awakening."

As she spoke he became conscious of her body, of her long slender legs against his, of her toes mutilated like her fingers, of her fur softer than his. Jancowski hopped out of the puddle and landed on a broken cooler beside the willow stump. His throat shone white and slimy in the moonlight as he puffed it out.

"Welcome to the zoo, Tigerman."

Tigerman stretched out in the square of sunlight, then yawned. Out back, Jancowski dove into the pond with a loud splash. Miranda *rrpwled* gently, then curled closer to Tigerman. The marble angel waited quietly for twilight and savored its dead fox offering. From the pond, a smaller toad harrumphed, then, after a squeaking croak, became silent.

Tigerman stroked her body, the small, pointy breasts and the breasts below them. She took his hand and teased it with her injured fingertips, gently forcing his claws from their sheaths. Tigerman remembered the places between places, and the places you go to put on skin. He found the soft damp place between Miranda's legs and rubbed gently. She arched back, all eight of her nipples stiffening.

This is the remembering country.

Miranda smiled, so broad that he could almost see past the caps, to the white sparkling fangs she was meant to have.

"It's the place we come for forgetting, too."

Her teeth pricked his neck as she rolled atop him. He pulled her close. Out back, another frog croaked, and Jancowski croaked in response. Miranda guided his cock inside her. Tigerman closed his eyes and wondered when he would dream again of being Doug McKenna.

Snowbound

by Ian R. Derbyshire

The car always broke down when it snowed. To be fair, it broke down in the rain quite a bit as well. The weather hadn't been too bad when he left the house, but it was a blizzard now.

A walk that took forty minutes during the summer had turned into an ongoing voyage that Luke figured must have surpassed three hours. Periodically, he wiped clean a street sign to figure out his location. His galoshes had frozen solid with a build up of snow inside. His eyelashes froze to each other, and his eyes seared with the pain of keeping them open while the biting wind and icy snow drove in.

Luke had passed numerous frozen car corpses that had ceased to operate or had been altogether abandoned. Sadly, he tripped over the body of a stray dog that hadn't been able to find adequate shelter when the storm hit.

He'd been walking four hours when he wiped clean a street sign that said 'Dremont'.

Was there even a street called Dremont in Felrush?

Panic and fear grabbed his insides. Now he was lost and blind, his entire body cold and numb.

He couldn't go back the way he'd come. Even if he figured out which way that was, there was no way to tell where he had missed the turn. Luke plodded onwards.

Thirty minutes later, dark clouds closed in from the corners of his eyes.

##

Warmth had become a foreign feeling to Luke. Before he opened his eyes, he felt heat spreading inside him. He remembered his grandfather, who had lived through everything during the war, telling him that the last thing you feel before you lose an extremity to frostbite is warmth. Now it had spread through his whole body. That couldn't be good.

Snowbound

Luke opened his eyes and tried shifting around. Something heavy pressed against his body and restricted his movement. Exhausted, he lowered his head slowly, the five blankets stacked on him making it so he could barely see the room. Flowery wallpaper. Copies of Monets. He was in a woman's bedroom.

What was that smell? It smelled like flowers. Stale flowers. An old lady's bedroom?

He heard creaking in the hallway getting closer and closer. The door opened, and a young, beautiful, dark-haired woman entered the room.

"You're awake! Excellent. Are you able to feel anything?"

"Uh, not really. I have pins and needles in my fingers and toes. Pain is seeping in as well."

"That's good though, Luke. You're making progress. I thought you might have been dead when I found you. Here, drink this hot tea." She carried a tray with a steaming teapot and a cup, both embossed with flowery designs much like the bedroom. Her clothes were similar; she wore a full length dress intricately designed with various flowers.

She removed two blankets so Luke could sit up enough to drink the tea. It didn't taste particularly good, but Luke felt it warming his insides immediately.

"You know my name?" Luke asked after he drained one cup and started on another. The woman sat in a chair next to the bed.

"Yes, I checked when I undressed you. I wanted to see if there was a contact number in your wallet so I could make sure your family wouldn't worry." Modesty caused Luke to blush as he looked at the pile of stacked clothes at the end of the bed, now clean and dry.

"No need to worry about that," he said. "I live alone." He took another sip of tea. "So what happened? The last thing I remember is losing my vision and collapsing."

"Well, I left the house to check the post and I saw you collapse on my front lawn. I dragged you back in and tried my best to raise your temperature quickly. I don't think you will lose any fingers or toes, your galoshes and gloves did a very good job. You should probably rest some more. You're still very white."

"One more question?" She nodded. "Who are you?"

Her face turned red and she laughed. "I'm sorry; I can't believe I forgot to introduce myself. My name is Julia."

"Thank you, Julia." She smiled and left Luke to rest.

##

Luke awoke the next day feeling better. He clambered out of bed and struggled to get dressed. It took awhile for his arms, legs, fingers, and toes to remember how to work normally. Eventually he got it together and stepped out of the door where the old flower smell seemed much thicker. Strange. In fact, there were a few strange things about this place he meant to ask Julia about. He should have been in more pain, bedridden for days from the exposure, but here he was, only a couple days later walking around. It had to be something in the tea.

He walked downstairs and wandered around the rooms until he found the kitchen. He saw Julia brewing another pot of tea.

"Ah Luke! You must be feeling better. Here, have some more tea."

Luke gingerly picked up the cup and drained its contents. He sighed as the warmth spread through his body.

"I was curious, Julia. Do you often check the post in crushing blizzards?" He tried to make it sound like an innocent question, but he knew he'd failed.

Julia paused as she put away the tea ingredients. She picked up an unmarked jar containing little black ovals floating in a clear liquid. The ovals seemed to have the consistency of jelly, and Luke wondered if that's why he couldn't taste them in the tea.

"Of course I check the mail frequently. I receive a lot of correspondence. Lucky for you, I checked the post...or you'd be dead." She smirked.

"Of course. I'm sorry, Julia. I didn't mean to offend you."

"No harm done, Luke."

"Alright, I'm going to lie down." Luke laboured out of the chair and slowly made his way to the staircase. He walked back upstairs, his mind roiling. Julia was hiding something, but what?

Luke stepped onto the second floor and tried to catch his breath. Unfortunately, the invasive smell of stale flowers overpowered him, and he gagged. Where was that coming from?

He sniffed around the hallway and determined it came from the door at the opposite end of the hall from his room.

He made his way there and looked to see if Julia was at the bottom of the landing. When he didn't see or hear her for awhile, he put his hand on the doorknob.

A blinding flare of stomach pain doubled him over, his hands grasping his belly. It was excruciating. Images of Julia hesitantly placing an unmarked jar into the fridge slipped into his mind and then out again.

Poison!

Luke fell through the doorway and wished he hadn't. Vases upon vases of stale flowers sat piled on a table in the middle of the room. The walls held human skeletons, and even a couple of dog skeletons. They hung side to side on all four walls: tall skeletons, small skeletons, some displayed in poses. The five skeletons on that wall closest to him were arranged like a portion of the Sistine Chapel. Skeletal finger reached for skeletal finger, and Luke tried to stagger to his feet but fell again as the pain intensified a thousand fold. He curled into a ball on the floor.

His stomach bulged outward. The tight skin of his belly ruptured, and beetles poured forth in a shower of blood. They started chewing at the ragged edges of skin, systematically devouring Luke's writhing body. He saw the bleached white bone of his sternum and cried as consciousness slipped from his grasp. Through the tears, he saw a dark form close the door.

HELPING HAND

by Curt Mahr

Mae stood on the corner of fourth and main, waiting for the red hand on the pedestrian signal to turn into a white stick figure. The last crossing to get home, and the worst. If she was at the front of the pack and stepped off the moment the stick figure appeared, she could make it across before it turned into an unblinking red hand.

That's when she felt a strong hand grab her arm.

"Need some help Ma'am?" asked a young man wearing a tan Boy Scout shirt. She almost felt like giggling.

Mae, all of seventy-two years, wasn't quite sure what to think. The boy must've been in his mid-teens, but his eyes didn't waver with the immaturity of puberty.

He looked down at her and smiled with shiny teeth that glinted from the late afternoon sun. She nodded at him, keeping her purse close and handing him the paper bag she had filled at the corner store.

If she tried hard enough, maybe she could get him to carry the bag all the way to her door. Would an offer of milk and cookies get the job done? She didn't know -- maybe nowadays it took beer and chips.

The stick figure popped up, and the throng enveloped her in a rush to get by. Sunlight flashed on the dark pavement between people's shadows, creating a strobe-like effect that caused Mae to second guess every step.

She didn't stop and ask for help once she had crossed; Mae had been around too long for that. She kept walking.

"Ma'am. Your bag."

"Right up here young man. Just a few more steps." She didn't look back, she didn't need to. Mae knew he would follow. She opened the door with the boy coming up beside her.

"Ma'am, your bag. You forgot I had it." Mae looked up at him, not so kind, a little irritated the young man thought she was absent-minded.

"Up here, young man." Her irritation turned into a smile as she pointed up the stairs. "You can help me with that, can't you?"

"Umm," he looked back to the street corner, a questioning look. "I guess I can."

She grabbed his chin and smiled. "Good, young man. I've got some milk and cookies for you." She let go and added in a murmur, "If you want."

He didn't respond, just followed in step behind her.

Mae opened her apartment door and walked in, leaving the door open for the young man.

Lavender and oleander, rosemary and the smell of old books blasted his senses. Enrapt in the sights and smells, Chuck didn't notice the door close behind him. He hadn't realized the size of the apartment. Cherry-wood bookshelves ten-feet-high lined the walls of the room to his right, appearing almost too large for the small apartment. Leather couches in the room center were stationed around large oak desks lit by chandeliers hung every hundred feet.

Books! He loved books and spent most of his time in the library. Not bookstores. No, he liked the feeling of opening an old book. One that had been read by many, a book that had the smell from years of being opened and closed, of delighting readers with its contents. That's what Chuck liked. Bookstores carried new books, fresh off the press, with no history of readership.

And the smell of leather. Few modern books were leather-bound. At first glance, Chuck believed every book here was. He touched a book to feel the soft leather binding. He felt something inside of him turn as the smell and the touch of the leather combined, overwhelming his imagination.

He looked again down the long room and noticed the large pictures hanging above the shelves. Oil paintings of elderly women in their seventies or even eighties.

"Young man, are you in here?"

"Yes, Ma'am. Right here at the front door. Where do you want your bag?"

"In here." Chuck yanked his attention away from the books and walked toward her voice.

The dark interior contrasted starkly with the sunshine in the kitchen, and he had to close his eyes for a moment. The smell of freshly baked cookies entered his nostrils.

"Right there. You can just put the bag on the counter." Mae pointed to where her bag sat. "Do you want some cookies and milk?"

"Thank you, Ma'am, but I think I should get going." Chuck set the paper bag down, noticing a large black handle sticking out of the lady's handbag.

"Ma'am, where did you get all those books?" he asked, unable to look away from the black handle.

"Generations of books, that's what's out there. Probably about a thousand years, each one handed down from generation to generation."

Chuck saw part of the blade that the handle was wrapped around, the part that shined in the light, shined with a red tint. The rest of it disappeared into her handbag, looking like it was stuck in the belly of a beast.

Mae noticed how the young man stared at her bag. Now what was she going to do? She needed more leather, what could she say?

He finally looked away and noticed the plate of cookies on the kitchen table. He sat down and took a bite. His fingers sunk into the warm dough, and strings of shiny chocolate stretched from the cookie to his mouth. That wasn't as good as the feel of cold milk rushing down his throat, mixing with the taste of the cookie.

"Do you like reading?" Mae whispered in his ear. Chuck swallowed hard, almost out of surprise.

"Yes," he croaked through a half-filled mouth.

"Why don't you take a look at the books then? I'm sure they won't mind. Take the cookies."

It wasn't long before Chuck lost himself among the sea of words contained on the shelves. Fearful of not having enough time to peruse every book, he quickly scanned the books that looked interesting. Time passed unnoticed.

By the time he'd finished the first shelf, the antique grandfather clock beside the first set of shelves rang eight times. His stomach turned when he looked at the empty cookie plate.

Chuck walked back to the kitchen looking for the old lady. He thought about calling out to her, then realized that he didn't know her name.

"Ma'am." His voice echoed back at him from the kitchen counters. He noticed the lady's bag still occupying the same place on the counter. "Ma'am!" he called a little louder.

He looked again at the bag. Something caught his attention; the black handle was gone. Looking around to see if his shouting caught anyone's attention, he went to the bag, curious as to its contents.

The zipper was open. Her bag was plastic, white with rainbow-colored daisies imprinted on it. Chuck tried to peer into the bag, moving his head around so it wouldn't block the light from the kitchen. He looked around and listened, making sure she wasn't near, then pushed on the opposing ends. The bag opened into a gaping maw, dark inside. He moved his head, only the shadow he thought he was casting didn't go away. Chuck backed up and bumped into something.

His heart lurched, his hand reaching behind. Chuck felt the wood of a chair, and sighed.

"Find anything interesting, Dearie?"

"Holy crap!" Chuck's heart skipped another beat. "N...No." He tried to reach for something to say.

"Good. Did you like the books?"

"Ye...Yes...you have an interesting collection. All leather-bound. Must be worth a lot of money."

"I'm sure they are. Want to borrow some?"

"I, I couldn't. I'd be too worried I might damage them."

"Nothing to worry about. Lots of people have borrowed them. I trust you. After all, you are a Boy Scout."

The last words slithered out of her mouth and ran down his spine like ice.

She held out her hand, showing the way to the living room. "Show me which books you would like."

Chuck squeezed away from her and walked out of the kitchen, watching her shadow bob along next to him.

"Where did you get all these books?" He tried not to sound nervous.

"I'm a librarian, or I was. As well as all my family, generations of librarians. It's just a collection."

"I saw one titled 'The Journal of King Henry the VIII'. Is that really his journal?"

"Yes, my great-great-grandmother was his librarian. She took it when he died."

Chuck thought about it for a moment. He was a history buff, and tried recalling the time period. Early sixteenth century, maybe?. She must have skipped a few greats in her description of the king's librarian.

Chuck made his way toward the first bookshelf and noticed her shadow change. It grew in size, both around and in height. It stretched past him causing the hair on his neck to stand up.

He glanced behind him, only to see her looking down at the slow steps she was taking.

Must have been the light, he thought. Then he saw the arm of the shadow raise up, but he didn't look again.

##

Mae brought the machete down, splitting Chuck's skull in half like a cantaloupe. The blade caught on his spine, and she cursed for the weakness in her arms. Chuck's blood squirted in several directions, including onto Mae's face. She released the blade, and his body slipped to the floor.

With one foot on his back, she wiggled the blade with both hands. The metal grinded and squeaked against bone until it broke free. She fell back a few feet from its sudden release.

"Oh, dear." She put her hand to her mouth. "What have I done now?"

Chuck's body lay in a spreading pool of blood, still jerking from a few remaining impulses.

Mae hurried to the kitchen and fetched a few towels. With a gentle touch, she lifted his split skull and put towels beneath it. She ran to the kitchen again, this time coming back with a rope that stretched from a kitchen cabinet. She tied it around his waist and ran back, all the time shouting, "Leather, leather, I have more leather."

Back in the kitchen, Mae threw the locking handle on her winch, then flicked a switch beside the cabinet door. The motor hummed and the rope wound onto the spindle.

Chuck's body left a snail's trail of blood which pooled together into little drops on the linoleum floor. Once his whole body was inside the kitchen, Mae retrieved her machete and went to work.

Blood again flew in all directions. It splattered on the wall, the counter, and even dripped from her eyebrows, mixed with her sweat. She removed his head, then his arms and lower legs.

Mae pulled out a tray of fillet knives and made cuts down what was left of his legs and up his belly. It took her some time; the sun would rise and set a few times before she would be done with it.

Chuck's body, without any skin, looked like a diagram of the human muscle system hanging on a doctor's wall. Only not as red -- most of the blood had flowed into the drain in the middle of the kitchen floor.

Mae dismembered the rest of the body with her electric knife, using her custom made -- twice than normal size -- food disposal to get rid of the pieces she cut off. Severed into two halves, the head fit in without much effort, and she kept thinking how fortunate it was that she had split the skull right down the center.

She hung the skin up to dry. Later, she tanned and stretched it, cutting out chunks of it for her new books. She had four books waiting to be bound and covered. It was then that she noticed a tattoo on one of the pieces she had cut off. After the tanning and stretching it wasn't very legible, but she could make out part of it.

She recognized the symbol, the pentagram that she had seen so many times in her work as a witch. Below the pentagram was the phrase: "My soul belongs to the devil."

No wonder he was so interested in her books, she thought.

"Well, how's your soul feeling?" She smiled joyfully as she worked the binding around her first book.

Dark and Stormy Wishes

by Bailey Hunter

"Jack! Put down that damn book and listen to me! I've been trying to tell you someone is in our yard."

Sherrie pulls the slats of the blind down just a hair to peek out again. "There. He's right there. I think he's up to something. Jack! Get over here." Sherrie's voice rasps as she yells at Jack in a whisper.

"Huh? Awww, Sherrie, calm down. It's probably some drunk or something. Come to bed."

"I'm telling you, he's up to something. Get out of bed and look for yourself!"

"All right, all right." Jack rolls his two hundred and fifty pound body out of the bed, muttering to himself "Jesus H Christ. A man can't even relax in his own damn bed any more. Some stupid drunk...gonna kick his ass...just wanna read my book..." Jack lumbers over to the window and pulls up the blind.

"See? Right there. What's he doing, Jack? Go talk to him. Tell him to leave or you'll call the police. Jack. Go on, Jack. Go tell him." Sherrie's voice rings shrill in Jack's tired ears. Sixteen years of marriage and he didn't like her any more than he did back then. Shotgun wedding was what he had. Complete with father-in-law and a 12-guage Winchester. Guess that's what he got for putting his pecker places it doesn't belong.

Jack grabs his old terry robe, shoves his feet in a pair of worn out slippers and heads down stairs. Anything to get away from her. Hell, he'd walk through a pit of deadly snakes if it meant she'd be gone. Sure he could divorce her, but he likes his lifestyle, and after sixteen years, she's bound to get everything. Not to mention the money is hers in the first place. A good education and a great job still can't match the money she has, and he knows it.

As he reaches the bottom of the stairs the first bit of fear begins to seep through. Jack grabs a golf club from the bag Sherrie had stuffed in the closet. A three wood ought to do the trick. With his sense of security now restored, Jack opens the door, prepared to confront the drunk in his yard.

"Hey you! What are you doing here? This isn't your house. You drunk or what?"

The man turns to Jack. He wears a tailored Armani suit and a fedora, is clean-shaven and sharp-witted. Jack can tell that from his eyes. Definitely not drunk. The fear starts to come back. Jack puffs himself up to look even bigger than his six-two stature, acutely aware of the breeze blowing up his robe and wishing he had put on some pants before coming out here.

"What do you want? It's awful late to be prowling around stranger's houses."

The man looks at Jack then smiles a large toothy grin. "Sorry to bother you, sir. I was looking for someone named Jessie Smythe. This is the address I was given." He flashes another large smile.

"How do you know her?" Jessie is Jack's pride and joy, the best thing to come out of his hellish union with Sherrie, and this man is far too old to be calling on his fifteen-year-old daughter.

"Oh, well, I don't really. She left a message for me." He continues to smile, unnerving Jack.

"Look, I don't know who you are or what you want, but I think you should leave. Now. If you don't I'll have to call the police."

"Terribly sorry to have bothered you, sir. Perhaps I have the wrong address. I will be going now." Tipping his fedora, he turns to leave then stops. "Oh, one more thing. If you happen to see this Jessie person, could you please give her this." He hands Jack a black card. "Dark and Stormy Wishes - Heman Black" written in silver foil, is all it says. Jack looks up to question the man only to find him gone, vanished without a trace.

"What the..." Jack scans the surrounding neighborhood for the man to no avail. Comfortable he is gone, Jack heads inside.

Sherrie stands at the bottom of the stairs. "Who was he? What did he want? Is he gone? Jack, answer me."

Jack thinks about the man and fingers the card in his robe pocket. "Nothing dear. Just had the wrong address. Go back to bed." Jack doesn't really want to get into a long discussion with Sherrie right now, so it's best if he leaves out the part about Jessie.

"What do you mean he had the wrong address? I think you should call the police. I think..."

"And tell them what?" Jack interrupts. "That a well dressed man was standing in our yard? That he apologized for the trouble and said he was at the wrong address? Don't you think the police have more important matters to handle? There's nothing to worry about. He's gone now and that's it. Go back to bed Sherrie. I'll be there in a few minutes, all right?"

"FINE." Sherrie whips around and stomps back up the stairs. How many times had Jack seen that act? It didn't matter. She'd be over it by morning and on to something new.

Jack pulls the card from his pocket and looks at it again. Who is this Heman Black?

What does he sell? Why would Jessie have called him?

"Dark and Stormy Wishes" Jack reads the card aloud, listening to the words, reflecting on the possible meaning. He flips it over and sees a phone number in very small type on the bottom. No wonder he missed it outside. Even now he'd need his reading glasses to make it out. There's a quote or something just above it too. Jack quickly goes to his office and retrieves his glasses.

"Ye shall be as gods, knowing good and evil." Weird. Sounds like something religious, not that Jack would know. Sherrie is the one who reads the Bible. Jack just uses it as a doorstop, coaster, fly masher, whatever the need is at the time.

Hmmmm... Maybe Jessie is joining a cult or something. He will have to bring it up with her tomorrow, that is if she doesn't run off before he sees her. Jessie is spending less and less time around her family. This last thought worries Jack. He had never really noticed it much before, just attributed it to being a teenager. Now, he isn't so sure.

Slipping the card into his pocket, Jack heads upstairs to bed. His mind is now full, and sleep will be a hard thing to come by. Hopefully Sherrie is asleep and he won't have to talk to her. Listen to her is more like it.

As he reaches the top, the bedroom door looms. Ever so quietly he walks toward it, careful not to step on the creaky spot just in front. Gingerly, he opens the door a crack. Sherrie's whistling breath tells Jack she's asleep. Thank God for pills. He stands at the door for a couple of minutes listening to her breathe, then decides there's no way he's going to go to sleep now. Carefully, he shuts the door and heads back downstairs. The card in his pocket feels as if it's heating up, drawing his attention to it again.

Jack goes to his study, pours three fingers of bourbon and eases himself into the overstuffed leather wing chair, tossing the card on the antique desk. The desk is the only thing in this house that is truly his. His great-great grandfather received it as a wedding present from his wife. It's an outstanding piece of furniture, handmade oak with a slate top. Even the brass handles are a masterpiece of craftsmanship.

Jack sits staring at the card and plays through fantastic scenarios of Sherrie having an untimely demise. If only she would have some sort of "accident" Jack could finally be rid of her. If only life were that simple.

"Daddy? What are you doing up? Everything OK?" Jack breaks from his daydream to see Jessie standing there.

"Hey sweetie. Well, there was a man in our yard tonight; he was looking for you. He left his card." Jack holds up the card for Jessie. "What's going on, Jessie? We never see you around the house anymore and now this strange man shows up."

Jessie takes the card from Jack and looks at it for a moment. In a small voice she says, "I was having problems with a kid at school. A friend of mine told me that this guy fixes problems like that. That he was some sort of wish granter. I called him, but I've changed my mind. I don't know how he fixes these things, so figure I'm better off to handle it on my own. Which I have." Jessie offers a soft smile.

"Jessie honey, if you were having troubles at school, why didn't you come to us? You know your mother and I love you. We would've tried to help." As Jack looks at his daughter, he sees the little curly blonde headed girl that used to sit on his lap and beg for piggybacks around the house. When did she blossom into a young woman?

"I know daddy. This was just something I needed to fix on my own. Everything's fine now. I've taken care of it. I'm gonna go back to bed now, school in the morning, ya know. You should go to bed too. Don't worry about this guy either. He won't bother us anymore. Night Daddy." Jessie leans over and gives Jack a kiss on the forehead, tossing the card onto the desk.

"G'night, sweetie. I'll be up soon." Jack sits back in the old leather chair and breathes a sigh of relief. It's not a cult. That's one good thing. He was going to have to make an effort to be more involved in Jessie's life.

Jack picks up the black card again. A problem solver, eh? Strange business. He wonders what kind of problems the man solves. Maybe he can solve Jack's.

"heh heh" Jack chuckles under his breath as he thinks of Sherrie sleeping upstairs. Wouldn't that beat all? Silliness. Jack slips the card back into the pocket of his old robe and heads to bed. Tomorrow he will call this Heman Black and let him know that Jessie changed her mind. Don't want him coming around anymore.

The next morning runs like every morning with the exception of Jessie actually staying long enough to have breakfast with Jack and Sherrie. Of course, Sherrie can't just let it be. She nags Jessie on her choice of clothing, her choice of make-up and the fact that her parents never see her anymore. At which point Jessie gets up from the table, winks at Jack and leaves.

"Damn it, Sherrie! What the hell is wrong with you? Jessie makes a point of sticking around this morning and you give her every reason not to do it again. Why do you always have to be such a BITCH?" Jack's heart races as the words he never dares to say spill out of his mouth. He can't believe the sense of release he gets with every syllable. Sherrie sits like a pink powdered lump of clay, staring in disbelief at the outburst.

It only takes a second before she explodes into her own tirade. "How dare you talk to me that way? I can show you who the real boss of this house is. Is that what you want? Do you really need me to show you? I am going upstairs to get dressed, and by the time I get back down here you had better be *blah blah blah blah blah*..."

Jack watches her lips move, not really hearing the words. Who cares anyway? By the time she gets finished applying the war paint, Jack will be at work and free of her for at least eight glorious hours.

##

Jack parks his Mercedes at the base of the twin office towers jutting upward like two mirrored pillars, splashing the morning sunshine on the subjects below. Sanctuary. Jack chuckles to himself. He wonders how many people in this world consider work a place of respite. 'Chirp Chirp' Jack slips the alarm remote into his pocket allowing his fingers to linger a second on the card. Just gonna call and tell him his services are no longer needed.

All morning Jack's thoughts are preoccupied with the card, and the explanation Jessie gave him. "A friend of mine told me that this guy fixes problems like that. That he was some sort of wish granter." Jack has only one wish: that his wife would disappear and leave him in peace. If only it were true, but that's just nonsense. It's one thing to fix a small problem at school, a completely different thing to have someone's wife removed. Besides the repercussions... Jack couldn't risk ending up in jail. Prison. Who would take care of Jessie?

Jack shakes his head, trying to get the thoughts out. "Nonsense," he whispers to himself. "Get a hold of yourself, Jack. You're acting like a madman."

Jack tries to do some paperwork, but can't focus. He strikes up a conversation with some of his coworkers, but his mind wanders. Finally, he decides the only way he's going to get it out of his head is to call this Heman Black fellow. He has to be careful with his words. Just feel the guy out. Find out what it is he really does. That's all. Just a fact-finding mission. Secure in his decision and having convinced himself it's harmless, he shuts his office door, closes the blinds and prepares to make the call.

His pulse quickens with every number pushed. Just getting some facts. Just getting some facts.

"Dark and Stormy Wishes, Heman Black speaking."

"Oh. Uh, hello. This is Jack Smythe. You were at my house last night."

"Yes hello, Mr. Smythe. What can I do for you?"

"Well, uh, I just wanted to tell you that Jessie solved her problem herself and that she no longer needs your services."

"That's fine, thank you for calling. Is that everything?"

Jack sits with the phone in his hand, momentarily unable to speak.

"Mr. Smythe? Is that everything?"

"Actually, no. I was wondering what it is that you do exactly. Jessie said that you're some sort of problem solver. A granter of wishes." Jack feels uneasy with this last statement. Granter of wishes. Stupid.

"Yes sir. That is correct. People come to me with all sorts of problems; things they wish would change or go away. I make it happen. It's really that simple."

"Uh, what sort of things? I don't mean specific details just..." Jack finds himself unable to finish.

"What's your problem, Mr. Smythe? Trouble with the boss? Gambling debts? Another woman?"

"No! I mean no, nothing like that. It's just...It's just my wife."

"What about your wife? Is she seeing another man?" Heman's voice is soft, soothing, almost hypnotic.

"No, at least not as far as I know. She's just a bona fide bitch. I know that sounds awful but it's true." Jack spills out all the things that he has never told anyone. How she controls the purse strings, how she belittles him in front of their family and friends, how she holds her power over him every chance she gets, how she is with Jessie--everything he has kept inside for sixteen years. It's like a dam has broken and the words flood out with nothing to stop them.

"I see. Well, Mr. Smythe, I believe I can help you. Do you wish my help?"

Jack weighs Heman's question, the thought of freedom dancing in his head.

"Depends," he answers cautiously.

"It always does, sir. It always does. Let's just say that I will fix your problem. The how's, what's and when's are left up to me. Your job will be simple; just live your life as usual. Is this acceptable to you?"

"What about payment? I assume this will cost me." Jack can't believe this conversation is happening. When did he cross that line? Why doesn't he feel more at this moment?

"The lines are drawn in sand, sir. Ever changing; and yes, it will cost you. But that's a matter we can clear up after I have completed my work."

Did Jack say that out loud? How did Heman...? Tingles inch up Jack's spine. "No, I need to know what the fee is now. If I'm going to go through with this I need to know that I'm not going to be bankrupted by it."

"I do not accept cash, Mr. Smythe. I prefer to do my business in trade. Less paper trails to worry about. Think of the most valuable thing you own. Your most prized possession. This will be my fee. Take your time. One more thing, Mr. Smythe--do not try to deceive me." With that the conversation is over.

Jack sits for a long time staring at the phone. Joy slowly wells up within him. Jack Smythe you have gone mad! Yet he feels no fear, no regrets, in fact he feels like a giddy schoolgirl. The rest of the day Jack walks on air. Not a single thing can touch him in this state. Hell, he even looked forward to going home for the first time, ever.

##

As soon as Jack walks in the door, Sherrie begins her nagging. Giving him shit for leaving before she was finished this morning and something about the gutters. Jack doesn't care. He grins through it all. This serves to drive Sherrie into near hysterics. Every word from her mouth confirms this was the right thing to do. No more would he have to put up with her. Never again. It was just a matter of time; and a matter of the fee. Jack already knew what the cost would be. It hurt him to give up the desk, but in the end it would be worth it. Great-great grandpa Smythe would surely understand.

All evening Jack smiles like the proverbial Cheshire Cat. He can't help himself. Even as insults and accusations are hurled at him, he beams. He wears the smile as a shield, and nothing Sherrie says or does affects him. He is at peace.

The couch is Sherrie's idea, and she figures it will smarten Jack up. If she only knew.

Around midnight, the front door slowly opens as Jessie tries to slip in late and unnoticed. Jack grins at her and gives her a kiss on the cheek. "You'd better go to bed very quietly, sweetie. Your mother is on a rampage tonight. She's asleep now, but I don't think you want to wake her."

"Uh, sure thing, daddy. You ok?" Jessie eyes her father curiously.

"I'm just fine. Nothing for you to worry about. You know how it is. Off to bed with you now. I'll see you in the morning." Jack flashes another smile and points up the stairs.

"All right then. Goodnight. Thanks for not freaking out on me for being late." Jessie blows a kiss at Jack and sneaks up the stairs to bed.

Jack curls up on the couch and sleeps better than he has in years. In the morning, his face is still stuck on perma-grin. Sherrie no longer has anything to say. She stares at Jack as if he was some sort of foreign insect she'd love to crush but is afraid to try. Jessie breezes through the kitchen stopping only to grab an apple and say "See ya!" as she rushes out to catch her ride.

Sherrie screams after her, "Where were you last night?" But Jessie is already peeling out of the driveway.

She turns to Jack. "What time did she come in last night? Did you say anything to her? Or did you just act like the spineless man that you are? I don't even know why I ask; I already know the answer. You make me sick." Sherrie seethes. Her face reddens when Jack doesn't answer and only smiles. "What the hell is wrong with you? You've been grinning like an idiot for two days now. Have you lost your mind?" Sherrie glares at Jack.

On any other day this would have Jack cowering within himself, wishing desperately for an escape. Today, however, she might as well be looking at him cross-eyed for all the effect it has. "Nothing dear. I'm perfectly fine. I'm off to work now. Have a great day." Stunned, Sherrie is at a loss for words as Jack puts on his jacket and leaves.

At work, everyone comments on Jack's unusually happy demeanor. "It's just a good day" he tells them, then heads to his office whistling. A couple of hours later, Mrs. Jackson's voice comes through the intercom. "Call on line two, Mr. Smythe."

"Thank You, Mrs. Jackson." "Hello, Jack Smythe here."

"Hello again, Mr. Smythe." Heman's voice answers back. "I need to see you, just to finalize the transaction. If you could please meet me at the old Apollo Theatre on Hibbard Street in one hour. Do you know the way?"

"Now? I don't know if I can get away. Yes, I know it, but why there? It's awfully far away." It is also a deserted section of the city, save for the squatters that live there, which makes Jack a little uneasy.

"Yes, now. I'm sure you can take some time off. It is a fair distance away, but discretion is the better part of valor, Mr. Smythe. It is also a place I am comfortable with. See you in one hour or I will assume you have changed your mind." This last statement is followed by a 'click' and then silence.

"Hello? Hello? Mr. Black?" Jack hangs up the phone and throws on his jacket. "I have to go out, Mrs. Jackson. There's a problem at the school. I may be gone for a couple of hours. Please tell my calls that I'm in a meeting and will get back to them later this afternoon."

"Yes, Mr. Smythe. Is Jessie all right?"

"She's fine, Mrs. Jackson. Thank you for your concern. I'll be back in a couple of hours."

Jack drives on as the city seems to crumble around him. The towers of mirror and glass disintegrate into gray, dirty stone. Even the sun barely reaches this forgotten land. It reminds Jack of so many dismal futuristic movies he's seen. Almost there. Jack sees the old theatre ahead. He pulls into the lot next to it, scanning the area for Heman Black. Warily, he gets out of the car and arms the alarm. Like that's going to help. Jack lets out an uneasy laugh. He never came to places like this, not as a young man and certainly not as an adult. He steps in through the broken door of the theatre. The place smells of rotting carpet and urine. A rat scurries off into the darkness causing Jack's heart to race.

"Mr. Black. Mr. Black, are you there. It's Jack Smythe. Mr. Black?" Jack calls out into the murky shadows. The moldy dankness of the hall starts to make his skin crawl and the bile to back up in his throat, threatening to force its way out of his mouth.

Jack scrambles from the building to the safety of his car, fumbling with the alarm remote. 'Chirp chirp' Jack rips open the door and jumps behind the wheel, locking the doors behind him. As he tries to calm himself, a small tapping on the window nearly sends him into total panic.

"Mr. Smythe, is everything all right?" It is Heman with his soothing voice.

At once Jack feels the fear subsiding and powers down the window to speak with him. "Yeah, fine. I don't like this place much though. Let's just get this over with." Jack wipes his forehead with a hankie.

"As you wish, Mr. Smythe. Have you decided what my fee will be?" Heman continues to speak in his gentle manner.

"A desk. It's been in my family for generations. It's the most important thing I own. It breaks my heart to lose it, but that's the price of freedom."

"Perfect. I will have the movers come by and pick it up when my work is done. Thank you, Mr. Smythe. Drive safely."

"Wait a minute. That's it? You have me drive all the way out here for that? I could have told you that on the phone."

"No, Mr. Smythe, I needed to see you in person. I had to be sure that this is what you wanted. If you have to work for it and still you want it, then I know you are certain. Good day, Mr. Smythe." Tipping his fedora like he did that first night, Heman vanishes into the shadows.

Jack doesn't care where Heman went this time. He just wants to get out of here. The car barely starts before Jack guns it, tires squealing. He drives back to the office in record time. What took an hour to get there took only thirty-five minutes to return from.

Rushing past his secretary, Jack enters his office and closes the door.

"Mr. Smythe? Jack? Do you want your messages?" Mrs. Jackson's voice asks over the intercom.

"Huh? Oh, yes please. Sorry about that. Had a scare on the way back to the office. Some people drive like maniacs in the city." Lies, lies and more lies. Jack never knew he could lie so effortlessly.

"Yes sir, it's a dangerous world out there. Glad to see you made it back safely. I'll get you a coffee and bring your messages."

"Thank you, Mrs. Jackson."

By the time Jack gets his coffee and messages he is feeling much better, the smile returning to his face. For the rest of the day he remains in his office cleaning up for the weekend, returning calls, finishing paperwork. At the end of the day he bids his secretary goodbye on the way out. "Have a nice weekend, Mrs. Jackson. See you Monday." Live my life as usual. That's what Heman said.

After a leisurely drive home, Jack pulls up to his house and parks. Before he is even out of the car, two men grab him.

"Jack Smythe, you are under the arrest for the murder of your wife, Sherrie Smythe."

Jack's head swims as the officers handcuff him and read him his rights.

"Sir, do you understand these rights as they have been read to you?"

"What? Yes I understand, but why are you doing this? What do you mean murder? Where is Jessie? Is she all right? Where…"

"We'll get into the details at the station," the fat one puffs out as he shoves Jack into the unmarked car.

Jack remains silent until he reaches the station and sees Jessie standing there, her eyes red, her face streaked with tears. When their eyes meet, the shame overwhelms Jack.

As the younger detective closes the interrogation room door, Jessie screams out "MURDERER! How could you do this?"

"Siddown," grunts the fat one. He is a mass of rolls stuffed into a cheap suit. The younger one is the opposite, lean, well-dressed and polite.

"Mr. Smythe, I'm not going to lie to you here. It looks pretty bad for you. Your own daughter thinks you did this. We've even got an eyewitness. He swears he saw you around the time of the murder dragging your wife out of your home. If you have anything to say, now would be a good time. The D.A. might go easier on you if you just tell us what happened."

Jack can't believe what he's hearing. Eye witness? To what? Jack hadn't done it. He'd set it up, but there was no way they could place him at the scene.

"I didn't do this! You guys got it wrong. You should be out there trying to find the real killer."

"OK then, Mr. Smythe. If this is how you want to do this, let's start with your whereabouts between eleven and one today? You told your secretary you had to go to the school. We called the school, Mr. Smythe. You were not there. No one called you to go there either. So where did you go?" The fat one stands over Jack, sweat beading on his upper lip, the smell of stale coffee and cigarettes on his breath.

"I just wanted to get out of the office is all. I just needed a break. I didn't think it was such a big deal. Everyone plays hooky once in a while. If I knew this would happen, I would have stayed at work." Jack struggles with the urge to shove his fist into the stinking, sweating mass standing over him.

The interrogation goes on for hours. "What were you so happy about today, Mr. Smythe? What did you do on your break? Did anyone see you? What caused you to be so upset when you got back? How was your relationship with your wife?" and so on and so on. Finally Jack comes to his senses and asks for a lawyer, but by then it's too late. A strong case has been built against him.

One month later at the Smythe home, movers are hauling out the contents to be packed away in storage until Jessie can decide what to do with them. The trial is over and Jack is in prison serving a life sentence for murder. One piece of furniture, a desk is being loaded into a separate truck. Jessie watches as the two men carefully lift it into the vehicle. Her dad loved that desk. She was going to have to go visit him soon.

"I want to thank you for all your help. I never could have got through this with out it. Since dad was convicted of the murder, the inheritance goes to me. Three million, not including the sale of the house and all this stuff. Of course it's mostly in trust until I reach eighteen, but I still get a pretty good allowance. My aunt and uncle have been really great. They do their best not to bring any of this up. I'm glad for that. It was a hard enough decision to make, giving up dad and all."

"It was my pleasure, Miss Smythe. Well I'd better be off now. Take care of yourself, and remember, be careful what you wish for."

"I will, Mr. Black. Thank you again."

Oɴᴇ Bᴜᴛᴛoɴ Eʏᴇ

by Jason Robert Beirens

She had a button for an eye. Her left eye. The other one was normal, a beautiful dark blue. Her lollipop-yellow hair fell in thick strings like yarn around her heart-shaped face. A short, pointy chin extended from the rest of her features. She wore a thin white shirt, dark blue overalls and no shoes. Her feet were covered in muddy clay, and she slopped the drying muck around the room. It smeared on the hardwood floor. The scent of mud and flowers wafted in the air. She waved her willowy arms in small circles, angrily making a point that we do not hear; about something that I am sure is none of our concern. She jabbered at the large lump of a man, an enormous elephantine figure, who towered over her five-foot frame.

His head was set a bit lower than his shoulders; almost what one could consider a hunchback. He wore a dark, finely-tailored suit with a crimson tie. His small, dark, bald head moved in whimsical circles as he stood listening to the vicious insults spat at him by the little angelic creature.

"How is your eye?" he interrupted gently.

She stopped talking and slowly ran her thin clay-covered white fingers over the little black button. "It's all right," she whispered, her voice decibels lower than what it was a moment before.

"Good. Please continue working on your sculpture." He paused, "Your way." His voice was far more gentle and kind than one would expect. He gingerly caressed one of the heads of the sculpture.

She silently stared up at the man.

"It is beautiful thus far," he said as he exited the room, his bulk slightly shaking the building around them.

When she was sure he had left, she slapped clay and other bits of material onto the growing piece.

The life-sized sculpture was of a large alligator man holding onto a beautiful young woman by the arms. The creature towered behind the normal looking woman. It could either be taken as a work of horror or of an odd romance. Either way she knew no one would like it, at least not as much as she did. She enjoyed working on the fantastic, the strange; it gave her a sense of normalcy.

After a few hours of working on the sculpture, she lost her muse. She wiped a thick layer of clay onto the woman's stomach, smoothed it out, and then left the piece. She wiped her clay-covered forearm across her dripping brow. A smear of blue-gray shone strangely on her forehead. She wrung her hair free of sweat and clay, and then pulled it back into a ponytail. She covered the piece and breathed a sigh of relief.

She was done for the day.

She went to the bathroom at the other end of the apartment, started the shower that was only just big enough for her, stripped down, and stepped inside. She washed away the mud, then let the hot water cascade over her, imagining the water cleaning her soul as well as her body.

She sat on the edge of her bed wrapped in a thick white towel. Her lollipop-yellow tangle of hair was pulled back in a loose ponytail. Her head rested in her hands. She gently tapped the button. It made a small clinking noise barely audible in the small room.

After an hour, she lay down and went to sleep.

In her dream she existed. She was one with society and the world. She interacted and cried and laughed and made love. She could smell roses in the distance. She smiled and pouted and felt her eye, it was the same as the other. The matte black button was gone. The large man was nowhere to be seen in her dream. She always knew when she was dreaming, and because of it, she never wanted to wake.

Returning to the real world was always as subtle as a car crash. Her eye darted open, and tears streamed down her cheek, from both eyes.

She awoke naked and alone. A pale blue light illuminated the room. Her towel was next to her, crumpled, and dry. She ran her hand through her hair and pulled out the small rubber band that held her hair up. She rubbed the stitches under her arm; they were tender and her eye was sore.

Walking to the bathroom like a sloth, she moved her stiff neck from left to right. Small snaps and cracks sang to her. The way was empty and cold. She turned back.

She put on a tunic splattered in paint and clay, and didn't bother with anything else. Her studio was warm. The sun shimmered in through small windows toward the ceiling. She wiped a bit of water on the sculpture. It was still moldable.

After a few hours of work, she decided to leave the house. She changed into a sundress, put on her dark sunglasses and walked out into the world. As soon as she exited the building she began to fall. The ground beneath her was gone. Around her was blue, the blue of the deepest sky, endless and forever. She looked back toward the house and it was no longer there. Only the whipping wind kept her company. Her eye shut tight.

When she hit the ground she was back inside her bedroom. She held onto the side of the bed as tightly as she could. The room was spinning and twisting in all different directions. She steadied herself and fought her way to her feet. Her button-eye glinted in the room's dim light. She climbed up the bed like it was a mile-high cliff. Every inch was endless.

She finally reached the top of the bed and pulled herself onto it; she was physically and emotionally exhausted.

The large man appeared again. "You tried to leave, didn't you?"

She fought to move her head to look at him, failed, and then said plainly, "Yes."

"Why'd you want to leave? It don't make no sense, Deary."

"To live, you bullock."

He shook his head in small circular patterns and slid his large hand from his bald head down to his smooth chin. "Tell you what," he said after a moment's hesitation. "When you finish the sculpture, I'll bring you some food from a nice restaurant. Some pictures as well. Of Paris, maybe Egypt."

"Promise?"

A smile grew across his large, round face. "Cross my heart and hope to die."

He knelt down and kissed her on the forehead. "For now though, sleep. You're tired again. I understand."

She knew as soon as she was done with the sculpture she would at last exist, and the man would be gone. She knew as well that the man didn't know this. The knowledge was new to her. She didn't know how she knew; it was simple fact. She smiled; her patchwork golem body would soon transform, and she would be free.

That night for the first time ever she was free from dreaming of being real. A smile cut its way across her face in her sleep.

Las Brujas Del Rio Verde

by M. Louis Dixon

Gerald watched El Viejo. He felt his face flush and wished the hotness away. The muggy Panamanian heat only made it worse, and he broke out in a sweat.

The old man laughed even louder than before. When his dentures slipped, he shoved them back into place and continued to chuckle with his thumb in his mouth.

Gerald gave his wife, Inez, a questioning look.

She smiled back at him. Her dark face framed by raven hair contrasted with the whiteness of her teeth. It was too bright, that smile, and it really bugged him.

"Papa says that your story isn't very scary," she said.

The old man spoke in his rapid-fire Spanish which Gerald didn't even bother to try and follow. Instead, he glowered at Inez and waited for the translation. This was how it had been for most of the two weeks during their trip to her homeland. Gerald knew enough to ask the important things like, "Where is the bathroom?" and "May I have some water, please?" He'd been able to master these phrases within the first two days, but after that he gave up. She spoke for both of them.

Gerald took a sip from the watery beer and grimaced at its warmth. He drummed his fingers along the neck of the bottle and watched Inez trade Spanish with her father. It appeared their conversation really tickled them.

Not scary, he thought; the scariest thing that ever happened to me and they think it's a joke.

"Papa says that for you it must have been terrifying to be held at gunpoint in your own home, but he's heard that in America things like this happen all of the time."

Gerald started to defend himself, but the old man cut him off.

Inez translated, "Mortal danger is always an uncomfortable experience, and he does not mean to offend you by making light of what you went through, but when you mentioned..." She broke off in a fit of laughter. Wiping at her tears, she took several deep breaths, but could not regain her self control.

Gerald waited.

"He's right," she said. "It is funny." With her accent, it sounded more like, "Eat tees funny."

"What's so funny?" Gerald couldn't keep the anger out of his voice.

"He said..." She giggled. "He said that he can't imagine why anyone would break into your house, hold you up with a gun." She made a gun out of her fingers and pointed at him. "Tie you up with..., what did you call it? Duck tape?" Her face screwed up in an obvious attempt to flatten her broad grin.

"That's duct tape, with a T at the end." Gerald gritted his teeth. "Not like the bird." He regretted telling his story. It wasn't funny; it was scary.

"He tied you up, took a few dollars in cash, and then stole your dog."

"Si, un perro," the old man said.

This father and daughter audience reacted to his traumatic tale like it was sketch comedy.

"Niño, no tengas miedo a algo o a alguien que pueda robarte la vida. Ten cuidado con tu alma. Ten cuidado con las cosas de inmortalidad." El Viejo wasn't smiling anymore.

Inez started to translate, but Gerald held up a hand. "I know what he said."

She raised her eyebrows.

She doesn't believe that I understood, he thought. She's testing me.

"He said I shouldn't be afraid to die... or something."

"He also said for you to take care of your soul. Be careful with things immortal, everything else is material."

"He didn't say that part about the material."

"No, I added that part."

Gerald frowned and looked around, plotting his escape.

"Mi amor," she said and placed a hand on his shoulder. She stroked him and leaned in close. "Don't be angry. He wasn't laughing at you. In Panamá, there are dogs everywhere." She swept an arm out. The gesture encompassed the long driveway and the dirt road. Palm trees of various heights and types lined these country lanes.

He looked in the direction she indicated and saw several dogs skulking about the landscape. The closest one was El Viejo's skinny mutt Paco. It sat so still it could easily be mistaken for a lawn ornament, except nobody would manufacture or purchase such a model of malnutrition. Its eyes did not blink and were focused on the plate of chicken bones which had not yet been cleared from the table.

"Nobody really thinks much about them. It's not like in the United States."

El Viejo leaned forward and grabbed the plate of chicken bones. With a snap of his wrist, he sent the bones scattering across the ground. They hit the packed dirt with a patter of soft taps.

The dog shot forth. His mouth already working before settling on the brittle objects.

Chicken bones? You don't feed dogs chicken bones, he thought.

Gerald shook his head and smiled at his wife. "If what happened to me isn't..." He snapped his mouth shut and sighed heavily. "What does he think is scary? Hmm?" He eyed the old man, waiting as she relayed the question.

El Viejo nodded and pointed toward the back of the property. Across the field a tall row of ficus trees marked the edge of the dense forest. When he spoke, his eyes drooped and his face went slack like a man beginning to drift off to sleep. His voice was soft and distant.

Inez snuggled closer to Gerald as she relayed the answer. Her voice was soft, almost a whisper.

"Sometimes at night, when there is no moon and no stars, and the wind is dead, you can hear strange sounds coming from the woods, from down by the river. Voices call, back and forth, but these are not the voices of people. Neither are they the calls of monkeys, nor the cries of birds. Then come splashing and smacking noises. The same sounds made when the women wash the clothes at the river. There are no lights in the darkness, and nobody dares to go and see. It is Las Brujas come to do their laundry."

"Brujas?"

"Witches," Inez whispered.

Despite the oppressive heat, Gerald felt her shiver.

"Has anyone ever gone to see what it might be?" Gerald stood to peer down the path that led into the woods. Woods? Hell, that's a jungle over there, he thought.

"No." Inez held onto his hand as if to keep him from walking off. "Anyone who sees the Witches will lose his soul."

Gerald smiled. His frustration from earlier vanished in the excitement of hearing this local myth. When he looked back at his wife, the smile faded.

Inez and her father were looking off into the woods. Her dark eyes were wide while the old man's were narrow, but both of them wore the same small frown.

The only sound was the snap and crunch of chicken bones.

##

Gerald wondered how long it took for the joke to spread around.

"¿Tu perro o tu vida?" said the cousin, or was he an uncle? His finger pointed at Gerald in the hand-as-gun gesture.

Gerald watched Cousin's thumb dropping repeatedly. This joke was getting old fast.

My dog or my life. Ha ha. Gerald pressed his lips tight and bit back his first response. With a sigh he said, "I'm just looking for the flashlight."

Cousin kept smiling, but he put his finger away.

"The flash—light." Gerald pantomimed sweeping a flashlight back and forth. He aimed into the darkness away from the house lights.

Cousin laughed.

Shit, he thought, what the fuck is the word. "Oh, yeah... Foco. Where? Donde es?"

"Se cayó en el servicio." Cousin pointed toward the outhouse.

"What?"

"Vaya." He pointed again and then spoke a whole string of words that Gerald couldn't follow.

"I need the flashlight to go to the crapper." Gerald looked at the small building standing at the edge of the light. He considered going to find Inez. She'd be able to help him find a flashlight.

Cousin gave him a push. "Vaya gringo." His smile was broad, but his eyes were humorless.

There was no way out for him. He managed a quick look back to the house and then walked down the path. Gerald felt the judgmental stare behind him all the way to the privy.

Inside, he saw light coming from the hole in the seat. Peering in, he spotted the flashlight. Several feet down it sat partially submerged in the viscous contents. The dark pool seethed with a noxious effervescence in the beam's illumination. Small shadows skittered along the walls in perpetual activity. Everything was in motion.

Once outside, he was able to breathe again. Cousin was no longer at the foot of the path. Shadows moved across the windows, and the house erupted in laughter.

The Panamanian winter brings repetitive rain showers providing short-lived relief before the humidity climbs back to levels where it acquires a texture that one can feel on the skin. This year they waited for the rain to come, but the moisture only hung in the air while the heavy clouds pressed down on them.

The night was pitch-black, the heat unforgiving. The drone of the oscillating fan filled the bedroom but provided little relief.

Next to Gerald, Inez slept. He listened to her soft snores. I should have brought some sleeping pills, he thought. He resisted an urge to poke her side and climbed out of the bed instead.

He stumbled through the darkness to the kitchen. When he opened the fridge, the light splashed into his eyes. He squinted and pulled out a jug of water. The drink was icy and delicious. He returned the water jug and shuffled away pulling the fridge door closed as he left. With a dull thump, he was once again in absolute darkness.

Gallina. The word surfaced in his mind and he considered it. Chicken. The filthy birds were always underfoot, but not always about when he heard the word in conversation. They were calling me a chicken, he realized, but tried to push the thought away before it led to more pointless anger. He'd be going home tomorrow and be done with this.

His bladder felt full, and he longed to be home with regular plumbing. He groped his way to the back door and out onto the porch. Outside was no lighter than in. A faint glow revealed the location of the outhouse.

The flashlight is still on, he thought with some surprise. He almost started in that direction, but paused when he recalled the images of the pit. No way am I going in there. He shuddered.

With his bare feet, he felt his way to the edge of the cement porch and pulled down the front of his gym shorts. The stream of urine splashing on the ground was the only sound in the night air.

What do they know? A bunch of macho assholes is all—

The silence was broken by a far off shout.

With a twitch, he snapped his shorts up and stepped back. A small remaining trickle of piss seeped into the material. He fingered the wet spot and wiped at the dampness absentmindedly.

Another shout. Could that be a "hey" and then a whistle? It sounded too far away for him to be sure.

He turned his head trying to find the perfect position to hear a little bit better.

A sound of splashing was followed by rhythmic smacking.

Gerald felt a tickle of adrenaline, and his heart beat faster.

The Witches, he thought. He groped his memory for the name El Viejo had called them. Another cry echoed up from the distance, and then he had it. "Las Brujas," he said aloud.

He stood there in the darkness listening to the noises coming from the woods. It has to be some kids making all that noise. What else can it be? He turned to go and wake Inez. *She just has to hear this.*

Excitement grew inside him as he inched his way through the darkened house. He wanted to wake everyone. Let them all come and hear the Witches play. He imagined their frightened faces and their superstitious dread. He could picture Cousin's fearful look as Gerald gave him a shove and told him to "vaya."

In their room, he swept his hand along the wall looking for the light switch, but encountered nothing except a smooth surface. A small green light winking in the far corner of the room caught his attention.

The video camera, he thought. It's charged and ready to go.

He banged his shin on a chair as he hurried to retrieve the camera. Ignoring the pain, he rotated the camera in his hands feeling for the power switch.

I'll get this all on tape, he thought. This is definitely worth recording.

His hands trembled with excitement. After pressing several different buttons, he was rewarded by a hum and a small flicker of light as the camera came to life. Cautiously moving back to the entryway of the room, he continued to fiddle with the camera buttons. One switch activated the night-vision mode, and the little viewfinder display came to life. The tiny screen delineated the contents of the room in an eerie green and black panorama reminding him of nocturnal military maneuver or police arrest videos.

A close-up of Inez's sleeping face disclosed a worried expression. The frown of her somewhat open mouth made her look sad. Beneath the eyelids, her eyes shuddered in fitful struggles.

This couldn't be the peaceful dreams of a good time at the river's edge -- recurring dreams she often told him about upon waking in the mornings. Tonight, perhaps her serene river was being invaded by Las Brujas. The idyllic scene cast in shadow, paralyzing her with fear on the river's rocky banks and then sending her gasping into a startled wakefulness.

A new idea came to him. He could use the camera to sneak out to the river and surprise the kids goofing around down there. He wouldn't need to use a flashlight, so they'd never see him coming. It would be easy to capture the whole thing on tape, and in the morning he'd show everyone the footage. He'd have the evidence for these superstitious people; he would show them that there are no such things as witches, and prove that this "Gringo del Norte" was no "Gallina".

He slipped on his sandals and made for the rear door of the house.

##

Through the camera viewfinder Gerald could see the well-worn path leading off into the woods. The image was clear, if somewhat spectral. With each step he took, the video display bounced, the trees jumped and thrashed upon the small screen. The shaky movement made him feel dizzy.

He stopped at the forest entrance and lowered the camera.

Without the aid of night vision, he stood in total blackness. He glanced back toward the house and saw nothing. Ahead, the night pressed in on his eyes like the cloth of a kidnapper's hood.

He twitched when a high-pitched whistle broke the silence. Despite the sweat that trickled down his body, and the hot humid air that enveloped him, he felt a chill and shivered.

Another couple of shouts drifted up to him followed by splashing water and a slapping sound that increased in tempo before cutting off completely.

What are those kids doing to make such loud splashes? Maybe they've got a horse or two down there.

Staring in the direction of the sounds, he still saw no lights ahead.

He wiped his face with his shirt, adjusted the camera and walked into the woods.

Several times he stumbled over rocks and roots that protruded from the ground. It was a struggle to keep switching back and forth between his steps and the path before him. He miscalculated the height of a log and fell sprawling to the forest floor. The camera slammed into the spongy substrate and flew from his hand. The image flicked off and Gerald was plunged into darkness.

He grunted from the impact of his fall, and with a string of muttered curses, scrambled in the direction he believed the camera had rolled.

A howl ripped through the night and froze him in the dark. It was very close. The tone was so low in pitch he could feel it in his chest, but quickly launched into a high-pitched wail, peaking at a teeth-grinding screech, trailing off into regions beyond the perceptions of human hearing.

His first reaction was to lay flat and still, but then the thrashing at the river sounded again, this time sounding so close he was certain he'd get wet in the spray. He felt the urge to run, but didn't know which way to turn. Everywhere was utter darkness. Sparked by fear and desperate to find the camera, he crawled forward casting about his hands in the way the blind are apt to do.

He struck the camera with the back of his hand and snatched it to him. With a prayer to the techno gods hovering in his thoughts, he fumbled for the power switch. He was rewarded by the ghostly green image of his dirty knees.

Several ratcheting clicks snapped from his right, and he turned the camera with a jerk.

He saw nothing but trees and plants on the screen. Several feet away, the terrain ended in darkness.

But it's coming from right there, he thought. He walked on his knees in that direction with the viewfinder only inches from his eyes. Each bit of forward motion caused the scene to sway back and forth. The sound of a waterfall nearby grew stronger as he continued to move closer to the dark area. Then it suddenly made sense. He recalled his trip to the river during the day. The river was at the bottom of a steep ravine. The darkness ahead was the edge of the cliff that overhung the river. He got to his feet but remained crouching. In this position, he duck-walked to the edge and aimed the camera down.

At first he couldn't tell what he was looking at. After the noises he'd heard, he no longer expected to see people. This was no late night swim party. The things that moved down there were some kind of animals. Walruses, he thought because of their size and shape. Their bodies undulated in forward lurches. The motion was awkward yet surprisingly swift.

Gerald thumbed the zoom lever on the camera. The field of vision tilted into darkness as the camera slipped in his damp grip. Using both hands, he steadied the image on one of the creatures.

What he had first taken as the smooth bulk of the aquatic mammal was, in fact, a segmented carapace. The thing lifted itself up and twisted momentarily as if searching about for something. Rows of twitching appendages fluttered in palpitating waves.

Its head dispelled Gerald's earlier misperception. A walrus never looked so deathly. Long, conical and sharp, these bone white features lacked any vestiges of eyes. It swung around and bounded off the screen splashing and whistling.

Gerald swung the camera to follow and stepped closer to peer around a bush blocking his view.

Five of the creatures capered in a pool at the base of a waterfall. At this distance the writhing shapes looked like grubs wriggling under a freshly turned stone. Howls, hoots, pops and clicks filled the air.

Witches my ass. It's nothing more than a bunch of giant worms.

He aimed the camera at his feet to find a way down to the river. He was too high to get a good close-up. The drop-off was only a few inches from where he stood. Peering over the edge, he noted that the down slope was steep but not impossible. Plenty of vegetation offered opportunities for hand and footholds.

Gerald checked the group of walrus-grubs once more and confirmed their distance. He was certain they wouldn't hear him climb down -- not over their own ruckus or the cascade of the waterfall. Since the camera was his only method of seeing in the inky night, he bent it to the task of guiding his descent. The sheerness of the declivity required him to occasionally use both hands. Those moments he would grab a plant or protruding root with the same hand that clutched the camera, and the light from the viewfinder would wash softly across the hard packed dirt. He explored with an extended foot for the next step downward and listened intently to the frolicking beasts. They remained at a distance.

Gerald's concentration was broken when a burst of commotion erupted from the opposite direction. He jerked in reflex -- his body trying to escape the impending attack. He lost his grip. The rough slide down the steep embankment was painful but brief. A thick root protruding from the side of the slope halted his short plummet. A burning sensation spread across his chest and the right side of his face where he'd scraped on the rocks.

The camera was still in his hand. Still running. Still recording. He clutched at it, pulled it to his eye and aimed it toward the screaming, splashing onslaught closing in on him.

The camera lens was still fully zoomed in. An enormous shape lurched in and out of frame. Shrieking filled the air. Its enormous bulk thrashed about the river sending sprays of water that jetted into view and then dropped away.

It must be on top of him.

Gerald scrambled backwards, trying to shove himself back up the wall of dirt and rocks. His heels gouged twin ruts in the crumbling surface and he slid back down to his prior perch, his arms flailing about as he tried to regain his balance.

The explosion of sound continued.

Certain that he would be snatched at any moment, Gerald cringed. The camera tucked tight against his chest.

Seconds dragged along and the bestial fracas continued.

When no insect-like jaws closed about his legs to pull him into the frenzy, Gerald hazarded a peek through the camera again. This time he had the presence of mind to pull back the zoom lens.

There were two of the walrus-grubs splashing down the river. They were bigger than the others he had witnessed.

Bulls, he thought.

For all their noise and movement, they made only a slow, steady progress.

Soon, the group at the other end of the river began to echo their behavior. Yodeling, whistling and beating the water, they closed in from the other direction.

Gerald swung the camera back and forth between the encroaching brutes. His panic resurfaced. The converging creatures would be upon him soon.

Smaller forms broke the surface of the river between the closing groups. Their appearance seemed to excite the giant grubs as they increased their fervor.

One of the beasts shot its head forward in a remarkable move that demonstrated the amazing elasticity of its structure. Its neck stretched out in a snakelike fashion -- lightning quick, and it snatched one of the fleeing forms as it made for the shoreline. It held its catch up in the air for a moment.

Gerald saw the wriggling shape of a small alligator.

The walrus-grub lunged forward and smacked the struggling reptile against a large rock at the shoreline. The strange vocalizations ceased as the other creatures snagged their own gators. Soon the crack and snap of reptile flesh being bludgeoned into submission was the only sound.

He adjusted the zoom to focus on the gruesome process. Each creature's head was made up of several appendages that worked in unison. The upper arms held the prey while the bottom mandibles picked it apart and shoved it back into the center dark hole of a grasping orifice.

The branch he stood on had taken his weight and would have been strong enough to support him all night, but after absorbing the impact of several hard landings from his frantic escape efforts, it had cracked in several places and was barely holding together.

Gerald leaned forward to try and get a closer shot of two of the walrus-grubs as they began to fight over a particularly large alligator.

The branch snapped.

Gerald dropped. The back of his head hit before his ass connected with the slope. A burst of light filled his vision. The tearing rocks that ripped at his back as he slid down the rest of the way felt muted as if happening on the other side of a thick wool blanket. When his legs entered the water, he raised the camera up over his head. He jolted to a stop waist deep in the river when his feet dug into the gravel at the bottom.

In the darkness, splashing exploded around, and then there was silence. Water rained down, dripping onto his upturned face and stinging when it entered his eyes. A heavy odor drifted over him. It coated the insides of his nose and mouth. The pungent smell was as heavy as eucalyptus but more musky -- like cat piss.

He looked through the camera.

The images on the screen swirled about in formless chaos.

Expanding the camera to a wider angle, he gasped when he discovered the enormous bulk of a walrus-grub only a foot away and looming over him. He tilted the camera upward.

The two big bulls towered above. Their massive facial appendages splayed out, hovering directly overhead like unearthly flowers reeking of musk and dripping contaminated nectar.

The camera made a soft buzzing sound as it adjusted the auto-focus and resolved the details of their alien countenance.

Quivering fans of membranous tissues unfurled from within the depths of these strange blossoms.

Under the fans of nictitating flesh, he saw their eyeless faces.

They watched him. Gerald could feel it. They didn't need eyes. They saw him better than any normal visual organ could.

Clicking and whistling as they swayed in a hypnotic rhythm, a resonant hum issued from deep within their dark folds. It grew rapidly until it vibrated his bones.

He wanted to scream, he might even have screamed, but the bass hum of their voices drowned out everything. They had him in their sonic grip. It was how they could see without having eyes. Nothing so superficial as eyesight could have been so penetrating. Each layer of tissue in his body reacted to their call and he felt their inspection as they observed all of him.

Behind them, the others moved with deliberate ease towards the waterfall.

Gerald held his breath. He dared not move. The bulls continued to sway, oozing over him. The rest of the herd pushed its way into the waterfall and disappeared beneath its flow.

His only thought was of how the creatures had dismantled the alligators. He prayed that they would not do the same to him. His cramped legs ached from holding such an awkward position at the river's edge.

Simultaneously, the bull walrus-grubs left their vigil and retreated.

They kept their dreadful heads in full bloom, swaying and watchful. When they were next to the waterfall, they twisted and leaped away, disappearing beneath the cascade.

Gerald did not relax until they had vanished beneath the falls; only then did he permit himself a soft sigh.

##

It began to rain as he made his way back through the woods, a tapping sound that pattered throughout the canopy. When large drops began to strike his head and wet the camera, he ran the rest of the way to the house.

Once inside, he stood dripping wet as the corrugated zinc roof amplified the sound of the falling rain into a pounding rumble. The dissonant tone made him shudder. Images of trembling veils of flesh splashed to the surface of his mind. With a shake of his head, he cast them aside.

In the bedroom, he watched his wife's sleeping form in the luminescent green of the display for a few minutes before he powered down the camera and placed it on the dresser. He changed out of his wet things in the total darkness.

The rough towel felt good on his naked flesh.

The potent scent of walrus-grubs had all but faded away.

He settled down next to Inez. She didn't stir. He lay on his back and listened to the crescendo of the rainfall.

Each wave of sound echoed within his body making his heart beat faster as if to keep pace. Then the shower became a torrent, the harsh downpour a deafening roar. In the inky darkness, the resonance took on a life of its own. It pulsated and swirled, reached out and pulled at him.

Gerald started to cry out, but found his lips sealed tight. His throat clicked with each attempted shriek, and from his nose he issued a quavering trill.

He sensed the soundless ripping as each minute connection to the world tore. He tried to reach out and grab hold of something, but he could not move his arms.

The vortex of sound enveloped him, and tumbled him into its abyss.

##

When Inez woke him, it was into a glaring brightness. He clamped his eyes shut.

"Gerald!" She pushed at his shoulder sending waves of electricity down the length of his body. He folded into a fetal position. "Wake up. We gotta start packing."

The light continued to bore into his head as he showered, shaved and dressed. It flooded his mind and plugged his thoughts. Later, on the back porch, he sat in a wooden chair. Inez had brought him a breakfast of corn tortillas and fresh coffee, but it sat cold on the table beside him.

Everywhere he looked was the vibrant color of green, so bright it seemed to eat into his mind. He felt dizzy. A shudder ran through his body. Squeezing his eyes tight he tried to drive away the force of energy, but it was already into his brain and would not let go. He tried to stand, lost his balance and collapsed into the chair. When he tried to rise again, the world washed away into darkness.

Sometime later, Inez woke him again. "Come on, you lazy guy." She sounded pissed. "Let's get moving."

Gerald stood and looked about. The clouds had rolled back in, and the humidity was rising.

Gerald felt nothing at all.

Gerald walked about the yard, taking a final stroll before leaving. Paco trailed behind him, which had lately become his habit. Passing a small shed, Gerald noticed the door was open. He peeked inside. Here were El Viejo's various tools. On the floor was a bright yellow jug of radiator coolant and a small pail with some dirty rags in it. He grabbed the pail and dumped its contents. He hefted the jug with his other hand. Outside he placed the pail on the ground and filled it with the fluid. The liquid was a radiant green.

"Here, Paco." He gestured to the dog with a snap of his fingers.

Paco trotted forward and began to lap up the liquid. He looked up at Gerald as he continued to drink. Gerald stood and walked toward the house.

"There you are." Inez held the video camera out to him. "Could you get a shot of everyone saying goodbye before we go?"

"Sure." He took the camera. "But let me put a new cassette in. I don't want to accidentally tape over anything."

On his way to the house, Gerald spotted El Viejo entering the outhouse.

The old man looked surprised when Gerald forced the door open. Maybe he thought it was an accident or that the gringo was just being rude. Whatever his thoughts were, he never once cried out.

When Gerald exited from the foul smelling toilet, he was alone. Rivulets of sweat ran down from his forehead and his armpits were soaked. A small cluster of flies broke ranks and zoomed past him.

Inez stood half way up the path. She smiled and shook her head.

She said, "You've been gone so long I thought you might have fallen in." When Gerald didn't react to her joke, she changed the subject. "So where's the video camera? Did you change the tape yet?"

He looked down at his empty hands, groped his sides like someone who had just been robbed then turned back to look at the outhouse.

"Oh my god," she said. Eyes widening she cried out, "No way." She ran past him and threw open the door.

Gerald watched her panic with serene detachment and walked calmly up behind her.

"Please tell me you didn't drop it down *there*." Her voice grew shrill as she pointed toward the dark hole and went inside.

Gerald looked about and saw they were alone and followed her into the small shack. The hum of a lone wasp hovering near the ceiling seemed to grow louder after he closed the door. The sound oozed into his ears. In the cramped space his body pressed her from behind and the unbearable heat was instantaneous. She pushed back into him—a subtle gesture of resistance.

Inez was holding her hands over her nose and mouth so that it muffled her voice. "I can't see anything. It's too dark." She shook her head. "I can't believe you did this. Go get a flashlight will ya. Maybe you can fish it out or something."

Gerald put his hands on her shoulders and peered past her into the dark opening. The drone grew louder and his nose began to bleed. The red drips splotched down onto her yellow blouse. Squinting his eyes, he saw that the pit wasn't completely black, but a soft glow lighted its depths. He leaned heavily on her back and guided her to the hole.

"We don't need a flashlight," he said. "Look."

THE PUPPET SHOW

by Rick J. Brown

Mark Petrov's face was chiseled like death itself, a blessing of sorts, since it would ensure his survival.

At the bus stop, Leyna squeezed his hand. Her fragility never escaped him, so that he couldn't let go of her -- not here, not anywhere. He wished he could wear her like a backpack, never losing sight of her. In this polluted air, she could disappear no less than twenty feet from him, forever lost behind a curtain of smoke the color of rust and bruises, where a Refurbished might stalk and capture her. How could he cope with that loss? In this world gone surreal and alien, she grounded him in a reality he priced to no end.

He bowed his wiry frame over the curb and counted the cobblestones. Those he could see. The foul-smelling smog, coughed daily by the Grinding Machines, swallowed the rest. He made a game of this, partly to track the thickening of the mist, partly to indulge in a number game. Perhaps this was not dignified of an aficionado of numbers and patterns, but it kept his mind busy. And in this simple act of faith that numbers always tell, he kept looking for clues wherever he could find them. There was hope in this. And it was all he could do to try to figure out The Grinding Machines, and whether the aerial release of human byproducts would ever stop.

The bus parted the smog in bellowing clouds, clanking its way down toward them. This brought color to his pale cheeks and he cracked parched lips into a smile long overdue. He knew how excited Leyna was, and if she would experience only one thing that a child *should* experience, it was this show.

"Is this it?" she squealed. "Is this it, daddy?" She'd never ridden on a bus. He pointed to the electronic sign above the windshield that said, "THE PUPPET SHOW".

She stared at him in puzzlement. "I can't read, daddy."

He shook his head impatiently. "You've seen this word before. What am I teaching you the alphabet for?" She delegated too easily, not realizing that her smarts might one day save her. She needed to hone her skills.

"Try harder."

She squinted, then burst into hops on the sidewalk. "Yes! Are we going to be able to take one home? Please, daddy? Please?"

"A puppet? I don't think so, Leyna."

The bus screeched to a halt and they climbed up the metal steps. The stench was worse inside. The copper smell of blood and odd sweetness now mixed with the odor of sweat, feet and feces. The driver hunched over the wheel, hair in disarray, and unshaven. His bloodshot eyes ringed with skin folds the size of handbags, were testimony to eyestrain from peering into the smog. He gave them an impatient head tilt toward the back, and the doors rumbled shut behind them.

They walked down an aisle strewn with crumpled paper, stomped Coke cans, and old beer bottles with half-torn labels. In the first seat on his right, a sizeable woman in a soiled gown cradled a baby that screamed while a streak of saliva ran down her hand. Beside her sat a small boy, the incredible shrinking man in his giant overalls, hair the color of rust and wild like campfire. To his left, an old man who seemed crooked at every turn of bone held onto the handlebar in front of him with a vacant stare. He sat beside a little girl who methodically banged her foot against the metal divider. A dark substance -- probably a homemade substitute for the long-gone chocolate -- caked the corners of her mouth. The rest of the bus was essentially a repeat of the first row. No one stood. They passed some faces marked with apprehension and restlessness. Some peeked ahead, craning their necks.

They insisted on glimpsing the invisible: landmarks of the old world buried in smog.

He sighed when he found two empty seats on the back couch. They were on either side of a young woman spruced up with erotic charm from the simplest of things: a turquoise silk blouse sewn-up at several places, and white jeans still hugging her thighs but thinning and graying at the knees.

Mark and Leyna stumbled toward her as the bus lurched forward, yet managed to keep their hands to themselves. He didn't want to have to touch the handlebars. He was sick enough, but proven not to be contagious. He didn't need an incurable disease he could pass on to Leyna, courtesy of a new wave of fools who tried to get sick to avoid the Grinding Machines.

The young woman was considerate enough to skew over and make space for two adjoining seats. Mark nodded in thanks, let Leyna hop on one side, and sat between the two He knew he didn't have to worry about Leyna touching anything. She was well-trained.

"Daddy?"

"Yes?" He self-consciously adjusted his shirt and counted the buttons (there were seven, as always). He'd been too weak lately to rub his fast dwindling supply of soap onto the fabric, and with renewed embarrassment, realized it was rumpled and soiled.

Leyna startled him. "How many seats on the bus?"

"Forty-six." He didn't need to count them.

She giggled. "Are you sure? I'm gonna count them!"

"Go ahead." But he looked at his hands now, self-conscious about them, too. They were cadaverous. The bones popped out under the stretched skin, making ridges with too many shadows. It scared him. He still wanted to live, if only for Leyna.

The bus bumped along, negotiating every turn with the passing shadows of leafless trees.

"You're okay, Leyna?"

She frowned and slapped him on the arm. "Stop asking that!"

He laughed. "Okay, okay."

"She's truly adorable," the woman beside him said. She was exotic, with slanted eyes and high cheekbones of Eastern ethnicity. Yet, the deeper tone of her skin and lips hinted at Latin heritage -- an extraordinary mix that made her brown eyes sparkle amidst a glow of golden hazelnut. She couldn't have been older than twenty, plump just enough to soften the curves -- a jewel in a world where the young and healthy were now as rare as diamonds.

"I can only agree," he smiled, "but I'm her dad, you see."

"No, no," she said coyly. Her hand was doing a lot of the talking. "She is beautiful. How old is she?"

He turned to Leyna. "It's okay," he said. "Tell the lady."

She showed an open hand, fingers sprawled.

"She's been doing that all morning She turned five today."

"Happy birthday, Leyna!" She turned to Mark and extended her hand. "I'm Nathalie."

He took it before he had a chance to wipe off his own, wishing he could strip off its boniness along with the sweat.

Nathalie nodded toward Leyna. "Shy?"

"That's an understatement." "And I bet," she said, "that she can't stop talking when she gets to know you."

He chuckled. "Do you have any of your own?"

"I was too young before the Invasion. Now it would be absurd." She recoiled, as if she realized what she'd just said. Her eyes shifted nervously between Mark and Leyna. "You seem like a good father," she said.

"She'll be fine."

"It's just a puppet show," he said, hearing the apology in his voice. "And I'm not letting go of her if the earth splits open."

They rode in silence. The smog redoubled its thickness, a forewarning that they were getting close to the Grinding Machines. The bus suddenly hushed, save for the crying baby up front. Before long, they heard the Machines' incessant screech and rumble, like un-oiled metal disks rubbing gravel. The passengers' gazes shifted to the floor, the seats in front of them, and their hands. Mark didn't have to see their faces. He'd seen them before.

Eyes would glaze over, throats would gulp, probably running dry, lower lips would curl in, and hands would wring -- the nervous discharges that came with dread.

Images would run through their heads. For some, they brought guilt; for others, despair; and for the rest, sheer terror. Who would be fed into the Grinding Machines next? Were people pulled at random? Was there a pattern? And what would it feel like? For Mark, when he heard the shrill sounds of abrading machines, it was inexorably linked with images of flesh tearing, slouching and granulating, with blood running down gutters to feed a giant cauldron of human pulp. *And out comes another Refurbished.*

The Grinding Machines ran in a circle that enclosed the city, with little gaps between them, so that once heading downtown, they couldn't be avoided.

You could shut your ears and look away, but you could never shut out their scream.

For the better part of his life, Mark had lived in a predictable universe -- one ruled by order that, if he really put his mind to it, he could glimpse right out of chaos. There were numbers, numbers everywhere. The magic of the modern world, they sparkled like gold amongst it and dispelled its mysteries. Except for the Invaders.

An elderly lady sat two rows up on a seat facing them. "Does she know yet?" she said. She had breasts like two giant bullets that bounced under a loose nylon top. She gazed at him with sleepy eyes, as if the ride made her groggy. "It will happen very quickly, you know. It will be subtle."

This was fact and unpreventable. Yet, he couldn't fathom why she would bring it up. It was unnecessary and obscene. The horror he felt at her callousness compelled him to look away and reach for Leyna's hand. He didn't have it in him to argue with the old hag.

They only take the young and the healthy, the flyers had said. These brave messengers regularly passed new ones around, whenever they learned something of importance that they glimpsed when spying on the Machines. But lately, the messages had become ramblings, less grounded in fact, and more fashioned out of fear and despair, with a growing obsession with false prophecies.

He retrieved a pack of Camel Lights from his shirt pocket, having long ago overcome the inhibition to smoke in public. No one cared anymore. The smog and its filth were far worse. He lit it and took a long draft, then blew the smoke as he tilted his head back, letting the calming rush take him to a better place that reminded him of a steaming bath when hot water was still available. "They'll kill you, someday," he said, "is what they used to say."

In front of them, heads bobbed in unison. The road was cratered with potholes. A man sporting a single tooth turned around and smiled at Leyna. Mark instinctively reached for her, then tried to hug her despite her complaints. She pushed him off, and he pushed back teasingly, then tickled her for good measure. She giggled and tried to run off, but Mark's reflexes kicked in and he grabbed her wrist before she made it down the aisle. Now that she felt comfortable, she was a bundle of energy. And this only pained him. In the bright green dress she wore for the occasion, she looked like an emerald brushstroke in a dark, macabre painting.

He felt Nathalie's gaze on him. She searched his eyes. "I went to a show like this," she said, "not too long ago. They're magicians, puppeteers, professionals out of Las Vegas, traveling circuses, things like that. They know how to put on a good show. It's admirable they do it for free now. I think it takes their minds off the Invasion. They really put their soul into it. She will like it."

"Oh, I don't doubt it. I made dolls out of cloth and buttons, even puppets out of paper and strings for her. She's crazy about them. She has a drawer-full now. Compared to mine - professional entertainers? Can't wait to see her face."

After a while, Nathalie added, "You know, you have that look."

"Oh?"

"I don't mean to pry. But before the Invasion, I'd say you were a teacher, maybe a professor or something."

He considered this. Maybe it was his eyes, the way they pierced and pried, although he didn't mean for them to. Maybe it was his Russian heritage, his nonchalant demeanor.

"I'm a mathematician. A bad one at that."

She winced. "Why do you say that? I'm sure there's no such thing as a bad mathematician."

"I failed at the only job I've ever had. I was part of the group at the Orion Search Center, a division of SETI. I tried every damned algorithm known to man. None of them worked."

"What are those? The algorithms."

"The thinking was that language based on mathematics is universal. We tried deciphering a pattern in the language of the Invaders. When we failed, we constructed our own message and sent it back. We never got a response. You wouldn't believe the pressure we were under. People with machine guns guarding the exits. We had to find a way to communicate anyway possible."

"The Invaders were a serious threat."

He found that he was out of breath. He must've explained this a million times. Yet, people didn't get it. *Why would you want to talk to them? They're evil! They're killing us! They're the devil!*

He caught a glimpse of the old woman staring at him, a smirk on her lips.

Leyna leaned across Mark and craned her neck at Nathalie with adult seriousness. "That's when daddy got sick!"

"*Shhhhhh*," Mark said. "That wasn't the question, Leyna."

"Sick?" Nathalie said.

"Leyna's been on my back about it. If you know of a doctor who's working pro bono -- hell, who's even still *working*, you'll make her happy."

"It's the smog, isn't it?"

"That's what I hear. I know I'm not the only one."

"THEY'VE BEEN TALKING TO US SINCE DAY ONE!" They both jumped and turned to the big-breasted lady.

She glared at them. A bump in the road loosened a white strand of hair from the bun in the back of her head. Her eyes beamed unrestrained spite, glistening deep in a halo of darkened skin. "You guys in your big towers with your big fancy computers don't get it, do you -- you don't get it and you never will I reckon because you're thick in the head."

She forced a smile. "Yeah, they've been talking, alright. You're just not listening."

Nathalie put a hand on his arm. It felt warm, and he liked it.

The bus came to a stop and deflated with a *pshhhhhhh*. They stepped out, reentering the smog, and the bus driver took the lead to guide them across the street. Mark felt apprehensive about crossing because there was no way to tell whether a vehicle might suddenly burst out of the fog and plough through them like bowling pins. Few people drove anymore, but some of the ignorant ones still did.

Finally, a giant drape striped blue and yellow broke out of the fog. The visibility was better vertically, so that the tent seemed to climb forever, paling to nothingness a hundred feet up or so. But once inside, the air was crystal clear. Mark breathed more easily. Tendrils of fog crawled low to the ground.

"The smog is heavy," Nathalie said. "When there's no wind to circulate it, it falls to the ground."

He felt her stare on him again, which lasted long enough that he had to acknowledge her. She pinched her lips, seeming to say, *did I just say something smart? Something that might impress you?*

They squeezed between two rows of seats, trying to avoid stepping on people's toes, and sat beside a heavyset lady who dipped enthusiastically into a pack of Doritos. She munched loudly while staring at the empty arena. He almost asked her where she'd gotten the prepackaged snack, but imagined she'd been prepared with wholesale boxes stacked to the ceiling -- gathered in the few hours during the supermarket rush before they closed forever.

He turned to Nathalie, hoping to catch her gaze on him. And he did. She had fake eyelashes, but the number of strands in the right eye didn't match the number in the left. A silver necklace followed the curves of her breastbones with twenty-eight visible links. All this he got in a flash.

She blinked twice as he scanned her face. Pressured to say something, he opened his mouth to speak but found he had nothing to say. She smiled weakly, eyes drifting to his lips. His mouth dried up, and his heart galloped. He felt apprehension and fear, all this mixed with an urge to kiss those full lips. There were six lone, fine hairs at the end of each eyebrow. He wondered how many crowns she had.

"How many stripes?" Leyna caught him off guard this time, but he took a moment to let the new environment sink in. The stadium around the arena was perfectly concentric, with seats arranged so they sat exactly between the two down from them. Four hundred chairs in all. Seventeen empty seats.

More than likely, ten buses outside. The lights dimmed, and something waddled out of hidden curtains. Seventeen camera flashes sprinkled the stadium like diamonds before stopping abruptly.

"Forty-eight." He yawned and she slapped his arm.

"You cheated!" She said.

Without looking, he grabbed her hand and squeezed it three times. *I love you.*

She squeezed right back. Three times. He squeezed again, twice, then once, and once again. *Tickle time!*

She giggled, then squeezed twice. No!

"Are they going to be like your puppets, daddy?"

"I doubt it."

As the figure advanced, still hidden by the darkness that cameras no longer obliterated with snapshots, Mark began to feel ill-at-ease. It was obscenely big, and dragged itself rather than walked. He'd been distracted when the cameras lit it, but the audience had apparently seen enough.

Spotlights snapped it into reality. Mark held his breath, as much for himself as for Leyna. What he saw was grotesque beyond description: a bloated lump of flesh, shaped to give a passing impression of an obese human figure, beamed at the audience. It was a thirty-foot tall puppeteer carrying two smaller versions of itself, two live fleshy horrors suspended on strings like greased dough balls. All three creatures were awkwardly designed in the crude human form typical of the Refurbished: two glistening puffy cheeks, a beaked protrusion carved in the likelihood of a nose. They leered with lips the color of liver through a jagged hole cut to give a rudimentary semblance of teeth.

"I don't know what's going on," Nathalie muttered, "but that's not the show I expected."

He didn't want to look at her, see the fright on her face, the validation of his own.

"They can come into our houses if they want," he whispered so Leyna wouldn't hear. "They can grab us off the streets. Why the charade?"

Mark finally found the strength to check on Leyna, whose face had gone expressionless, lips slightly apart, gaze darting across the creature. He scanned the tent, hoping to glimpse signs of protests, but found only confused fascination. Clearly, no one knew whether to stay or leave. Mark sat on the edge of his seat, heart pounding, ready to spring and run the moment things turned ugly.

On closer inspection, he could now easily pick out several of the traditional Refurbished. Like the giant and his puppets, they were parodies of the human shape. They sat there, inconspicuous in their immobility. In the early part of the Invasion, they'd been chased, killed and burned, but their numbers only grew. Finally, they stopped appearing altogether. But here they were, insidious as ever, partaking in a silent chorus of open mouths that doughnuted their faces.

As the monster pulled strings seemingly at random, raising wobbly limbs, the Refurbished stretched their mouths even further. Finally, they uttered a piercing shriek that felt like a needle digging into a root canal. Brief clinks of shattering glass popped all around him: watches and eyewear were breaking.

The monster of the arena slowly turned to face the audience, the leer on its face taking on a strange, inquisitive appearance.

Something was happening here, leaving Mark frustrated as to what it was.

The concern on Nathalie's face matched the general, growing uneasiness that permeated the air. It was as if the entire tent breathed fumes that could blow up with the accidental strike of a nail. People were on the brink of darting out to howl their pent-up terror. They were just waiting for the first person to shout fire.

Mark agonized over a deciphering frenzy. He tried counting the pulls of strings by the monster -- *a musician directing a symphony playing a silent melody; the shriek of the Refurbished provided a background chant* -- but no, he couldn't detect a regular beat, a pattern. He tried extracting a sequence, maybe one that repeated, and searched the underlying algorithm -- *something like Morse code* -- but nothing repeated, nothing seemed contrived.

In his peripheral vision, he saw a blurry shape staring at him. It was the elderly lady from the bus. With the knowing eyes and that smirk, it was clear what she was saying: *I told you so*. As she turned back around, he noticed that locks of hair dislodged from her scalp and stuck to her pullover, leaving cranial spots that glistened pink like burned skin covered with medicated gel.

He reached to his own scalp. His hair was still firmly attached. Suddenly, the Refurbished stopped screaming.

People looked at each other, but no one said anything. It was the silence before the storm. Something was about to happen, and Mark took a firm hold of both Leyna and Nathalie's hands, ready to bolt.

The Refurbished slowly turned to the audience, and in a guttural voice like a forced whisper, pronounced in unison the first utterance to ever breach their lips.

Hello.

Over the hush, nervous shuffling could be heard clear across the arena.

Everyone waited for what was to follow. Yet nothing came. The puppeteer had stopped pulling strings, the Refurbished had returned to their previous blank stares, and that was that.

"What, that's it?" Nathalie whispered. Mark winced. He feared her voice might disrupt something. But the monster and its puppets turned and left.

Mark let go of both hands to wipe his own on his jeans and burry his face in them. The chatter volume steadily rose as the spectators slowly disengaged from their trance.

Mark shrugged. "So... they were just saying *hello*."

"So..." Nathalie parroted in shock, "that's what the Refurbished are for?

They're translators?"

Mark suddenly had a vision of the Grinding Machines regurgitating flesh puppets: interpreters programmed to capture and translate the language of the Invaders. It was outrageous, yet there it was: they had just clearly communicated a simple greeting. There was strange hope in that. It wasn't *we will kill you all*, or *we will enslave you*, or *you will obey us*.

It was a simple *hello*.

"And what if," he said, "they had much more to say to us? Won't they need a new batch of humans to process through their Grinding Machine to say it?"

Finally someone screamed, then a child across the stadium followed suit until it infected the audience, reminding him of the nocturnal canine frenzy before the Invasion. Mark rose to his feet in the middle of a cacophony of screams, hands grabbing and pushing, people tripping over seats and themselves. Nathalie's hand firmly in his, he strained to hear what people were screaming about.

"What happened to him?" Female voice. "He was sitting right here!"

Male voice. "Oh my God! She's gone!"

Female voice. "I told her not to go anywhere! Please please please please, Mary Ann WHERE ARE YOU?"

As the realization of what was happening dawned on him, he spun toward Leyna and found only an empty seat. "LEYNA!!!!!"

He searched for her frantically in the aisles, screaming her name, but the panicking audience carried him toward the exit like a tsunami. He pushed his way through the crowd, but lost more ground than he gained, and finally spilled outside.

The emerging crowd eventually thinned. With still no sign of Leyna, he fought his way back inside. He found himself among a couple of dozen people in the arena center, some on their knees, face in hands, some running around to look under seats. But she was nowhere among them. He scanned the tent for the exit taken by the monster, but couldn't find a single break in the tent material.

A hand rested on his shoulder. It was Nathalie. Without enthusiasm, she said, "Let's look for her outside."

For months, he looked for Leyna. He looked for her where the world was slowly unwinding, losing its familiarity, and shrouding her -- at least in his mind -- like the strange world of Alice in Wonderland. He frequented bars where the last drops of booze were freely distributed, churches, and the dreary, candle-lit hallways and classrooms of high schools and universities. There, various groups met regularly to organize plans of action. But his questioning only met the knowing stares of the demoralized. They were veterans; they knew people were never recovered. He looked for her in buses that also ran freely, and for free. He looked in parks where prowlers, shielded by the smog and the conspicuous absence of law, were unstoppable. He looked in alleys where the homeless now cherished the diseases and mental illnesses that rendered them untouchable. Sometimes a Refurbished would crystallize out of the fog with fear on its doughboy face, or maybe an unknowable emotion inherited from the aliens. He would peer at the thing, at the absence of eyes in the malformed crevasses, to wrench some recognizable feature that would tell him that Leyna was in there, somewhere, lost in the cellular soup of a dozen, a hundred -- a thousand?

But the only certainty was the faraway sound of the Grinding Machines playing in the background like eternal thunder. And one day, as he fell to his knees in front of one of them, its tall walls without doors rising in the smog, he screamed. Because he knew he would finally search no longer.

One morning, he found Nathalie sitting at the edge of the bed as he woke to her touch. She used a sponge soaked in cold water to cool his face.

"Did you have bad dreams again?" she said. She didn't use the name *Leyna*.

But the way he avoided her eyes said it all. She lay down by his side, and he breathed deeply. The weight on his chest was heavier than usual, the fever had come back, and he'd lost more weight. The weakness he had felt when moving about he now felt upon waking, and all he could do was ride the fatigue until he fell into a slumber.

Nathalie curled up to him and rested her head on his chest. He knew what she was doing. but the Illness wouldn't spread. It would kill him, not her, and she would eventually be alone, waiting for her time at the Grinding Machines, waiting to dilute into the human ocean.

Her instructions once he was gone were simple. There were razors in the cabinet and a bottle of Vodka to ingest for a cottony departure. Of course, neither Mark nor Nathalie knew with any certainty whether she would have time to take that route.

Blue and yellow canopies had gone up throughout the city, a clear sign that a new message was to come -- the impulse to count them had evaporated with Leyna's departure. He gathered that the people most likely to venture in the tents would be the curious: the physicists, the psychologists, the mathematicians, and the linguists; people with cameras and equipment; people with a desperation greater than their fear.

In the middle of the night, Mark often woke up in sweat. His worst dream resurfaced again and again: a child without a face crouched by a writhing mass in the grass, holding a kitchen knife over it. The bulk was a cat, skinned and bloody, with a dying squeal. Every time the child removed some skin, the cat shrieked. Every time the cat shrieked, the boy turned its face to Mark, as if asking for a translation. Mark screamed, "It's not talking to you! It's crying in pain!" The boy stared eyelessly for a moment, then went back to the cat to cut some more.

Whatever the Invaders were trying to say must've been of enormous importance, for they were killing life by the masses to do it. Perhaps Leyna, with her inherited love of numbers, might pass on enough enthusiasm about patterns to bring attention to a new means of communication for the aliens.

But for now, with the distraction of numbers out of the way, Nathalie looked splendid and carried a subliminal message of her own that needed no encryption: *I will be here with you, no matter what.*

In Nathalie's embrace, Mark daydreamed about what that next message would be. He also wondered if there was anything in that message that would have something recognizable of Leyna in it. And even though the likelihood was slim that a recognizable pattern would emerge, there might still be a coded question in the strange voice of the

Refurbished. One that only she and he would know, like a particular pattern from their hand squeezes. He would wait, however long it took.

He would wait for anything.

How many seats in the tent, daddy?

How old am I now, daddy?

Anything at all.

SURRENDER

by Vince Churchill

His rough hand worked frantically under her skirt, her hips lifting to allow him easier access. The lurid symphony of his grunts and her own panting thundered in her ears. Her eyes squeezed tight as passion seared through her. She was under the complete, merciless control of the substance he had forced into her body. Mentally, she floated outside herself, unable to stop from reacting in such a reckless, shameful fashion. Every inch of her delicate, pale flesh had become a super-sensitive erogenous zone. Flames of unquenchable, wanton desire burned from the wetness between her legs to the base of her skull where the rough concrete scraped her skin raw.

He was very, very strong -- whether from the parasite's chemical influence on his system or just from being a large man, she wasn't sure. He pushed her onto her back, moving her further from the dimly lit path that wound its way through the park. He bent over her, one hand tearing at the moist crotch of her panties, the other hand pulling at her brand-new, sheer-black blouse. She had a vague thought about how she almost didn't buy the top because she could see her bra right through it. Her hard nipples throbbed under the lacy fabric, and she wished he would hurry and free her breasts to the chilly night air. She felt her matching lacy underwear ripped and pulled free. Had she known the man on top of her, this might actually have been a dark, secret passion come true. This was the classic rape fantasy combined with having sex in a public place, except the man savagely forcing himself on her was a diseased, psychotic stranger, and she was beginning to wonder if she might have made an error in judgment.

Mary had closely followed the news, carefully listening to reports of the parasitic virus spreading throughout the Western Hemisphere. LF X13 was a man-made microorganism combining the biological devastation of HIV and rabies. It had the extra ingredient of a two-pronged sexual behavioral enhancer that drove the host to sexually transmit the virus with an uncontrollable psychopathic urgency. The other by-product of the virus was a potent psychosexual venom the host could use on his or her intended victim to breakdown resistance to the assault, maximizing the chance for infection. Any type of body fluid passed between host and victim transmitted the venom. Newscasts reported the sharp rise of sex assaults, coupled with the lack of victims pressing charges. Reports poured in from major metropolitan hospitals detailing the sudden glut of emergency room patients, many of them still in a zombie-like trance. Most victims, male and female, had disturbing, wistful smiles plastered on their faces.

LF X13 had been a top-secret chemical warfare option until the general population experienced an accidental exposure. The government wasn't talking, but there didn't appear to be an antidote. After a couple of long, sleepless nights, Mary knew what she had to do to make things right for herself.

Feeling her body responding to the man's rough handling, including the series of blood-drawing nips at her throat, she realized with distant fascination that her hips, with seemingly a will of their own, were grinding up against the man. She hadn't felt the slightest discomfort when he initially penetrated her. At thirty-two, she'd still been a virgin, but was way beyond that now. As the man's rutting took her to the brink of her very first orgasm, her eyes popped open and she looked into the face of her lover/rapist. It was difficult to tell if he was handsome because his face was distorted in animalistic passion, the parasite driving him to spread the virus before his brain was completely eaten away. He grunted and drooled, spittle splattering her face as he plunged himself in and out of her with no regard beyond reaching his own release. Her body responded by locking itself around him. Her thigh muscles flexed and clamped around his waist, and her fingernails clawed through his shirt and into his back, spurring him on.

Beyond the information from television, radio and newspaper, she received a lot of very interesting tidbits from the Internet. Rumors were becoming fact -- while this organism was lethal, it also drove its host and the host's victim into an abnormal state of sexual frenzy. Several cults had popped up, using the virus and the Bible to pronounce doom to pagan western civilization. Some Internet junkie had nicknamed it the "fuck bug". LF X13 was a radical, mercurial germ, and it had reached epidemic levels in mere days. Rape statistics had catapulted hundreds of times the norm, and aggravated assaults and attempted rapes had skyrocketed. The plague was spreading beyond country borders like a raging brush fire, with the population of the United States, and maybe the world, as its tinder. The virus ran its course in less than a week, during which time the organism devoured and liquefied the internal organs of the host while replicating itself. Early symptoms were similar to the flu. Why did everything start out feeling like the flu? Was this nature's all-purpose smoke screen when something new was introduced into the world to thin out the human herd? Or was this just some devilish form of biological bait and switch?

It had all seemed right to Mary. She was just another faceless person on the planet; a mere social security number in the world computer. Estranged from her small family, Mary was void of any social relationships outside her work. She had a job, paid taxes, gave out candy on Halloween, but in the greater scheme of things, she felt like she didn't really matter. She'd never been on a date, never had a boyfriend, and had never been kissed. A boy named Dirk Baumgarten had tried in high school, but she'd chickened out at the last moment, and his slobbering mouth and tongue had found the side of her face. She never afforded him a second opportunity.

The idea of having sex with a man, of getting naked in front of someone else, of playing all the social-sexual games had terrified her for most of her life. Despite comments of co-workers and acquaintances, she'd always felt ugly. Well, maybe not exactly ugly, but just a very uncomfortable plain.

For her, things hadn't been the same since she started developing breasts and hips. Already shy, the attention she garnered made her into a champion wallflower and super self-conscious. She showered in near darkness, and she wore very bland, unflattering clothing. She stayed away from bright colors, high heels, cutting-edge fashion and any make-up that would draw attention. She'd never worn a swimsuit or a pair of shorts in public since she had been in control of her wardrobe. Throughout her school P.E. years, she wore sweat pants and over-sized sweat tops and never showered in the presence of other girls. But despite the crippling fear and anxiety, she recognized a tiny part of her hungered for intimacy and sexual pleasure much like her occasional late-night craving for exotic chocolate ice creams.

There had been a short period of time when she had allowed a girl from her high school to stay with her while she was in town for a job interview. Mary spent one of those nights listening to the girl and a strange man "doing it" on her living room floor. Disgusted at first, she had been frightened by the sounds the pair made, fearing a date rape might be in progress. But soon fascination grew out of the couple's grunts and moans and primal bursts, and Mary found herself pressed against her bedroom door. Before long, excitement had made her breathing a soft pant, their escalating guttural passion urging her hand down between her legs, her fingers forcing their way between the tightly squeezed thighs. By the time the sounds had quieted from the living room, Mary was on her bedroom floor, eyes squeezed shut and gasping for breath as a near orgasm wracked her nervous system. Her hand rubbed mindlessly at her wet junction until she couldn't stand it anymore, her stomach muscles cramping at the exertion. Come morning, the scent of their lovemaking still lingered in the air. The girl had apologized for the late-night activity, but seeing Mary's embarrassment and confusion, left later the same day. A tiny but growing part of Mary had wanted to ask the woman questions. What was it like having a man kiss you hard? What did it feel like to have a man inside you? But those questions would have gone unasked no matter how long the girl had stayed.

So why not? Why not just do it? Why not find out how it felt to be with a man and finally put an end to the gray, unsatisfactory cycle she plodded through day after day? Suicide wasn't a new thought for Mary. Ideas of ending her life had comforted her like stuffed animals for as long as she could remember. There didn't seem to be any real purpose to continuing this empty charade, and she knew without the hope of experiencing love or a family of her own she was only going through the motions of having a "real" life. She understood why these sex/death cults were gaining such popularity; she just wasn't social enough to join one. Like everything else, this would have to be something she did alone. And it wasn't until she was bucking and squirming like a rodeo bronco under this strange man that she realized she'd probably be alone in death too.

As she felt his hot, sticky seed and virus unleashed inside her, the man cried out in a jumble of what sounded like both pain and pleasure. His body continued to shove inside her, and she felt something strange happening between her legs. Inside... An overwhelming, exquisite pressure strained for release. She imagined a time-lapsed red rose blooming, then the pleasure exploded within her and she screamed, her voice joining his as her body thrashed and shook, hungrily accepting his fatal seed.

As the spasms subsided, he stared down at her, blood and saliva from his slack jawed mouth stringing down to her face. He heaved himself off her, clutching his stomach and groaning in agony. The wet peeling sound their bodies made when they separated struck a cord deep inside her, and the beautiful rose in her mind began to wither and die. She was puzzled that the wet sound didn't seem very human. She lay there, feeling the sweat cooling on her exposed inner thighs, her breasts, and her throat. Her continued state of arousal made her ache for the sticky, diseased touch of the man. She tried to close her eyes to make those feelings go away, but the echoes of his fevered, dirty fingers remained. On its own, her tongue darted out, licking the blood from her busted lip. It barely stung from when he had first attacked her.

She had gone to a high-end department store to buy the short skirt and the sheer top she had on to make her appear more desirable. She'd had trouble walking in her first pair of high heels, but she stayed in the shoe department until she was confident she wouldn't fall and twist an ankle. It felt strange leaving the store, feeling the eyes of strange men on her, knowing they followed her. But she was beyond their affectionate glances and smiles. Where had they all been the day before?

When she had arrived at the park she couldn't help but feel nervous. What if even with all the make-up and skimpy clothing and the expensive trip to the beauty shop no one thought she was pretty enough to attack? That thought didn't stay with her long because the maniac had stepped out of the bushes and blocked her path before she had walked two minutes. Her attacker mumbled something she couldn't understand under his hot, putrid breath, and she flinched, turning away from him, suddenly afraid. She couldn't help but notice the bloody spit dripping from his chin, and she couldn't ignore the jolt in her gag reflex. In the next instant, his first and only blow had sent her reeling to the sidewalk, and then she made it easy for him, spreading her legs and sealing her deal with the devil.

Mary multiplied her sins by having sex outside of marriage and committing suicide in exchange for a few moments of feeling something, of feeling anything...intimate. And as Mary lay there in the fading afterglow of a powerful orgasm, she wished she'd made the deal years ago, even if the purchase price had included her soul.

Her attacker had long since crawled away, and for the first time Mary felt the damp chill of the ground seep into her flesh. Skirt bunched up around her waist, she struggled to pull it down and cover herself. She shivered, reaching for her torn, wadded panties. Staggering to her feet, she tried to gather herself, her body stiff and bruised from the violent encounter. There was little doubt the aphrodisiac part of the venom was well on its way to wearing off. As she stepped toward the path, something caught her attention and she turned, peering over a thick bush to her right.

A huddled figure lay on the ground. A small woman -- no, a girl -- curled up in a fetal position, whimpered softly. The chirping crickets nearly drowned out her tiny, protesting voice. The girl stared at Mary with a huge, teary, blue eye, her other eye swollen shut. Dried tears streaked the girl's dirty cheeks. Her clothing was in tatters, her tender young skin torn and bloody. Meekly, she whispered to Mary.

"Did he hurt you too?" The girl's voice had the tone of a dying baby bird. Mary watched a fresh tear spill down the girl's face. Her trembling body and the stolen innocence of her expression would haunt Mary for the remainder of her severely abbreviated life.

In her mind, like the ringing of giant church bells, Mary heard the devil laughing, and she knew there was no place in this world for her when she couldn't even cherish her pain and her death as her own.

Wings with Hot Sauce

by Fran Friel

"Look, Hillary," he said. "I'm only one guy. Unlike some people, I can't be in more than one place at a time." He threw up his hands and bit his lip. A bead of blood trickled down his chin, dripping onto his heart with a sizzle. "War, starvation and disease are sweeping the planet. What more do you want, woman?"

Clad in a navy blue pinstriped suit, his wife stood in the center of the cavernous room, hands planted on her hips. Unimpressed, she tilted her head and raised an eyebrow.

He knew he could never win an argument with a politician, so before all hell broke loose, he turned and stomped out of the house, slamming the heavy planked door behind him. The muffled sound of shattering china followed behind him. With a snarl, he kicked a pile of bleached bones off the steps. Taking a deep breath of the hot wind, the sand of the nearby burial pits buffed his radiant skin. With the burning hillside lighting his way, he stalked off to the local pub.

##

The sign for the Horns and Ale swung back and forth above the door of the pub; its rusty hinges squealed their rhythm into the night. Opening the door, he dipped his horns and folded his fleshy wings to enter. "Lu!" came the resounding greeting from the crowd of patrons. With a scowl and a dismissive wave, he plopped down on his stool at the bar. Familiar with his moods, the crowd turned back to their drinks, rolling their eyes at each other.

In the back of the room a bold raven-eyed demon whispered, "Another domestic dispute, no doubt."

Lu shot him a sharp glance and engulfed the demon with a snatch of fire, leaving a neat pile of ash in his place. In the hush that followed, the curt cadence of Adolph's accent broke the silence.

"Vat vill you have, Lu?" he said, polishing the surface of the long granite bar. He paused to serve his most prominent patron. While Lu continued to brood, the bartender straightened the belt across his uniform and swiped back an errant piece of hair from his brow.

"Single malt, and make it a double. No ice," said Lu, with a growl. He sat, elbows on the bar, with his shoulders hunched forward.

"How about some vings, Lu?" asked Adolph. "Ve got a shipment of dat hot sauce you like from da immigration boys. Seems da blood from illegal border crossers is plentiful dese days."

Lu nodded, "Sounds good A. I shouldn't, but screw the agita!"

"Marilyn, get Lu some vings!" Adolph shouted back to the kitchen. "And be sure to bring da Inferno sauce."

In a snap the platinum blonde, Marilyn, appeared - low cut red chiffon flowing. With the enormous barbequed wings piled high on a platter, she sauntered around the bar and delivered them in person. Straddling the barstool beside the massive Dark Angel, she leaned into him with a coy smile.

"Want some hot sauce, Lu?" With a wink, she reached two fingers into her cleavage and slowly withdrew a bright red bottle. "It's all warmed up for you, baby."

A bashful grin broke at the corner of Lu's crimson lips. Marilyn sat the bottle on the bar in front of him, then reached back to stroke his leathery wings. He shivered at her touch.

"Go on, Honey," she said. "Eat your wings. They came from a special seraphic culling at the Vatican."

"I wonder if they're anyone I know," said Lu, with a smile and a low chuckle. Dousing the wings with sauce until they dripped red, he dug in, ripping and slurping at the meat and bones. Marilyn's petting continued as Lu devoured the entire platter of wings; the glut of sweet meat made him light-headed.

Smoothing the ebony hair around his horns, Marilyn whispered, "Trouble at home again, big boy? Marilyn can make it all better, you know." She reached over, taking hold of his hands.

Lu watched with anticipation as she guided his fingers to her lips. With long slow strokes of her tongue, one by one she licked his fingers clean. He felt the warmth of her mouth and her dreamy gaze melting his restraint. His eyes closed and his head drifted back with pleasure. A tingle began in his spine and pulsed out through the veins of his fleshy wings. Suddenly, a jolt ran through his body.

A deep grunt escaped Lu's throat, "Unh!" His eyes popped open; his face flushed hot with embarrassment.

With gaping mouths and eyes wide, the crowd stared at the spectacle as enormous white-feathered wings unfurled behind the Dark Angel. Trying to regain his dignity, Lu stood up and glared at his minions.

"Damn it to hell! My Allergies!" he shouted, eyeing the lush plumage over his shoulder. "Must have been an Archangel in that batch!"

And Mother Makes Five

by John Mantooth

Cleveland Walker watched as Donnie Tunnel scooped the pizza off the restaurant floor. Donnie was careful not to get it on his new, well-pressed, Pizza Shack shirt. He deposited what was left of a large pepperoni with green peppers into a little black sack he kept tied to his cart.

Cleveland, owner and operator of Pizza Shack for just over two weeks now, thought again about firing Donnie, or Dummy, as the other employees had taken to calling him.

Donnie finished table four and pushed his cart past table five. Then instead of turning left to avoid the salad bar as Cleveland had instructed him to do, Donnie kept going straight. Cleveland winced as Donnie tried to squeeze his cart past a large black woman who was pouring ranch dressing on her salad. The cart hit one gelatinous hip, and a glob of marinara sauce sloshed off the cart and landed on the woman's shirt, staining it blood red.

By the time Cleveland reached the salad bar, Donnie was already laboring over an apology. The woman, who looked as if she could benefit from more lettuce and less dressing, smiled at him. "No problem, sugar," she said. "It happens."

"Not thirty times a day, it doesn't," Cleveland said. "Ma'am, your salad bar is on the house today. I apologize for this unfortunate incident." The woman frowned at Cleveland as if he were the one that had bumped her. Cleveland had only known Donnie a little over a week, but he'd already learned the two most important things about him: he was a total fuck-up, yet people felt sorry for him. Well, not Cleveland. He wasn't obligated to make his restaurant a charity organization.

He turned to Donnie, who was already trying to disappear under his red Pizza Shack hat, which said, "Pizza: Grub of the Gods". Another one of the many idiosyncrasies that Cleveland meant to change about this place. But nothing changed before the name. Pizza Shack had to be the worst name he'd ever heard. It was a blatant rip-off of Pizza Hut and completely unappetizing. Who wanted to eat pizza in a shack? Yes, he'd change the name first. He looked at Donnie, cowering below the brim of his hat, his ragged little goatee hiding at least some of his vitriolic acne. *Check that*, he thought. *First I fire Donnie Tunnel.*

"Donnie, see me in the men's room." Cleveland spun on his heels and walked away smartly, the way he thought a manager should move before firing an incompetent employee.

He reached the men's room and opened the door. He didn't want to do this in the kitchen because even though the rest of the employees liked to make fun of Donnie, they all felt sorry for him and wouldn't want to see him fired. At least this way Cleveland could soften it when he explained it to them.

"I gave him two options," he might tell them later. "Shape up or ship out. He chose the latter. Unfortunate, really."

Something shifted inside one of the stalls. Funny, he could have sworn the place was empty. He scanned the bottoms of the stalls, but didn't see any feet. He was about to step closer to investigate when Donnie came in.

His head hung in despair, and Cleveland felt a little sorry for him. Suddenly he remembered something Arlo Smits, the previous owner, had told him a few weeks ago, just before he signed the last paper.

"Donnie Tunnel's a little different, but he's a hard worker. Give him a chance."

Cleveland had nodded and smiled. "Yeah," he had said. "He seems like a nice enough kid."

"He loves this job," Arlo said.

Don't get all sentimental, Cleve, he thought. *It's no way to run a business.* He looked Donnie in the eye and said in his best, owner/boss voice, "Donnie, your performance has been unacceptable. I hope you'll realize this isn't personal---"

"I'm sorry, boss." Donnie looked like he might cry.

"Like I said, Donnie, it's not personal, but---"

"It won't happen again, boss. I'm really, really sorry."

"Now listen here, Donnie. I'm trying to tell you that I won't be needing you to come back to work tomorrow." *Real professional, Cleveland. That a way to stick it to him.*

Donnie's face dropped. Something shifted in the stall again. Cleveland was sure of it. *Some old bastard taking a shit, listening to it all.* Inspired by the realization that someone might be listening, Cleveland decided to let Donnie have it. "You're fired, Donnie. Go home, now. You're a disaster waiting to happen."

A tear welled up in Donnie's eye.

"Take a minute to compose yourself and then get the hell out. Tough luck, Donnie."

Cleveland stepped out of the restroom quickly and returned to the kitchen, sorry that he'd had to do it, but also glad that it was done. Now he could start figuring out what to call this damn place.

#

Two nights later, Cleveland was adding up receipts after closing when the phone rang. Too tired to move, he let it go. The answering machine would pick it up. At this hour it was probably a wrong number anyway.

The machine clicked on. "Howdy. This is Arlo at The Pizza Shack, and I've got one question for you today: Pizza: Is it in you?" There was a pause and then Arlo added, "Leave a message at the beep." Cleveland sighed. *One more thing to change.*

The machine beeped and gruff laughter rang out over the line. "I see you ain't had time to change the message yet, Cleve. This is Arlo. I was sitting up in bed, thinking on a few things, and thought I'd call you before they slipped my mind. Let's see, I got my list here somewhere." Cleveland heard papers shuffling in the background. "Here she is. Top of the list. There's something wrong with the toilet in the men's room. It's been acting funny for quite awhile now. Sorry, I forgot to mention it. I've tried three different plumbers and they all said it checked out, but sometimes it won't flush. Worse still, sometimes all the shit just comes back up. Oh well. Your problem now." He let loose a great gale of laughter that quickly turned into a vicious sounding coughing fit. When he finally regained his voice he said, "Also, Francine Peabody's been filching from the Shack for years, but its just small change. She mainly takes it so she can afford new shoes for her kids. I let it go because she's a good worker."

Cleveland dropped the stack of receipts in his hand in utter amazement. He'd be firing her first thing in the morning. Of course, he'd have to get out a help wanted sign.

"...said he wanted to set up a meeting. I told him I didn't own the place anymore, he'd have to call you" What the hell was Arlo talking about now?

"...Anyways, that's about it. Good luck with it all. And be good to Donnie Tunnel. He's the first kid I ever hired. The real heart and soul of that place. He ain't that smart, but he's got a heart of pure gold. I like to think of him as the place's good luck charm."

Cleveland shook his head. He didn't need this kind of misery. He'd done the right thing, and that was all there was to it. Still, he couldn't help but think of Donnie's face when he'd fired him.

The line went dead, and Cleveland felt completely alone. He glanced at his watch. It was only 9:30 p.m. Why weren't they still open on a Friday night? One more thing to change. He peered out through the darkened window at the cars speeding by on Highway Seventeen. Rain streaked the glass. A low growl of thunder sounded somewhere in the distance, and Cleveland rested his head on the table.

#

He was awakened thirty-five minutes later by someone pounding on the door.

Groggy, he stood and took a few tentative steps to the door. Storm winds gusted full speed now, and squinting through the rain-soaked glass, he could just make out a tall, lean man dressed in dark clothes. He waved at Cleveland impatiently.

Cleveland shook his head and tapped his watch, mouthing the words, *We're closed.*

The man shook his head in frustration and pounded on the door again. Cleveland wondered if there might be some emergency. He stepped forward to open the door and stopped. He'd heard last week about a murder at a convenience store just a few blocks away. The clerk had been carved up like a Halloween pumpkin. His body was found behind the counter the next morning. His head was still missing.

The stranger pounded on the door again. "I only want to talk!" he shouted. "Arlo sent me!"

Cleveland considered telling the guy to come back in the morning, but something in the man's haggard expression made him think the matter might be urgent.

As if reading his mind, the stranger said, "It's urgent."

Reluctantly, Cleveland opened the door.

A gust of rain came in with the stranger. Cleveland slammed the door and locked it before turning to address the tall man.

He was thin with a jaw sharp enough to slice an orange. His skin looked like somebody had stretched it too tightly over his bones. He had big ears and a heavy nose over which peered a set of sleepy blue eyes. "Cleveland Walker, I presume?" He held out a wet hand.

Cleveland took it. It felt slick and cold. "That's me. What can I do for you?"

The man strode over to table number fourteen and sat down. He pulled off his jacket and draped it over the chair next to him. He wore a pistol, holstered on his side. Cleveland let out an audible gasp.

"Don't worry, Mr. Walker. I'm harmless. And as to your question: it isn't what you can do for me, it's what I can do for you."

"Okay," Cleveland said, surprised that he was more irritated than afraid. "What can you do for me?"

"Much better," the stranger said, smiling "I'm James Turner. I'm here about the toilet."

Cleveland frowned. "You don't look like a plumber."

Another smile. Was this one slightly wolfish? "I never said I was a plumber, only that I was here about the toilet."

"Okay, Mr. Turner. Would you mind getting to the point?"

"Certainly. I have a few questions."

Cleveland rolled his eyes. "I really would like to know what this is all about."

James Turner ignored Cleveland's request. He pulled a tiny case from his pocket and laid it flat on the table. It opened with a click. Inside were two crosses. "Take your pick," he said. He shrugged. "I'm already wearing one."

Cleveland shook his head. "You've got ten seconds to get to the point, buddy, or I'm calling the police."

Still nonplussed, Turner smiled. "Sure, I'll get to the point. Be very quiet, Mr. Walker, and tell me what you hear."

"What the---"

"Very quiet, or you won't hear it."

Despite himself, Cleveland fell silent. He heard the wind chasing the cars down the interstate and the pitter-patter of rain and somewhere far in the distance, a train hitching through the night. And there was another sound. High pitched, whining. Like a baby crying. Or chanting. What was it saying?

"I see from your expression, Mr. Walker, that you hear it. It's getting louder. Even since I've been here, it's gotten louder."

Cleveland barely heard Turner speaking. Instead, he listened to the high whining noises. He was so close to hearing what they were saying. If he could listen just a little harder...

Something struck him on the side of his face. His cheek stung badly. The sounds disappeared. He focused his eyes on James Turner, who looked ready to slap him for a second time.

"Look at me," Turner said. "I need you to concentrate and answer my questions. It's getting stronger. It will be here soon."

Cleveland, despite being struck by this strange man, found he wanted to listen now. Turner might hold the answer to what the strange sounds meant. They were so...so... otherworldly.

"How long have you owned this restaurant?" Turner said, his hand still ready to slap Cleveland if the need arose.

"Two weeks."

"Have you ever heard those sounds before?"

"Not until tonight."

"Anything strange happen recently?"

"I don't know."

"Think, damn it."

"No, just you."

Turner drew his hand back as if to slap Cleveland again but dropped it instead. "You ever used the shitter here at work?"

"Yeah. Once or twice. I try to go at home if I can. It's not very clean here." Suddenly, Cleveland remembered the sounds in the bathroom stall. Would that count for unusual? It was worth a try. "Today, I took an employee into the restroom to fire him, and I heard someone in the stall. Except I didn't actually see anyone. I don't know if that's the kind of thing you---" Cleveland broke off. Turner was shaking his head. Cleveland sat down hard in his chair.

"Tell me about the employee you fired."

"He was severely stupid. He kept bumping into customers and spilling things. I had to do it. About that noise---"

"What was his shift like?"

"On a day, off a day, lunch to close."

"Would this have been his day on?"

"Yeah, I suppose."

"Sweet Jesus," Turner said and pulled his cross out from beneath his shirt.

"What's wrong?"

"I would really recommend you putting one of those on," Turner said. "It won't keep you completely free from harm, but if I'm wearing one and you're not, I can promise you who it will go for first."

"It?"

"Take a fucking necklace, Walker."

There was something in Turner's tone that made Cleveland pick up a cross and put it around his neck. What the hell was going on? Was this one of Arlo's wacko friends come to torture him? Was it some kind of sick joke? He remembered the sound. The sound had been real. What was it saying?

"About that noise..."

"Never mind the noise. Get on the phone and call the employee you fired. Get him the hell up here right now."

Cleveland shook his head. "No. You either tell me what's going on, or I'll make good on my promise to call the police."

"Go ahead, call them," Turner said. "With what's coming out of that, we'll need all the help we can get."

"For God's sake, what are you talking about?" Cleveland flung his hands up in exasperation.

"Demons," Turner said quietly. "I'm talking about demons from hell."

#

A few disorienting moments later, Cleveland stood in the kitchen with his cell phone to his ear. He had laughed when Turner said the thing about demons. Literally thrown his head back and busted a gut. He had stopped laughing when Turner had grabbed him by the wrist and walked him over to the men's room door. "Listen," Turner had said, pushing the door open just a little. "It's hatching."

The sound with the door open was painful. The high whining sound had turned into a grotesque screech, like uncut nails on a chalkboard. Except it sounded like words. A chant. *I'm coming. I'm coming. I'm coming.* Cleveland had shuddered and stepped away from the door.

That had been enough. Seconds later, he was dialing Donnie Tunnel's home number.

A woman answered. She spoke quietly as if she was unsure why someone might have phoned.

"Donnie?" she said. "He's asleep."

"This is Cleveland Walker from Pizza Shack. It's urgent that I speak to him." Cleveland glared at Turner. If he had more information, he might be more effective at this.

Turner shook his head and twirled his fingers impatiently. *Get on with it.*

"Cleveland Walker. Pizza Shack. Urgent." She sounded as if she were reciting terms for a big test. "I don't think I want you to talk to him." She paused, breathing into the receiver. "Unless you mean to give him his job back."

Again, Cleveland glared at Turner. This was ridiculous. He felt like hanging up and telling Turner to get the hell out. But then he remembered the sounds from the bathroom: *I'm coming. I'm coming.* And he knew hell was trying to get in.

"Yeah, that's why I called, actually. I've been thinking about things today, and I realized that I made a mistake firing Donnie."

"Seems a little late to be calling about this sort of thing."

"Like I said, it's just been on my mind today. I'd feel much better if I could only talk to him. Let him know that I was wrong."

"Well..."

"Please, Mrs. Tunnel. It'll only be a few minutes."

"This better not happen again. Donnie's a *special* boy, and I don't mean Special Olympics kind of special. I mean real special. Oh, I know he's not sharp or quick or any of those other things. And I know he makes more than his fair share of mistakes, but he's got a good heart. That's a special thing in this world."

Cleveland, despite wanting to say about a hundred other things, found himself saying, "Yes ma'am. That's exactly why I felt bad."

"Hold on. I'll get him."

A few minutes later, Donnie Tunnel was convinced that he would have his job back by simply coming down to the Pizza Shack. Cleveland was just about to ask Tuner to explain why Donnie was so important when something exploded in the bathroom.

"Get in the kitchen," Turner said.

Cleveland didn't move. Instead, he turned to face the bathroom. He wanted to see what came out. The explosion was followed by a loud clatter. It sounded like a football team was trashing the bathroom.

He watched the door.

He expected it to blow off its hinges, so when it opened slowly and a small, gray-bearded old man emerged naked, he was surprised. The man bled from his head and chest. He appeared very disoriented. Cleveland felt the bizarre urge to go help the man. He looked so frail, so disoriented. He took a step forward.

"Get the hell in the kitchen!" Turner shouted.

Cleveland took a step back. A low rumble came from the bathroom. The naked man's eyes widened as if remembering something. Behind him, the door opened again.

A whip lashed out and struck the naked man's back, causing him to sink to his knees in anguish. Another crack of the whip got the man up and moving. Turner pulled out his gun. He aimed it at the old man as if trying to decide if he was worth killing. Another lash of the whip and the old man started forward. Turner fired.

The bullet struck the naked man in the top of the head. His scalp exploded. The man fell to his knees. Turner fired again. This shot hit the man just below the chin. His neck opened, and a stream of blood spilled out. The old man fell face forward in the doorway, his body holding the men's room door open. The thing behind him with the whip fell silent.

Turner ran forward. He grabbed the dead man's wrists and pulled him clear of the threshold. The bathroom door clanged shut.

"Help me," Turner said. Cleveland grabbed the man's right arm and helped Turner drag him across the restaurant. They dropped his body between tables nine and ten.

"Disaster averted. At least for the time being," Turner said, sliding the pistol back in its holster.

"Okay," Cleveland said, casting a watchful eye at the bathroom door. "I'm out of here."

He turned to exit the restaurant when Turner said, "We're safe now. Wait, so I can at least explain what happened."

Cleveland stopped. Despite the fear and confusion he felt, another emotion gripped him: curiosity.

He looked at the bathroom door again. "What the hell just happened?"

"Like I said before. Demons. Or at least one. Luckily, we contained it. See, it's a funny thing about demons -- they can't cross the first threshold without a human clearing the path. Lots of reasons why." He pointed at the old man. "This poor fellow was supposed to cross the threshold. I shot him before he could. Now the demon's locked away in the men's room."

As if listening, the demon bellowed a deep throaty snarl that shook the walls.

"Are you telling me that thing can't open the men's room door?"

"That's what I'm telling you." Turner paused, as if unsure how to proceed. "But it could still get out."

"How?" Cleveland wasn't sure he wanted to know.

"By summoning another person to cross the threshold. See, old man river here was a member of this world before he went into your bathroom and got sucked into hell to become a thresher."

"A thresher?"

"Short for threshold crosser. Weird how they're always naked."

"So where's the next thresher going to come from?" Cleveland asked.

"Anywhere," Turner said, touching his gun. "Might be me, might be you. Might be the next person to walk through that door."

"This is incredible," Cleveland said. "Fucking incredible."

"You could say that."

"So what is this, like your job? I mean, are you like part of a secret task force on demon control or some shit?"

Turner chilled Cleveland with a slight smile. "No, nothing so grand. I work with two other gentlemen. Our goal is to contain all demons before they get out of control."

"Out of control? Must not happen that often. I've never heard about an out of control demon on the six o'clock news"

"Sure you have. Ever heard of Osama Bin Laden? How about Hitler? See, once a demon successfully crosses the first threshold, then it clings to a carrier, eventually becoming one with the person, almost always resulting in massive destruction and totalitarian evil."

"Shit." Cleveland was speechless, considering the implications. "What about the police?"

"No good. We want to keep people away from the demon. The more people that are around, the greater chance it has of finding a compatible soul, a soul mate if you will."

"A soul mate?"

"Yeah, the demon can't cling to just anyone. See, evil needs evil. It takes a pretty dark soul to accept a threshold crossing demon. Wouldn't describe you would it? I mean, you sounded like you were pretty low down to fire this Donnie kid."

Cleveland thought about the look on Donnie's face. He'd been pretty hurt, but did that make Cleveland evil? He was pretty sure it didn't. "No, it doesn't describe me." Then, despite himself, he added, "I don't think."

"No, me either. I don't see it on you."

"See it on me?"

"Yeah, you can see these folks a mile away. The evil just oozes off them. Remember the kid in grammar school that always wanted to kill small animals? You know, pin the wings of a butterfly to the ground with tacks and watch the thing suffer. You usually can see it pretty quickly." Turner holstered his gun and sat down on his jacket.

"So what do we do?" Cleveland felt exhausted, like his mind had just stepped off a roller coaster ride—the one with loops and hairpin curves that left a person puking their cotton candy in the parking lot.

"We wait. There's only one way to banish a demon."

"And that would be?"

"Get the employee you fired back down here. Send him in the bathroom. Nine times out of ten, that's all it takes."

"So what's so special about Donnie?"

"Well, there are the folks like you and me. We fall in the middle. Ninety nine percent of the world is like us. We're flawed. We try to do the right thing most of the time, and sometimes we even succeed. We're capable of greatness and we're capable of plumbing the depths of depravity. But we're not good all the time, nor are we filled with pure hatred toward others either. See, the best I can figure is that it's all about balance. There's us. We're the majority. And then there's the other one percent. Half of those are made up of the Jeffrey Dahmners of the world. The Adolph Hitlers, the John Wayne Gacys. The other half are made up of people who have pure hearts, almost blameless in the eyes of God."

"Let me guess. Mother Teresa and all the saints?"

"Not all of them. Some of those so-called saints were less saintly than you and me. But that's not the point. The point is balance. There's us, the dumbfucks that can't do right to save our lives, but we wish we could. We balance each other out. Some of us continue to fuck up. Some of us become ministers or teachers. The other one percent has to balance too. The demons versus the angels, if you will."

Cleveland let out a sigh. He was scared. Whatever still lurked in the men's room had fallen silent for the moment, but it had sounded big, very big. And that whip... "So what if Donnie can't get the job done? I mean, you said it works nine times out of ten."

"True. I did say that" Turner pursed his lips and stared at the bathroom door. Cleveland waited for him to say more, but Turner stayed silent. His expression was grim.

Someone rapped on the front entrance. Turner jumped up, pulling his piece out.

The door opened.

"Shit. You didn't lock it back?" Turner aimed his pistol at a pretty blonde, soaked from the rain. He hair and face glistened with rainwater. She flashed them a bashful smile that changed to a frown when she saw Turner's gun.

"Not a good time, lady," Turner said slowly.

"Yeah," Cleveland said. "We're closed."

"I'm sorry," she said. "I just need to use the bathroom. It's an emergency."

"Lady," Turner said "You need to leave."

She smiled again. "Okay, sure I'll just go on down the road a little. Find another place."

"Sounds like a plan," Turner said.

She reached back for the door and froze. Slowly, she turned back to face them, a new look in her eyes. "You know, boys, the real reason I stopped in is because I'm horny as hell. If you'll let me in the men's room, I'll do whatever you want beforehand." She took a step forward and dropped one hand to her crotch and the other to her right breast. "I'll even let you both do me at the same time," she gasped.

"And then," Turner said, "after we've gotten our jollies, we both get eaten alive by what's in that bathroom. I think we'll pass on the sex." He cocked the gun and aimed it at her head. "Get the hell out, lady."

She shrieked at them and wheeled around. She ran hard at the bathroom door, diving headlong for it before two bullets entered her back, one on either side of her spine, dropping her to the floor in a lifeless heap.

The thing in the bathroom growled, and it sounded like thunder.

"I hate having to do that," Turner said, almost to himself, as he went over and grabbed her wrists and began pulling her away from the door. "Call your boy back. Tell him if he doesn't get down here pronto, you'll fire him again."

Cleveland didn't move. He couldn't peel his eyes off the two dead bodies in his restaurant.

"Move!" Turner said. He was already back at the door, twisting the lock tight. "Otherwise there'll be more. That demon's sending out a signal to anybody and everybody with a soul dark enough to listen. Somebody else will be by soon, or maybe even..." He trailed off.

"Maybe even what?"

"Never mind. Just get on the horn."

Cleveland opened his cell phone and dialed.

There was another knock at the door.

Turner's gun came back out, a blur of cold steel.

Another knock. Cleveland squinted, but could only make out a shadow behind the rain streaked glass. "You locked it, remember?"

Turner lowered the gun slightly. "It doesn't matter. When a demon calls, people will do anything to answer it. I doubt that glass will be much of an obstacle."

Another knock. Louder.

"It could be Donnie," Cleveland suggested

Turner nodded. "Or it could be somebody else I'll have to kill."

"Good point."

"Go to the door and see if it's your boy. Don't open it until you're sure, though"

Cleveland dragged his feet across the floor. He couldn't remember being so terrified... *And of what?* Even if it wasn't Donnie, he didn't have to let them in. Or did he? He suddenly felt an intense urge to open the door wide, to let whoever was out there in, and more, to shield them from Turner's inevitable bullets. He shook his head, trying to toss off these urges. They stuck. He came to the door and leaned against the glass.

"Call out to him," Turner said. "But don't open it until you're sure."

Cleveland nodded, even as he decided that opening the door quickly would be most effective. He gripped the handle hard and pulled.

"What the fuck!" Turner cried. "Shut the door, Walker! Shut the fucking door!"

Cleveland thought about shutting the door, but it was too late. A burly figure pushed through the door, knocking Cleveland to the ground. Cleveland looked up and saw a large man of Asian descent. He looked like a Sumo wrestler and wore a plain white t-shirt that hung down almost to his knees. He cast a baleful glance down at Cleveland and broke into a sprint toward the men's room.

No tricks this time, Cleveland thought. *And if he succeeds, it'll be my fault.*

Turner shouted at the man, but he kept running. He reached the door. Why hadn't Turner shot him yet? Cleveland rolled over and saw Turner struggling with his holster Somehow, his pistol had gotten wedged in his holster. He yanked it hard, but it wouldn't come out. Cleveland turned back over and saw that Mr. Sumo had pulled the door open wide. Inside, through the threshold, Cleveland could make out a scaly black hand, one crooked finger beckoning the large man inside. The nails were dark red.

At the exact moment Cleveland knew his death was imminent, he heard the sweetest sound he would ever hear: the deafening retort of Turner's pistol. The slug hit Sumo in the back of the neck. He fell forward, filling the doorway like a cork in a bottle of wine.

Cleveland watched as the hand snaked around the corner, revealing a spiky black arm. The hand clutched one of Mr. Sumo's big feet, and with a flick of its powerful wrist, jerked the heavy man through the threshold and into the men's room, leaving the door to swing shut with an empty thud.

##

After a few moments of silence, Turner said, "Demon talking to you?"

Cleveland still lay on the floor. He'd forgotten about his role in the large man's death. He sat up, shamed by what had happened. "I'm okay," he said. "It won't happen again."

Turner didn't speak.

"It won't happen again."

Turner nodded slowly.

"How'd you get the gun out?" Cleveland said, hoping to change the subject.

"I just took my holster off," he said, holding up the gun still in the holster.

"Good thinking."

Turner said, "It can use that dead guy."

"What?"

"Yeah. The demon can raise him. It'll take about thirty minutes. We'll have to find an axe. Only way to slay the undead is to cut their head off."

"You're kidding."

Turner flashed him a sharp look. "Don't question me anymore. Everything I tell you is the fucking truth. Got it?"

Cleveland swallowed. He was sweating. Something buzzed inside his ear. It sounded like... "I got it," he said firmly, hoping he could dismiss the sound in his head. The buzzing shrunk, but he was still dimly aware of it.

A cool breeze struck Cleveland. He whirled in time to see Donnie Tunnel walking through the door. He still wore that stupid Pizza Shack shirt. Did he sleep in it?

"Is this your boy, Walker?" Turner said. He held his holstered pistol in the air, aiming it at Donnie's head.

A strange thought came over Cleveland. He almost said, "No, never seen him." Perhaps he would have said this if not for the door swinging open again, and a small, pale woman entering the restaurant. She stood beside Donnie and glared at Turner.

"What's this?" she said. "Why are you pointing a gun at my son?"

Turner lowered the pistol to the table. "So it is him." He nodded to the woman, Donnie's mother. "Sorry, ma'am, but we have a situation on our hands."

"Well, we can leave," she said, taking Donnie's arm.

"No," Cleveland said. He found that he had to force the word through his larynx and out over his tongue. "Stay."

Donnie's mother looked over at Turner again and down to the holstered gun on the table.

"No, we'll go." She turned to open the door and Turner, quick as a cat, fired a warning over her head. It shattered the glass above the door. Donnie's mother shrieked, but did not go any further.

"Move away from the door," Turner said.

Minutes later, Turner had managed to tie Donnie's mother to a chair with his belt. She cried a lot. Turner looked very solemn.

Donnie stood there blankly. He didn't understand, and no one had bothered to explain it to him yet. Finally, Turner swung around and addressed Donnie. He had his pistol free from his holster now, and he waved it when he spoke.

"Look kid, I need you to do something for me." He paused, taking time to study Donnie closely. The open mouth, slumped posture, and unsuspicious eyes must have confirmed what Turner already suspected. He pushed on. "All you have to do to get your mother out of this chair and to get your job back is walk in that bathroom."

Donnie furrowed his brow. His eyes shaded with something between confusion and suspicion -- uncertainty, perhaps. "Why?" he asked.

Turner glanced at Cleveland as if to say, "Wanna help me here, or what?"

Cleveland's mind raced. He wanted to think of something, but thinking had become difficult, lately. The demon pried at his mind again like a criminal in the teeth of the night, picking at a lock. Would the lock hold until morning? Cleveland told himself it would. It had to.

Turner, visibly frustrated now, turned back to Donnie and brandished the gun. "Sorry kid, but I don't have to tell you why. Just get your ass in the bathroom or I'll shoot you." Turner spoke like he meant it, and Cleveland had no doubt that he did. A voice rattled around inside his head. *He's going to shoot you, too.*

No, he responded. *This is almost over. Donnie will finish it. Then I'll give him his job back and sell the place to first buyer. After that, I'll get the hell out of town and never come back.*

The voice came again louder, bolder: *He's going to shoot you tonight if you don't do something to stop him. He's the demon. Look at how many people he's killed already.*

Cleveland let his eyes drift to the other side of the restaurant where Turner had dragged the girl and the old man. How many had he shot? There was the naked man, and then the girl, and after that, there was Mr. Sumo. Three in less than an hour.

And Donnie will be four, the voice just outside the door of his mind said. *And mother makes five. And...*

Stop it, Cleveland said. *No one else dies.*

He forced his attention back on Donnie. The boy's mother screamed at the top of her lungs, but Donnie didn't seem to notice.

The door swung shut behind him. His mother stopped screaming and resumed crying.

Cleveland closed his eyes. The thief was back. This time he brought his tools. He poked and prodded and twisted at the threshold to Cleveland's mind, and soon Cleveland found himself locked in a struggle of wills: his own against the demon's. It felt like a thousand little voices urged him to go in the bathroom and take Donnie Tunnel's watermelon head and crack it over the nearest porcelain sink. His foot slid toward the door. He grabbed his knee with both hands, guiding his leg back in place again.

Riches and power and riches and power for just a moment of your time serve me. The reasoning had stopped. The demon was desperate now. Cleveland knew this, but it didn't make his battle any easier. The voices were so persuasive. They sounded so real. *Twist his neck in two. Slam his head against the hard stone wall. Like a cantaloupe. Ever seen a cantaloupe on concrete? Riches. Power. Sex.* On and on the chorus went in his head. He remembered the cross hanging from his neck and he clutched it. He squeezed it hard. The voices dimmed. His mind cleared long enough to look around. He saw Donnie's mom sitting in the chair, crying. Turner stood over her, holding his pistol, trying to soothe her with soft words.

In the bathroom, Donnie wailed. It was a long, mournful sound like foghorn on a deep dark night or the howl of three-legged dog whose hard life had been matched only by its harder death. It sent a melancholy into Cleveland so deep that it seemed to be bottomless; all of his life's hopes and dreams and optimism fell into that melancholy. When the long sound ceased, the hole sealed shut, trapping all of those things deep within him. He had just enough time to wonder if he'd ever get them back when he heard Turner's voice.

"He was pure of heart, bless him."

Cleveland turned away from the bathroom and saw Turner had backed up to the far side of the room. He was in the corner of booth number nine, pointing the pistol at Donnie's mother.

Cleveland said, "You act like he's dead."

"He is." Turner had reached a new level of grimness. His jaw was set so hard that it seemed a great effort for him to speak.

"But you just said he was pure of soul."

"He was." Turner kept the gun pointed at Donnie's mother. "Look," he said. "I couldn't tell you everything. These demons are a pain in the ass to kill. Remember earlier when I talked about balance?"

"Yeah."

"Well, that's what happened. They cancelled each other out."

Cleveland felt his eyes well up with tears. "Then why are you still pointing the gun at her," he said.

Turner shook his head. "The demons dead, but there's still a residue of evil---"

The men's room door flew off its hinges. Cleveland ducked, and it sailed over his head shattering glass on the other side of the restaurant. There was a great intake of air and a noise that sounded like a zipper. A dirty, filmy thing, like bacteria viewed under a microscope, floated through the threshold. It buzzed like a throng of bumblebees. Donnie's mother, her head cradled in her hands, never saw it snake up her ass, shimmy her spinal cord, and slither around her neck into her open mouth.

Turner waited until she'd inhaled it all before firing. One shot was all it took. The bullet hit her between the eyes, knocking her chair over. She landed on the floor with a heavy thud.

Cleveland no longer tried to hold back his tears. This was unthinkable. But now at least it was over. He turned back to Turner.

Turner still held his pistol.

"It's over, right?"

Turner looked at his pistol and said nothing.

"The residue is gone, right?"

"Yeah," Turner said. "It's gone."

Cleveland glanced at Donnie's mother again. Five dead bodies and one dead demon.

"You call this balance?"

"Yeah. I didn't want to tell you everything involved in killing a demon because I thought you might get queasy. But the hardest part is over now." Turner rotated the pistol in his hand, studying it.

"So what do we tell the police?" Cleveland said, taking his eyes away from Donnie's mother at last. He wanted to go into the bathroom and see what remained of Donnie. Would there be a demon carcass? He thought of the long, spiked black arm and shivered.

Suddenly the room seemed too quiet. Cleveland sensed something behind him. A fly? No, bees. A wet mist stroked the back of his neck. He turned and saw through a vapor, Turner standing up, holding the pistol in both hands, aiming it at Cleveland's head.

"I'm sorry, Walker. You know I wish I didn't have to kill any of you, but it's my job." He cocked the pistol.

Cleveland was too shocked to speak. Not only because Turner was about to kill him, but also because of the shock his mind was experiencing. He realized at once that the evil had entered him just as it had Donnie's mother. He mind-hiccupped, going blank for a second. When he regained consciousness, he felt cold and slimy. He felt like running. He turned and sprinted for the door.

Something slammed into his back and he fell to his knees. He heard Turner speaking: "If you can still hear me, Walker, I'm sorry. Rule of thumb is that you have to kill a demon twice. Donnie and the mother should have been enough. Sometimes demons are stubborn though. Tough luck, Walker. You seemed like a good enough guy. You know, I really hate this part of the job, but I can't let you live. You did a good job, Walker, but now you're fired."

James Turner pulled the trigger again.

A short time later, Turner's cell phone rang.

"Turner here."

"James, it's Frank. Everything okay?"

Turner sighed. "Situation contained. Threat eliminated."

"Good. How many?"

Turner counted the bodies. "Six."

"Powerful bastard."

"Yeah."

Frank was silent for a moment.

"What do you have?" Turner said.

"A red eye flight to Paris, James. A grocery store with a toilet that won't flush."

Turner made a mental note of the flight time, clicked off his cell phone, and reloaded his gun.

Insensitivity

by Sunil Sadanand

"So things are going well then, Dennis?" the doctor asks. He looks at my chart, looks down at me, nods and smiles.

"Yeah, things are going all right."

"So you're gaining some feeling back, then? Some sensation?"

"In a manner of speaking."

"We have a very high success rate with this procedure. But the length of time it takes to heal is entirely dependent upon the nature of the injury. A C-3 patient, for example, will naturally take a longer road to recovery than say a T-6 or an L-1."

"I know. You don't have to placate me," I say even though we both know he damn well better placate me, because my insurance policy doesn't cover embryonic transplant surgery, so when I come into this office, it better be all smiles, platitudes and fucking placations.

"I'm not trying to placate you, Dennis," he says. "I just want you to stay positive. We have seen some regeneration -- not at the optimal growth level of one centimeter a week, but close to that -- definitely close. With continued treatment, and transplantations every two weeks, I'm optimistic about your chances."

"Good," I reply. "Glad to hear you're optimistic. Because I am, too, doctor. I am, too."

He nods and puts his hands behind his back and smiles. His chubby face is getting red again. It's almost as if he's embarrassed about what he has to do next.

"So...whenever you're ready," he says.

"Right. I'm ready now."

He nods and then he and the nurse move to help me out of my chair and into the bed. They lay me flat on my stomach. I bury my face into the pillow and wait.

Insensitivity

And I'm still waiting.

I try to visualize this doctor, pudgy little man, white beard, pink face, eyes like slits, holding up that large, dripping syringe, filled with live embryonic cells extracted from a blue shark.

I'm waiting for that little pop that sounds out when he pokes it right through my partially transected spine.

"I want to talk to you about these cuts and burns, Dennis."

"Just give me the shot. We can talk about them later."

Pop.

And I'm still waiting.

For anything now.

A little pressure. An involuntary muscle spasm. A twitch -- the faintest echo of a tactile sensation as that needle burrows its way into the coiled knot of severed nerves and broken sensory pathways.

But there's nothing. Everything is gone down there. I'm what they call a 'complete.' Can't feel a goddamn thing below the injury site, where that needle now pumps little shark embryos through crushed bone, bullet fragments, cysts, and husks of scar tissue, withered and atrophied, bereft of nutrients and precious spinal fluid.

And five minutes later, he says, Okay Dennis, I'll see you in a couple of weeks.

And then I tell him I need a refill on my prescription.

And then he says, I don't know, those were only supposed to be for temporary usage, and I'm thinking this guy must be out of his fucking gourd if he thinks he's not going to write a prescription for me when I need one -- with all the money I'm dishing out to this clinic.

Yeah right, buddy. Give me some more of those fucking pills.

So he shakes his head, looks to the ground and says I don't know one more time and sighs.

"Come on, Doc."

He stands there a little while longer and rips a piece of paper off a pad and scrawls out a prescription for oxicodones, still shaking his goddamn head, muttering something about how this is the last time he'll do this for me.

"Thanks, pal," I tell him.

"Take care, Dennis." And then he waddles his way out of there with his nurse following close behind him.

##

"Hey, Dennis."

"Hey, Charissa."

Now it's nine o'clock and I'm at my desk in the wonderful, equal opportunity financial institution called Global Consulting.

This is what I do to earn money. I sit in a cubicle with a flat screen computer and a cold-call list sitting on my desk. I go through the list and disturb people at their homes. I disturb people while they eat dinner. I disturb mothers as they scold their children. I disturb children while they watch television. I disturb men while they masturbate. Fuck them, I haven't been able to whack the plant in seven years, I don't have a family and I hate kids. So I can't really sympathize. When they answer the phone, I recite a pitch. This is what I say:

"Mr. or Mrs. So and So, I'm sorry to bother you, but I have great news. We're conducting a survey that will only take a few minutes of your time and might save you a tremendous amount of money on your mortgage payments."

Ninety percent of the time I hear a click and a dial tone before I get half way through my spiel. Some people listen to the whole thing and then tell me to fuck off before they hang up. About three percent of them are actually willing to take the "survey." But it's not actually a survey. I'm just trying to get their social security number. I'm trying to sell them a mortgage.

"So how was your appointment with the doctor?" Charissa asks me.

The woman standing above my desk? Well, she is the reason I get up every morning. She looks down at me with eyes so blue you'd think they might have been dabbed across her face with a brush soaked in fluorescent paint. Her skin is like polished porcelain. Her hair is long and black and silky and today she wears it loose, and if she was my girlfriend, I would have her wear it like that every day.

"Same as always," I tell her.

She smiles and I feel butterflies flapping around in my stomach. Her perfume drifts down, floods my nostrils and its effect is like a shot of morphine -- instantly hypnotic and intoxicating.

"No new feelings yet?"

"Feeling is a highly subjective term."

"What's up, Dennis?"

Ah, and here comes the black cloud that hangs over me.

Clint stands next to Charissa, gently puts his hand on her shoulder and kisses her cheek. She blushes, smiles and looks away coyly, and now the butterflies in my stomach wither, rot and convulse against my intestinal walls, dying slowly. I feel a sinking feeling down there and this is the closest thing I've had to pain in seven years.

And guess what, pal.

It hurts.

Like a motherfucker.

"Hey, gorgeous. Have lunch with me today?"

"Sure," she says.

"Good. I'll see you later."

And then he walks away.

Fucking Clint.

Six foot three, young, tanned, blonde, steely gray eyes, muscles within muscles, which he has been forging in his expensive health club for most of his adult life.

Worst of all? He's the current object of my Reason For Living's affection. He's the best salesmen in our brokerage. He makes about fifteen thousand dollars a month, five thousand more dollars than me -- the second best salesman in our firm. I know this because every time one of us closes a deal, our names go up on the board. Our office manager seems to think that this promotes healthy competition. Healthy competition, my ass. All it does is make us hate each other. Clint drives a beamer and has a Rolex. I hate him the way an albino might hate the sunlight.

Charissa turns back to me and says, "Don't worry, honey. I'm sure you'll start feeling again soon. Just stick with the program. Don't lose faith."

She walks away and leaves me alone at my desk and I'm wondering how it's possible that I can love this woman and desire her so much even though my dick can't even get hard. Her perfume still lingers in the air, and I close my eyes and attempt to suck in every last droplet of moisture.

It's pure affection, I realize. Nothing sexual.

I open my eyes, pick up the phone and call one of the names on my cold-call list.

Federico Hernandez. 188th Street, Washington Heights.

The phone rings three times.

On the third ring, "Allo?"

"Mr. Hernandez!" I say. "Sorry to disturb you this evening but I have great news! We're conducting a survey that will only take a few minutes of your time and might save you a tremendous amount of money on your mortgage payments."

Tremendous.

Gotta love that word.

Silence.

"Mr. Hernandez?"

"Fuck off, puta."

Click.

##

Everyone has at least one of them.

A pivotal turning point in their lives; the one that changes everything.

Mine was seven years ago on July 23rd.

I left my favorite bar on Third Avenue and headed over to the grocery store to buy a loaf of bread and some cold cuts. Back then I was this rich, cocky, Jewish kid from the suburbs who thought he had the world by the balls.

The truth was, I was miserable then, too, but I just didn't know it. I was doing really well in my job, I had a girlfriend with a great body and the IQ of a Down syndrome-afflicted bunny rabbit, a dog named Chester and a nice little bachelor pad on the Upper West Side.

But I was missing something. I couldn't be happy. Despite the fact that I had things that most guys can only dream of having, there was this empty hole in my life that I didn't know how to fill. A void. I was depressed in the truest sense of the word.

I just wasn't aware of it.

So anyway, I go into the supermarket, pretty hammered, and I grab a loaf of bread and some Virginia ham, and then I head on over to the express line and see this black kid holding a .38 caliber snub-nosed pistol to this little old white lady's head.

"Hurry the fuck up," he says through gritted teeth. "I'll blow your brains all over the counter."

And what does my drunk ass do? Turn around and run? Scream for help? Hide behind a stack of cereal boxes?

Nah.

I say, "Hey man, leave her alone."

The big fucking hero, over here.

So the kid turns around and his eyes are red-rimmed and he looks at me and maybe he sees some privileged white asshole, the kind that has looked down on him all of his life; the kind that got everything handed to him on a silver platter, the kind of pompous, well-dressed honkey that has always kept him down and now, even now -- even though he had a gun in his hand -- this motherfucker still has the audacity to tell him what to do, like maybe he owned him or something.

So without saying a word, the kid raises that hand cannon and shoots three times.

Bang, bang, bang.

The explosion drowns out all the other sounds and leaves my ears ringing for the next seven years, and I feel like I've been hit in the chest by a cinder block and there's this horrible burning sensation and I'm falling.

Forever.

Insensitivity

There was pain. The worst pain I've ever felt in my life.

And the best pain I ever felt... that too.

And what was I thinking once I crumpled to the ground?

I'm too young to die? God please spare my life? Give me another chance?

Nope.

I'm thinking, thanks, pal. I'm thinking, thanks a million. I needed that. I really fucking did.

##

Wednesday night in New York City means that it's time for my weekly night on the town.

And what do I do on Wednesday nights?

Catch a Broadway Show? Go out to a nice restaurant? Have drinks at the Marriot Marquis?

Nah.

I go to this little dive over on Second Avenue between Thirteenth and Fourteenth Street. It's called the Flesh Theatre; it's where fellow perverts and sadomasochists get together; where house performers with names like Lady Malice and Mistress Sophia parade around in leather outfits and simulate acts of torture and domination onstage. The bartenders here call me the wheelchair guy behind my back and Dennis to my face. I'm the only real freak in here, and I think they're just jealous. I didn't choose the life of an outcast; it was thrust upon me. I'm a freak by nature, and they're freaks by choice. There's a difference.

So it's always dimly lit in here and tattooed mutants with multiple piercings and faces like cadavers drift through the stage fog like graveyard revenants. I'm at the bar sipping on a coke -- I can't drink alcohol as it interferes with the salad of antidepressants and sleeping pills that currently keep me from rolling my ass into the East River.

The music is Gothic/techno trash with synthesized keyboard sounds mingled with a pulsing bass drum. I hate it the way a guy with no hands hates an unexpected hard on.

Just have to try and will it away...

"On time as usual. Good boy."

"I'm Mr. Punctuality."

"Buy me a drink."

"Usual?"

"Yes."

"Excuse me," I say to the large, bald bartender with a ring through his septum. "Can you get the young lady here a Cosmopolitan, no ice?"

He nods and saunters off.

I turn to my right.

Monica is dressed in her usual dominatrix get up. She has her pretty black face painted white and more rings in her cheeks, eyebrows, ears, nose and chin than a fisherman's tackle box. She is wearing a black leather body suit with stiletto heels that add about two inches to her already formidable six-foot-three stature.

The bartender places the drink in front of her and tells her it's on the house. Not like she was going to pay for it anyway. Monica is a regular in the Flesh Theatre. Usually she 'performs' onstage with Lady Malice and company. But tonight she's mine.

She downs that loathsome concoction in two gulps along with a couple of Benzedrines.

I reach into my pocket, pull out a check for two thousand dollars and place it on the bar. She grabs the check and slips it into her purse (yeah, she's got a fucking Louis Vuitton bag with that outfit, doesn't get more New York than that, pal) and then she offers me a wink.

"Ready when you are," she says.

"Right. I'm ready now."

My Mistress stands over me, a shadow in the darkness.

She raises a gloved hand in front of my face to show me what she's holding. It's a razor.

"Now lay very still," she says with her eyes narrowing cruelly, her voice thick with lust and something else. She's a sick puppy, my Mistress.

Sick, of course, being a highly subjective term.

"Hurt me," I tell her.

She puts the razor against my chest, presses lightly, and then slides it down. Slowly.

Crimson wells up and dribbles down my chest tracing the path of the razor. The scars are too many to count. Scabbed, blistered, and oozing, they crisscross down my chest and legs, corrugating my flesh like little chasms.

"How does that feel?" she asks.

"It doesn't."

"Lower?"

"And deeper."

She wipes off the razor and soaks it in iodine.

"Prop my head up please, Mistress," I tell her. "I want to see it."

She helps me into an upright seated position.

She presses the razor into my inner thigh, running the blade along a wound that has only just begun to scab over. Pus mingled with blood trickles down and soaks my bed sheets. The scab crackles as it comes apart like a piece of paper tearing.

"I'm running out of space here," she mutters.

"Use something different."

She nods and then reaches into her purse and pulls out a cigarette and a lighter. She lights the cigarette and blows smoke into my face. I watch her as she presses the burning ember into the flesh above my knee.

I close my eyes...

...and think of Charissa.

I visualize her and Clint lying in bed together. There's nothing perverse or sexual about my fantasy.

Pure affection.

They laugh and hold each other's hands. He runs his hand through her long black hair. He gently brushes her cheek with his finger. He kisses her forehead and she smiles.

My stomach starts sinking. I imagine her walking down Fifth Avenue—too beautiful to be out in the world. I imagine how every man she passes falls in love. I imagine how the doorman loves her and the concierge and the guy who lives across from her and everyone who brushes by her and everyone who smells that perfume; how they are intoxicated, starving for her. Everyone in the office loves her. Everyone around her imagines that they'll have a shot at her, that once in a lifetime golden opportunity that will never happen, and no matter how unrealistic their fantasies are, and no matter how ugly some of these guys might be, their chances at having her are a hundred times better than mine will ever be.

"I love you, Clint," she says.

"I love you, Charissa"

They kiss and pull the covers over each other, and my stomach clenches and sinks down into my groin. I love her and I'll never have her and Clint will. He's probably having her right now.

And then...

##

"Christ."

"What? What is it?" Monica asks. The sadistic bitch is sweating and breathing heavy and looks like she has just awakened from a deep trance. She has removed her panties and is fingering herself while she burns me with the cigarette.

I look down at my leg and a fresh sore is centered in a perfect circle of burn marks.

"Christ," I repeat, wiping the sweat that has suddenly appeared on my brow.

"What is it, Dennis?"

I run my hand over the sore and wince.

"What's wrong?"

I look at her and smile, even as my eyes well with tears.

We both laugh when we see my penis suddenly rise up, harden, shudder and then spurt out a stream of jizz, some of which hits her chin.

"It burns," I tell her, laughing and crying and jizzing all at once. "It burns."

"See, see! I knew you'd start making progress."

"You were right, doctor."

"Pretty soon you'll be jogging to work every morning."

We both have a laugh.

The doctor sits down, frowns, and then looks at me with what he probably thinks is a stern expression.

"So, are you ready to talk about..."

"No. Look Doc, my therapist and I are discussing this in private and it's not a topic I'm ready to talk about outside of our sessions just yet."

"Okay, I see."

He nods, clears his throat, taps his foot, looks away, looks down at his chart, and then we share a brief, awkward silence.

"Well," he says after a few moments. "I'm glad you are still attending psychotherapy, Dennis. You are now on the road to recovery."

"I'm gonna need more of those pills, doctor. The antidepressants aren't enough these days."

"Now, Dennis," he says taking off his glasses and shaking his head.

"Last time, doctor," I say holding up my palm. "I promise. After today, I'll never ask you for another prescription again."

"You promise?"

"When have I ever promised you this before?"

"Never again?"

"Never."

"This is the last time. After this, never again!"

"Sure."

##

Clint whispers something in Charissa's ear, and she giggles before pushing him away. He tries to grab her and she moves away and wags her finger at him.

Naughty boy.

I turn to my cold call sheet and grab the phone. I'm on a roll this morning. I've been in the office for an hour and I've got three social security numbers; all of them have good credit scores, all of them are stuck in high-interest mortgages, and all of them are looking to refinance their homes.

Bang, bang, bang.

"Hey Dennis, slow down," Clint says walking up to me and putting a hand on my shoulder.

Even this asshole can't ruin my mood today. I think about how easily I could reach out and just rip his arm right out of its socket, and then I feel a little better.

"Save some for the rest of us, tiger," he adds.

I force a smile and I guess something about it makes him uneasy because he walks away without another word.

"Hey, Dennis."

"Hey love," I say. My heart races, my stomach clenches. She's wearing my favorite black dress and her hair smells like cinnamon. Today is a day for golden opportunities.

"Wow, you look great, Dennis," she says. "Did you do something different?"

"I feel great."

"How's the therapy going?"

"I think it's working."

"Really?" she asks genuinely interested. Did I tell you she's an angel?

"I'm getting some feeling back in my legs," I tell her. "Not much, but it's a start."

"That's wonderful, Dennis!"

"Yeah. Look, I'm about to go get a coffee. You wanna come along?"

"Uh..." she laughs and shakes her head.

"Come on, you're the only one in this office who doesn't look at me like I'm a half crushed animal on the side of the road. Let me buy you a coffee and celebrate my little breakthrough."

"No one looks at you like that, Dennis."

"Well then just give a lonely old cripple the company of a pretty girl."

She smiles and shakes her head.

"You're terrible," she says. "All right, let me just get my purse."

"Great. I'll be in the car."

##

The thing about pain, when it's properly distributed, in all its forms -- emotional, spiritual, physical -- is that it affects all of your senses simultaneously. When it's pure, you can taste it, smell it, feel it, see it, touch it; it's yours and it's personal and no one understands it but you. In this regard, it's not much different from pleasure.

##

"Ready."

"Almost, Mistress. Almost."

"She's beautiful."

"I know. I love her."

Silence.

"Her body is flawless. Not a single blemish."

"I know. She's my angel."

"Will she be awake soon?"

"Give it a few more minutes, those sleeping pills are pretty potent."

"Must be. She's been out for a while now."

"She's moving."

##

After all, the same chemical signals responsible for letting your body know it is in pain are the same ones responsible for letting you know when you are feeling pleasure. Same endorphins, same neurotransmitters, the same nerve receptors receiving the signals and sensations. The same mechanism allows you to process the stimuli -- only the interpretation is different.

Insensitivity

"Dennis? Dennis, what happened? Dennis, who is she, Dennis?"

"Start with the razor?"

"What is she saying? What did you do to me? Dennis, where am I? Somebody help me!"

"Should I gag her?"

"No," I say. "I want her to tell me..."

##

I don't know.

##

"So the razor, then? "

"No, use a cigarette."

"No Dennis, tell her to stop, please..."

##

Maybe I'm just insensitive.

##

"Go ahead, darling. Tell me how it burns."

THE MOTHER

by jOhn lOverO

The sign was plain white paper and black Sharpie medium-point marker. "Missing Child: 16 years old - 777-8762".

And that was all. No description, no details, not even a picture. A disgrace to milk cartons everywhere. Ed saw it plastered to the men's room door at his favorite bar. In fact, he saw it so many times he finally scrawled the number on his forearm so he could call it when he got home.

It would offer him such unique entertainment.

The woman who answered the phone whispered so lightly he couldn't make out a word. She cried, whimpered, sobbed, and retched in tiny squeaks, but made no attempt at clarity, despite Ed's insistence. Enraged, he shouted into the phone. Silence followed, the receiver going cold on his ear. Eventually the woman spoke in her tiny, worried voice.

"My daughter is gone. And I know you have her...please, I won't tell anyone...just tell me where she is...please..."

Ed slammed the phone down and backed away from it. What the hell was that all about? Some freakshow, no doubt, a lonely old lady with nobody to gum at night leaves up a sign to entice random callers.

Ed was a telemarketer. He knew all about the old farts who took up his time on the phone talking about their children who lived far away and never called instead of talking about how they could take advantage of 2.8% financing for the next eight months. His job was hard enough without lonely people talking his ear off and not refinancing their house.

But the woman on the phone was different. Maybe she was crazy enough to not even have any kids outside of her imagination. Maybe she got the idea from an episode of Magnum PI. At least the old boogers not buying his telemarketer schmeal had families to talk about; this woman was severely compensating.

He blew it off.

The Mother

It took a few days of convincing himself, but halfway through a desolate workout at the sweaty gym, he decided to try again. The same woman, still very distressed, answered.

"Please...don't hurt her, she's all I've got..."

"Listen, lady. What's your name?"

"She didn't tell you?"

"Who?"

"Clarissa... my little girl."

"Look, I just want to know your name."

"Grenda."

"Okay, Grenda. I want you to listen to me. I do not have your daughter. The sign---"

"Damn the sign! I just want her back."

He moved the phone nervously to his other ear and spoke swiftly, trying to get a few important words in to gain a foothold in the conversation.

"I understand that, but I need more information."

"Are you the police?"

"What? No."

"Oh thank god, I'm sure you'd kill her if I'd talked to the police."

"What are you talking about?"

"Please don't kill her. I swear I didn't talk to the police."

"I don't want to kill her."

"Have you raped her?"

"Oh god, lady. NO! I don't even know her, I don't have her, I'm just trying---"

"You don't have my daughter?"

"No."

And the phone went dead. He looked up to see a line of gym-goers staring at him, waiting to use the phone. A man twice his size loomed over him, even the man's "mom" tattoo looked like it could kick Ed's ass.

"There's a two minute limit on that phone, pal," the big man said.

Ed handed it over and walked away. He went about his workout, only attending the gym once a week because he had to pay for it another two years, three months, two weeks and four days. As he pressed the unforgiving bar over his throat, the same hysterical mom voice counted the reps out in his mind.

After the workout, he sat in the car and smoked a cigarette. The phone number was still on his forearm. He couldn't get away from it throughout the workout. Every upper body exercise he wasted time on gave him a view of the number. He had it memorized.

What really got to him was that she had the nerve to hang up on him. Here he was trying to help, and she cut him off. Anybody else would have just hung up on her crazy ass after the first phone call. Most would have called the cuckoo squad with the big nets and jackets with heavy strings.

He drove to his bar and went directly to the payphone in the back by the men's room door. The sign was still there, looking out of place amidst the half-peeled pin-ups and dried beer labels. As he dialed the number, a warm smell of rot wafted out of the men's room.

"Please..."

"Shut up and listen, lady. I got your daughter."

The phone was silent except for the buzz of the telephone line, somehow louder than before.

"You there? Cuz if you ain't there, I'm hanging up forever."

"I'm here."

"Good. Listen up. I want the following items in one big bag. You bring two bags, I never call again. Got it?"

"Yes. Is she okay?"

"Wha -- yeah, she's fine. This is what I want. Write it down." He held the phone away from his ear and stifled a huge laugh. He pounded a quick shot and went back to the phone.

"I want a large sausage and eyeball pizza from Aldos on the corner of 5th and Walnut, a pair of men's Goldtoe socks, a bag of cat hair, and a small chalkboard with your address on it. Got it?"

She repeated everything back the moment he finished speaking. Her voice was brighter, almost shrill with either excitement or fear, Ed couldn't tell which.

"Let me speak to her please...just for a second."

"Not today. You make the drop first, and then you talk to her."

"I just need to know if she's okay, please!"

"No. I said---"

"I'm BEGGING YOU, sir, for the sake of my sanity."

"Sanity, woman you are out of your---"

"DAMMIT I WANT TO SPEAK TO MY DAUGHTER NOW!!!" She shrieked at him in a voice that sounded like a mountain lion with a fishhook in its balls.

He hissed into the phone, careful so no one would hear. "Don't you fucking curse at me, bitch I've got your damn daughter, and if you wanna see her..."

"NO. You let me speak to her now or so help me I will rip out your heart and consume it in front of

you!"

"You don't know---"

"No, you don't know. I've killed thousands like you, better than you. I've scooped brains out of their heads, violated them with thick branches, I've eaten men's genitalia in front of their emasculated, enslaved yet still living bodies, and I've broken legions...legions of men better than you."

His ear was red from pressing the phone too tight against it. His hands went a pale white as the blood rushed out of them. Ed hung up the phone.

And immediately it rang again.

He backed away from it. He looked to the sign, hanging there innocently. The door opened and a massive man in a painter's uniform came out of the bathroom, adjusting his sloppy white overalls. He answered the phone. Ed lifted a hand to stop him, but he answered anyway. He listened for a moment, looked at Ed, and then listened for another moment.

When he hung up the phone, the painter walked right up to Ed, smelling of turpentine, canvas, and cigars. His breath made Ed gag.

"Why don't we have a drink or five? I'm buying." He had a deep, rusty voice like an old cowboy.

"I don't think so," Ed said.

"I don't care if you don't think so, I ain't asking. Sit down." Ed sat down.

"Whadd'ya drinking Ed? You a whiskey man? A beer fella? What is it?"

"Well, if you're buying, I like Scotch. Black Label."

"Black Label it is." The painter dropped a hundred on the bar. "As much as that will get us, ma'am."

"Who are you?" Ed asked.

"I don't know. I never met me before tonight." He chuckled at that. "Not important who I am. I wanna talk about you. What do you do?"

"I'm a telemarketer."

"Well, ain't that something. That what you set out to do, partner?" The bartender opened a bottle and left two glasses. The painter poured two glasses to the rim and handed one to Ed.

"No. I went to school I wanted my own business."

"And what would that be?"

"Toy store, you know, custom made toys. High dollar stuff, like the crap I never got as a kid. You need money to do that kind of thing, though."

"I'm sorry to hear that, I really am. Do you have parents, Ed?"

Ed gulped his drink.

"Why are you asking me this? Who the hell are you? What did she tell you on the phone?"

The painter smiled, his stubbly face stretched and worn. "She...she wants to know about your parents. About your mother."

"My father lives in Cleveland with another family. He's sixty years old and has twelve grandkids. My mother's been living in the dirt for thirty some years now."

The painter winced and ran his paint-speckled fingers across his wrinkled eyes.

"Well damn, Ed. I didn't know."

"Car accident. I survived because I was in a car seat. My mom went through the windshield. Later on, my dad told me she left a bloody streak on the pavement a hundred feet in front of the car. He told me that on my 18th birthday. He left the next day."

The painter capped the scotch bottle and rolled it to Ed. He got off the barstool and put a hand on Ed's shoulder.

"I am sorry. Nobody should be without a mother."

And with that the painter walked away.

After finishing most of the Scotch, Ed walked home and tried to forget everything. He knew it was futile if a bottle of Black Label couldn't cover his memories, but a walk wouldn't kill him.

When he arrived home, his front door was kicked in, the stainless steel deadbolt so much scrap metal on the floor, and the heavy door split in several places. When he pushed the door open it fell to the ground in three separate chunks.

Whatever had burst through the front door had cut a swath through the living room and into the dining room. It was dark except for a light in the kitchen on the far end of the apartment. The sofa looked like it had been through a trash compactor. The air was thick with gypsum dust and debris.

There was a large black bag on the kitchen table. The scotch abandoned him, filtering itself through his liver to avoid being a part of this discovery. He approached it slowly.

The pizza box was the first item he had asked for and the first item he pulled out of the bag. Sure enough, the sausage pizza was peppered with eyeballs. He tossed it off the table, afraid to look at it.

He found the men's socks with feet still in them. The bag of cat hair was full of dead cats. He shoved everything back into the bag and tied it shut. He hefted it over his shoulder and headed out the door.

His body heaved in pain from the hangover and shock at the gory findings, making it so that he couldn't go far. He stuffed the bag into the complex dumpster and went back home.

His phone was ringing.

He stood outside the apartment, listening to the phone sound like some distant cricket playing a death song on its hind legs for him. Somehow he had messed up like he had never messed up before. And now he was going to pay for it.

It continued to ring. Compelled, he went inside and moved through the darkness toward the phone. His muscles twitched under his cold skin, his breath came in gasps. He was crying. Snot ran down his nose. It rang again.

And again. And again.

He picked up the phone and it almost slipped from his clammy hand. He couldn't bring himself to say hello.

"*You don't have my daughter do you?*" The woman's voice was heavy, but calm.

He couldn't answer; he was too afraid.

"*Please, just be honest with me. Do you know where my daughter is? Do I have a daughter?*"

"I... I don't know."

"*I didn't think so. You know, I try so hard, I miss her so much. You made me terribly angry. I haven't been that angry in centuries. Not since...well, when I get angry I see things how they really are.*"

She paused, and Ed gulped air and swallowed.

"*I don't have a daughter. I never did. But I'm so old, so old, I spent so many years alone thinking about a little girl of my own to love and cherish and nurture and teach and hold. But I am the only one of my kind, and when I'm gone, you will be the only one who will know I ever existed. Well, there's a painter who may have some dreams about me. I wish you could have known me a long time ago, before I got so old. I could do such wonderful things. I could have been a good mother to you as well. I still could be, but I'm afraid I've ruined that with my temper, haven't I? I'm so sorry. Please, find some way to forgive me. I'll leave you now. Please, take down the sign you found. It's the only one left. I wish to cause no further harm. Good luck to you.*"

Ed listened until he passed out with the receiver pressed against his ear. He slept deeply, full of dreams he wouldn't remember.

The next day, he took a cab to his favorite bar and peeled the sign off the men's room door. He tore it up and burned the little pieces in an ash tray. He ordered a club soda and a cheeseburger.

When he finished eating, he walked over to the phone and dialed a familiar number.

A Violent Descent into Livid Territories

by Esteban Silvani

Ten more minutes and Frank was to shut down his notebook, hit the lights, lock up and head out the door. Having sat on his duff all day putting together a comprehensive quote for a business insurance policy on Chambers, Inc., whom he'd been fighting to do business with for years, he was ready to get home to that crock pot and a cold one.

This project had been much more desirable than anything among yesterday's chain of events. Yesterday seemed like hell; the girls had been out of the office, and taking call after call from pathetic late-payers, crusty lien holders, and obnoxious nickel-and-dimers had taken its toll. Today, locked away in his office adorned with football helmets and trophies, Frank had concocted number games on big accounts, a task which soothed the psyche so much better.

Frank was about to click the SHUT DOWN option when the telephone suddenly pierced through the monotony.

One phone call won't hurt.

"Good afternoon...evening rather, this is Frank McGraw."

"Hey Frank, this is Mitchell Stevenson."

Frank forced a chuckle, pretended to be a go-lucky guy and leaned back in his plush office chair.

"Mitchell," he schmoozed, "Buddy, what's going on? Déja vu, man, I was just thinking about you, wondering where you've been. I was just about to check the obituary for your name. What's new?"

A silence ensued from the other end. Frank leaned forward.

"Hello, Mitchell, you still there?"

Frank thought he heard sobbing.

"I'm sorry, it...it's been a hellacious day."

"I hear you, man. Been swamped here myself. So, what you got, buddy?"

"Uhm...could you check my auto policy and tell me what coverage I have, please?"

Frank crunched his round, good 'ol boy features and obligingly brought up the agency's business book on the screen.

"Let me pull that puppy up here, it'll be just a sec."

"No problem," Mitchell responded with a slight trace of indecision.

Trained to probe and discourage possible claims to avoid unfavorable numbers in the loss-ratio column, Frank put on his detective cap.

"Is everything okay, Mitchell?"

"Everything's fine, just fine. I just wanted to know because I'm trying to evaluate all my expenses, y'know. My oldest is graduating from Barkersville come May and---"

"Ah, gonna be a college boy, egh? Can't say I blame you. I've got nieces and nephews; believe me, I know how it is."

He wasn't sure to take Mitchell's lack of response as a sign of annoyance or of going along, nodding his head on the other line, forgetting the recipient couldn't see him.

"Well, Mitchell...Mitchell Stevenson, policy number M613733, the '99 Explorer, '96 Grand Am, and a '96 Civic. $100 deductible on comp, $500 on collision for the Explorer, liability only on the rest, $2000 in medical payments, you got towing and labor and loss of use---"

"Frank?"

Frank knew what was coming. He'd been down this road many times before during his nine years in the business. The customer finds a better rate, but just doesn't have the balls to come right out and say so. Next thing you know, he's going to ask for a faxed copy of his coverage to send to the new carrier, with the lame-ass excuse that some employer is requiring it.

"Yes?"

"Uhm...what is today's date?"

"Oh...good question, well, let's take a look here. Today is...December 18th, Buddy. Damn, thanks for reminding me, I haven't bought even one single gift for any of my nieces or..."

"Frank?"

Well, maybe he was going to come out and say it after all.

"Yes?"

"I need you to remove a driver from the policy."

Relieved that he wasn't losing the business altogether, he perked up and responded, "Oh, sure. That would be your son, right? Getting him on his own, egh? That's great; I always recommend that children learn to manage bills while still under their parents' roof."

Again, the sobbing sounded faintly in the background.

"C'mon, Frank! Don't tell me you don't remember what we spoke about last time!"

Last time? Last time he'd spoken with this guy had been a while back to say the least. Mitchell Stevenson had been insured with Frank for nearly five years, no problems, no claims, called a couple years back to add on his son who had just gotten his license, but other than that...

"Mitchell, I'm going to be brutally honest with you. I have had a really tough week, and I'm looking here in my notes, and I don't see anything."

He nearly swallowed his tongue as Mitchell roared, "Cut this shit out, Frank! Cut it out!"

"Wh...what are you talking about? Just tell me."

"You going about your job like nothing ever happened makes me sick! Why don't you step outside, asshole."

It dawned on him that this man was either stoned, drunk off his ass, or was going postal. If he was on his cell phone, he might be outside the agency waiting. Frank gulped upon recalling the article in the latest Insurance Monthly Journal about an agent in Kentucky getting stabbed after hours.

"Mitchell, I have to go now, my friend. I have an evening appointment which I'm late for. Why don't you call me first thing in the morning and we'll discuss this, alright?"

The line had gone dead.

"Wha--?"

He fiddled with the caller id, then pressed another line but got no dial tone.

Did that horse's ass tell me to step outside?

The parking lot was well lit, and Gregorio's bakery/check cashing business was open till eleven with tons of Latinos in and out of the place nonstop, not to mention the security camera sweep. Shouldn't have to worry, besides, according to his recollection, Mitchell Stevenson was a short, geeky type; not much of a match for a former NC State Lineman.

The computer shut down with a few taps. Frank grabbed his jacket. What a day. He stepped into the restroom before heading out. After a therapeutic piss which left more than several drops on the seat, he washed his hands and stared himself down in the mirror.

What the fuck...?

This could not be real. He nearly fell backwards as his heart accelerated out of control. Black veins had spidered out from what appeared to be a clean bullet hole in the center of his forehead.

Fumbling for the door handle, he backed out of the restroom and ran toward the front door. Fuck setting the alarm. The front door to the McGraw Insurance Agency swung open, but not to the strip mall parking lot he had expected. A barren, sinister desert, greyer than the desolate moon's surface, flung its odious winds at the solitary figure standing at the brink of his existence. A purple, starless sky was barely visible beyond the violent windstorms which spiraled about the vast emptiness.

After taking this in, he instinctively stepped back into the suite and gazed out the glass. The bullet hole seemed to glow in the reflection.

What is this? God, please tell me what this is!?

His cell phone rang.

"Hell-hello?"

Prominent static invaded his ear with a sobbing sound nestled somewhere in it.

"You remember now?"

"Mitchell, listen, tell me---"

"What were you doing yesterday, Frank?"

"Yesterday the girls were out of the office, I took lots of calls, non-stop all day."

"What about that last call? Seven o'clock, Frank?"

"I didn't answer the phone after six-thirty."

"Frank, don't start with me! The parking lot, Frank! They got me, and I see they got you too!"

Static laughter invaded his earpiece.

He burst out in tears, flipped his cell phone shut, fell to the floor, and bawled like a spanked infant. He had told himself it was all a dream. No client of his had run over a four-year old girl. He had not been confronted with a client. His parking lot had not been the scene of a homicide/suicide. He was still alive, damn it.

I'm in hell, I'm in hell, oh sweet Jesus, help me...

Shadows

by D.X. Williams

-I-

The city had changed.

Natalie Edwards sat in the back of the limousine and watched the endless procession of faces drift past the window. They all looked so empty, so alone. Natalie felt a slow chill spread through her chest and she reached for the St. Anne medal around her neck. She closed her eyes and pressed the charm against the underside of her chin, saying a quick prayer for the lost.

A moment later she felt Jack's hand on her thigh.

"Thoughts?" he asked.

Natalie turned away from the window. "Too many," she said. "I can't think of a time I've been more frightened." She let go of the St. Anne, letting it slide gently between her breasts. "Not even when we knew we were losing her."

"But we didn't lose her."

Natalie nodded. She didn't speak.

Jack moved closer and reached for her hands. "Nat," he said. "Claire is alive and she is healthy. We have our second chance."

She watched him, scanning his face for any sign of uneasiness or doubt. There was none. "You really believe that."

Jack smiled. "Of course. Don't you?"

"I'm not sure." She looked down and ran a finger along the back of his hand, slowly tracing the familiar galaxy of age spots on his skin. "So much time has passed."

"Nonsense."

"It doesn't worry you?"

"Of course not."

She turned back to the window. "It worries me."

"So, you'd prefer not to have her back, is that what you're saying?"

"I'm saying she needs parents, Jack, not grandparents." She paused, whispered, "Great-grandparents more like."

"You're not serious?"

"She's a child, Jack. How can we pretend?"

"We're her parents."

"But for how long? And how fair are we being to *her*? She's eight years old, and you're eighty-two. She's been dead to us for forty years."

Jack narrowed his eyes. "She's never been dead to me."

Natalie stopped. It was true, he'd never let her go, and she knew it. He'd kept her alive inside of himself just as he had inside that goddamn tube. He was incapable of letting her go, emotionally or physically. "Please, Jack," Natalie said, inching closer to him. "We should consider Dr. Kelly's recommendation, especially if what he said was true."

"We'll be fine," Jack said. "We'll employ a nurse, and Kelly can recommend one he feels would be adequate."

"Jack, I—"

"I want her home, Natalie, and I don't care what Kelly says is best and I don't care if you think we're too old. She is our daughter and she belongs with us, not in some regeneration facility. Those places are nothing more than asylums, and you know that."

"That's not true," Natalie said. "Not anymore. Times have changed."

Jack didn't answer, and she realized the discussion was over. She'd never known him to be so uncompromising, especially when the decision involved them both. Then again, she'd never expected to have to make this particular decision at all. She'd always believed -- hoped -- that death would take her first.

Natalie turned back toward the window and the people moving along the walkway. She noticed a child running along side the car, waving, pushing through the crowd, trying to keep up. Natalie smiled and raised a hand to the window, pressing her palm against the glass. For a moment, the child's face became clear, then the limo turned and the child disappeared into the crowd.

Natalie reached for the St. Anne and squeezed as hard as she could.

LZI Cryogenics was tucked up against the foothills outside town, and when the limousine turned into the parking lot Natalie felt her stomach spin. This was the first time she'd been back in decades, and the emotions came all at once. Jack noticed, and he leaned close and whispered. "Everything is fine, Nat. Please, no worries."

But everything was not fine, and she knew it. Up until they'd arrived she'd been able to distance herself from the situation, but once the building came into view, everything changed.

"I'm not sure I can do this."

Jack didn't answer. She wondered if he'd even heard her.

The limousine stopped at the front entrance of the building. A young man with pomegranate red hair waited in the doorway.

Jack pushed the door release, and the man came forward at once, hand extended, smiling. "Mr. Edwards," he said. His voice was high and scratchy. "I wanted to meet you personally when you arrived."

"That was kind of you, Doctor," Jack said. He was using his boardroom voice, and Natalie smiled despite herself. She'd known the man for three quarters of his life, seen him at his worst, and it still made her laugh to witness this side of him. She wasn't sure which was more foolish, him trying to intimidate others, or the fact that it worked.

"Mr. Edwards, I must ask you to reconsider your decision. Claire is not ready to leave the hospital."

Jack reached back and offered Natalie his hand. She took it and stepped out. "Dr. Kelly, you said three weeks was more than enough time for anyone to complete regeneration It's been nearly four. We're taking her home." He stepped past Dr. Kelly and led Natalie toward the entrance.

Dr. Kelly moved in front of them. "I tried to explain to you on the phone that Claire is a special case," he said, walking backward, holding his hands in front of his chest. "There is so much we don't know. Suspension has different effects on children. If you remove her too soon it could be dangerous."

Jack stopped. "Is it still— is the cancer?"

"No, no," Dr. Kelly said. "She's taken to treatment very well. All signs of the disease are gone. She's in perfect physical health."

Jack looked back at Natalie and smiled. "Good," he said. "Then we're taking her home." He sidestepped Dr. Kelly and pushed toward the doors.

The look on the doctor's face made Natalie sad for the man. She could tell he was used to being in control of these situations, and he seemed unsure of what to do next. She smiled at him, trying to let him know he wasn't the first to feel that way around her husband. Dr. Kelly returned the smile, nodded, and followed Jack inside.

The building was silent and deserted. The only sound in the lobby was their footsteps echoing off the mirrored marble floor. Several dim lights, placed at intervals along the walls, burned behind frosted glass fixtures. None of it was the way Natalie remembered. Before, it'd been bright and professional and clean, alive with noise and activity. Now it was different, sterile, mechanical.

"Mr. Edwards, we have serious concerns," Dr. Kelly said. "When your daughter was suspended, the procedure was still very new. Many practices at the time were dangerous. We've lost several clients in regeneration simply because of mistakes made during the initial handling."

Jack slowed, giving Natalie time to catch up. When she did, he turned back toward Dr. Kelly. "Is she in danger?"

"We don't know yet," Dr. Kelly said. "All we know is that suspending a child is a much more delicate process than an adult. When working with a brain that isn't fully developed at the time of suspension, certain symptoms tend to be more pronounced."

"What symptoms?"

"Emotional swings, mostly. Hysteria, depression, violent episodes all the way to uncontrollable laughter. I've had patients run through them all, moving from a near catatonic state to violent psychosis and back, all within minutes."

"And Claire?"

"She has good days and bad days."

Natalie stepped forward and placed her hand on Jack's arm. "How much longer do you think she needs to stay?" She felt Jack tense, but she didn't look at him. "Until you'd feel comfortable releasing her?"

The muscles in Dr. Kelly's face seemed to relax all at once. He almost smiled. "Another three, maybe four weeks."

"Out of the question," Jack said. "She can complete the transition with us, at home."

"Mr. Edwards," Dr. Kelly said. He pressed his palms together in front of his mouth. "Under normal circumstances we keep the patient in isolation for a few days after the initial regeneration, careful not to introduce any stimuli at all. Then, slowly, we build up, as we deem necessary, eventually re-introducing them into social situations. Claire is not at that stage, and we cannot rush the process."

"You said all of that would only take a couple weeks."

"Under normal circumstances, yes, but she is one of only a handful of children who've gone through this. There is so much we don't know."

"What happened with the others?"

Dr. Kelly paused. "Of the three I'm aware of, one is functioning semi-normally with his family. The other two are institutionalized."

"Semi-normally?"

"Heavily medicated."

Jack shook his head. "I want to see her."

"Mr. Edwards, I—"

"I want to see my daughter." His voice was harsh. He glanced back at Natalie. "We'll decide then."

-IV-

The observation level overlooked a round room that reminded Natalie of a pre-school playroom. Bright colored balls and toys were spread across activity mats along the floor. Easels held what looked to be finger paintings, and a table covered with oversized books and drawings occupied the center of the room. Two nurses stood off to the side, talking, whispering.

Natalie searched the room for Claire, and all at once she felt the sensation of being at a zoo, waiting for the animals. The feeling made her nauseous and she leaned forward on the railing.

"Are you okay, Mrs. Edwards?" Dr. Kelly put his hand on her shoulder. "Would you like a chair?"

Natalie shook her head. "I think this is just a little too much." She looked up at Jack, but he was focused, staring intently into the room. She straightened herself and stood back. "I'll be fine."

"Where is she?" Jack asked.

Reluctantly, Dr. Kelly turned away from Natalie. He pointed. "She's under the table."

Natalie didn't want to look, but she couldn't stop herself. For a moment there was only the table, the books, the drawings. Then she saw her -- huddled underneath, a blue and green hospital gown, her knees, a long draping of black hair.

Natalie felt her breath catch in her throat. She wanted to look at Jack, but she couldn't turn away. They were all silent for a moment, then she heard Jack's voice.

"Claire?"

The knees under the table twitched, then froze. The nurses looked up at the observation level and frowned.

"Can she understand me?" Jack asked.

"Communication comes and goes," Dr. Kelly said. "Good days and bad."

Jack leaned over the railing. "Claire, sweetheart?"

This time she spoke. Her voice was small and quiet. "Daddy?"

Natalie couldn't breathe. She felt her legs give out, but she didn't fall. She stood, gripping the railing, never taking her eyes off the figure under the table. She didn't let go, not even when she saw Claire lean forward and stare up at them. That face, those eyes, the child she watched die, watching her.

This time she felt her legs fold and her body slide to the floor. Dr. Kelly stood over her, holding her hand. She closed her eyes hard, and felt the tears push back harder. Somewhere behind her she heard Jack's voice, calm, final.

"We're taking her home," he said.

-V-

The ride home felt clouded and broken. Dr. Kelly had given Natalie something to help her relax, but all it did was remove her from the situation, make her not care.

That was fine.

There were voices through the haze. Slow and thin, drifting in and out.

"Your room is ready for you." It was Jack's voice, calming. "It's different from your old one, but you'll like it."

Natalie tried to open her eyes; she wanted to see them together, but the medication covered her like a wave and after a while she stopped fighting and let it pull her under, into sleep.

-VI-

She awoke to purring.

Isabel was on her chest, her claws slowly kneading against her blouse. Natalie pushed her off and sat up. She'd been dreaming about Jack, but already the images were fading. She tried to hold on to them, but it was too late. They were gone.

Natalie's head throbbed. She massaged her forehead with her fingertips and looked around the room. It was dark except for a gray morning glow pressing through the curtains. Isabel sat at the foot of the bed, staring, her eyes blinking slowly.

"Sorry, baby." Natalie reached down and ran her hand along Isabel's white fur. The purring picked up immediately. So easy to please.

After a while Natalie stood up and wrapped her robe around her shoulders. She was wearing her nightgown, but she didn't remember putting it on. Whatever Dr. Kelly gave her really did the trick.

She reached down and picked up Isabel. The cat didn't protest. Natalie listened for sounds of movement in the house, but there was nothing. Jack hadn't come to bed, and she wasn't surprised. She knew where he'd be.

Claire's room was across the hallway, and Natalie pushed the door open, careful not to make a sound. Jack was asleep in a rocking chair by the window. He'd stayed with her through the night, and Natalie knew he'd feel the repercussions of that decision today. His back was bad enough without deliberately making it worse.

In the middle of the room was a large, white canopy bed. Natalie saw the small shape of her daughter under the covers. As she got closer she reached down and touched Claire's leg, feeling the warmth of her skin through the sheet. Isabel's purring was loud, and Natalie set her on the floor.

Once down, Isabel immediately jumped on the bed. Claire rolled over and opened her eyes. She stared up at Natalie then noticed Isabel and jumped back, pushing herself toward the headboard.

"No, no." Natalie sat on the edge of the bed and picked up Isabel. "It's okay."

Claire's eyes didn't move from the cat.

"This is Isabel." She set her back on the bed. "She won't hurt you."

For a second, Natalie thought she saw her smile, and she felt it deep in her chest. Claire looked at her, then immediately back at Isabel.

"Do you want to pet her?"

This time Claire did smile. She reached out and grabbed Isabel's fur, pulling the cat across the bed.

"Gently," Natalie said, but it was too late. Isabel hissed and squirmed away, scratching the back of her hand in the escape.

Claire screamed, and Isabel was gone.

Jack sat up fast. "What happened?"

Natalie reached for Claire, but she pulled back. "Isabel scratched her," she said. "She's fine, just scared."

Claire squeezed her hand against her chest and rocked back and forth on the bed, moaning.

"What the hell was Isabel doing in here?" Jack pushed himself up, slowly, never quite straightening. He leaned against the post of the canopy and reached for Claire's hand. "Let me see, sweetheart."

Claire pulled away. Jack tried to grab her hand. "How could you let that cat in here, Nat? What were you thinking?"

"It's a small scratch," Natalie said. "It's nothing."

Jack ignored her and tried to coax Claire's hand away from her chest.

"Just leave her be," Natalie said. "She's fine."

"What if it becomes infected? What then?" He motioned toward the door. "We need to get rid of that animal."

Natalie laughed out loud. The sound surprised them both. "I am not getting rid of Isabel, Jack. You're being ridiculous. It's only a scratch."

Jack pointed to the door. "You need to call Kelly and find out what we need to do."

Natalie waved him off. "I'll get the disinfectant. If you want to call Dr. Kelly, then you call." As she turned away she saw a flash of movement as Claire leaned forward and bit into Jack's hand.

Jack screamed and struggled, finally pulling his hand away. Blood dripped on the white sheets. "Get the fuck away from me," Claire said, teeth clenched, the words forced and angry.

Jack backed up, cradling his hand. The room was silent except for the wheeze of Claire's breathing.

"Claire?" Natalie took a step closer to the bed.

Claire turned toward her and Natalie stopped. There was blood on her teeth, and a bright pink smear on her cheek. Her eyes were wide and focused. She stared at Natalie for a moment, then opened her mouth and screamed.

The sound was piercing, and Natalie put her hands to her ears. A moment later she felt Jack pulling her away, out of the room. She followed him down the stairs and into the kitchen.

"My God, Jack," Natalie said. She sat at the kitchen table and stared at the ceiling. Claire was still screaming. "What are we going to do?"

Jack ran his hand under the faucet. "We need to call Kelly."

"She attacked you," Natalie said. "Claire never would've done something like that"

"It's obviously a reaction to the new environment, maybe to the cat."

"That had nothing to do with Isabel." Upstairs, the screaming stopped, and Natalie paused, lowering her voice as she spoke. "That is something deeper than a scratch. That is something we can't handle."

"Just stop," Jack said. "She's our daughter, and we'll handle her."

"That is not our daughter."

Jack slammed his hand against the counter. "Goddamn it, Natalie. We'll handle this." He yanked a towel from the rack by the sink and pushed past her, out of the room.

Natalie sat for a moment, watching him disappear down the hallway, then took a towel from the drawer and ran it under the faucet. She wondered why she let him convince her of everything. Why, in all the years they'd been together, she'd never questioned him. When the towel was soaked, she wrung it out and turned back to the stairway.

Claire was at the top of the stairs, giggling.

Natalie went up, bracing herself on the railing. "Why'd you do that?" she asked.

Claire didn't answer.

-VII-

"Mrs. Edwards?" Dr Kelly stood as she entered his office, his face turning somber. "Has something happened?"

"There was an incident this morning," she said. "Claire attacked Jack."

Dr. Kelly motioned toward the couch along the wall. "Is he okay?"

Natalie nodded, sitting down. "Claire never would've acted that way. She was never a violent child."

Dr. Kelly came out from behind his desk and sat next to her. "Mood swings are a common side effect," he said. "Sometimes they're violent, and that was a particular concern with me in regards to you and your husband."

"Why is that?"

Dr. Kelly adjusted himself on his chair. "Violent mood swings are accompanied by a surge in adrenaline and an increase in physical strength. A person experiencing this can be very hard to handle, and my concern had to do with your age and ability to control her when she's in that state."

Natalie felt the tears coming on and ran her fingertips under her eyes. "What can I do?" she asked. "He's trying to pretend all of this is normal, and I can't take it anymore. He's unreasonable."

"I can provide you with the medication that will help control her outbursts."

Natalie shook her head. "Jack won't want her drugged."

"Mrs. Edwards," Dr. Kelly said. "Claire will get worse before she improves, if she improves at all. The situation this morning will only be the beginning. Once she feels more comfortable with her new surroundings and realizes you don't pose a threat, the outbursts will get worse. She is a very bright girl; all she is doing is testing the waters."

"Are you saying she's doing this on purpose?"

"No, I don't believe she is," he said. "I think she lacks the ability to control her emotions in the same way she lacks the ability to communicate properly. Her reactions to emotions such as fear or anger will be extreme. The medication will help her, calm her."

Natalie looked down at her lap. "Sedate her."

Dr. Kelly nodded slowly. "That is an effect of the medication."

This time when the tears came she couldn't stop them. "I never expected to see her again," she said. "I only agreed to any of this for Jack. He was so devastated when she died."

Dr. Kelly remained quiet, waiting for her.

Natalie took a deep breath and tried to collect herself. "How long will she need to be on the medication?"

"I don't know." He stood and opened a cabinet behind his desk, removing a small, black tube. "Like I said, we have very little experience with children. She could improve rapidly or not at all." He handed the tube to Natalie. "This is a self injector. Put it against her thigh and press this button. A pre-set dose is automatically administered. You should only use it once a day. If she still has problems, call me and we'll set her up on something else."

"How soon does it take effect?"

"Immediately."

-VIII-

The house was quiet when Natalie opened the front door. She set her purse on the entryway table and removed the injector. She hoped Claire was in her room. The house was too big and there were far too many places to hide. The last thing she wanted to do was search for her. She walked into the foyer and looked up at Claire's bedroom door. It was closed, a good sign.

Natalie palmed the injector and made her way upstairs When she got to the top she heard the news report coming from Jack's den at the end of the hallway. She knew without checking that he was asleep, spread out over the couch, book tented over his chest. It was what he'd done every afternoon for the past fifteen years since he'd retired, and she knew this as well as she knew anything in her life.

She pressed her ear against Claire's door and listened. Claire was singing, but the sound was low and wavering, unnatural. Natalie pushed the door open. Claire was sitting on the bed, head down. "Claire?" She squeezed the injector in her hand as she walked.

"How are you feeling?"

Claire didn't look up. She was still making that sound, and as Natalie got closer she saw the blood covering her arms and the sheets around her. "Oh my God," Natalie said, reaching for her. This time Claire didn't pull away, and Natalie grabbed her arms, checking them for injury. "Where are you bleeding?" she asked. She ran her fingers along the skin, searching, but there was nothing there.

It wasn't her blood.

Natalie looked down at Claire's hands and froze. She was holding two bloody handfuls of white fur.

Natalie's breath caught in her throat. She reached down and pulled the covers away.

Claire had divided Isabel into several piles, separating bones from flesh as methodically as any butcher, and stacking them according to size.

Natalie couldn't move; she stared at the blood and the bones and the child smiling up at her, and all she could think of was one question:

Where was Isabel's head?

Natalie grabbed Claire's arm and pulled her off the bed. "Where is it?" She was screaming. "Goddamn you, what did you do with it?" She tore the sheets from the bed, the bones scattered across the floor. Behind her, she heard Claire laugh then begin to sing again, the same monotonous hum.

She's purring, Natalie thought. She's trying to purr.

Natalie turned toward her and slapped her, hard across the face. Claire screamed, and Natalie struck her again, over and over.

"Natalie!" Jack was in the room. He grabbed her arm and pulled her back. "What the hell are you doing?" She tried to get away, but he held her hands tightly. Then he saw the blood. "My, God, what did you do to her?"

"Isabel," Natalie said. "She killed—"

Jack took the injector from her hand. "What the hell is this?" he asked. "Where did this come from?"

Natalie looked back at Claire. She'd pushed herself into the corner of the room. She was staring at them. "We have to give it to her, Jack." Natalie's voice shook. "You have to see that now."

Jack let go of her hands. "Stay away from her. Do you hear me?"

"Will you listen to yourself?" She pointed at the sheets. "Can't you see what's happening?"

Jack ignored her and turned toward Claire. When he saw the bed he stopped. He didn't look away. Natalie waited, then reached out and gently touched his arm. She felt him shudder beneath her fingers. "We can help her," she said

Jack didn't say anything. Instead, he turned and walked out of the room.

Natalie chased after him. "We don't have a choice."

Jack stopped at the top of the stairs and held up the injector. "How dare you go behind my back." His voice was loud. "Were you going to give her this? Were you going to keep it from me?"

"We don't have a choice. You have to see that now." She reached for his hand, and he pulled away. "We have to give her the medication. It'll help her."

"It'll drug her into catatonia, maybe kill her." Jack said. "That would make you happy, wouldn't it? You could watch her die again."

Natalie slapped him, hard.

Jack's eyes went wide. He seemed to look past her, through her, and then he drifted backward. Natalie tried to reach for him, but it was too late. He hit the stairs and rolled down, hitting the foyer tile with a wet crack.

Natalie ran down the stairs. Jack's left leg was bent under him, and his hips looked as though they were turned backward. She knelt over him at the foot of the stairs, his eyes following her movements. "Jesus, Jack," she said, brushing his hair from his face.

Jack didn't speak. There was a bubble of red saliva on his lips that expanded and fell with his breath.

"I'll call the ambulance." She ran to the kitchen and hit the Med-Alert button on the phone. Jack had installed the feature earlier that year, and Natalie prayed it worked The Alert flashed red and sounded a slow-beeping alarm. Hopefully that was a good sign.

When she got back to the foyer, Claire was sitting on the stairs above Jack. She had her feet on his face and neck, gently needing her toes against his skin. As Natalie got closer she could tell it was too late for the ambulance. Jack's eyes were vacant.

Claire was giggling.

Natalie leaned over him and pushed Claire's legs away.

Claire moved them back.

Now the tears came in bursts. Natalie leaned over Jack's body, feeling the fading warmth of his skin. A moment passed, and she felt a light tap on her back, then a small voice.

"He hated you."

"Shut up, Claire."

Silence for a moment, then, "I hated you."

Natalie sat up, slowly wiping the tears with the back of her hand. "You don't belong here."

Claire smiled, showing teeth.

Natalie looked around for the injector tube. She saw it in the middle of the foyer and crawled toward it on hands and knees. She heard Claire's footsteps on the tile behind her, and when she grabbed the injector, Claire struck her, hard.

Natalie fell forward and Claire was on top of her, hitting her over and over. She tried to scream, to turn over, but she couldn't move. Claire pushed her down, her hair draping over her face like a veil. "Claire?" Her voice was weak and breathless. "Please."

Claire leaned forward and bit into her cheek.

Natalie screamed, and when Claire pulled back, she took flesh with her.

This time Natalie managed to turn over. Blood streamed down her face, swelling into a stain on her blouse. She pushed Claire back and pressed the injector into her leg. There was a click and Claire screamed and twisted away. A moment later her eyes changed, and she walked slowly toward the stairs.

Natalie tried to stand, but her legs wouldn't hold. The floor was covered in her blood, and she couldn't catch her breath. A sharp pain radiated through her chest and into her arm. She lay still for a moment, listening to the slow, steady pace of the Med-Alert in the next room, and wondered how soon the ambulance would arrive. The thought got her going again, and she pushed herself up, moving toward the stairs.

Claire was sitting by Jack, and when Natalie sat next to her, she didn't seem to notice. When Natalie held the injector against her thigh and pressed the button, Claire barely jumped. A moment later her eyes drifted again.

The pain in Natalie's chest was getting worse, and she reached up, gently touching Claire's face. After a moment she leaned in close and whispered, "I'm so sorry, Baby." She pressed the injector into Claire's thigh and pushed the button, waited, then did it again, and again, and again.

When she was sure Claire had stopped breathing, Natalie eased herself down against Jack's chest and stared at the ceiling. Her vision faded in and out, and each breath was a struggle. The Med-Alert still pulsed in the kitchen, and she thought she heard a siren in the distance.

Natalie closed her eyes and reached for the St. Anne medal around her neck. She squeezed it, feeling the familiar raised surface between her fingers, and prayed the ambulance wouldn't arrive too soon.

THE EXTERMINATORS

by Sara Joan Berniker

"Hon, you awake?" Richard shouted up the stairs.

Yawning, Molly struggled to shake off the dream that still ensnared her: Samantha's dwindling cries; Richard's shining smile; the silent beach and a sky filled with stars, each worth a wish.

As she dressed, she noticed the bottle of sleeping pills on the windowsill: Richard was having the dream again, too. This was getting weird. They were going to have to have a talk.

"I've got to go, Molly! You up?"

"Yeah, Richard."

"Good, then I'll let them in."

"Who?"

Down the hall, Samantha began to cry, obscuring his reply.

So tired she could barely walk, Molly went into the nursery and picked up the wailing baby. Samantha's forehead felt a little cooler, but that didn't mean much. She could tell from those snotty, labored gasps that her daughter was still sick.

In the silence that fell when Samantha paused to gulp a breath, Molly heard voices downstairs: more contractors, she guessed. They'd been taking bids for remodeling the kitchen, and lately the house had been crawling with burly men in tool belts.

Molly hurried down the stairs, smiling at the waiting men as she jiggled Samantha to try and ease the cries that came in out-of-breath bursts.

"You and your husband called?" the taller one said. "I'm Grady. This is Stan."

She blushed under Grady's unblinking gaze. He wasn't a bad looking guy, with those muscular arms and straight white teeth. "You're here to look at the kitchen?"

"No, we're the exterminators." He held out a clipboard. "Just need your signature..."

Exterminators? Had she and Richard talked about this? Who could remember? For weeks, Molly had been running on weird dreams and too much caffeine. Richard must have called them because of the ants in the pantry. They'd charge a bundle, these guys, and that meant another raid on the vacation fund. They were never going to get away, never going to get a break.

Molly felt warmth on her neck, and when her fingers came away they were wet with milky spit-up.

"A signature, Mrs. Bindley?"

"Yeah, just give me a sec." She shifted Samantha to her other arm and dabbed at the mess, the smells of used milk and talcum powder making her dizzy. The dream had been so real this time. Every part of her craved to be back on that sandy beach with Richard at her side, the two of them rapturous under the canvas of glittering stars. If only Samantha would stop crying for two fucking seconds so she could think straight…

"Here, let me," Grady said, holding out his arms. "Don't worry. Kids always take to me."

"You'll be sorry," Molly muttered, trading the squalling baby for the clipboard. She stared at the contract, unable to make sense of it; she wasn't much good before her first cup of coffee, and the writing was so very dense. "Wasn't my husband supposed to take care of this?"

"Yeah, he did. Put your John Hancock beside his, and we'll be good to go."

Molly looked up, startled at the sudden silence: Samantha was *smiling*. "I guess she likes you."

"Yeah, I'm good with babies. That's why they hired me."

For the life of her, Molly couldn't grasp how being good with children was linked to being an exterminator, but Grady had the kindest eyes she'd seen in a long while. No sense in looking stupid by asking. She squinted at the contract, a mess of legal jargon gobbledygook, and found her husband's cramped, hurried signature. Using the pen tied to the clipboard, Molly signed her name.

"There you go," she said, handing it to the other man. "Let me show you where the ants have set up house. You'll have to excuse the mess; Richard didn't tell me he'd called you."

"You both called us, Mrs. Bindley," Grady said softly, but Molly didn't hear him -- she was busy wondering if she should offer them coffee and whether they could tell she hadn't bothered to put panties on under her jeans.

It wasn't until she reached the kitchen that she realized the men weren't following her. She turned just in time to see them cross the front lawn towards a white van, Samantha's little hand waving over Grady's broad shoulder.

"*Wait!*" Molly cried, running through the hall and out onto the porch. Stan climbed behind the wheel, while Grady opened the van's back door and placed Samantha inside.

Stumbling down the stairs, she saw that the van's interior was crowded with racks of big guns and cruel-looking spiked mallets.

"*Stop! Stop!*"

Grady stared at her. There was nothing threatening in his gaze, only mild confusion. "Ma'am?"

Molly sprinted across the lawn, her breath coming in harsh bursts. "*Give her back!*"

"Shit, not again," Stan said. "We don't got time for explanations. That last one put us forty minutes off schedule."

"There's no need to be upset, ma'am," Grady said. "Everything's in order. She'll be fine."

"Sure she will," Stan said, winking. "Tell the nice lady what she wants to hear."

"We'll bill you in two to four weeks, Mrs. Bindley," Grady said, ignoring his partner.

"What? No, the *ants*! That's why you're here!"

"I didn't say that."

"*Give me my daughter back!*" Molly reached for the van's back door, meaning to wrench it open and rescue Samantha, but Grady held her back, smiling patiently as if she were an ill-tempered child.

"You signed, ma'am," he said. "You and your husband both. Have a nice day."

Pushing hard, he sent Molly sprawling to the ground, then climbed into the van. In the moment before the engine growled to life, Molly heard her daughter laugh and wondered when she'd last heard Samantha sound so happy.

The van roared away from the curb.

Skull Farmers

by Matt Samet

If one sees a car broken down by the side of the road, does one stop? It's lonely there, and cold, and the wind screams uninterrupted across the gray expanse of the Plains, freezing the fine hair on your arms while you wrestle with an obstinate lug nut. You twist, you invoke the gods, you stand on the wrench and make small hopping motions, but the nut remains fixed, caked to the hub of the wheel with ice and greasy mud. Semi trailers whip past, and it seems that each one comes closer than the last. They threaten to clip you while you hunch there, sweating, on the trash-strewn shoulder. You struggle to catch your breath in their diesel wake.

And me, I sharpen a blue pencil. I look out my window, the square one near the kitchen table. The road is distant, a smudge of noise diluted by the tangle of shrubbery and threadbare elms that line the ditch below the highway. I have lived here a long time and no longer hear the highway, except when it falls silent during those death-like hiatuses. I grind the tip of my pencil in a small child's sharpener; it is white and shaped like a Scotty dog. The pencil is a wax pencil, and I press hard; blue shavings drop to the floor where they collect at my feet.

You recall a sign you've seen a few miles back, something about a high wind warning or the potential for crosswinds, you're not sure which. This far north the wind has a real sting to it, a particular volition and viciousness. Neophytes liken this wind to a malevolent consciousness; I know better. The wind is indifferent if not persistent, and you get used to it, just like the highway.

I step into the entryway and draw a sheet of crisp white paper from an oak drawer. I look into the living room and it is quiet there. I no longer use this room, and I have unscrewed all the light bulbs from their fixtures. Sightless lamps of latticed iron stand sentinel over vertical pillars of dust, motes stirred up by my passing caught in the sun's waning rays. The pillars are square and sturdy, so thick with flecks of dirt and dead skin as to be almost palpable.

Your technology betrays you. *Out of range*, bleeps your cellular phone. You've been out of range since you crossed the scrubby spine of the continental divide an hour ago. You curse the phone and jam it into your hip pocket. It's a small telephone, sleek and black.

You will repeat this ritual every five minutes for the next half hour until you finally give up. Frustrated, you refocus your energies on the faux-chrome of the lug wrench, torqueing and yanking, anticipating the sweetness of the moment when the nut breaks and the wrench cranks earthward under the pressure of your grip. The nut refuses to break free, and though you are chilly, the odor of a nervous, caffeine-sour sweat wafts upward from your armpits.

I carry my sheet of paper back into the kitchen and drop it on the battered table beneath the low window. It hovers for one weightless moment over the slab of pitted wood, then settles. Names are carved in the table, oaths and imprecations. I think I should recognize these names, but I don't. It's shaping up to be one of those evenings, a dismal gloaming where earth and sky meet in a razor-thin, orange-black meridian so low in the west as to be almost invisible. I lay my blue pencil across the paper and sit.

The predicted half hour passes, and you give up on the phone and the wrench. You try flagging down passers-by instead. No luck. It's a winter evening, and you hesitate to step more than an inch or two across the white line that demarcates the shoulder lest a trailer flatten your toes. The trucks won't stop anyway; they breeze past, all bluster and efficiency. You fare no better with passenger cars. Though a few might slow at the frantic waving of your arms, the drivers can't read your face in the gloom. You could be a robber or a serial killer, your face a pinched and withering mask of desperation. You're flushed like a speed freak, and your eyes flash madly in the glare of the oncoming headlights.

I poke my tongue through a gap in my lower front teeth. I feel the soft meat of my gums and wince. The injury is an old one, yet I still lament the loss of the teeth. As I child, I heard a wailing from the basement and had to investigate: I crept halfway down the wooden staircase and watched my father slaying the family dog with an axe. He was a cruel man and had always hated that dog. The dog was being punished for stealing steaks off the kitchen counter. It tried to drag itself across the packed earth of the floor on its forepaws, pie-shaped wedges of flesh missing from its flanks and back. There was blood everywhere, and my father lost his footing. He went down, laughing. The dog, a cow-spotted mutt, gave off a low hissing noise. I heard the clanging of the hot-water heater from the kitchen above me. I turned to run back upstairs, but a forceful hand stayed me, grasping me tightly about the neck. *Tell no one*, said my father, and the hand slammed me face-forward into the wooden riser. I awoke with a headache, minus two teeth. We buried the dog behind the barn the next day, just me and my father. The wind blew hard that day, just like all the other days.

Ten minutes pass and no one has stopped to help. Frozen claws, your hands are cramped from your battle with the lug wrench. You open the trunk of your civilized sedan and replace the tools. You root around in the back seat, looking for a hat, gloves, anything to insulate you from the elements. There's nothing, only the light beige windbreaker on your back. You're dressed for the city and you hadn't planned to stop except for gas.

I press the blue pencil against the paper and begin to sketch, heavy lines criss-crossing to form a lattice of hair, a subtle spray of cross-hatching giving breadth to the flesh. The fine tip of the pencil homes in on the nuclei that are the seven portals of the head. I cup it loosely between my bent fingers and the base of my palm, feeling it bounce off the table beneath the paper. I stare out the window at you, and you are a distant figure on the horizon, bending and swaying with the pressure of the wind as you lock your car and begin to walk. Skin stretches; you can insert just about anything into any bodily orifice if you're patient -- or strong -- enough. There are seven holes leading into the head. These stretch too.

You are an obsessive man and it bothers you to leave your car unattended by the highway like some hunk of derelict metal. You've seen abandoned cars before -- they're either stolen or they are completely degraded shells of rust that their owners had no choice but to leave behind. Your car isn't like that. It's late model, foreign, well cared-for. You take it to the best garages and cover it with a nylon sleeve at night. You skip down the embankment, your flat-soled shoes skating on a patch of dirty ice, depositing you in a crumpled heap on the soft mud by the ditch. You kneel, then stand, swatting madly at the soiled fabric of your pants. A snag catches you below the eye, and a few drops of blood trickle down your face. You've seen the lights of my house from the freeway and hope to use my telephone.

You have no way of knowing this, but I had the phone disconnected after my parents died. If I'd left it on, it would have rung incessantly -- sympathy calls from relatives and neighbors. I don't need that sympathy. My parents died down at the creek behind our house. A beaver dam broke upstream, releasing a three-foot-high wall of water studded with dagger-sharp tree limbs and great chunks of ice. We're Plains people -- we don't know how to swim. They say from the way my dad's legs were broken, that even if he'd known how, he'd never have escaped that flood. He had splinters of shin fanning out below one knee, a pink-tipped femoral bone projecting above the other. My mom was run through with a stick. She died first. They went down there to see a sculpture I'd made on a thin shelf of ice overhanging the near bank. I'd scooped a handful of stones from the streambed -- those weighty, slick ones shaped like ovals without the moss -- and fashioned a sort of tower by freezing them together. After the deluge passed, my tower was still standing. When spring came, the stones flaked off and slid back into the river. I'm not sure why that dam gave out when it did, but I feel like I should remember.

You're intimidated by the sudden onset of the Plains night. It's not like the city, where even as the sky darkens, thousands of street lamps flicker to life, maintaining the constant if not artificial presence of light in much the same way a heated pool remains a steady sixty-eight degrees. Raspberry bushes snatch at your jacket as you push to the edge of the ditch. You step gingerly onto the ice, and your feet punch through. You're wet to your knees with irrigation water, cursing, your pleated slacks plastered to your shins. You initiate a standing long jump and punch through the ice again. Water reaches your thighs, your hands skittering about for purchase, as ineffectual as flippers. I hear a faint crackling noise and your frenzied cursing. To me this is funny, the way you flap and flail like a dying fish. If you're smart, you'll take hold of a branch and hoist yourself from the ditch.

I know the smell of that water, the tickle of its sulfurous breath. Grind your toes into the muck and feel the twigs and rotting leaves. If you cut your toe on a rock, you'll have to limp home across the furrows of a newly seeded alfalfa plot, trailing blood and fresh mud into the kitchen where your goggle-eyed mother backhands you with a wooden spoon for dirtying her floor.

You regroup on the far side of the ditch and cast a worried glance up at your car. It's still there, but you feel nauseous with cold. You pick your way through the copse of elms and emerge at the edge of a field. Soil in neat rows leads toward a dilapidated farmhouse, crusts of snow filling in grooves that rise roundly to low ridges of earth. You're not sure if this field has been tilled recently; perhaps the wind has worried it into its present state.

I can see your face now, fifty yards away and glowing. The sun has shed its cloak of scuddy winter cloud and glows a vibrant orange, warming your frost-speckled face and lending an almost alpine crispness to the miniature mountain ranges at your feet. There is urgency now and I sketch madly, my eyes glued on your advancing form. The seven portals are complete. I take a first look at my sketch and know that it is you. There is hollowness to my portrait, a hunger or depletion around the eye sockets that I cannot discern at this distance. You come closer, your feet crunching in the snow, and I see a healthy burning in your eyes that I do not like. There's something vaguely familiar about your features...a thinness of lips or droop to the mouth that recalls a face I can't quite remember. It's like you're a caricature of yourself.

I abhor caricatures because they're vulgar. Smiling or not, the out-sized, toothy heads make me nervous. They conjure up images of hydrocephalic freak-children lolling about in special chairs or trauma victims stewing in medically-induced comas. When I look at my picture of you, the seven portals are complete, but the head swells to fill the page.

You knock on the door.

I stand up to answer it.

You knock harder, desperate with hypothermia.

I step softly into the hall.

You're pounding now, shouting something about a telephone.

I open the door.

You're not there.

Q: How do you frighten a banshee?

A month after my parents died, they placed me in the state mental hospital. I stayed there for two years. I read books and learned to sketch. When they brought me in, they said I was dangerous. They said they had found me out by the highway, bare-chested and bloody, flinging handfuls of rocks into oncoming traffic.

They told me that I had shat all over the floor of my house, that I had written the word "evil" in feces across the yellowing wallpaper of the living room. That I had flooded my basement with irrigation water siphoned from the ditch via a long, green hose. That I had smashed all the mirrors, then flayed myself open with the jagged shards. That the oven was littered with small, brittle bones that once belonged to cats.

They showed me photos of a wooden rack I had supposedly crafted in my bedroom. It was a crude affair, all jutting nails and awkward angles. Woven stirrups of horse hair hung from a supporting beam. There was even a length of rope to tie the feet. They asked me if I had used this rack on anybody, if I was a torturer. Is there blood on this device; are there slicks of body grease? I asked them. No, they said. How about grooves scratched by fingernails? No, they said. Then I'm not a torturer, I told them.

I didn't want to go home just then, so I made sure they kept me there. I knew about the trifecta of sociopathy: bed-wetting, fire, animal abuse. I didn't have access to critters or matches, so I did my best with the bed-wetting. This seemed to please my doctor, an overworked little fellow with the vein-riddled nose of a drunk. Soon they gave me rubber sheets and moved me to a room of my own, one with a drain in the floor and stretching mats glued to the walls. I studied the androgynous figures painted on the mats, memorizing their blank-faced poses even as the paint cracked with age and the lines began to chip and fade. I tore down a mat and moved through the poses. They threatened to take my mat away, but when they saw how the stretching made me smile, they let me keep it.

Months went by, then a year. I never complained, never touched myself nor tore at my flesh. They began to trust me and reward me with books despite my frequent and sloppy micturition. I asked them for paper and a pencil. We can't trust you with a lead pencil, they told me, you'll try to jab your eyes out. They gave me wax pencils instead, black ones, blue ones, always with soft tips. I ate the black ones, so they stopped with those. I had blue pencils and paper and books. I drew the faces of the characters in the books and honed my pencils in an ineffectual little child's sharpener. I couldn't have a real sharpener -- I might remove the blades and cut myself.

When my doctor learned of my artistic bent, he demanded I draw a picture of him. I resisted, then tried a realistic likeness in broad, blue strokes. The man was sallow and jowly and this came across in my picture, in the blue rolls of neck, the blubbery blue cheeks, the blue wisps of hair covering the blue liver-spotted dome of the skull. He hated the picture and threatened to confiscate my drawing materials. I laughed at this and told him he was bluffing.

Even during that first year, before I had the pencils, the man's daily visits were nothing but hurried check-ups. There were always other patients to attend to, most of them sicker and more boisterous than I had ever been, even at my "psychopathic" worst. Once we began with the posing, he rarely asked me about my condition, as if it were ancillary to the matter at hand. Though my symptoms were mostly fake, I began to resent such negligent care. I was the doctor's slut cum artist, sketching my way out of a self-imposed imprisonment that, had I been thinking, would have ended much earlier.

We repeated this ritual every day for the next year, each successive sketch incrementally more flattering until what I held before me was no longer the reality of the man but a balloon-headed caricature with gargantuan, flashing teeth. I finished the sketch with trembling hands and mourned this capitulation, this final loss of integrity. Ever since he had imposed his patronage on me, I had wanted to take my pencil and stab it into the doctor's head -- into his cauliflower ears so he could no longer hear my querulous voice, into his nose so he could no longer smell the sour tang of my degradation, into his mouth so his aged tongue would cease with its pat, formulaic questions, into his eyes so he would no longer see nor care about my drawings. But I couldn't. It would simply extend my stay. I handed the doctor his sketch and waited.

He looked it over and held it to the light. A slight smile flickered across his lifeless features and he extended his hand to me.

"You're cured," he said, "you're cured!" He folded the portrait up and placed it in his pocket.

They discharged me the next day.

##

A: By nigger-knocking.

Pardon my language; I don't know what else to call it. You sneaky bastard, you had a peek through the frosted glass adjacent the front door and you didn't like what you saw (an egg-eyed, balding man with sloped shoulders and simian arms). I know I'm not pretty. You've gone around to the back of the house. You shouldn't have done that. I left the hall light on so you could see me through the glass. You're hiding now, hunkered down near the woodpile. If you look a few yards to your left you'll see a basement window with missing panes.

I shut the door behind me and go back to the kitchen for my sketch. I'll put it with the others down in the basement. They're arranged in chronological order in a flimsy aluminum filing cabinet the height of a circus midget. It rests unsteadily on an eroding hump in the corner farthest from the staircase. It's dark back there where I store the whips and the rack.

I descend the rickety staircase and tip-toe across the earth. Even though the roar of the wind is enough to mask the pitter-patter of my passing, I must be careful. You seem skittish, and until I've filed your sketch, there's nothing I can do to help you. Run away and I'll have to tear it up.

Muscle memory carries me across the uneven floor and my eyes attune to the pitch. I slide the bottom drawer of the cabinet open and place your sketch in a clean manila folder. There are a handful of sketches already in the folder, but not enough. I've had to rip too many up. Usually I don't file my drawings until after I'm done with the pencils, but I feel confident about you. It's an arctic evening and you're beginning to freeze into place, your clothes soaking wet, severe bouts of shivering wracking your city-soft frame. I keep a bundle of seven lead pencils in every room, each pencil honed to a needle-sharp point by an electric sharpener in the kitchen. It's nice to have real pencils again, though I prefer to draw with the wax ones. The top drawer of the filing cabinet, too, is packed tightly with pencils, all sharpened and kept at ready. I grab one of these bundles and go back upstairs. You'll knock again soon.

I know you will.

##

You crouch by the neatly-stacked wood and ponder your options. You could pick your way back to the freeway, but it's completely dark and you don't want to drown in the ditch. If you made it unscathed across the ditch you could sit in your car with the heat on, but eventually you'd run out of gas. Then there's the trucks. You'd be a sitting duck on that shoulder the way those semis are sloshing around. You scan the horizon, hoping to spy another house, one with a less menacing tenant. Something red flickers about a mile away and you study it, your eyes tearing up with the cold and the wind. You shield them and blink. Your nose is running and the light leaps with your shivering. Seized by spasms, your lower back begins to stiffen. You squint; the light crisps. It's nothing but a blinker at a railway crossing.

You attempt to clarify what you've seen in the house, your flow of thought as clotted and sluggish as an ice-choked stream. First, as you approached via the field: a smear of still, pink flesh glimpsed through a window. The figure was set back from the window then it moved! You could just see the hands, thick and purposeful, as they maneuvered some unseen object. You paused to decipher these motions: slicing, perhaps, or writing. Their rhythm is lethargic yet unwavering and makes you uneasy. The light pouring from the window is yellow, meaning kitchen. To be benign, the figure should be stirring or washing with the quick hand action that signals a jolly, down-home love for work . . . but it isn't.

What did you see through those slats of glass framing the doorway? An ogre? A spectre? The Phantom of the Opera? Or just something unexpected? On a nervous night with Stygian overtones, you would people this house with docile grandparents, sugar-sweet rustics who offer you a slice of pecan pie while you wait for a tow truck. Or the proverbial farmer and his three daughters -- blonde as sand and ripe with unfulfilled country sexuality. Or a Bohemian couple, malcontent college types who've fled the city to "get back to the land."

But not with monsters. Not some lug-headed giant with a meter-long stride and hands the size of hams. Not some snaggle-toothed behemoth with a penis like a lead bat who dances into brittle focus before your startled eyes (you standing on his rotted porch and monitoring his approach with a mounting sensation of horror and disbelief).

Because this is what I'd do to you: I'd skull farm you, city boy, I'd skull farm you.

I proffer no underlying philosophy, nor diabolical screed (that would be trite). I speak with action.

The human head is an obdurate thing, noisome and vile. Severing it presents an exhausting challenge. Under tension, the lengths of gristle and sinew that hold the head fast to the body yield nicely to a saw. It's another matter when the body has gone slack with unconsciousness, or death. The head lolls obnoxiously on the stalk of the neck, and I must two-hand the saw and bear down with all my weight just to make the first cut (it helps to drive a knee into the solar plexus). Tendon, meat and bone alike become rubbery and flimsy, sucking at the saw, which now drips black with gore. If the heart is still aflutter, I'll find myself drenched in an arterial spray. I lick my lips and resume the cut.

Just because one can fill a ditch with skulls does not make one a skull farmer. I do not confer this title upon pretenders like Adolf Hitler or Pol Pot, those fucking dilettantes. Death merchants maybe, but not skull farmers. My concern is with the quality of the act, not the quantity. The method of killing and even whether the victim is alive at the time of decapitation are secondary considerations. You, you seem quick on your feet so I'll just gut-shoot you.

You must know this, which is why you continue to hide. Others I've kept around the house for days. I lash them to the wooden rack in the basement or affix them to a kitchen chair with my nail gun. They scream the most when I go through their feet -- lots of nerves there -- and claw missives of hope into the kitchen table until their hands, too, must be nailed down.

I don't like the smell of death, so I drag the bodies far from the house, across the hard slab of river ice and into the woods beyond. I'll go to some pains to take your head off. I can see it now in my freezer, ready to be sown. Though I'm jittery with the killing, I make myself wait for this pleasure.

I remove your head from the icebox and place it in a large, plastic dish.

You stare up at me, surprised.

I remove the bundle of pencils from my pocket and snap the elastic off by crooking my index finger.

You stare up at me, surprised.

The rubber band makes a small popping noise that resounds throughout the house. It's one of those rare moments when the highway is quiet.

You stare up at me, surprised.

I've covered all my parent's furniture with sheets because I do not like to sit in it.

You stare up at me, surprised.

The only rooms I use now are the basement and the kitchen.

You stare up at me, surprised.

The first thing to go is your ears. I jam a pencil into each and watch as a viscous fluid the color of semen leaks from the base of the pencils, hard against the walls of your skull.

You stare up at me, surprised.

I jam two pencils up your nose, one for each nostril. The nostrils dilate then close around the glossy shafts.

You stare up at me, surprised.

The mouth is tricky; it takes some thought. Do I stuff it with pencils until the cracked blue lips can stretch no further or do I adhere to the perfection of the number 7? I've tried both ways. There was something bothersome about filling the mouth, about spoiling the count. I gently place a single pencil on your tongue and it looks like you're sipping on a straw.

You stare up at me, surprised.

I finish with the eyes, ramming home the last two pencils with an athletic flourish. They leak a clear liquid not unlike tears.

You stare up at me, surprised.

I jack off onto your skull, slathering your matted hair with baby juice, and take you out to the garden. I plant you in a small hole so that just the crown of your head is exposed. I will fertilize it every day with my seed and wait to see what grows there. I pray for a child -- a loyal homunculus -- the bastard offspring of my sociopathic spermatozoa and your sun-dried scalp.

I've planted three heads and nothing has grown except maggots.

Something is wrong. You should have knocked again; you're not the kind to just freeze to death out there. You haven't gone back to your car because I would have heard you crunching through the alfalfa field. Had you come around to the front porch, I'd have heard you too, treading cautiously up those worm-eaten stairs which translate stress to the rest of the house, making the ancient planks groan. My shotgun leans against the table and I hoist it to my shoulder, filling my pocket with red, plastic shells from a box on the tabletop. You must be down in the basement. You must have squeezed through that window with the broken panes.

I have an advantage. Though your eyes are attuned to the dark, I've known this basement my whole life. I keep it deliberately uncluttered for situations like these. There's nowhere to hide. I will walk my grid and find you and shoot you in the gut.

I begin at the base of the stairs and hug the wall on the right, my right arm trailing along the rugosity in the plaster while my left braces the shotgun at chest height. I work my way around all four walls in this fashion, sidestepping the filing cabinet and the rack. It is absolutely black down here; not so much as a whisper of starlight enters through the ground level windows that line the west wall. I'm back at the stairs, in the cobwebby space behind the risers. I expect you to be here, but you're not. You must be in the middle of the room, meditating on your breath like some blissed-out monk. I admire your presence of mind. I step out from behind the stairs and fire a shell into the black heart of the basement.

The flash of the gunpowder lights up the room, and there you are, crouched in a ball, pinned onto the earthen floor by a sickly white glow. I've shot too high, and as the odor of cordite osmoses with the weedy stench of the basement, I feel you rushing me, your hands upon my throat. Your grip is firm, as strong as my own; with such strength, you should have been able to free that lug nut.

I heave the shotgun upward against the bottoms of your arms, trying to break your hold. You drive a knee into my scrotum, and I feel a leaden sickness boiling like constipation rippling through my bowels. You're more combative than the others, resourceful and quick -- I saw this in my portrait and I should have been more cautious. You stand above me, throttling me, warming with the exertion of your task. You're no longer shivering. A second shell remains chambered in the shotgun, whose barrel rests lightly across the palms of my hands. I'm gagging now and the shotgun feels too heavy to lift. I fumble with the trigger and squeeze off that last shot. It sprays harmlessly into the wall, and in that split second of brilliant light, I see your hunger up close. It is as my own -- unfocused, raw -- yet lacks the unflinching profundity of genuine psychopathy. Rootless and situational, it is a mere by-product of your fear, a knee-jerk reaction. I shoot a foot out and hook you behind the shins, dragging you toward me.

Your grip falters, just for a moment, and I suck a quick breath through my nostrils, a snort almost. It's enough. I lock my elbows and swing the shotgun up toward your face, clocking you just under the chin with the oily heft of the wooden stock. You drop to the earth and I stand above you, the butt of the shotgun poised above the egg of your skull, ready to stave it in should you choose to rise. You remain still, your breathing ragged and irregular I drop the shotgun and hook my hands under your armpits, dragging you toward the rack. Your head sags low between your shoulders, and I can tell that you have a heavy one, dense with brain matter and bone.

I spit in my palms and rub them together, wiping the grime off on my pants. I want my hands to be clean for that first touch, the one where I finger-stir the mucous of your eyeballs in the bowls of their orbits. An incipient erection presses against the denim of my pants and I pause, squaring my shoulders and inhaling deep until the jitters pass. I need to be relaxed if I'm going to do this right; I need to pace myself. Because this matters. Because this matters to me. Because this is what I do.

SCAVENGER HUNT

by R.J. Cavender

The Weed-Master Plus was slapping up a beautiful mess of what used to be Amanda's face.

I mean, I say the name like I knew the girl. She was just as nameless as anyone else. Names were never of any importance. You make friendly with an ocean of skin. You hear and forget an army of names.

Imagine the things two swirly-eyed boys of just fourteen could buy with five-large a week. That's each. It was like we had all the money in the world. We were unstoppable. Every moment was a murder-junkie-rockstar dream. Children and demons and armed and drugged, we raped the city streets.

When referred to, if ever, the gutterpunks and bindlekids called us The Scavenger Hunt. We had a list, we were paid well, and we asked no names. Oft times we traded psychedelics and powders for useful information. We were effective and precise. We were shadows on the cold city concrete.

So's her magna-tag labeled her Amanda, not that either of us ever called her by name. We swiped her sweet and clean on her darkened walk to her shitmobile, and one nastily laid 'BONK' upside her crannie later...and we've got our newest star. Never underestimate the powers of a brick in a pillowcase, friend.

See, we've got her tied tight and right, and my good man Dodger and I were ready to earn our keep. Old Stu had set up the entire operation, and no matter what his claims may be, both Dodge and I knew quite well he was pocketing more bills than he gave us. Which was acceptable. At first.

After all, the scrot-wrinkled old fuckleknuck was about as daft as they come. But, he had indeed orchestrated the entire project, so some props should be given for that if nothing else.

Those who do the dirty work sometimes need a bit more green. We had habits to feed, and admittedly got greedy. It's like kings in our world. Kill your teacher. Destroy all idols. Climb up to the throne. To us, Stu had become dust.

We killed, he made the money. The dusty desert was pregnant with graves we'd dug by hand.

The old fuck had us connected with the right of the wrong people. Old Stu had the hook-ups on everything of worth; drugs, tech weaponry, contraband pornographics, and deathshows. We signed on with Stu for the latter of the list. It was his farm where the deeds were done, and his digividcams were the ones steeped in hour upon hour of our bloodied footage.

Which brings us back to Amanda, and the goulash mess she once called a face. She was number three on our list for the night. Just a messy interlude sandwiched between a hit-and-run and a better than worse interrogation. Just goes to show you, you never know what moment exactly will be your last.

This one was a fighter. No one could ever diss this dolly, as she was most assuredly the strongest female I'd ever put to rest. She spat and cursed with the best of them, even with her face falling off in sloppy, wet chunks. A wildcat.

The vidi-film Stu was recording tonight was given the working title of "Deep Red." We'd already burnt two hours on Amanda, and still found ourselves far from done. The list we'd been given was rather specific on what was to be done to her. Stu's "clients" were very exact in what they wanted.

So's, you find yourself at the fork in the road. Less taken path seemingly oh so perverse and unbearable, yet still you know if ye dare not tread...it'll stay stuck in your head. You know I did something utterly repulsive to sweet and holiest of Amanda. That name itself just screams victim. We've all known an Amanda once. Was your Amanda a hapless waif who'd lost her way? Mine was.

There still stands this truth. To continue on only perpetuates violence, yes? Are you an enabler? I think, yes. But, you read on nonetheless. Just another rubbernecker. Just another consumer in this human machine.

It reminds us that we're alive, when people die.

That's why people like you pay to read stories of "true crime." You want to hear what beasts other citizens can be. You want to know the fear and death that demons can bring. Death makes you cling to life. Love your life.

That's why people buy the vidi-films. These cruddy-fucks with their tech-connects and shareburns sending data and collecting pain at an astonishing rate. A million broken lives and dreams all saved and savored and sent. And I break these lives. And I break these bodies. I am the spiller of the blood.

It almost makes me proud. My best work has been seen worldwide.

A white sheet. White robes. A freaker strobe made our every move all nightmare fucking beautiful. A sparkling razor-sharp knife in each hand, hot liquid sex and metal. Stu was watching from somewhere behind the mirrored glass. Digi-vid burnt film. Blood spattered, frozen, all stop-motioned under the strobe.

Dodger twisted the skin on Amanda's back with a jagged broken bottle. He used the pliers next.

It was more like some trippy creepjoint performance art piece than murder. Fuck yes a girl died that night. Fuck yes we destroyed her. She was recreated as a piece of art, as well.

The finale. With surgical precision she was flayed. Skin parted from muscle, muscle parted from bone. That little dolly was quite aware as her stuffing was pulled out. Hating the whole time. Cursing us with her last breath. An amazing specimen. Almost a shame to snuff, really.

Not that there wouldn't be retribution. All within a week, Stu and Dodge both dead. Me thrown into a "center" all locked and caged and raped and rotting. So, don't you fog up your ghoul eyes with tears for sweet Amanda. She was lucky. Even the death we gave her betters my everyday excuse for a life.

Stu had provided the list. His client had specific tastes. He wanted us to abduct a waitress. Young. Blonde. Pretty. Catch it all on vid from beginning to end. And the end. The fucking end.

The white sheets had set Stu back a couple of stones. Expenses to be absorbed in the cost of the vid. White sheets everywhere. Cotton and silk.

Turn white to red. Specific directions for acquired tastes. Take her apart. We did as requested.

Here's the part that got to me. This skirt is just getting off work. She's had a long day. I could see when we got her shoes off just how sore her feet looked. Waitresses work hard, they deal with muppets and creeperfreaks all day, and they bring us food. They make next to nothing. For some reason, this client had a grudge against waitresses.

Howmotherfuckingever, this particular diner-bitch deserved nothing like this. What, you stuff a meager twenty-spot or so in your greasy apron and call it another day, and you somehow fall into someone else's sick electric nightmare. You find yourself at the mercy of a couple of powerdusted murder-junkies with knives and boners and rope. No matter how well you've planned out your life, you still end up with your head planted on a wooden spike in the middle of a dirty barn.

We pulled her apart. More specifically, we disassembled her entirely and made a hollow cavity where her chest used to be. That's what we were paid for. That's what they paid to see.

We cut her long ways, down the middle and displayed her peeled open and pinned. Struggling and jiggling and fighting the whole time. I've yet to see someone hang onto life quite like Amanda did. She must have really loved her life.

Specific tastes. Take her insides out, display them as they are removed, and pin her open like a bug on a board. Dodge produced a hammer and nails. Her guts already scooped out and strung about the barn like Christmas garland. Her heart in a jar.

Even though we enjoyed our jobs, neither of us were shits and giggles while we worked. Pure professionalism. Complete concentration. Precision. With every knife stroke, with every gun blast. We were tops at what we did, even for mere boys. I've lost track of how long it's been now. I've been moved from one correctional facility to another to another to another. Now that I'm sick, they have finally left me in one place, presumably to die.

But, I don't die. Or I can't die. I've tried on several occasions, believe you me. But still my heart beats, slow and murmurous in my chest. My blood still flows. My flesh still lives. But every waking second is an excruciating parody of life itself.

Hunger consumes me. So hungry I could eat a scabby baby. Once, in this hellhole, I even pulled out patches of my own hair just for something else in my stomach. Fortunately, I am no longer plagued with the company of the other 'offenders' in this zoo. They tend to steer clear of me now. They can smell me rotting. They don't want to catch whateverthefuck I have.

I lost all my teeth last week. Just by brushing. They all fell right out like pretty pearls clinking in the sink.

My thumb turned black and just sort of fell off. I can feel myself crumbling from the inside. The smell of decay covers me.

And even though I don't know why this is happening, I find at the same time I don't care. I just want it done. I want it over. Whatever curse the diner-witch put on me, whatever flesh-eating disease I've contracted, whatever this is, it's a blessing.

My every dream is filled with bodies and arms and mouths, all scratching and biting. I rarely sleep. When I do, I awake to find another part of me rotten. Another part of me gone. And all I really want to be is gone. If I cannot die, at least I can disintegrate and rot. Soon I will be gone completely.

Dust. Nothing at all.

You make friendly with an ocean of skin. Children and demons and armed and drugged we raped the city streets. We were angels of death in a time of everlasting chaos.

I only remembered one name ever.

Also from Cutting Block Press:

Butcher Shop Quartet
Novella Anthology